THE BLIND MAN OF SEVILLE

THE BLIND MAN
OF SEVILLE

Robert Wilson

HARCOURT, INC.

Orlando   Austin   New York   San Diego   Toronto   London

www.HarcourtBooks.com

Library of Congress Cataloging-in-Publication Data
Wilson, Robert, 1957–
The blind man of Seville/Robert Wilson.—1st ed.
p. cm.
ISBN 0-15-100835-3
1. Police—Spain—Seville—Fiction. 2. Seville (Spain)—Fiction.
I. Title.
PR6073.I474 B57 2003
823'.914—dc21 2002068495

Text set in Postscript Linotype Janson

First published in England by HarperCollins*Publishers*

Printed in the United States of America

First U.S. edition
A C E G I K J H F D B

For Jane
and
Mick and José

ACKNOWLEDGMENTS

Before I could start writing this book I had to find out how the police and the judiciary worked and I interviewd a number of people who were all friendly and helpful. I would like to thank Magistrado Juez Decano de Sevilla Andrés Palacios, los fiscales de Sevilla and the Inspector Jefe del Grupo de Homocidios de Sevilla Simon Bernard Espinosa, who was also very informative about his approach to murder cases. The characters who appear in this book with these titles are in no way representative of the real people nor are the professional relationships between them at all typical.

I would also like to thank Dr Fernando Ortíz Blasco who not only helped me with my hip but was also very informative about bull-breeding and bullfighting.

On the Tangier end of things I was very fortunate to be introduced by Frances Beveridge to Patrick Thursfield, who in turn put me in touch with Mercedes Guitta who lived in Tangier during and after World War 2. I thank them all for their help.

My friend Bindy North was good enough to run her professional eye over the psychological dialogues and give me her opinion, for which I am very grateful.

The main reason why this book was written was because of my two friends who live in Seville, Mick Lawson and José Manuel Blanco Marcos. Over many years they have decanted, consciously and inadvertently, massive amounts of information about Spain, Andalucía and Seville. They have also been incredibly supportive of me throughout my writing career, rebuilding me when I've turned up broken and celebrating with me when things have gone right. I have dedicated the book to them, which is a small way of saying that no man could wish for better friends.

Finally I want to thank my wife, Jane, who doesn't see much more of me than a hunched back over a desk but, as always, has helped me with research, given me the benefit of her very sure editorial eye and despatched my frequent doubts to the abyss. I cannot conceive of writing a book without her, which must make her my muse.

L'art, c'est le vice. On ne l'épouse pas légitimement, on le viole.

Art is vice. You don't marry it legitimately, you rape it.

EDGAR DEGAS

'You have to look,' said the voice.

But he couldn't look. He was the one person who couldn't look at it, who would never be able to look at it because it started things up in that part of his brain, the part that would show up bright red on a cerebral scan while he was asleep, that tunnel of the brain maze which laymen would name 'wild imaginings'. It was the danger zone which had to be closed off, barricaded with whatever came to hand, nailed up, chained, padlocked, key hurled into the deepest lake. It was the dead end where his big-boned, mule-knuckled peasant frame was reduced to the shivering nakedness of a little boy, face pressed into the dark, hard, narrow comfort of a corner, legs and buttocks raw from sitting in his uncontrollable urine.

He wouldn't look. He couldn't.

The sound from the TV switched back to an old movie. He heard the dubbed voices. Yes, he'd look at that. He could look at James Cagney speaking Spanish while his eyes darted in his head and his lips said things differently.

The tape whirred in the video player as it rewound, clicked off at the beginning. A horizon slopped in the back of his head. Nausea? Or worse? The tidal wave of the past rising up. His throat tightened, his lip trembled, a fuzziness converged on James Cagney's manic Spanish. He curled the toes of his bare feet, gripped the arms of his chair, his wrists already cut from the flex that secured them. His eyes filled and blurred.

'Tears before bedtime,' said the voice.

Bedtime? His brain juggled with the concept. He coughed a muffled thump into the socks stuffed in his cheeks. The end? Is that what bedtime means? The end would be better than this. Time for bed. Deep, dark, endless bed.

'I'm going to ask you to try again . . . to try to *see*. But you must look first. There's no seeing without looking,' said the voice, quiet in his ear. The 'play' light winked red out of the black. He shook his head, squeezed his eyes tight shut. James Cagney's voice was swallowed by the scream of laughter, the wild giggling holler of a small boy. It *was* laughter, wasn't it? He rolled his head from side to side as if this might deafen him to the sound, the confusing sound that he refused to believe could be agony, shrieking agony. And the sobbing aftermath, the helplessness, the terrible weakness as when the tickling stops . . . or was it the torturing? The sobbing. The concentrated panting. The recovery from pain.

'You're not *looking*,' said the voice, angry.

His chair rocked as he tried to throw himself back from the screen, away from the piercing sound. James Cagney's perfect staccato Spanish returned and the whirr of the rewind, the acceleration to the thump at the end of the tape.

'I have tried,' said the voice. 'I have been patient and . . . reasonable.'

Reasonable? This is reasonable? Tying my feet and hands to the chair, stuffing my stinking socks into my mouth. Forcing me to watch this . . . my . . . this . . .

A pause. The muttered expletive behind his head. Tissues ripped from the box on the desk. The smell in the room again. The one he remembered. The dark patch coming towards him, but not on a rag, on tissues. The smell and what it meant. Darkness. Lovable darkness. Give it to me. I'll take that over this.

The hard smack of the chloroform tilted him back into space.

A snick of light, small as a star, punctured the high vault. It grew to a circle and drew him up from his dark well. No, I'll stay. Leave me here in the dungeon dark. But it was inexorable, the drag, the wrench into the widening circle until he was reborn into the living room with James Cagney and a girl now, which wasn't the only thing that was different. There was flex cutting into his face. It had been pulled tight under his nose and fastened to the high back of the chair so that he could feel the carved contours of some ancient coat of arms digging into his scalp. And there was more. Oh Mary, Mother of Christ, *Virgen de la Macarena, de la . . . de la Esperanza . . .* what have you *done* to me?

The tears were warm on his cheeks, down the sides of his face, in the corners of his mouth. They dripped thickly on to his white shirt. There was the taste of a sugary blade between his teeth. What have you *done* to me? The screen rolled on its casters towards him, stopping at his knees. Too much was happening at once. Cagney kissing the girl, nastily. The flex cutting up into his septum. The panic rising from his feet, ripping through his body, collecting more panic on the way, funnelling up through his organs, shunting up his narrowing aorta. Irrepressible. Unswallowable. Unthinkable. His brain was livid, his eyes on fire, the tears blazing away. His lids – lines of stubble burning in the dark – advanced towards his black and shining pupils, blistering the whites of his eyes.

A dropper appeared in his torched vision, a quivering bead of dew hanging from its glass tube. His eyes would drink that down. Drink it down and take more.

'Now you will see everything,' said the voice. 'And I will provide the tears.'

The drop flashed on to the eye. The tape engaged and squeaked on its reels. James Cagney and his girl were consumed by a creeping blizzard. Then came the screaming and the administering of considerate tears.

1

Thursday, 12th April 2001, Edificio del Presidente, Los Remedios, Seville

It had started the moment he'd walked into that room and had seen that face.

The call had come at 8.15 a.m. just as he was preparing to leave home – one dead body, suspected murder and the address.

Semana Santa. It was only right that there should be at least one murder in Holy Week; not that it would have any effect on the crowds of people following the daily convergence of quivering Holy Virgins on board their floats en route to the cathedral.

He eased his car out of the massive house that had belonged to his father on Calle Bailén. The tyres rattled on the cobbles of the empty, narrow streets. The city, reluctant to wake up at any time of year, was especially silent at this hour during Semana Santa. He entered the square in front of the Museo de Bellas Artes. The white-washed houses, framed in ochre were silent behind the high palms, the two colossal rubber trees and the tall jacarandas, which had not yet flowered. He opened his window to the morning still fresh from last night's dew and drove down to the Guadalquivir River and the avenue of trees along the Paseo de Cristóbal Colón. He thought he might be approaching contentment as he passed by the red doors of the Puerta del Príncipe in the baroque façade of the Plaza de Toros, La Maestranza, which was about to see the first bullfights in the week leading up to the Feria de Abril.

This was as close as he got to happiness these days and it held firm as he turned right after the Torre del Oro and, leaving the old part of the city behind, crossed the river, which was misty in the early-morning sunshine. At the Plaza de Cuba he veered away from his regular route to work and headed down Calle de Asunción. Later he would try to recapture these moments because they were the last of what he'd thought, until then, had been a quite satisfactory life.

The new and very young Juez de Guardia, the duty judge, who'd been waiting for him in the pristine, white-marbled entrance hall of Raúl Jiménez's large and expensive apartment on the sixth floor of the Edificio del Presidente, did try to warn him. He remembered that.

'Prepare yourself, Inspector Jefe,' he'd said.

'For what?' Falcón had asked.

In the embarrassed silence that followed, Inspector Jefe Javier Falcón had minutely scrutinized the surface detail of the Juez de Guardia's suit, which he decided was either Italian or a leading Spanish designer, someone like Adolfo Dominguez, perhaps. Expensive for a young judge like Esteban Calderón, thirty-six years old and barely a year in the job.

Falcón's apparent lack of interest decided Calderón that he didn't want to appear naïve in front of the forty-five-year-old Inspector Jefe del Grupo de Homicidios de Sevilla, who'd spent more than twenty years looking at murdered people in Barcelona, Zaragoza, Madrid and now Seville.

'You'll see,' he said, with a nervous shrug of his shoulder.

'Shall I proceed then?' asked Falcón, maintaining proper procedure with a judge he'd never worked with before.

Calderón nodded and told him that the Policía Científica had just been let into the building and that he could go ahead with his initial observations of the scene.

Falcón walked down the corridor leading from the entrance hall to Raúl Jiménez's study thinking about preparing himself without knowing how it was done. He stopped at the door to the living room, frowned. The room was empty. He turned to Calderón who had his back to him now, dictating something to the Secretaria del Juez while the Médico Forense listened in. Falcón looked into the dining room and found that empty, too.

'Were they moving out?' he asked.

'*Claro*, Inspector Jefe,' said Calderón, 'the only furniture left in the apartment is a bed in one of the kids' rooms and Sr Jiménez's complete study.'

'Does that mean Sra Jiménez is already in the new house with the children?'

'We're not sure.'

'My number two, Inspector Ramírez, should be here in a few minutes. Send him straight through to me.'

Falcón proceeded to the end of the corridor, suddenly conscious of each footstep on the polished parquet flooring in the empty apartment. His eyes were fixed on a hook on the bare wall at the end of the corridor under which was a square lighter than its surrounds, where a picture or mirror had been hanging.

He eased his hands into a pair of surgical gloves, snapped the cuffs against his wrists and flexed his fingers. He turned into the study, looked up from his cloudy latex palms to find Raúl Jiménez's terrible face staring at him.

And that was when it had started.

It wasn't a question of looking back at that moment and realizing later that it had been a turning point. The change was not subtle. A difference in body chemistry has a way of making itself immediately felt. Sweat came up inside his gloves and at a spot high on his forehead just out of the hairline. The taut pattering of his heart stopped him and he began to find oxygen in the air difficult to come by. He hyperventilated for some seconds, pinched at his throat to try to encourage a better intake. His body was telling him that there was something to fear while his brain was indicating otherwise.

His brain was making the usual dispassionate observations. Raúl Jiménez's feet were bare, his ankles secured to the chair legs. Some furniture was out of place, at odds with the rest of the room. Indentations in the expensive rug, Persian, showed the normal position of the chair. The lead to the TV/video was stretched taut because the rolling cabinet was some metres from its normal position by the wall socket in the corner. A ball of cloth, which looked like socks tracked with saliva and blood, lay on the floor by the desk. Windows, double-glazed, were shut, curtains drawn back. A large soapstone ashtray sat on the desk, full of pinched stubs and whole, clean filters which had been broken off from the cigarettes whose pack lay alongside, brand name Celtas. Cheap cigarettes. The cheapest. Only the cheapest for Raúl Jiménez, owner of four of the most popular restaurants in Seville, with two others in Sanlúcar de Barrameda and Puerto Santa María down on the coast. Only the cheapest for Raúl Jiménez in his ninety-million-peseta apartment in Los Remedios, overlooking the Feria ground, with his celebrity photographs hanging on the wall behind his leather-inlaid desk. Raúl with the torero El Cordobés. Raúl with the TV presenter Ana Rosa Quintana. Raúl, my God, Raúl with a carving knife behind a *jamón* which had to be a top quality *Pata Negra* because he was flanked by Antonio Banderas and Melanie Griffith, who was looking completely appalled at the cloven hoof pointing at her right breast.

Still the sweat didn't stop but appeared elsewhere. Top lip, small of the back, trickling down to his waist from his armpit. He knew what he was doing. He was pretending, persuading himself that it was hot in the room, that the coffee he'd just taken . . . He hadn't had any coffee.

The face.

For a dead man it was a face with presence. Like El Greco's saints whose eyes never left you alone.

Were they following him?

Falcón moved to one side. Yes. Then the other. Absurd. The tricks of the mind. He pulled himself together, clenched a latex fist.

He stepped over the taut lead from the wall to the TV/video and went behind the dead man's chair. He looked up to the ceiling and let his eyes fall on to Raúl Jiménez's wire-wool hair. The back of the head was matted thick, black and red, from where he'd rammed his head repeatedly against the carved coat of arms on the chair back. The head was still secured to the chair with flex. Originally it must have been tight but Jiménez had gained some slack through his struggle. The flex had cut deeply into the flesh beneath his nose and had ridden up until it had bitten into the cartilaginous material of the septum and it had even sawn through that to reach the bone of the bridge. The nose was hanging off his face. The flex had also cut into the flesh over his cheekbones as he'd thrown his head from side to side.

Falcón turned away from the profile only to see the full frontal in the blank TV screen. He blinked, wanting to close those staring eyes, which, even in reflection, penetrated. His stomach leapt at the thought of the horror images that had forced a man to do this to himself. Were they still there, burned on to the retina, or further back in the brain in some cubist digitalized state?

He shook his head, unused to these wild thoughts interfering with his investigative coolness. He moved around to confront the gory face, not quite full on because the TV/video cabinet was up against the man's knees, and, at this moment, Javier Falcón came up against his first physical failing. His legs would not bend. None of the usual motor messages could get beyond the roiling panic in his chest and

8

stomach. He did what the Juez de Guardia had advised and looked out of the window. He noted the brightness of the April morning, remembered that restlessness as he'd got dressed in the shuttered dark, the uneasiness left after a long, lonely winter with too much rain. So much rain that even he had noticed how the city's gardens had burgeoned to the density of jungle, to the richness of an abundant botanical exhibit. He looked down on the Feria ground, which two weeks from now would be transformed into a tented Seville crowded with *casetas*, marquees, for the week-long session of eating, drinking fino and dancing *Sevillanas* until dawn. He breathed in deeply and lowered himself to meet Raúl Jiménez's face.

The terrible staring effect was produced by the man's eyeballs bulging out of his head as if he had a thyroid problem. Falcón glanced up at the photos. Jiménez was not bug-eyed in any of them. This was caused by ... His synapses shunted like cars crunching into each other nose to tail. The visible ball of the eye. The blood down the face. The coagulation on the jaw line. And these? What are these delicate things on his shirtfront? Petals. Four of them. But rich, exotic, fleshy as orchids with these fine filaments, just like fly-catchers. But petals ... here?

He reeled backwards, his feet kicking at the rug edge and the parquet flooring as he fell over the television lead, yanking the plug out of the wall socket. He crabbed on the heels of his hands and feet until he hit the wall and sat legs splayed, thighs twitching, shoes nodding.

Eyelids. Two top. Two bottom. Nothing could have prepared him for that.

'Are you all right, Inspector Jefe?'

'Is that you, Inspector Ramírez?' he asked, getting up slowly, messily.

'The Policía Científica are ready to move in.'

'Send the Médico Forense down here.'

Ramírez slipped out of the doorframe. Falcón shook himself down. The Médico Forense appeared.

'Did you see that this man had had his eyelids cu— his eyelids removed?'

'*Claro*, Inspector Jefe. The Juez de Guardia and I had to satisfy ourselves that the man was dead. I saw that the man's eyelids had been removed and ... it's all in my notes. The *secretaria* has noted it, too. It's hardly something you'd miss.'

'No, no, I didn't doubt that . . . I was just surprised that it wasn't mentioned to me.'

'I think Juez Calderón was about to tell you, but . . .'

The bald head of the Médico Forense rolled on his shoulders.

'But what . . . ?'

'I think he was in awe of your experience in these matters.'

'Do you have any opinion about the cause and time of death?' asked Falcón.

'The time, about four, four-thirty this morning. The cause, well, *vamos a ver*, the man was over seventy years old, he had been over-weight, he was a heavy smoker of cigarettes which he preferred with the filter removed and, as a restaurateur, someone who enjoyed a glass of wine or two. Even a young and fit man might have found it difficult to sustain these injuries, that physical and mental distress, without going into deep shock. He died of heart failure, I'm sure of it. The autopsy will confirm that . . . or not.'

The Médico Forense finished, flustered by the steadiness of Falcón's look and annoyed by his own idiocy at the end. He left the frame, which was instantly reoccupied by Calderón and Ramírez.

'Let's get started,' said Calderón.

'Who called the emergency services?' asked Falcón.

'The *conserje*,' said Calderón. The concierge. 'After the maid had . . .'

'After the maid had let herself in, seen the body, ran out of the apartment, and taken the lift back down to the ground floor . . . ?'

'. . . and hammered hysterically on the door of the conserje's flat,' finished Calderón, irritated by Falcón cutting in. 'It took him some minutes to get any sense out of her and then he called 091.'

'Did the conserje come up here?'

'Not until the first patrol car arrived and sealed off the crime scene.'

'Was the door open?'

'Yes.'

'And the maid . . . now?'

'Under sedation in the Hospital de la Virgen de la Macarena.'

'Inspector Ramírez . . .'

'Yes, Inspector Jefe . . .'

All exchanges between Falcón and Ramírez started like this. It was his way of reminding the Inspector Jefe that Falcón had moved down from Madrid and stolen the job that Ramírez had always assumed would be his.

'Ask Sub-Inspector Pérez to go down to the hospital and as soon as the maid . . . Does she have a name?'

'Dolores Oliva.'

'As soon as she is sensible . . . he should ask her if she noticed anything strange . . . Well, you know the questions. And ask her how many times she turned the key in the lock to open the door and what *exactly* were her movements before she found the body.'

Ramírez repeated this back to him.

'Have we found Sra Jiménez and the children yet?' asked Falcón.

'We think they're in the Hotel Colón.'

'On Calle Bailén?' asked Falcón, the five-star hotel where all the toreros stayed, only fifty metres from his own . . . from his late father's house – a coincidence without being one.

'A car has been sent,' said Calderón. 'I'd like to complete the *levantamiento del cadaver* as soon as possible and get the body down to the Instituto Anatómico Forense before we bring Sra Jiménez up here.'

Falcón nodded. Calderón left them to it. The two Policía Científica, Felipe in his mid fifties and Jorge in his late twenties, moved in murmuring *buenos días*. Falcón stared at the TV plug lying on the floor and decided not to mention it. They photographed the room and, between them, began to put together a scenario, while Jorge took Jiménez's fingerprints and Felipe dusted the TV/video cabinet and the two empty slipcases on top. They agreed on its normal position and the fact that Jiménez would usually have been watching it from a leather scoop chair whose swivel base when lifted revealed a circular mark on the parquet. The killer had incapacitated Jiménez, swivelled the leather chair, which was unsuitable for his purposes, and moved one of the high-backed guest chairs so that he could shift the body in one turning movement. The killer had then secured the wrists to the arms of the chair, stripped the socks off the feet, stuffed them in Jiménez's mouth and secured the ankles. He then manoeuvred the chair by pivoting it on its legs until he achieved the ideal position.

'His shoes are under here,' said Jorge, nodding to the footwell of the desk. 'One pair of ox-blood loafers with tassels.'

Falcón pointed to a well-worn patch on the parquet in front of the leather scoop. 'He liked to kick off his shoes and sit in front of the TV rubbing his feet on the wooden floor.'

'While he watched dirty movies,' said Felipe, dusting one of the slipcases. 'This one's called *Cara o Culo*.' Face or Arse I.

'The position of the chair?' asked Jorge. 'Why move all this furniture around?'

Javier Falcón walked to the door, turned and held his arms open to the forensics.

'Maximum impact.'

'A real showman,' said Felipe, nodding. 'This other slipcase has *La Familia Jiménez* written on it in red felt-tip and there's a cassette in the machine with the same title, same handwriting.'

'That doesn't sound too horrific,' said Falcón, and they all looked at Raúl Jiménez's blood-streaked terror before going back to their work.

'*He* didn't enjoy the show,' said Felipe.

'You shouldn't watch if you can't take it,' said Jorge from under the desk.

'I've never liked horror,' said Falcón.

'Me neither,' said Jorge. 'I can't take all that . . . that . . .'

'That what?' asked Falcón, surprised to find himself interested.

'I don't know . . . the normality, the portentous normality.'

'We all need a little fear to keep us going,' said Falcón, looking down his red tie, the sweat tumbling out of his forehead again.

There was a thump from under the desk as Jorge's head hit the underside.

'*Joder*.' Fuck. 'You know what this is?' said Jorge, backing out from under the desk. 'This is a chunk of Raúl Jiménez's tongue.'

Silence from the three men.

'Bag it,' said Falcón.

'We're not going to find any prints,' said Felipe. 'These slipcases are clean, as is the video, TV, the cabinet and the remote. This guy was prepared for his work.'

'Guy?' asked Falcón. 'We haven't talked about that yet.'

Felipe fitted a pair of custom-made magnifying glasses to his face and began a minute inspection of the carpet.

Falcón was amazed at the two forensics. He was sure they'd never seen anything as gruesome as this in their careers, not down here, not in Seville. And yet, here they were . . . He took a perfect square of ironed handkerchief out of his pocket and dabbed his brow. No, it wasn't Felipe and Jorge's problem. It was his. They behaved like this because this was how *he* normally behaved and had told them it was the only way to work in a murder investigation. Cold. Objective. Dispassionate. Detective work, he could hear himself in the lecture theatre back in the academy, is unemotional work.

So what was different about Raúl Jiménez? Why this sweat on a cool, clear April morning? He knew what they called him behind his back down at the Jefatura Superior de Policía on Calle Blas Infante. *El Legarto.* The Lizard. He'd liked to think it was because of his physical stillness, his passive features, his tendency to look intensely at people while he listened to them. Inés, his ex-wife, his recently divorced wife, had cleared up that misunderstanding for him. 'You're cold, Javier Falcón. You're a cold fish. You have no heart.' Then what is this thing thundering away in my chest? He jabbed himself in the lapel with his thumb, found himself with his jaw clenched and Felipe looking up with fish aquarium eyes from the carpet.

'I have a hair, Inspector Jefe,' he said. 'Thirty centimetres.'

'Colour?'

'Black.'

Falcón went to the desk and checked the photograph of La Familia Jiménez. Consuelo Jiménez stood in a floor-length fur coat, her blonde hair piled high as confectionery while her three sons cheesed at the camera.

'Bag it,' he said, and called for the Médico Forense. In the photograph Raúl Jiménez stood next to his wife with his horse teeth grinning, his sagging cheeks looking like a grandfather and his wife, a daughter. Late marriage. Money. Connections. Falcón looked into Consuelo Jiménez's brilliant smile.

'Good carpet, this,' said Felipe. 'Silk. Thousand knots per centimetre. Good tight pile so that everything sits nicely on top.'

'How much do you think Raúl Jiménez weighs?' Falcón asked the Médico Forense.

'Now I'd say somewhere between seventy-five and eighty kilos, but from the slack in his chest and waist I'd say he's been up in the high nineties.'

'Heart condition?'

'His doctor will know if his wife doesn't.'

'Do you think a woman could lift him out of that low leather scoop and put him in that high-backed chair?'

'A woman?' asked the Médico Forense. 'You think a woman did that to him?'

'That was not the question, Doctor.'

The Médico Forense stiffened as Falcón made him feel stupid a second time.

'I've seen trained nurses lift heavier men than that. Live men, of course, which is easier . . . but I don't see why not.'

Falcón turned away, dismissing him.

'You should ask Jorge about trained nurses, Inspector Jefe,' said Felipe, arse up in the air, practically sniffing the carpet.

'Shut up,' said Jorge, tired of this one.

'I understand it's all to do with the hips,' said Felipe, 'and the counterweight of the buttocks.'

'That's only theory, Inspector Jefe,' said Jorge. 'He's never had the benefit of practical experience.'

'How would you know?' said Felipe, kneeling up, grabbing an imaginary rump and giving it some swift thrusts with his groin. 'I had a youth, too.'

'Not much of one in your day,' said Jorge. 'They were all tight as clams, weren't they?'

'*Spanish* girls were,' said Felipe. 'But I come from Alicante. Benidorm was just down the road. All those English girls in the sixties and seventies . . .'

'In your dreams,' said Jorge.

'Yes, I've always had very exciting dreams,' said Felipe.

The forensics laughed and Falcón looked down on them as they grovelled on the floor, rootling like pigs after acorns, with football and fucking fighting for supremacy in their brains. He found them faintly disgusting and turned to look at the photos on the wall. Jorge nodded his head at Falcón and mouthed to Felipe: *Mariquita*. Poof.

They laughed again. Falcón ignored them. His eye, just as it did when he looked at a painting, was drawn to the edges of the photographic display. He moved away from the central celebrity section and found a shot of Raúl Jiménez with his arms around two men who were both taller and bigger than him. On the left was the Jefe Superior de la Policía de Sevilla, Comisario Firmin León and on the right was the Chief Prosecutor, Fiscal Jefe Juan Bellido. A physical pressure came down on Falcón's shoulders and he shrugged his suit up his collar.

'Aha! Here we go,' said Felipe. 'This is more like it. One pubic hair, Inspector Jefe. Black.'

The three men turned simultaneously to the window because they'd heard muted voices from behind the double-glazing and a mechanical sound like a lift. Beyond the rail of the balcony two men in blue overalls slowly appeared, one with long black hair tied in a ponytail and the other crew cut with a black eye. They were shouting to the team eighteen metres below who were operating the lifting gear.

'Who are those idiots?' asked Felipe.

Falcón went out on to the balcony, startling the two men standing on the platform, which had just been raised up a railed ladder from a truck in the street.

'Who the hell are you?'

'We're the removals company,' they said, and turned their backs to show yellow stencils on their overalls which read Mudanzas Triana Transportes Nacionales e Internacionales.

2

Thursday, 12th April 2001, Edificio del Presidente, Los Remedios, Seville

Juez Esteban Calderón signed off the levantamiento del cadaver, which had uncovered another piece of baggable evidence. Underneath the body was a piece of cotton rag, a sniff indicated traces of chloroform.

'A mistake,' said Falcón.

'Inspector Jefe?' questioned Ramírez, at his elbow.

'The first mistake in a planned operation.'

'What about the hairs, Inspector Jefe?'

'If those hairs belonged to the killer . . . shedding it was an accident. Leaving a chloroform-soaked rag was an error. He put Raúl Jiménez out with the chloroform, didn't want to put the rag in his pocket, threw it on the chair and then dumped Don Raúl on top of it. Out of sight, out of mind.'

'It's not such an important clue . . .'

'It's an indication of the mind we're working against. This is a careful mind but not a professional one. He might be slack in other areas, like where he got the chloroform. Maybe he bought it here in Seville from a medical or laboratory supplies shop or stole it from a hospital or a chemist. The killer has thought obsessively about what he wants to do to his victim but not all the details around it.'

'Sra Jiménez has been located and informed. A car will drop the kids at her sister's house in San Bernardo and bring her on alone.'

'When will the Médico Forense do the autopsy?' asked Falcón.

'Do you want to be there?' asked Calderón, weighing his mobile. 'He said that he was going to do it immediately.'

'Not particularly,' said Falcón. 'I just want the results. There's a lot to do here. This film, for instance. I think we should all watch the *La Familia Jiménez* movie now before Sra Jiménez arrives. Is there anybody else from the squad here, Inspector?'

'Fernández is talking to the conserje, Inspector Jefe.'

'Tell him to collect all the tapes from the security cameras, view them with the conserje and make a note of anybody he doesn't recognize.'

Ramírez made for the door.

'And another thing . . . find somebody to check all the hospitals, laboratories and medical supply shops for chloroform sold to odd people or missing bottles of the stuff. And surgical instruments, too.'

Falcón rolled the TV/video cabinet back to its normal position in the corner of the room. Calderón sat in the leather scoop chair. Falcón plugged the equipment back in. Ramírez stood by the dead man's chair, which was wrapped in plastic, ready to be taken down to the Policía Científica laboratories. He murmured into his mobile. Calderón ejected the tape, inspected the reels, put it back in and hit the rewind button.

'The removals men are still here, Inspector Jefe.'

'There's no one to talk to them now. Let them wait.'

Calderón hit 'play'. They took seats around the room and watched in the sealed silence of the empty apartment. The footage opened with a shot of the Jiménez family coming out of the Edificio del Presidente apartment building. Raúl and Consuelo Jiménez were arm in arm. She was in an ankle-length fur coat and he was in a caramel overcoat. The boys were all dressed identically in green and burgundy. They walked straight towards the camera, which was across the street from them, and turned left into Calle de Asunción. The film cut to the same family group in different clothes on a sunny day coming out of the Corte Inglés department store on La Plaza del Duque de la Victoria. They crossed the road into the square, which was full of stalls selling cheap jewellery and shawls, CDs, leather bags and wallets. The group disappeared into Marks & Spencer's. The family group were shown again and again until two of the three men were stifling yawns amidst the shopping malls, the beach gatherings, the *paseos* in the Plaza de España and the Parque de María Luisa.

'Is he just showing us he did his homework?' asked Ramírez.

'Impressively dull, isn't it?' said Falcón, not finding it so, finding himself oddly fascinated by the altering dynamics of the family group in the different locations. He was drawn to the idea of the family, especially this apparently happy one, and what it would be like to have one himself, which led him to think how it was that he had singularly failed in this capacity.

Only a change in the direction of the movie snapped him back. It was the first piece of footage where the family didn't appear as a group. Raúl Jiménez and his boys were at the Betis football stadium on a day when, it was clear from the scarves, they were playing Sevilla – the local derby.

'I remember that day,' said Calderón.

'We lost 4–0,' said Ramírez.

'You lost,' said Calderón. 'We won.'

'Don't tell me,' said Ramírez.

'Who do you support, Inspector Jefe?' asked Calderón.

Falcón didn't react. No interest. Ramírez glanced over his shoulder, uncomfortable with his presence.

The camera cut to the Edificio del Presidente. Consuelo Jiménez on her own, getting into a taxi. Cut to her paying the taxi off in a tree-lined street, waiting some moments while the car pulled away before crossing the road and walking up several steps to a house.

'Where's that?' asked Calderón.

'He'll tell us,' said Falcón.

A series of cuts showed Consuelo Jiménez arriving at the same house on different days, in different clothes. Then the house number – 17. And the street name – Calle Río de la Plata.

'That's in El Porvenir,' said Ramírez.

'This *is* the future,' said Calderón. 'I think we have a lover here.'

Cut to night-time and the rear of a large E-Class Mercedes with a Seville number plate. The image held for some time.

'He doesn't move his plot on very well,' said Calderón, reaching his boredom threshold quickly.

'Suspense,' said Falcón.

Finally Raúl Jiménez got out of the car, locked it, stepped out of the street lighting and into the dark. Cut to a fire burning in the night, figures standing around the leaping flames. Women in short skirts, some with their suspenders and stocking tops showing. One of them turned, bent over and put her bottom to the fire.

Raúl Jiménez appeared at the edge of the fire. An inaudible discussion ensued. He strode back to the Mercedes with one of the women following, stumbling in her high heels over the rough ground.

'That's the Alameda,' said Ramírez.

'Only the cheapest for Raúl Jiménez,' said Falcón.

Jiménez pushed the girl into the back seat, holding her head down as if she were a police suspect. He looked up and around and followed her in. The frame held the rear door of the Mercedes, shadowy movements beyond the glass. No more than a minute passed and Jiménez got out of the car, straightened his fly and held out a note to the girl, who took it. Jiménez got back into the driver's seat. The car pulled away. The girl spat a fat gob on to the dirt, cleared her throat and spat again.

'That was quick,' said Ramírez, predictable.

More night-time footage followed. The pattern was the same, until an abrupt change of scene put the camera in a corridor with light falling into it from an open door at the end on the left. The camera moved down the corridor gradually revealing a lighter square on the wall at the end with a hook above it. The three men were suddenly transfixed, as they knew they were looking at the corridor outside the room where they were sitting. Ramírez's hand twitched in that direction. The camera shook. The suspense tightened as the three lawmen's heads surged with the horror of what they might be about to see. The camera reached the edge of light, its microphone picked up some groaning from the room, a shuddering, whimpering moan of someone who might be in terrible agony. Falcón wanted to swallow but his throat refused. He had no spit.

'*Joder*,' said Ramírez, to break the tension.

The camera panned and they were in the room. Falcón was so spooked that he half expected to see the three of them sitting there, watching the box. The camera focused first on the TV, which, at this remove, was running with waves and flickering but not so much that they couldn't see the graphic performance of a woman masturbating and felating a man whose bare buttocks clenched and unclenched in time.

The camera pulled back to a wide shot, Falcón still blinking at the confusion of sound and expected image. Kneeling on the Persian carpet looking up at the TV screen was Raúl Jiménez, shirt-tails hanging over his backside, socks halfway up his calves and his trousers in a pile behind him. On all fours in front of him was a girl with long black hair, whose still head informed Falcón that she was staring at a fixed point, thinking herself elsewhere. She was making the appropriate encouraging noises. Then her head began to turn and the camera spun wildly out of the room.

Falcón was on his feet, thighs crashing into the edge of the desk.

'He was there,' he said. 'He was . . . I mean, he was here all the time.'

Ramírez and Calderón jerked in their seats at Falcón's outburst. Calderón ran his hand through his hair, visibly shaken. He checked the door from where the camera had just been looking into the room. Falcón's mind bolted, didn't know what it was looking at any more. Image or reality. He started, went on to his back foot, tried to shake his vision free of what was in his head. There was someone standing in the doorway. Falcón pinched his eyes shut, reopened them. He knew this person. Time decelerated. Calderón crossed the room with his hand out.

'Señora Jiménez,' he said. 'Juez Esteban Calderón, I am sorry for your loss.'

He introduced Ramírez and Falcón, and Sra Jiménez, with mustered dignity, stepped into the room as if over a dead body. She shook hands with the men.

'We weren't expecting you so soon,' said Calderón.

'The traffic was light,' she said. 'Did I startle you, Inspector Jefe?'

Falcón adjusted his face, which must have had the remnants of that earlier wildness.

'What was that you were watching?' she asked, assuming control of the situation, used to it.

They looked at the screen. Snow and white noise.

'We weren't expecting you . . .' started Calderón.

'But what was it, Señor Juez? This is my apartment. I should like to know what you were looking at on *my* television.'

With Calderón taking the pressure, Falcón watched at leisure and, although he was sure he didn't know her, he at least knew the type. This was the sort of woman who would have turned up at his father's house, when the great man was still alive, looking to buy one of his late works. Not the special stuff, which had made him famous. That was long gone to American collectors and museums around the world. This type was looking to buy the more affordable Seville work – the details of buildings: a door, a church dome, a window, a balcony. She would have been one of those tasteful women, with or without tiresome wealthy husband in tow, who wanted to have their slice of the old man.

'We were watching a video, which had been left in the apartment,' said Calderón.

'Not one of my husband's . . .' she said, hesitating perfectly to let them know that 'dirty' or 'blue' was unnecessary. 'We had few secrets . . . and I did happen to see the last few seconds of what you were watching.'

'It was a video, Doña Consuelo,' said Falcón, 'which had been left here by your husband's murderer. We are the three officers of the law who will be running the investigation into your husband's death and I thought it important that we saw the film as soon as possible. Had we known that you would be so prompt . . .'

'Do I know you, Inspector Jefe?' she asked. 'Have we met?'

She turned to face him full on, her dark fur-collared coat open, a black dress underneath. Not someone to be inappropriately dressed for any occasion. She gave him the full force of her attractiveness. Her blonde hair was not quite so structured as in the desk photograph but the eyes were bigger, bluer and icier in reality. Her lips, which controlled and manipulated her dominating voice, were edged with a dark line just in case you might be foolish enough to think that her soft, pliable mouth could be disobeyed.

'I don't think so,' he said.

'Falcón . . .' she said, feeling the rings on her fingers as she looked him up and down. 'No, it's too ridiculous.'

'What is, may I ask, Doña Consuelo?'

'That the artist, Francisco Falcón, should have a son who is the Inspector Jefe del Grupo de Homicidios de Sevilla.'

She knows, he thought . . . God knows how.

'So . . . this film,' she said, turning on Ramírez, sweeping her coat back and fitting her fists into her waist.

Calderón's eyes flashed across her breasts before they locked on to Falcón over her left shoulder. Falcón shook his head slowly.

'I don't think this is something you should see, Doña Consuelo,' said the young judge.

'Why? Is it violent? I don't like violence,' she said, without unfixing Ramírez from her gaze.

'Not physically,' said Falcón. 'I think you might find it uncomfortably intrusive.'

The reels of the video squeaked. It was still playing. Sra Jiménez picked up the remote from the corner of the desk and rewound the tape. She pressed 'play'. None of the men intervened. Falcón shifted to catch her face. Her eyes narrowed, she pursed her lips and gnawed at the inside of her cheek. Her eyes opened as the silent film played. Her face slackened, her body recoiled from the screen as she began to realize what she was watching, as she saw her children and herself become the study of her husband's killer. When they reached the end of her first taxi ride, to what everybody now knew was 17 Calle Río de la Plata, she stopped the tape, threw the remote at the desk and walked swiftly from the room. The men tossed silence between them until they heard Sra Jiménez retching, groaning and spitting in her halogen-lit, white marble bathroom.

'You should have stopped her,' said Calderón, pushing his hand through his hair again, trying to shift some of the responsibility. The two policemen said nothing. The judge looked at his complicated watch and announced his departure. They agreed to meet after lunch, five o'clock in the Edificio de los Juzgados, to present their initial findings.

'Did you see that photograph on the end there by the window?' asked Falcón.

'The one of León and Bellido?' said Calderón. 'Yes, I did, and if you look a bit closer you'll see there's one of the Magistrado Juez Decano de Sevilla in there, too. Old hawk eyes, Spinola, himself.'

'There's going to be some pressure on this case,' said Ramírez.

Calderón chucked his mobile from one hand to the other, slipped it in his pocket and left.

3

Falcón told Ramírez to interview the removals men – specifically to ask them when they arrived and left, and whether their gear was unattended at any stage.

'You think that's how he got in?' asked Ramírez, the man incapable of just doing something.

'This is not an easy building to get into and out of without being seen,' said Falcón. 'If the maid confirms that the door was double locked when she arrived this morning, it's possible he used the lifting gear to get in. If it wasn't then we'll have to scrutinize the closed-circuit tapes.'

'That takes a lot of nerve, Inspector Jefe,' said Ramírez, 'to wait in here for more than twelve hours.'

'And then slip out when the maid came in to find the body.'

Ramírez bit his bottom lip, unconvinced that that sort of steel in a man existed. He left the room as if more questions were about to turn him back.

Falcón sat at Raúl Jiménez's desk. All the drawers were locked. He tried a key from a set on the desk, which opened all the drawers down both sides, while another opened the central one. Only the top two drawers on either side had anything in them. Falcón flicked through a stack of bills, all recent. One caught his attention, not because it was a vet's bill for a dog's vaccinations, and there had been no evidence of any dog, but rather that it was his sister's practice and it was her signature on the bill. It unnerved him, which was illogical. He dismissed it as another non-coincidence.

He went through the central drawer, which contained several empty Viagra packets and four videos. From their titles, they seemed to be blue movies. They included *Cara o Culo II*, the sequel to the video whose slipcase had been left empty on the TV cabinet. It occurred to him that they hadn't found the porn video that was showing on the TV while Raúl was with the prostitute. He shut the drawer. He began a detailed inspection of the photographs behind him. He thought that Raúl Jiménez might have known his father. He was, after all, a famous painter, a well-known figure in Seville society, and Jiménez seemed to be a celebrity collector. As he worked his way from the centre out to the edges he realized that this was a collection of a different order of celebrity. There was Carlos Lozano, the presenter of *El Precio Justo*. Juan Antonio Ruiz, known in the bullring as 'Espartaco'. Paula Vázquez, the presenter of *Euromillón*. They were all TV faces. There were no writers, painters, poets, or theatre directors. No anonymous intellectuals. This was the superficial face of Spain, the *Hola!* crowd. And when it wasn't, it was the bourgeoisie. The police, the lawmen, the functionaries who would make Raúl Jiménez's life easier. The glamour and the graft.

'Did you find who you were looking for?' asked Sra Jiménez from behind him.

She was out of her coat, wearing a black cardigan and leaning against a guest chair. Her eyes were pink-rimmed despite the make-up repair.

'I'm sorry you saw that,' he said, nodding at the television.

'I'd been warned,' she said, taking a packet of Marlboro Lights out of her cardigan pocket and lighting one with a Bic from the desk. She threw the pack on the desk, offering him one. He shook his head. Falcón was used to this ritual sizing up. He didn't mind. It gave him time, too.

He saw a woman about the same age as himself and well groomed, maybe over groomed. There was a lot of jewellery on her fingers whose nails were too long and too pink. Her earrings clustered on her lobes, winking from the nest of her blonde helmet. The make-up, even for a repair job, was heavily slapped on. The cardigan was the only simple thing about her. The black dress would have worked well had it not had a hem of lace which, rather than bringing grief to mind, brought sex awkwardly into contention. She had square shoulders and an uplifted bust and was full-bodied with no extra fat. There was something of the health club fitness regime about her, the way the straps of muscle in her neck framed her larynx and her calf muscles were delineated beneath her black stockings. She was what the English would call handsome.

She saw a fit man in a perfectly cut suit with all his hair, which had gone prematurely grey but belonged to a class of person who would never think of returning it to its original black. He wore lace-up shoes and the tightness of the bows led her to believe that this was someone who rarely unbuttoned his jacket. The handkerchief in his breast pocket she assumed was always there but never used. She imagined that he had a lot of ties and that he wore them all the time, even at weekends, possibly in bed. She saw a man who was contained, trussed and bound. He did not give out, which may have been a professional attitude but she thought not. She did not see a Sevillano, not a natural one anyway.

'You said earlier, Doña Consuelo, that you and your husband had few secrets.'

'We should sit,' she said, pointing him into her husband's desk chair with her cigarette fingers and pivoting the guest chair round with some dexterity. She sat quickly, slipped sideways on to one of the arms and crossed her legs so that the lace hem rode up her calf.

'Are you married, Inspector Jefe?'

'This is an investigation into your husband's murder,' he said flatly.

'It's relevant.'

'I *was* married,' he said.

She smoked and counted her fingers with her thumb.

'You didn't need to tell me that,' she said. 'You could have left it at "Yes".'

'These are games we should not be playing,' he said. 'Every hour that goes past takes us an hour away from your husband's death. These hours are important. They count more than the hours, say, in three or four days' time.'

'You've separated from your wife?' she said.

'Doña Consuelo . . .'

'I'll be quick,' she said, and batted the smoke away from between them.

'We are separated.'

'After how long?'

'Eighteen months.'

'How did you meet her?'

'She's a public prosecutor. I met her at the Palacio de Justicia.'

'So, a union of truth hunters,' she said, and Falcón searched her for irony.

'We are not making progress, Doña Consuelo.'

'I think we are.'

'I might be satisfying your curiosity . . .'

'It's more than curiosity.'

'You are reversing the procedure. It is *I* who have to find out about *you*.'

'To see whether I killed my husband,' she said. 'Or had him killed.'

Silence.

'You see, Inspector Jefe, you're going to find out everything about us, you're going to dig into our lives. You're going to strip down my husband's business affairs, you're going to probe his private life, uncover his little uglinesses – his blue movies, his cheap whores, his cheap . . . cheap cigarettes.'

She leaned over and picked up the pack of Celtas and threw them across the desk so that they skidded into Falcón's lap.

'And you won't let *me* alone. I'll be your prime suspect. You saw that horrible thing,' she said, waving at the television behind her.

'Number 17 Calle Río de la Plata?'

'Exactly. My lover, Inspector Jefe. You'll be talking to him too, no doubt.'

'What's his name?' he asked, getting out his pen and notebook for the first time, down to business at last.

'He is the third son of the Marqués de Palmera. His name is Basilio Tomás Lucena.'

Did he detect pride in that? He wrote it down.

'How old is he?'

'Thirty-six, Inspector Jefe,' she said. 'You've started before I've finished.'

'This is progress.'

'Did she meet somebody else?'

'Who?'

'The public prosecutor.'

'This isn't . . .'

'Did she?'

'No.'

'That's hard,' she said. 'I think that's harder.'

'What?' he asked, instantly annoyed with himself for snatching at her bait.

'To be dumped because she would rather be alone.'

That slid into him like a white-hot needle. His head came up slowly.

Sra Jiménez looked around the room as if it was her first time in it.

'Were you aware that your husband was taking Viagra?' he asked.

'Yes.'

'Did his doctor know?'

'I imagine so.'

'You must have been aware of the risks for a man in his seventies.'

'He was as strong as a bull.'

'He'd lost weight.'

'Doctor's orders. Cholesterol.'

'He must have been very disciplined.'

'I was disciplined for him, Inspector Jefe.'

'I should have thought as a restaurateur, with all that food around . . .'

'I hire and run all the staff in the restaurants,' she said. 'They were threatened with the sack if they gave him so much as a crumb.'

'Did you lose many?'

'They are Sevillanos, Inspector Jefe, who, as you probably know, rarely take anything seriously. We lost three before they understood.'

'I'm a Sevillano.'

'Then you must have been abroad for a long time to learn your . . . gravity.'

'I was in Barcelona for twelve years and four years each in Zaragoza and Madrid before I arrived back here.'

'It sounds as if you've been demoted.'

'My father was ill. I asked to be transferred to be close to him.'

'Did he recover?'

'No. He didn't make it to the new millennium.'

'We *have* met before, Inspector Jefe,' she said, stubbing out the cigarette.

'Then I don't remember.'

'At your father's funeral,' she said. 'We *are* talking about Francisco Falcón.'

'You couldn't believe it before,' he said, thinking: Let's see how this changes your tune.

'Was that who you were looking for in the photographs?' she asked, and he nodded. 'You wouldn't find him there. He was not Raúl's kind of celebrity. He never came to any of the restaurants. I doubt they knew each other. I went to the funeral because *I* knew him. I own three of his paintings.'

He imagined his father with Consuelo Jiménez. His father had liked attractive women, especially if they bought his stupid paintings . . . but this one? Maybe that would have interested him. The showy, slightly tacky dresser with a razor tongue and a well-honed intuition. The usual crowd who bought his paintings always tried to say something 'intelligent' about them, when there was nothing intelligent in them. Consuelo Jiménez wouldn't have done that. She would have found something different to say to his father, perhaps made a personal observation, even attempted a small perception, which most people, standing under the fierce reflection of his colossal fame, would never have dared. Yes. And his father would have risen to that. Definitely.

'So you were completely involved in your husband's business affairs?' he said.

'What happened to his house on Calle Bailén?'

'I live in it,' he said. 'And you would know if your husband had any enemies.'

'On your own?'

'Just as he did,' said Falcón. 'Your husband . . . he must have trodden on people on his way up to the top. There are probably people out there who would . . .'

'Yes, there are people out there who would gladly see him dead, especially those he'd corrupted and who are now free from the weight of their obligation.'

She flicked a derisory fingernail at the functionary end of the photograph gallery.

'If you know something . . . it would help.'

'Ignore me. I'm being facetious,' she said. 'If there had been any corruption I would not have known about it. I ran the restaurants. I designed the interiors. I organized the flower arrangements. I made sure the produce for the kitchens was of the highest quality. But, as you can probably imagine, even without knowing my husband, I did not make contact with a single peseta of real money, nor did I deal with any of the powers, legal or otherwise, who let Raúl build, who licensed him, and who made sure there were no . . . unforeseen circumstances.'

'So it is possible that . . .'

'Very unlikely, Inspector Jefe. If something goes wrong in that department the stink soon gets into the restaurants and nothing reached my nose smelling that bad.'

Falcón decided he'd let this woman run free for long enough. It was time she understood what had happened here. Time she stopped looking at this as a news item that didn't affect her. Time to bring her inside.

'Your husband's body is undergoing an autopsy at the moment. In due course we will have to go to the Instituto Anatómico Forense for you to identify the body. You will see for yourself that your husband's murder was extraordinary, more extraordinary than any I have seen in my career.'

'I saw the killer's little production for myself, Inspector Jefe. To spy on a family like that you would have to be profoundly disturbed.'

'You happened to see the last few moments of the video when you first arrived. Perhaps you were not aware of what you were looking at,' he said. 'Your husband was entertaining a prostitute in here last night. The killer filmed it. We think that he may have got into this apartment much earlier, around lunchtime, using the removals company's lifting gear, and that he was hiding in here, waiting for his moment.'

Her eyes widened. She grabbed for the cigarettes and lit up, spanned her forehead with her hand.

'I was here yesterday afternoon with the children before we went to the Hotel Colón,' she said, on her feet now, pacing the length of the desk.

'We found your husband sitting in the twin of that chair,' said Falcón, not taking his eyes off her. 'His forearms, ankles and head had been secured with flex. He was barefoot because his socks had been used to gag him. He was being forced to watch something on the screen, something so horrific to him that he fought with all his strength not to see it.'

As he said this it occurred to him that it was only half true. The on-screen horror might have been the start of it, but what made Raúl Jiménez writhe convulsively was coming round in agony to find that a madman had cut his eyelids off. After that he'd have known there was nothing to lose and he'd have fought like a dog until his heart gave out.

'What was he being forced to watch?' she asked, confused. 'I didn't see . . .'

'What you saw had a certain amount of horror for you personally. Being stalked is creepy, but it's not something that you would fight to the point of self-mutilation not to see.'

She sat down straight in the chair, knees pressed together like a good little girl. She leaned forward, grasping her shins, holding herself in.

'I can't think,' she said. 'I can't think of anything like that.'

'Nor can I,' said Falcón.

She drew on the cigarette, spat out the smoke as if it was disgusting. Falcón searched for any hint of pretence.

'I can't think,' she said it again.

'You *have* to think, Doña Consuelo, because you have to go over every minute that you spent with Raúl Jiménez plus everything you know about his life before you met him and you must tell it all . . . to me and then perhaps between us we can find the small crack . . . the . . .'

'The small crack?'

Falcón's mind went blank. What crack was he talking about? An opening. A chink. But into what?

'We might find something that will give us an insight,' he said. 'Yes, an insight.'

'Into what?'

'Into what your husband feared,' said Falcón, losing his thread.

'He had nothing *to* fear. There was nothing frightening in his life.'

Falcón reined in his thoughts. His fear? What was he thinking of? What was this man's fear going to tell him?

'Your husband had certain . . . tastes,' said Falcón, fingering the pack of Celtas. 'Here we are in one of the most prestigious apartment buildings in Seville, or at least they were fifteen years ago . . .'

'Which was about when he bought it,' she said. 'I never liked it here.'

'And where were you moving to?'

'Heliopolis.'

'Another expensive place to live,' said Falcón. 'He has four of the most well-known restaurants in Seville attended by the rich, the powerful and the celebrated. And yet . . . Celtas, which he smoked with the filters broken off. And yet . . . cheap prostitutes picked up in the Alameda.'

'That was only a recent development. No more than two years . . . since . . . since Viagra became available. He was impotent for three years before that.'

'His taste in tobacco probably goes back to a time when he had no money. When was that?'

30

'I don't know, he never talked about it.'

'Where does he come from?'

'He never talked about that either,' she said. 'We Spanish don't have such a glorious past that his generation would choose to wallow in it.'

'What do you know about his parents?'

'That they're both dead.'

Consuelo Jiménez was no longer maintaining eye contact. Her ice-blue eyes roved the room.

'When did you and Raúl Jiménez meet?'

'At the Feria de Abril in 1989. I was invited to his caseta by a mutual friend. He danced a very good Sevillana ... not the usual shuffling about that you see from the men. He had it in him. We made a very good pair.'

'You would have been in your early thirties? And he was in his sixties.'

She smoked hard and trashed the cigarette. She walked to the window where she became a dark silhouette against the bright blue sky. She folded her arms.

'I knew this would happen,' she said, mouth up against the cold glass. 'The digging. The turning over. That's why I wanted something from you first. I didn't want to spew my life into the police machine, the one that encapsulates lives on a few sides of A4, the one that doesn't have space for nuance or ambiguity, that doesn't see grey but only black or white and really only has an eye for black.'

She turned. He shifted in his seat, trying to get the light to catch her face. He turned on the desk lamp and began a reappraisal of Consuelo Jiménez in this warmer light. Perhaps the initial toughness she'd shown was what she'd learned from being with and working for Raúl Jiménez. The dress, the jewellery, the fingernails, the hair – maybe that was how Raúl Jiménez wanted her and she wore it like armour.

'My job is to get to the truth,' he said. 'I've been working at it for over twenty years. In that time I ... and police science, have developed hundreds of techniques for helping us get to the provable truth. I'd like to be able to tell you it is now an exact science, that it *is* actually scientific, but I can't, because, like economics, another so-called science, there are people involved and where people are involved there's variability, unpredictability, ambivalence ... Does that answer your concern, Doña Consuelo?'

'Maybe after all your job is not so different from your father's.'

'I don't understand.'

'Forget it,' she said. 'You were asking me about my husband. How we met. Our age disparity.'

'It just struck me as unusual that an attractive woman in her thirties should . . .'

'Go for an old toad like Raúl,' she finished. 'I'm sure I could think up something suitable about the emotional and economic stability of the mature man, but I think we've come to an agreement, haven't we, Inspector Jefe? So I'll tell you. Raúl Jiménez pursued me relentlessly. He cornered me, pressured me and begged me. He broke me down until I said "Yes". And having spent months avoiding that word, in fact saying "No, no, no", once I'd said it . . . it untangled me.'

'What was there to untangle?'

'I imagine you've known disappointment,' she said. 'When your wife left you, for instance. How old was she, by the way?'

'Thirty-two,' he said, no longer resisting her digressions.

'And you?'

'Forty-four then.'

She sat in the leather scoop chair, crossed her legs and swivelled from side to side.

'As you've probably gathered, I'm not a Sevillana,' she said. 'I've lived with them for more than fifteen years but I'm not one of them. I'm a Madrileña. In fact I come from a *pueblo* in Estremadura, just south of Plasencia. My parents left there when I was two. I was brought up in Madrid.

'In 1984 I was working in an art gallery and I fell in love with one of the clients, the son of a duke. I won't bore you with details . . . only that I became pregnant. He told me we couldn't marry and he paid for me to go to London for an abortion. We separated at the Barajas Airport and the only time I've seen him since is in the pages of *Hola!* I moved to Seville in 1985. I'd been here on holiday. I liked the city's *alegría*. Four years later and not much alegría, it has to be said, I met Raúl. I was ready for Raúl. Disappointment had prepared me.'

'You made it sound as if he was crazy about you. You've had three children by him. You seem to enjoy your work. Your choice in finally accepting him must have, as you said yourself, simplified things.'

She went to the desk, ripped through the drawers until she came to a pile of old creamy-coloured black–and–white photographs which she shuffled through rapidly, choosing one, which she held to her chest.

'It did,' she said, 'until I saw this –'

She handed him the photograph. Falcón looked from the photograph to her and back again.

'If it wasn't for the mole on her top lip you wouldn't be able to tell us apart, would you, Inspector Jefe?' she said. 'Apparently she was also a little shorter than me.'

'Who is she?'

'Raúl's first wife,' she said. 'Now you see, Inspector Jefe, once a Consuelo always a Consuelo.'

'And what happened to her?'

'She committed suicide in 1967. She was thirty-five years old.'

'Any reason?'

'Raúl said she was clinically depressed. It was her third attempt. She threw herself into the Guadalquivir – not off a bridge, just from the bank, which has always struck me as a strange thing to do,' she said. 'Not snuffing yourself out with sleeping pills, not savagely punishing yourself with slashed wrists, not diving into oblivion for all to see, but throwing yourself away.'

'Like rubbish.'

'Yes, I suppose that's it,' she said. 'Raúl didn't tell me any of that, by the way. It was an old friend of his from the Tangier days.'

'I was brought up in Tangier,' said Falcón, his brain unable to resist another non-coincidence. 'What was your husband's friend's name?'

'I don't remember. It was ten years ago and there've been far too many names since then, you know, working in the restaurant business.'

'Did your husband have any children from that marriage?'

'Yes. Two. A boy and a girl. They're in their fifties now or close to it. The daughter, yes, that's interesting. About a year after we got married a letter came here from a place called San Juan de Dios.'

'That's a mental institution on the outskirts of Madrid in Ciempozuelos.'

'As any Madrileño would know,' she said. 'But when I asked Raúl about it he invented some ridiculous story until I confronted him with a direct debit to the same institution and he had to tell me that his daughter's been an inmate there for more than thirty years.'

'And the son?'

'I never met him. Raúl wouldn't be drawn on the subject. It was closed. A past chapter. They didn't speak. I don't even know where he lives, but I suppose I'll have to find out now.'

'Do you have a name?'

'José Manuel Jiménez.'

'And the mother's maiden name?'

'Bautista, yes, and she had a strange first name: Gumersinda.'

'The children were both born in Tangier?'

'They must have been.'

'I'll run it through the computer.'

'Of course you will,' she said.

'Did he ever talk about his Tangier days . . . your husband?'

'Now *that* was a very long time ago. We're talking about the early forties and fifties. I think he left there shortly after independence in 1956. I don't think he came straight here but I can't be sure. All I do know was that by 1967, when his wife killed herself, he was living in a penthouse in one of those blocks of flats on the Plaza de Cuba. They were new then.'

'And near the river.'

'Yes, she must have looked at that river a lot,' she said. 'It can be quite mesmerizing, a river at night. Black, slow-moving waters don't seem so dangerous.'

'What do you know about your husband's . . . ?'

'Call him Raúl, Inspector Jefe.'

'Raúl's personal and business relationships between, say, the death of his first wife and your meeting in the Feria in 1989?'

'This is ancient history, Inspector Jefe. Do you think it's relevant?'

'No, I don't, just background. I have to learn a life in a morning. I have to establish a victim in his context if I'm to have a chance at discovering motive. Most people are killed by people they know . . .'

'Or thought they knew.'

'Exactly.'

'The killer knew us, didn't he? The happy Family Jiménez.'

'He knew *about* you.'

Out of nowhere her face crumpled and she started crying, burst into wracking sobs and collapsed forwards on to her knees. Falcón moved towards her, unsure how to act in these situations. She sensed it and held up her hand. He held out a box of tissues, hovering like a bad waiter. She slumped back into her chair, panting, her eyes black and glistening.

'You were asking about his personal and business relationships,' she said, staring off out of the window.

'He was forty-four when his first wife died. I can't believe he went twenty years without . . .'

'Of course there were women,' she said savagely, angry now, possibly at him for his curiosity and his uselessness. 'I don't know how many there were. I imagine lots, but none of them lasted. Quite a few of them came to look at me . . . the winner of Raúl's devotion. Most had their nails dipped in spite, ready to scratch. You know how I dealt with them, Inspector Jefe? I gave them the satisfaction of thinking me a silly little tart. You know, a little bit *cursi*, twee. It made them happy. They were superior. They left me alone after that. Some of them are friends now . . . in the Seville sense of the word.'

'And business?'

'He didn't start the restaurants until the tourist boom in the eighties when people found there was more to Spain than the Costa del Sol. It was a hobby to begin with. He was very sociable and he didn't see why he shouldn't make money out of it. He started with that one in El Porvenir for his rich friends, then the one in Santa Cruz for the tourists, likewise the big one off the Plaza Alfalfa. After we married he added the two on the coast and last year we opened that one in La Macarena.'

'Where did the money come from in the first place?'

'He made a lot of money in Tangier after the Second World War when it was a free port. There were thousands of companies there in those days. He even had his own bank and a construction company. It was an easy place to get rich then, as I'm sure you know.'

'I was very young. I have no memory of the place,' said Falcón.

'He started a barging company here in Seville in the sixties. I think he even owned a steel-pressing factory for a while. Then he got into property and went into partnership with the construction company Hermanos Lorenzo, which he pulled out of in 1992.'

'Was that amicable?'

'The Lorenzos are regular clients of the restaurants. We used to take the children to their house in Marbella every summer until Raúl got bored.'

'So since the death of his first wife and his daughter going insane you don't think there's been any major disturbance in Raúl's life?'

She remained silent for some time, staring out of the window, her foot nodding, the shoe working loose from her heel.

'I'm beginning to think that Raúl was the quintessential Spaniard, maybe the quintessential Sevillano, too. Life is a fiesta!' she said, and held her hands out in the direction of the Feria ground. 'He was as you see him there in the photographs. Smiling. Happy. Charming. But it was a cover, Inspector Jefe. It was a cover for his total misery.'

'An antidote, too, maybe,' he said, not agreeing with her, thinking that he was Spanish, too, and he didn't consider himself miserable.

'No, not an antidote, because his alegría didn't counteract anything. It never remedied his essential condition which, believe me, was one of *abject* misery.'

'And you never got to the root of that?'

'He didn't want me to and I didn't want to. He quickly discovered that while I was the visual replacement of his wife I was not her clone. Having pursued me relentlessly, he totally failed to love me. I think, in fact, I made him even more miserable by constantly reminding him of her. Still, he kept his side of the bargain, I'll say that for him.'

'What was that?'

'He absolutely didn't want any more children and I very much wanted them. I said I wouldn't marry him if he wasn't going to give me children. So we . . . copulated, I think that's the right word, on the three occasions necessary. He only just made it for the youngest. Those were pre-Viagra days.'

'And so you found Basilio Lucena.'

'I'm not finished about the children yet,' she said, snapping. 'Having said he didn't want children, he then completely doted on them and was incredibly, obsessively protective of them. He was security mad. He made sure they were picked up from school. They never walked around alone. They never even played unsupervised. And have you seen the front door to this flat? That was put in after the last one was born. There are six steel bolts within the body of the door, which by five turns of the key are driven into the wall. We don't even have a door like that to the office and there's a safe in there.'

'Who normally locked the door at night?'

'He did. Unless he was away and then he'd call me at one or two in the morning to make sure I'd done it.'

'Would he have locked it if he was alone?'

'I'm sure he would have. He was always going on about making it routine so that it would never be forgotten.'

'Did you ever ask him about this unusually obsessive behaviour?'

'I was touched he cared so much about the children.'

Ramírez called him on his mobile. He'd finished with the removals men. It had taken some time to break them down, but they'd finally admitted that they went for lunch leaving the lifting gear in place because they had one more chest of drawers to bring down. They'd said that the gear wouldn't work without the truck engine running, but the platform went up on rails, which was as good as a ladder. Once they'd brought the chest of drawers down nobody went back into the apartment. Falcón told him to join Fernández viewing the CCTV tapes with the conserje and hung up.

'I'd like to talk about Basilio Lucena,' he said.

'There's nothing to tell.'

'Did you have any plans?'

'Plans?'

'Your husband was an old man. Didn't it occur to you . . . ?'

'No, it didn't . . . ever. Basilio and I have a nice time together. It involves some sex, of course, but it is not a great passion. We don't love each other.'

'I was thinking back to that duke's son you mentioned earlier.'

'That was different,' she said. 'I have no intention of developing my relationship with Basilio. In fact, I think this might even finish it.'

'Really?'

'I should have thought that you, with a famous father, would know how the eyes of society will come down on me. There will be talk and malicious thinking not dissimilar to the suspicions that you are paid by the state to have. It will all be idle . . . but vicious, and I will protect my children from that.'

'Is it you or your husband who has the enemies?'

'I am perceived as undeserving, as a rider on my husband's coat-tails, as someone who would have failed in life were it not for Raúl Jiménez. But they will see,' she said, her jaw muscle tensing in her cheek. 'They will see.'

'Were you aware of the contents of your husband's will?'

'I never saw him sign one, but I knew of his intentions,' she said. 'Everything would be left to me and the children and there would be some provision made for his daughter, his *hermandad* and his favourite charity.'

'What was that?'

'Nuevo Futuro, and the particular part of it that interested him was *Los Niños de la Calle*.'

'Street children?'

'Why not?'

'People support charities for reasons. A wife dies of cancer, the husband puts money into cancer research.'

'He said that he began contributing after a trip to Central America. He was very moved by the plight of children orphaned by the civil wars in those countries.'

'Perhaps he himself was orphaned by the Civil War.'

She shrugged. Falcón's pen hovered over his notebook where the word *putas* was underscored.

'And the prostitutes?' he said, punching the word out into the room. 'You haven't seen the section of the video where your husband is filmed frequenting the Alameda. He could have afforded better in less dangerous surroundings. Why do you think . . . ?'

'Don't ask me why men go to prostitutes,' she said, and, as an afterthought, '. . . his misery, I should think.'

'And you can't shed any light on that.'

'People will only talk about those things if they want to, if they know how to. Something that could make my husband that wretched was probably buried so deep that he didn't know it was there any more. It was just his condition. How would you start talking about something like that?'

Consuelo Jiménez's words induced a trance in Falcón. His mind tumbled back over those first hours of the investigation and he hit that fear again, the surge of panic. He was on the walk down the corridor, the double walk, because it was his and the killer's same strides towards that blank wall with its empty hook lit by the light from the horror room. Then the face, and the eyes in the face, and the terrifying relentlessness of what they'd seen.

'Don Javier,' she said, which snapped him back to reality because she hadn't used his rank.

'Please excuse me,' he said. 'I was lost. I mean I was elsewhere.'

'It didn't look like somewhere I would want to be,' she said.

'I was just running over some things in my mind.'

'Then you must have seen some terrible things. You said yourself, about Raúl's murder, the most extraordinary of your career.'

'Yes, I did say that, but this wasn't anything to do with that,' he said, and found himself on the brink of a confession, which was not, he thought, a place the Inspector Jefe del Grupo de Homicidios should ever be.

4

Thursday, 12th April 2001, Edificio del Presidente, Los Remedios, Seville

He offered her a car. She turned him down and said she'd make her own way to her sister's house. He asked for her sister's details just to keep the pressure on, and reminded her that he would pick her up later to go to the Instituto Anatómico Forense for the identification of the body. He wanted to interview her then, once she'd been shocked out of any residual complacency by the sight of her husband's dead body. He asked her to think about anything unusual in Raúl's business or personal life in the last year and told her to call the restaurant to get the names and addresses of the three people who'd been fired for feeding her husband against orders. He knew they would be dead leads, but he wanted to induce a fear in her of his thoroughness. They shook hands at the door of the apartment; his were damp, hers dry and cool.

Ramírez followed him back into Raúl Jiménez's study from the hall.

'Did she do it,' he asked, slumping into the high-backed chair, 'or have it done, Inspector Jefe?'

Falcón turned his pen over and over in his fingers.

'Any news from Pérez at the hospital?' he asked.

'The maid's still out cold.'

'And the CCTV tapes?'

'Four people unidentified by the conserje. Two males. Two females. One of the females I would say is the whore, but she looks very young. Fernández has taken the tapes down to the station and we'll get some digitalized print-outs to show around the building.'

'What about people leaving the building by alternative exits? The garage, for instance.'

'Neither of those cameras are working. The conserje called the technicians this morning but they still haven't arrived. Semana Santa, Inspector Jefe,' he explained.

Falcón gave him the names and addresses of the fired employees and told him to have them interviewed as soon as possible. Ramírez left. Falcón picked up the photograph of Raúl Jiménez's first wife – Gumersinda Bautista. He called the Jefatura and asked them to run a check on José Manuel Jiménez Bautista, born in Tangier in the late 1940s, early 1950s.

He sat back with the other photographs, flicked through the nameless people. He came across a shot of Raúl Jiménez on the deck of a yacht. He was barely recognizable. No hint of the toadiness to come. He was handsome and confident and stood as if he knew it, hands on hips, shoulders braced, chest puffed out. Falcón brushed his thumb over that chest, thinking there was a speck on the photograph. It stayed and on closer inspection looked to be some kind of wound to his right pectoral near the armpit. He flipped it over – *Tangier, July 1953* was written on the back.

His mobile rang. The police computer had come up with a Madrid address and telephone number for José Manuel Jiménez. He took them down and asked after Serrano and Baena, two other officers from his group. They were off for Semana Santa. He ordered them to be sent down to him at the Jiménez apartment.

Instead of reviewing his notes and planning his next assault on the cultivated defences of Doña Consuelo Jiménez, who, he couldn't deny it, was still his prime suspect, he found himself reaching for the sheaf of old photographs. There were some group shots, again from Tangier, in 1954 according to the dates on the back. He looked over the faces, thinking that he was trying to find his father in there until he realized that he was concentrating more on the women and was wondering if his mother, who'd died seven years after these photographs were taken, was amongst these strangers. He was fascinated at the prospect of finding a shot of her he'd never seen, in the company of people he'd never heard of, in a time before he was born. Some of the faces were too small and grainy and he decided to take them home and look at them under his magnifying glass.

He took a cigarette from the pack of Celtas, sniffed it. He hadn't smoked for fifteen years. He'd given up when he was thirty, on the same day he'd terminated his relationship of five years with Isabel Alamo. She'd been heartbroken, not least because she'd assumed their private talk was going to be a marriage proposal. In the ghastliness of that memory he broke off the filter, picked up the Bic and lit the cigarette. It was horrible even without inhaling and he set it down on the ashtray. He leaned back in the chair as his mind shot back to another memory back in Tangier on New Year's Eve 1963. He was standing by the stairs in his pyjamas, waist height to all the leaving guests, who were going down to the port for the firework display. Mercedes, his second mother, his father's second wife, picked him up and took him back upstairs to bed. This smell was in her hair, Celtas; somebody must have been smoking the same brand at the party. There were still plenty of Spaniards in Tangier in those days, even though the really good times were long over. Mercedes had put him to bed, kissed him hard, squeezed him to her bosom. He left the memory at that point. He never took it forward from there because . . . he just didn't. He was interested to find that this new smell could take him back to that time. Normally he only ever thought of Mercedes when he came across Chanel No.5, her perfume of choice.

A knock at the door brought him back. Serrano and Baena stood in the corridor.

'You were quick,' said Falcón.

The two men shuffled in, uneasy with their boss who they assumed was being sarcastic. They'd been forty minutes.

'Traffic,' said Baena, which solved the problem both ways.

Falcón was mystified by the sight of the cigarette reduced to an ash snake in front of him. A glance at his watch left him stunned to find that it was past eleven o'clock and he'd achieved nothing. He checked his notes to see when Ramírez had timed the removals men's lunch break and ordered Serrano and Baena to go out on the streets to try to find a witness who'd seen someone, probably in overalls, climbing up the lifting gear to the sixth floor of the Edificio del Presidente.

Sub-Inspector Pérez called saying the maid, Dolores Oliva, had finally come round. She wouldn't speak until she had a rosary in her hand and throughout the interview she fingered a key ring of the Virgen del Rocío. She was convinced she had come into contact with pure evil and that it might have found a way in. Falcón tapped the desk. It was always like this with Pérez. The academy and eleven years in the field had not been able to break down his need to tell a story in a report. It took eight minutes for him to reveal that Dolores Oliva had opened the door with five turns of the key.

Falcón cut Pérez off and told him to get down to Los Remedios as soon as possible to work the apartments in the block with the print-outs of the unidentified persons from the CCTV tapes. The prostitute had to be identified and found, too. He hung up and saw that there was a message for him from the Médico Forense saying that the autopsy was complete and a written report was being typed out. He thought for a moment about whether he should let Consuelo Jiménez see the body in its full horror and decided that it would be better to keep the eyelid removal as police information only. He called the Médico Forense back and asked him to make the body clean and presentable.

He arranged to pick up Consuelo Jiménez from her sister's house in San Bernardo and went down to his car calling Fernández and telling him to make contact with Pérez to work the apartments.

It was fiercely bright outside after the darkness of the apartment and nearly warm. It was always the same around Semana Santa and the Feria, a most ambiguous time of year. Neither hot nor cold. Neither dry nor wet. Neither religious nor secular. He got into his car and threw the sheaf of old photographs on the seat. The one of Gumersinda, Raúl's first wife, was on top. It was a formal shot and she was staring earnestly into the camera, but it was Consuelo Jiménez's words that came to mind: 'He totally failed to love me.' Two bizarre thoughts clashed in his mind, squirting adrenalin into his system, which made him start the car and pull out without looking. Tyres squealed. A muffled shout of 'Cabrón!' reached him.

He made a U-turn and crossed the river over the Puente del Generalísimo. The port railway tracks streamed beneath him and the cranes formed a guard of honour down to the massive Puente del V Centenario, which rose out of the urban mist. His thoughts burgeoned as he headed northeast past the Parque de María Luisa and he desperately wanted that cigarette he'd let burn to ash in Raúl Jiménez's study. What had come into his mind were the words of his wife, Inés, whom he, too, had failed to love: 'You have no heart, Javier Falcón,' and this had been entangled with the sight of Gumersinda, a woman from his mother's era, which had made him think of his blood mother, Pilar, and then his stepmother, Mercedes. All these women, immensely important to him, he now thought he'd somehow failed.

The idea was so new and peculiar it made him quite desperate to be active and unconscious.

He sat at the traffic lights, his fingers jittering over the steering wheel, muttering: 'This is madness' because this did not happen to him. He did not have random inexplicable thoughts. He had never been by nature a daydreamer. He had always been calm and methodical, which characteristics could not be applied to him now. From the moment he'd seen Raúl's terrible face there'd been something no less cataclysmic than a genetic mutation. His mind was flooding with uncomfortable memories, sweat welled up from his forehead and dampened his hands, his concentration was shot. He hadn't even got this investigation under control. He hadn't checked the windows and doors out on to the balcony in the Jiménez apartment. First steps. And that business with the TV, yanking the cord out of the wall and not mentioning it. It was unprofessional. It was not him.

He cruised up Calle Balbino Murrón right to the end, to a building that overlooked the soccer pitch in the Colegio de los Jesuitas. He put the photos in the glove compartment. Consuelo Jiménez came out on her own before he reached the house. A child, probably the youngest, stood in the window. She waved and the boy waved frantically back. It saddened Falcón. He saw himself in the window, left behind.

They set off, cutting across the main arterial roads going into the centre of town. She looked straight ahead, not taking much in beyond the glass.

'Have you told the children yet?' he asked.

'No,' she said. 'I didn't want to tell them and then leave them to go to the hospital.'

'They must know something is wrong.'

'They see I'm nervous. They don't know why they are with their aunt. They keep asking me why we aren't in the house in Heliopolis and when is Daddy going to bring the present he promised.'

'The dog?'

'You can be quite impressive, Inspector Jefe,' she said. 'You don't have children, do you?'

'No . . .' he said, wanting to fill that out somehow.

They continued in silence, heading north towards La Macarena.

'How is the investigation going?' she asked, polite, distant.

'It's early days.'

'So you only have the obvious motive to go on.'

'Which is?'

'Wife wants to get rid of unloving older husband, inherit his fortune and disappear with younger lover.'

'People have killed for less.'

'*I* gave you that motive. There's no one who could have told you that Raúl Jiménez didn't love me.'

'What about Basilio Lucena?'

'He only knows that Raúl was impotent and that I have physical needs.'

'Do you know where he was last night?'

'Ah, yes, of course. It would be the lover who would do the deed,' she said. 'You'll meet Basilio and then you must tell me what you think he's capable of.'

They passed the Basilica de La Macarena and a few minutes later pulled up by an austere grey building on Avenida Sánchez Pizjuan that housed the Instituto Anatómico Forense. A crowd of people were gathered outside the doors. Falcón parked up inside the hospital barrier. Consuelo Jiménez put on a pair of sunglasses. The crowd were on them as soon as they got out of the car, Dictaphones pointing. Loose words blasted out from the cacophony and cut like shrapnel – '*marido*', '*asesinado*', '*brutalmente*'. Falcón took her by the arm and pushed past them, got her through the door and slammed it behind him.

He walked her through the corridors to the office of the Médico Forense, who took them to the viewing room. The official pulled back the curtain and, beyond the glass panel, lit from above, lay Raúl Jiménez under a sheet that was pulled down over his chest. Two candles burned by his head. His eyes, clean of blood, stared up at the ceiling. There was nothing in them. The back of his head, previously matted with gore, had been washed clean. The nose had been miraculously reattached and the scarring from the flex on his cheeks had gone. The old wound to his right pectoral, seen in the photograph, now looked like the worst thing his body had suffered. Consuelo Jiménez formally identified the body. The curtain was closed. Falcón asked her to wait while he had a short discussion with the Médico Forense, who told him that Raúl Jiménez had died at three in the morning. He had suffered a brain haemorrhage and heart failure. There was an extremely high level of Viagra in his blood. It was the doctor's conclusion that the increased blood pressure and high degree of distress combined with the clogged condition of the victim's arteries had caused the Raúl Jiménez to more or less internally burst. He gave Falcón his official typed report.

They ran the gauntlet to the car and rather than go back through the barrier, which was blocked by the journalists, he headed through the grounds of the faculty and out past the main hospital building on to Calle de San Juan de Ribera.

'They should have closed his eyes,' said Consuelo Jiménez. 'You cannot be at peace with your eyes still open, even if they don't see anything.'

'They couldn't close his eyes,' he said as the traffic lights released them to turn left on to Calle Muñoz León.

He drove past the old city walls and found a parking space in the busy street. Sra Jiménez clung to the roof grip, her knuckles whitening, her face already beginning to shrink from the words that she knew were coming her way. The worst of his career.

He told her how it was, with no soft focus, giving his own appalled version. Yes, it had been the worst of his career. There were scenes he'd had to 'process' which perhaps sounded worse – walking into an apartment in a high-rise block in an *urbanización* on the outskirts of Madrid, four dead in the sitting room, blood up the walls, two dead in the kitchen, needles, syringes, tinfoil floating on gore and, in the bedroom, a child whimpering on a soiled cot. But that was all expected horror in a culture of brutality. The torture of Raúl Jiménez was something he could not be objective about and not just because he was sensitive about eyes, which were so important to his work. It was how the killer's punishment of his victim had worked on his own imagination. It terrified him, the notion of the sheer relentlessness of reality, the lack of visual respite. As Sra Jiménez had noted, not even in death could he be seen to enjoy the big sleep but had to lie in eternal, wide-eyed horror at man's capacity for evil.

Sra Jiménez had started crying. Really crying. This was no dabbing at the mascara but a bawling, retching, snot-streaked breakdown. Javier Falcón understood the cruelty of police work. He was not the man to comfort this woman. It was he who had put the images in her head. His job, the point of his job at this moment, was to observe not just the veracity of the emotional display but also to perceive the opening, the crack in the carapace where he would jam in his lever. It had been his conscious tactic to get her in a car, in an enclosed bubble in a busy street with nowhere to go, while an indifferent world crashed by, oblivious to the enormity.

'You were in the Hotel Colón last night?' he said and she nodded. 'Were you alone after your children had gone to bed?'

She shook her head.

'Was Basilio Lucena with you last night?'

'Yes.'

'All night?'

'No.'

'What time did he leave?'

'We had dinner in the room. We went to bed. He must have left by two o'clock.'

'Where did he go?'

'Home, I suppose.'

'He didn't go to the Edificio del Presidente?'

Silence. No answer, while Falcón looked into the structure of her face.

'What does Basilio Lucena do for a living?' he asked.

'Something useless at the university. He's a lecturer.'

'What department?'

'One of the sciences. Biology or chemistry – I can't remember. We never talked about it. It doesn't interest him. It's a position and a salary, that's all.'

'Did you give him a key?'

'To the *apartment*?' she said, shaking her head at him. 'Meet Basilio before you even . . .'

'How do you know I haven't?'

Silence.

'Have you been in touch with Basilio Lucena this morning?' he asked.

She nodded.

'What did you tell him?'

'I thought he should know what had happened.'

'So that he could prepare himself?'

'You might think, Inspector Jefe, if you saw Basilio Lucena on paper that he was an intelligent man. He is certainly educated and sophisticated. But his intelligence is very finely tuned to a narrow waveband and his sophistication admired by a small clique. He has been made lazy by the lack of challenge in his job. His house and car have been paid for by his parents. He has no dependants. His income allows him an irresponsible lifestyle. He isn't somebody who's ever had to think on his feet because most of the time he's lying down. Is that the profile of a murderer?'

Falcón's mobile rang. Pérez made an elaborate report on the unidentified people picked up by the CCTV cameras. Two positive identifications, one negative, and the girl they assumed to be the prostitute had been referred to Vice. He told Pérez to follow up on the girl and asked Fernández to go through the apartments again over lunchtime.

The moment with Consuelo Jiménez had passed. He pulled out into the traffic, did a U-turn and headed west to the river. He glanced at his hostage to see how her thoughts were progressing. He sensed a crisis point, began to have that feeling that this could all be over before his first meeting with Juez Calderón. That was how this work went in his experience. All over in twenty-four hours or they went into months of long, bleak slog.

'Are you taking me back to the apartment?' she asked.

'You're an intelligent woman, Doña Consuelo.'

'Your opportunity to flatter me has long passed.'

'You spend your life amongst people,' he said. 'You understand them. I think you understand the demands of my job.'

'That you have to be so disgustingly suspicious.'

'Do you know how many murders there are in Seville every year?'

'In this city of joy?' she said. 'In this city of handclapping in the streets, of *cervecitas y tapitas con los amigos*. In this city *de los guapos, de los guapísimos*? In this godly city of the Holy Virgin?'

'In the city of Seville.'

'A couple of thousand,' she said, tossing the number up into the air with her ringed fingers.

'Fifteen,' he said.

'Back-stabbing is metaphorical murder.'

'Drugs account for most of those murders. The remaining few come under the heading of "domestic" or "passionate". In *all* of those murders – *all* of them, Doña Consuelo – the victim and the perpetrator knew each other and in most cases they were intimate.'

'Then you have an exception, Inspector Jefe, because *I* did not kill my husband.'

They went through the underpass by the old railway station at the Plaza de Armas and continued along the riverside on the Paseo Cristóbal Colón past the Maestranza bullring, the Opera and the Torre del Oro. The sun was bright on the water, the high plane trees in full leaf. It was no time to be confessing to murder and spending a lifetime of springs behind bars.

'Denial is a very powerful human condition . . .' he said.

'I wouldn't know, I've never denied anything.'

'. . . because there are no doubts . . . ever.'

'I'm either a liar or completely deluded,' she said. 'I can't win, Inspector Jefe. But at least I always tell myself the truth.'

'But do you tell it to me, Doña Consuelo?' he said.

'So far . . . but perhaps I'm changing my mind.'

'I don't know how you persuaded your husband's old flames that you were a silly tart.'

'I dressed like one,' she said, tinkling her fingernails. 'I can talk like one, too.'

'You're an accomplished actress.'

'Everything counts against me.'

Their eyes connected. His soft, brown, tobacco. Hers frozen aquamarine. He smiled. He couldn't help liking her. That strength. The inexorable mouth. He wondered what it would taste like and shot the thought straight out of his head. They crossed the Puente del Generalísimo and he changed the subject.

'It's never occurred to me before what a Francoist little corner of town this is. This bridge. This street is named after Carrero Blanco . . .'

'Why do you think my husband was living in the Edificio del Presidente?'

'I thought most people were following the Paquirri fashion.'

'Yes, well, my husband liked *los toros*, but he liked Franco even more.'

'And you?'

'He was before my time.'

'Mine, too.'

'You should dye your hair, Inspector Jefe, I thought you were older.'

They parked up. Falcón called Fernández on his mobile, told him to go to the Jiménez apartment. He and Sra Jiménez took the lift to the sixth floor, nodded past the policeman at the door. They paced the empty corridor towards the empty hook, that double walk still snagging in Falcón's brain. They sat down in the study and waited in silence for Fernández to arrive.

'Just run your pictures past Sra Jiménez, please,' he said. 'In order of appearance on the CCTV tapes.'

Fernández counted them out, each one getting the negative from Consuelo Jiménez until the last one when her eyes widened and she blinked the double take.

'Who is that in the picture, Doña Consuelo?'
She looked up at him, entranced, beguiled as if it had been magic.
'It's Basilio,' she said, her mouth not closing.

5

Thursday, 12th April 2001, Edificio del Presidente, Los Remedios, Seville

How to play this? Falcón resisted the temptation to run his fingers up the edge of the desk like a concert pianist in full flourish. He rested his chin on his thumb, tensed his jaw and brushed his cheekbone with a finger while the adrenalin flashed down his arteries. This was it, he thought. But how to make it come out? Separate or together? He felt inspired. He decided on the cockpit approach. Throw them in together, let them flap and cut, peck and stab.

'Sra Jiménez and I are going to El Porvenir,' he said to Fernández. 'Contact Sub Inspector Pérez and help him find the prostitute. Tell him we've identified the unknowns from the CCTV tapes.'

Sra Jiménez crossed her legs, lit a cigarette. Her foot wouldn't keep still. Falcón went into the corridor to call Ramírez on his mobile. He wished he liked him more.

Ramírez was bored. He'd taken on the fruitless task of interviewing the fired employees himself and, so far, after two had come up with nothing other than they were glad to get away from Sra Jiménez. Falcón watched her while Ramírez blew off steam. She was clicking the fingernails of her thumb and forefinger, playing things over in her mind. Falcón briefed Ramírez and gave him Basilio Lucena's address, told him to get down there and be ready to maintain the pressure on the two protagonists.

Falcón took Consuelo Jiménez back across the river to 17 Calle Río de la Plata. The traffic was heavier around lunchtime. The joggers were out in the park; girls with their hair tied in ponytails bobbed along beyond the railings, gay in the sunshine. These moments of police work were fascinating to him – driving along while a suspect endured some massive internal struggle between denial and truth, between acting out the lie or embracing the relief of retribution and absolution. Where did the impulse come from that started the body chemistry into a decision of such magnitude?

He turned right up Avenida de Portugal behind the high towers of the Plaza de España. The building which had been the centrepiece of the '29 Expo was so normal to him that he wouldn't have noticed it except, on this day, with the red brick against the blue sky and the explosive greenery all around, it amazed him. It brought back a memory of his father throwing himself out of his seat as they watched *Lawrence of Arabia* on television to point out that David Lean was using the building as the British Embassy in Cairo.

'You can talk if you like,' he said.

She started out aggressive and pulled back after the first syllable. She found a lipstick in her handbag and reshaped her mouth . . . nicely.

'I'm as curious as you are,' she said, which unnerved him.

They parked down the street from the house. No Ramírez. Falcón took out the autopsy report and read it through, blinking in the detail. The instruments used, the technical know-how demonstrated, the chemicals and solutions evident on the victim's clothes – all reaffirmed his suspicions.

A car pulled up alongside. Ramírez nodded and parked up at the end of the street. He walked back down, through the gateway and rang the bell to number 17. Lucena opened it. There was a discussion. Ramírez showed his ID card. He was let in. Minutes passed. Falcón and Sra Jiménez got out of the car, rang the bell. Lucena came to the door, harassed. He walked straight into Falcón's eyes and caught the blue flash of his lover's. The fear was unmistakable, but of what Falcón wasn't sure. They went in, the man definitely crowded out in his own living room with the pressure of three pairs of eyes on him. Falcón positioned himself next to the television set, which had a video camera connected to it. Ramírez stood by the door. Lucena sat down on the edge of an armchair. Sra Jiménez occupied the sofa opposite, looked at him out of the corner of her eye, crossed her legs and set her foot nodding.

'We've already established from Sra Jiménez that you were with her last night,' said Falcón. 'Can you remember when you left?'

'It was about two o'clock,' he said, running his hand through his thin, brown hair.

'Where did you go after leaving the Hotel Colón?'

The foot stopped nodding.

'I came back here.'

'Did you leave your house again that night?'

'No. I went to work this morning.'

'How did you get to work?'

He faltered, stumbled over the beginner's question.

'By bus.'

Ramírez took over and tied him in knots about bus routes. Lucena clung to his lie until Falcón quietly put the print-out from the CCTV tapes into his hands.

'Is that you, Sr Lucena?' he asked.

He jiggled his head in nervous affirmation.

'What subject do you lecture in at the university?'

'Biochemistry.'

'So you'd probably be working from one of those buildings on Avenida de la Reina Mercedes?'

He nodded.

'Very close to Heliopolis, where Sra Jiménez is moving to?'

He shrugged.

'In your faculty would it be easy to get hold of such a chemical as chloroform?'

'Very easy.'

'And saline solution and scalpels and cutting scissors?'

'Of course, there's a laboratory.'

'You see those figures in the bottom right-hand corner of the picture . . . what do they say?'

'02.36. 12.04.01.'

'Who were you going to see in the Edificio del Presidente at that time?'

He pinched the bridge of his nose, squeezed his eyes shut.

'Can we talk about this in private?' he asked.

'We're all interested parties here,' said Ramírez.

'Twenty-five minutes after you entered that building Raúl Jiménez was murdered,' said Falcón, who saw now that Lucena, rather than considering him as a persecutor wanted him as a friend. It was the woman he feared.

'I went to the eighth floor,' said Lucena, throwing his hands up.

An unexpected answer, which had Ramírez reaching for his notebook.

'The *eighth* floor?' said Sra Jiménez.

'Orfilia Trinidad Muñoz Delgado,' said Ramírez.

'She must be ninety years old,' said Sra Jiménez.

'Seventy-four,' said Ramírez. 'And there's Marciano Joaquín Ruíz Pizarro.'

'Marciano Ruiz, he's the theatre director,' said Falcón.

Lucena nodded up at him.

'I know him,' said Falcón. 'He's been to see my father, but he's . . .'

'*Un maricón*,' said Sra Jiménez, deep-voiced, brutal.

Ramírez, like some mugging comic actor, took a quick step back, stared down at Lucena. Falcón used his mobile to call Fernández, who told him that there'd been no reply from the Ruíz apartment when he'd called that afternoon.

'He's not in today,' said Lucena. 'He dropped me off at work and went to Huelva. He's rehearsing Lorca's *Bodas de Sangre*.'

The air thermals changed in the room. Sra Jiménez charged out of her chair before there was any chance of intervention. Her hand swung back and made nasty contact with the corner of Lucena's head. It wasn't a slap, more of a thud. All those rings, thought Falcón.

'*Hijo de puta*,' she roared from the door.

Blood trickled down the side of Lucena's face. The front door slammed. Heels split the paving stones.

'I don't get it,' said Ramírez, more relaxed now that the woman was out of the room. 'Why were you fucking her if you're a . . .'

Lucena took a packet of tissues out, dabbed his forehead.

'Can you just explain that to me?' said Ramírez. 'I mean, you're one or the other, aren't you?'

'Do I have to put up with this imbecile?' Lucena asked Falcón.

'Unless you want to spend a long time down at the Jefatura, yes.'

Lucena got to his feet, put his hands in his pockets, walked to the centre of the room and turned to Ramírez. His weakness had been replaced by an aristocratic, vindictive smoothness of the sort employed by fops who've been asked for the satisfaction of a duel.

'I fucked her because she reminded me of my mother,' he said.

It was a calculated offence, which had its desired effect of shocking Ramírez, who Lucena could see was from a different class to his own. The Inspector was from a conservative, working-class Sevillano family and lived with his wife and two daughters in his parents' house. His mother was still alive and living with them and when his father-in-law died, which would be any week now, his mother-in-law would join them. Ramírez balled his fist. Nobody talked like that about mothers to him.

54

'We're leaving now,' said Falcón, gripping Ramírez by his swollen bicep.

'I want to get . . . I want to get the phone number of the other maricón,' said Ramírez, the words bottling in his throat. He wrenched his arm away from Falcón.

Lucena went to the desk, slashed a pen across some paper and handed it to Falcón, who manoeuvred Ramírez out of the room.

Outside the Calle Río de la Plata was moving as slowly as the river through Buenos Aires. Sra Jiménez was down at the end of the street, her rage bristling in the sunlight. Ramírez was no less angry. Falcón stood between them, no longer the detective, more the social worker.

'Get Fernández on the mobile,' he said to Ramírez. 'See if they've found the girl yet.'

Lucena's door slammed shut. Falcón headed down the street to Consuelo Jiménez thinking: Was that the sophistication you were talking about that so entranced you? What are we now? Where are we? This society with no rules of engagement.

She was crying, but from anger this time. She gritted her teeth and stamped her feet in humiliation. Falcón drew alongside her, hands in pockets. He nodded as if agreeing with her but thinking: This is policework – one moment on the brink of cracking the case and packing up early for celebratory beers and the next back on the street wondering how you could have been so facile.

'I'll run you back to your sister's house,' he said.

'What did I do to him?' she asked. 'What did I *ever* do to him?'

'Nothing,' said Falcón.

'What a day,' she said, looking up into the perfect sky, all serenity a long way off, beyond the stratosphere. 'What a fucking day.'

She stared into the mash of tissue in her hand like a haruspex who might find reason, clarity or a future. She threw it in the gutter. He took her arm and turned her towards the car. As he helped her in, Ramírez said they'd found the girl from the Alameda and were taking her down to the Jefatura on Blas Infante.

'Tell Fernández to interview that last employee that Sra Jiménez fired. Pérez should leave the girl to sweat until we get there. I want all reports filed at four-thirty before we go to see Juez Calderón at five.'

Falcón called Marciano Ruíz's mobile and told him he would have to come back to Seville to make a statement tonight. There was a protest from Ruíz, which was followed by a threat from Falcón to arrest Lucena.

'Are you calm?' he asked Ramírez, who nodded over the roof of the car. 'Take Sr Lucena down to the Jefatura and get a written statement out of him . . . and don't be rough.'

Falcón led Lucena out of his house and put him in the back of Ramírez's car. They all left. Falcón hunched over the steering wheel, muttering in his head as the tyres hissed down Avenida de Borbolla. Everybody was mental today. Some cases did this. They grated too much. Normally the child cases. The kidnapping followed by the wait and the inevitable discovery of the abused body. This was the same . . . as if something terrible had been added to the excesses of the human experience and had subtracted something greater which could never be replaced. The daylight would always be a little dimmer, the air never quite as fresh.

'Do you see a lot of this?' asked Sra Jiménez. 'Yes, I suppose you do, I suppose you see it all the time.'

'What?' said Falcón, shrugging, knowing what she meant, not wanting to get into it.

'People with perfect lives, who see them destroyed in a matter of . . .'

'Never,' he replied at the edge of vehemence.

That word – 'perfect' – hardened him and he remembered her earlier words which had flayed his 'perfect' life alive: 'I think that's harder. To be dumped because she would rather be alone.' He felt cruel and fought the urge to retaliate: 'I think that's hard . . . to be dumped for a male lover.' He filed it in his mind under 'Unworthy' and replaced it with the thought that maybe Inés had ruined women for him.

'Surely, Inspector Jefe . . .' she said.

'No, never,' he said, 'because I've never met anybody with a perfect life. A perfect past and a pristine future, yes. But the perfect past is always brilliantly edited and the pristine future a hopeless dream. The only perfect life is the one on paper, and even then there are those spaces between the words and lines and they're rarely patches of nothing.'

'Yes, we are careful,' she said, 'careful of what we show to others and of what we reveal to ourselves.'

'I didn't mean to be so . . . intense,' he said. 'We've had a long day and there's more to come. We've had some shocks.'

'I can't believe I'm still such an idiot,' she said. 'I met Basilio in the lift of the Edificio del Presidente. He was probably on his way down from the eighth floor. I didn't think. But . . . but why would he . . . *bother* to seduce me?'

'Forget him. He's not important.'

'Unless he's given me something.'

'Take a test,' said Falcón, more brutal than he intended. 'But start thinking too, Doña Consuelo, about who could possibly have a motive for killing your husband. I want names and addresses of all his friends. I want you to remember, for instance, who it was who told you how much you resembled the first wife. I want Raúl's diary.'

'He had a desk diary in the office which I kept up. He threw away his address book when he got his mobile phone. He only spoke to people on the phone anyway. He had no use for paper and he always lost pens and stole mine.'

Falcón did not remember a mobile phone. He called the forensics and the Médico Forense. No mobile. The killer must have taken it.

'Any other records?'

'An old address book in the office computer.'

'Where's that?'

'Above the restaurant off the Plaza de Alfalfa.'

He handed her his mobile and asked her to arrange for him to pick up a print-out in half an hour.

He dropped her outside her sister's house in San Bernardo just after 3 p.m. Ten minutes later he parked up by the east gate to the Jardines de Murillo and continued on foot, half running through the crowded streets of the Barrio de Santa Cruz, where tourists gathered for the Semana Santa processions. The sun was out from behind the clouds. It was hot and he was soon sweating. The air in the enclosed streets smelt strongly of Ducados, orange blossom, horseshit and the vestiges of incense from the processions. The cobbles were spattered and slippery with candle wax.

He stripped off his mac and cut down the backstreets he knew from the few times he'd managed to attend the English classes he kept paying for at the British Institute on Calle Frederico Rubio. He came into the southeast corner of the Plaza de Alfalfa, which was packed with all the tribes of the world. Cameras nosed at him. He sidestroked through the crowd, trotted up Calle San Juan and was suddenly carried forward by a crush of people surging down Calle Boteros. He realized his mistake too late, saw the procession coming towards him, but couldn't break free of the herd. They bore him onwards to the flower-decked float, which had just negotiated a difficult corner and was now beetling forward under the power of the twenty *costaleros* underneath. The Virgin, demure beneath her white lace canopy, was shimmering in the intense sunlight, while incense from the burners shifted this way and that in the thermals of the street, filling his head and chest so that air was difficult to come by. The drums from the band behind the float beat on, hammering out their portentous rhythm.

The crowd shoved forwards. The *paso* bore down on their awe-struck faces, the Virgin towering above them, her whole body shuddering from right to left under the straining costaleros. Earsplitting, discordant trumpets suddenly blasted out the passion. The sound in the confines of the narrow street reverberated inside Falcón's chest and seemed to open it up. The crowd gasped at the glorious moment, at the weeping Virgin, at the height of ecstasy . . . and the blood drained rapidly from Falcón's head.

6

Thursday, 12th April 2001, Calle Boteros, Seville

The paso veered away. The high Virgin's pitiful eyes moved off, fell on others. The crush slackened. The final blast of the trumpets ricocheted off the balconies. The drums beat out to silence. The costaleros lowered the float from their shoulders. The crowd clapped at their feat of engineering. The procession of *nazareños* in their high-pointed hats put down their crosses, rested their candles. Falcón held on to the handle at the back of an old woman's wheelchair, a hand on his knee. The old woman was waving at one of the nazareños, who'd lifted the flap of his hood. He smiled, revealing the normal human being beneath, nothing more sinister than a bespectacled accountant.

Falcón loosened his tie, wiped cold sweat from his face. He pushed through the edge of the crowd, staggered through the files of nazareños. The people on the other side parted for him. He found some pavement and bent his head to his knees, felt the blood thump back up his cerebral cortex, refresh his brain.

Haven't eaten all day, he was thinking, but he knew that wasn't it. He looked back at the paso, the Virgin staring off down the street, unconcerned with him now. Except, this was it ... she had been. For that moment, for that fraction of a second, she'd got inside him, filled him out. It had been an experience he could nearly remember having had before, but he couldn't quite get to the memory of it. It was too distant.

He found the office above the Jiménez restaurant, picked up the print-out and drank a glass of water. He left the old city, avoiding all processions. He drove down to the river and crossed over to the Plaza de Cuba feeling empty and hungry. He stopped at a bar on República Argentina and bought a *bocadillo de chorizo*, which he ate too quickly so that it stuck in his chest, the crust as hard-edged as the pain of loss, which was odd because he hadn't lost anyone since his father died two years ago.

The Jefatura was on the intersection of Calle Blas Infante and Calle López de Gomara. He parked at the back of the building and made his way up the two short flights of stairs to his office, which had a view over the ordered ranks of cars. His office was spartan with not one personal item in it. There were two chairs, a metal desk and some grey filing cabinets. The light came from a neon strip above his head. He did not hold with distractions at work.

There were thirty-eight messages for him and five were from his immediate superior Jefe de Brigada de Policía Judicial, Comisario Andrés Lobo, who was no doubt reacting to pressure from his boss Comisario Firmin León, whose relationship with Raúl Jiménez Falcón had noted from the photographs. He went straight to the interrogation rooms, where Ramírez was standing over Basilio Lucena, holding his fist as if he wanted to punch him. He called Ramírez out, briefed him on the interrogation strategy for the girl and told him to send Pérez down. He went in to see Lucena who looked up and went straight back to writing his statement.

'What you said to Inspector Ramírez back there . . .' Falcón started, the nastiness of that line still bothering him.

'Any student will tell you that lecturers react very badly to morons.'

'Was that all it was?'

'I'm surprised you're concerned, Inspector Jefe.'

He was, too, and wondered if he was making a fool of himself.

'I doubt my mother was ever as good in bed as Consuelo, if that's what you were wondering,' said Lucena.

'You're a confusing man, Sr Lucena.'

'In a confused age,' he said, waggling his pen at Falcón.

'How long had you been seeing Sra Jiménez?'

'A year or so,' he said. 'That was the first time I'd been back to the Edificio del Presidente since we met . . . Such is my luck.'

'And Marciano Ruíz?'

'You're as curious as the Inspector, aren't you?' he said. 'I'm easily bored, Don Javier. Marciano and I see each other when my ennui peaks.'

Pérez came in, told Falcón which room the prostitute was in and took over.

The girl was sitting at a table smoking while she stacked and unstacked two packs of Fortuna. Her hair was cropped unevenly on her head as if she'd done the job herself without a mirror. She stared at the dead TV screen straight ahead of her, blue eyeshadow, pink mouth. A blonde wig hung off the back of an unused chair. She wore a tartan miniskirt, a white blouse and black boots. She was tiny and still looked of school age, but the depravity she'd seen on her extended truant was worn into her dark brown eyes.

Ramírez turned on the tape, introduced her as Eloisa Gómez and announced himself and Falcón.

'Do you know why you're here?' asked Falcón.

'Not yet. They said it was a few questions, but I know you guys. I've been here before . . . I know your games.'

'We're different to the usual guys,' said Ramírez.

'That's right,' she said, 'you are. Who are you?'

Falcón shook his head a fraction at Ramírez.

'You were with a client last night . . .' said Falcón.

'I was with lots of clients last night. It's Semana Santa,' she said. 'It's our busiest time of the year.'

'Busier than the Feria?' asked Ramírez, mildly surprised.

'Without a doubt,' she said, 'especially the last few days when everybody comes from out of town.'

'One of your clients was Raúl Jiménez. You went to see him last night in his apartment in the Edificio del Presidente.'

'I knew him as Rafael. Don Rafael.'

'You'd met him before?'

'He's a regular.'

'In his apartment?'

'Last night was maybe the third or fourth time in his apartment. Normally it's the back of his car.'

'So how did it work this time?' asked Ramírez.

'He called the mobile. My group of girls bought three mobiles last year.'

'What time?'

'I didn't take the call. I was with someone else . . . but it must have been midnight. The first time.'

'The first time?'

'He only wanted to speak to me, so he called again around twelve-fifteen. He asked me to come to his apartment. I told him I was making a lot of money on the plaza and he asked me how much I wanted. I told him one hundred thousand.'

Ramírez roared with laughter.

'That's Semana Santa for you,' he said. 'The prices are ridiculous.'
The girl laughed too, relaxed a notch.
'Don't tell me he paid that,' said Ramírez.
'We settled on fifty.'
'*Joder.*'
'How did you get there?' asked Falcón, trying to settle it down again.
'Taxi,' she said, lighting up a Fortuna.
'What time did it drop you off?'
'Just after half past twelve.'
'Anybody around?'
'Not that I saw.'
'What about in the building?'
'I didn't even see the conserje, which I was glad about. There was no one in the lift or on the landing and he let me in before I rang the bell, as if he'd been watching me through the spy hole.'
'You didn't hear him unlock the door?'
'He just opened it.'
'Did he lock it once you were inside?'
'Yes. I didn't like that, but he left the keys in the door so I didn't protest.'
'What did you notice about the apartment?'
'It was almost empty. He told me he was moving. I asked him where and he didn't answer. Other things on his mind.'
'Talk us through it,' said Ramírez.
She grinned, shook her head as if men the world over were all the same.
'I followed him up the corridor into his study. There was a TV on in the corner with an old movie playing. He took a video out of the desk and loaded it into the machine. He asked me to wear a thick blue skirt which came down to my knees and a blue jumper over my blouse. He told me to tie my hair in bunches. I was wearing a long black wig,' she said. 'He preferred brunettes.'
'Did you see him take a pill?'
'No.'
'You didn't notice anything strange apart from the place being empty?'
'Like what?'
'Anything that made you feel nervous?'
She thought about it, wanting to help. She held up a finger. They leaned forward.

'He wasn't wearing any shoes,' she said, 'but that didn't exactly make me panic.'

They slumped back in their chairs.

'Hey! It's your fault. You're making me see things where there's nothing.'

'Keep going,' said Ramírez.

'I asked him for my money. He gave me some five thousand notes which I counted. He picked up the remote and a porno movie started up on the TV. He took off his trousers. I mean he dropped his trousers and stepped out of them. And we got down to it.'

'What about the windows?' asked Ramírez.

'What about them?'

'You were facing the windows.'

'How do you know?'

'He *assumes* you were facing the windows,' said Falcón.

'The curtains were drawn,' she said, suspicious now.

'So you had sex with him,' said Ramírez. 'How long did it last?'

'Longer than I expected.'

'Is that why you turned round?' asked Ramírez.

The brown eyes hardened in her head. These were not the usual games.

'Who *are* you?' she said.

'Inspector Ramírez,' he said, dry as fino.

'We're from the Grupo de Homicidios,' said Falcón.

'Somebody *killed* him?' she asked, her head switching between the two men, who nodded.

'The person who killed him was in the apartment while you were there.'

She wrenched the cigarette from her mouth, puffed hard.

'How do you know?'

Ramírez had prepared the tape earlier and clicked the remote so that the screen was instantly filled with the empty corridor, the bare hook, the light falling from the study doorway while the soundtrack blared the mixture of the two fake ecstasies. The hairs came up on Falcón's neck. The girl was transfixed. The camera turned the corner and she saw herself kneeling in front of Raúl Jiménez, who was staring up at the screen while she confronted the curtains. As her head turned, the camera toppled back into the darkness.

The girl knocked her chair back flat and paced the room. Ramírez returned the screen to black.

'That is very weird,' she said, pointing at the screen with her cigarette fingers.

'Did you notice anything?' asked Falcón.

'I don't know whether you've put things into my head, but I do remember something now,' she said, closing her eyes. 'It was just a change of light, a shadow wobbling. In my business that's what I'm frightened of . . . when the shadows move.'

'When darkness has a life of its own,' said Falcón, the words out unsupervised so that Ramírez and the girl checked him for oddness. 'But you didn't react . . . to these shadow moves?'

'I thought it was something in my head and anyway I think he reached his moment about then and that distracted me.'

'And afterwards?'

'I cleaned up in his bathroom and left.'

'Did he lock the door behind you?'

'Yes. The same as when he locked it the first time. Five or six turns. I heard him take the keys out, too. Then the lift came.'

'What time was it?'

'I don't think it was much after one o'clock. I was back in the Alameda with another client by half-past one.'

'Fifty thousand,' said Ramírez. 'That's a good hourly rate.'

'It might take you a while before you could earn that amount,' she said, and they both laughed.

'What's your mobile number?' asked Falcón, and they both laughed again until they saw he was serious and Eloisa rattled it out for him.

'So,' said Ramírez, still good-humoured, 'that seems to be everything . . . except I'm sure she's left something out, aren't you, Inspector Jefe?'

Falcón didn't react to Ramírez's brutal game. The girl looked away from him and back to where she'd suddenly felt the threat.

'I've told you everything that happened,' she said.

'Except the most important thing,' said Ramírez. 'You didn't tell us when you let him into the apartment.'

It took a few seconds for the implication of that mild statement to penetrate and then her face went as hard as a death mask.

'I thought you were too good to be true,' she said.

'I'm not good,' said Ramírez, 'and nor are you. You know what the guy did – the one you let into the apartment? He tortured an old man to death. He put your Don Rafael through some of the worst suffering that we've ever come across in our police careers. No, it wasn't just a shot to the head, not a knife in the heart, but slow, brutal . . . torture.'

'I didn't let anyone into that apartment.'

'You said he left the keys in the door,' said Falcón.

'I didn't let anyone into that apartment.'

'You said you saw something,' said Ramírez.

'You made me think I saw something, but I didn't.'

'The light changed,' said Ramírez.

'The shadows moved,' said Falcón.

'I didn't let anybody in,' she said slowly. 'It happened just as I told you.'

They terminated the interview just before 16.30. Falcón sent Ramírez off with the girl to find a policewoman to supervise a pubic hair match with the Policía Científica. As they left he heard Ramírez talking to her as if she were an old friend and they were heading for a *cervecita* except the words were different.

'No, I tell you, Eloisa, if I was you I'd drop the guy, drop him like a hot rock. If he can kill a guy like that he can kill you. He can kill you without feeling a damn thing. So you watch yourself. You get any suspicions, any doubts, you give me a call.'

Falcón went to his office and called Baena and Serrano to see if they'd found any witnesses outside the Edificio del Presidente. None. Few people around. Shops closed. Most of the locals in the centre of town for the processions.

He hung up, cracked his knuckles one after the other, a habit that Inés had loathed but it was an unconscious act, something he did to steady his brain. It had made her writhe.

Falcón called Comisario Lobo, who told him to make an appearance in his office. On the way to the lift he saw Ramírez and told him to get the paperwork ready for the meeting with Juez Calderón. He went up to the top floor. Lobo's secretary, one of those minimalist Sevillanas who reserved all her extravagance for after office hours, sent him in with a flick of an eyelash.

Lobo was facing the window, hands behind his back, doing knee bends while he took in the greenery of the Parque de los Principes across the street. He was short and stocky with large, hairy agricultural hands. He had a bull neck and grey, industrial hair. He'd always worn heavy black-framed glasses from a lost era until last year when his wife had persuaded him into contact lenses. It was an attempt at image improvement which had failed because his eyes were the colour of mud and the lack of frames had made his nose look more hooked, revealing more of his brutal face than most wanted to see. He had thin lips, which were only two shades darker than his cumin complexion. He looked more criminal than most of the people in the holding cells, but he was a good manager and a direct talker, who always supported his officers.

'You know what this is about?' he said, over his shoulder.

'Raúl Jiménez.'

'No, Inspector Jefe, it's about Comisario León.'

'He was in the photographs in Jiménez's study.'

'Who was he in bed with?'

'They weren't those sort of . . .'

'I'm joking, Inspector Jefe,' said Lobo. 'You probably saw a lot of other *funcionarios* in those photos.'

'Yes, I did.'

'Did you see me?'

'No, Comisario.'

'Because I'm not in them, Inspector Jefe,' he said, walking quickly to his desk.

They sat down; Lobo clasped his hands as if about to crush small heads.

'You weren't here at the time of the 1992 Expo?' he said.

'I was in Zaragoza by then.'

'A very different situation existed here at Expo '92 than at the Barcelona Olympics. There, I'm sure you will recall, the Catalans made a profit. Whilst here, the Andalucians made a staggering loss.'

'There was talk of corruption.'

'Talk!' roared Lobo savagely. 'Not just talk, Inspector Jefe. There *was* corruption. There was so much corruption that if you *weren't* making millions it was an embarrassment. Such an embarrassment that those who *hadn't* managed to stuff their pockets went out and hired Mercedes and BMWs to make it look as if they had.'

'I didn't realize.'

'And it wasn't just the locals. The Madrileños were down here in force, too. They could see a certain attitude was prevailing. A slackness. A lack of attention to detail that could be financially exploited.'

'How is this relevant ten years later?'

'Do you remember how many people were brought to book over that?'

'I don't recall, Comisario.'

'None!' said Lobo, whacking the desk with his clasped hands. 'Not one.'

'Hermanos Lorenzo,' said Falcón. 'Construction.'

'What about them?'

'Raúl Jiménez had a business relationship with them, which terminated in 1992.'

'Now you're beginning to understand. Raúl Jiménez was on the Expo de Sevilla Committee. He was on the board of directors responsible for the development of the site. Hermanos Lorenzo was not the only construction company he was connected to.'

'I'm still not sure how this can be relevant to his murder nearly ten years later.'

'Possibly it isn't. I doubt there will be any connection. But you'll be stirring up the shit pot, Inspector Jefe. Nasty things will come to the surface.'

'And Comisario León?'

'He doesn't want any unpleasant surprises. You must tell me if you come across "sensitive" information and . . . no leaks, Inspector Jefe, or we'll all be broken on the wheel.'

Another reason why Lobo's men liked him was his unique ability to help them understand the seriousness of a situation. Falcón got up to leave, headed for the door knowing that there was something else, that Lobo always liked to spring things on his men as they were leaving. It made a more lasting impression.

'You probably thought, with all your experience in Barcelona, Zaragoza and Madrid, that your application to a second division murder city like Seville would be well received.'

'I don't take anything for granted, Comisario. Politics plays its part in every appointment.'

'I had to work very hard on your behalf.'

'Why did you do that?' he asked, Lobo unknown to him before he arrived.

'For that very unfashionable reason that you were the best man for the job.'

'Then I thank you for it.'

'Comisario León was a great admirer of the tenacious talents of Inspector Ramírez.'

'As am I, Comisario.'

'They keep in touch, Inspector Jefe . . . informally.'

'I understand.'

'That's good,' said Lobo, suddenly cheerful. 'I knew you would.'

7

Thursday, 12th April 2001, Edificio de los Juzgados, Seville

'I think Eloisa Gómez let him in,' said Ramírez as they crossed the river.

'Baena and Serrano haven't got anybody outside the Edificio del Presidente,' said Falcón. 'And I prefer that scenario to the killer climbing up the lifting gear and hiding in the apartment for half a day, even though it was empty apart from a short visit from Sra Jiménez. Was the girl scared?'

'Didn't say a word to me after we finished the interrogation.'

'Does she believe us?'

'Who knows?'

The Edificio de los Juzgados was next to the Palacio de Justicia, just opposite the Jardines de Murillo. It was well past five o'clock when Falcón and Ramírez parked up at the back of the court building. Falcón, who hated to be late, wanted to break the comb that Ramírez was putting through his black, brilliantined hair into ten little pieces. His murderous glare had no effect on the Inspector, who considered that they were early and his coiffure a priority – there could be secretaries about.

The two men in their dark suits, white shirts and sunglasses went to the front of the dull grey building – the monochrome of justice in the garden city. They put their briefcases through the X-ray machine and showed their ID. The place was quiet; almost everything happened in the morning. They went upstairs to Juez Calderón's office on the first floor. The building was dark, even grim, on the inside. Nothing pretty about justice even when it was good and true.

Ramírez asked about Lobo and Falcón told him that pressure was already coming down from Comisario León and mentioned the corruption angle. Ramírez looked bored.

Calderón was not in his office. Ramírez slumped in a chair and played with a gold ring he had on his middle finger which was set with three diamonds. The ring had always bothered Falcón, too feminine for the mahogany muscularity of Ramírez.

'We're going to have to make something of that time-wasting maricón, Lucena,' said Ramírez brutally, 'or we're going to look like incompetents in our first meeting with the new boy.'

Falcón let his eyes ripple over the book-lined room. Ramírez stretched out.

'You know, I think even if you fuck both women and men, that deep down you're a maricón,' he said.

'Even if it was just a one-off?' said Falcón.

'It's not something you can experiment with, Inspector Jefe. It's in your genes. If you can even think about it . . . you're a maricón.'

'Let's not get into this with Juez Calderón.'

The young judge arrived at a quarter to six, sat at his desk and got straight down to business. He was now in the role of the Juez de Instrucción, which meant that he had ultimate responsibility for the direction of the case and bringing the necessary evidence for a conviction successfully to court.

'What have we got?' he asked.

Ramírez yawned. Calderón lit a cigarette, chucked the pack at Ramírez, who took one. They smoked while Falcón wondered how these two men had got to know each other . . . until he remembered the football. Betis losing 4–0 on the day the killer shot his movie of Raúl and his sons. Where did that ease come from? He tried to remember if he'd ever had it. He must have done and lost it somewhere in his youth when his work had become too serious, or perhaps he'd become too serious about his work?

'Who's going to begin?' asked Calderón.

'Let's start with the body,' said Falcón, and gave a resumé of the autopsy.

'How did he think the eyelids were removed?' asked Calderón.

'Initial incision by scalpel, and the cutting done by scissors. He thought it was a good job.'

'And we think this was done to force him to watch something on the television?'

'The severity of the self-inflicted wounds would suggest that the man was horrified by what had been done to him as well as what he was being forced to watch,' said Falcón.

'I'd go along with that,' said Calderón, unconsciously fingering his eyelids. 'Any thoughts on what the killer showed him?'

Ramírez shook his head. No room for that sort of conjecture in his hard cranium.

'I think we only know our *own* worst nightmares, not those of others,' said Falcón, trying not to be patronizing.

'Yes, I hate rats,' said Calderón cheerfully.

'My wife can't be in the same room as a spider,' said Ramírez, '. . . even if it's on television.'

The two men laughed.

'This is something a little stronger than a phobia,' said Falcón, stuck in the schoolmaster role. 'And conjecture isn't going to help us right now, we need to concentrate more on motive.'

'Motive,' said Calderón, nodding the task into himself. 'You've spoken to Sra Jiménez?'

'She *gave* me her motive for killing her husband or having him killed,' said Falcón. 'Their marriage was not successful, she had a lover, and she and the children would inherit everything.'

'The lover,' said Calderón, 'did you speak to him?'

'We did, because he was recorded as entering the Edificio del Presidente about half an hour before Raúl Jiménez was murdered. He's also a lecturer in biochemistry at the university.'

'Opportunity *and* expertise,' said Calderón.

'As well as access to chloroform and lab instruments,' said Ramírez, so that Calderón had to check him for irony or stupidity.

'So?' asked Calderón, hands open, waiting for the obvious.

Falcón gave him the bad news that Lucena was on his way up to Marciano Ruíz's apartment on the eighth floor.

'I know that name,' said Calderón. 'Isn't he a theatre director?'

'And a well-known *mariquita*,' finished Ramírez.

'I don't understand,' said Calderón.

'He was fucking them both,' said Ramírez. 'He said he was fucking *her* because she reminded him of his mother.'

'What's all this about?'

'Lucena was trying to offend Inspector Ramírez,' said Falcón.

'But not you,' said Calderón smoothly. 'Are you going to arrest him?'

'First of all, I don't think these people are stupid enough to walk into the security cameras . . .'

'Unless they're being very intelligent and subtle about it,' said

71

Calderón. 'For instance, we never see the lover in the *Familia Jiménez* movie, do we? We only see his address.'

'You're forgetting the prostitute, Eloisa Gómez,' said Falcón. 'If Lucena was the killer he would have been in the apartment, filming her having sex with Raúl Jiménez as we saw on the movie. The girl was taped leaving the building at three minutes past one and was back on the Alameda at one-thirty. Basilio Lucena was still in the Hotel Colón with Sra Jiménez. I've worked on the timings to see if it's still possible, and it is, but highly improbable.'

'Well, that was nearly exciting,' said Calderón. 'When did Lucena leave the building?'

'No record,' said Falcón. 'He says he left in the morning with Marciano Ruíz.'

'Why no record?'

'The camera links in the garage had been cut,' said Ramírez, which was news to Falcón. 'According to the Policía Científica they were severed with pliers.'

'So that was the way in?' asked Calderón, trying to get through to more interesting information.

'It was definitely the way out,' said Falcón. 'The problem, though, was not just to get into the building without being seen, but to get into the apartment as well. Raúl Jiménez was very security conscious. He always locked his door, which needed five turns of the key – and that was confirmed by the prostitute, who heard him while she was waiting for the lift.'

'So how did the killer get in?'

Falcón gave him the theory of the lifting gear on the back of the Mudanzas Triana removals truck. Calderón played with that idea in his head.

'So he gets into the apartment, which admittedly is empty, but he hides in it for twelve hours and he's even brought his video camera with him to record Raúl Jiménez with a whore? That doesn't sound . . .'

'If that was the case, I don't think that part of it was planned,' said Falcón. 'I think he did that in a moment of arrogance. He wanted to show us that he'd been there all the time. If he hadn't filmed them we'd have known much less. We'd probably still be wasting our time with Basilio Lucena. So we can thank the killer for that small slip, along with the forgotten chloroform rag, because with each of these mistakes he's telling us something about himself.'

'That he's an amateur,' said Calderón.

'But an amateur with nerve,' said Falcón, 'He'll take risks and he likes to tease.'

'Psychopathic?'

'Driven and playful,' replied Falcón. 'With not a lot to lose.'

'And some surgical expertise,' said Ramírez.

Falcón gave him the second scenario – Eloisa Gómez letting in her lover or low-life friend to kill Raúl Jiménez.

'Nothing was stolen,' said Ramírez. 'The place was practically empty, so the only reason for getting in there was to kill Raúl Jiménez.'

'How did she stand up to the interrogation?'

'She toughed it out,' said Ramírez.

'You'll go back to her though, won't you?' said Calderón.

In the quiet that followed their nods Falcón gave Calderón a short report about his discussion with Lobo on the level of corruption in the building of Expo '92 and Raúl Jiménez's involvement. He mentioned the warning he was given by the Comisario.

'If there's corruption associated with this murder I have to be free to talk about it,' said Calderón, eyes alight, suddenly the crusading judge.

'You are, of course,' said Falcón. 'But there are some sensitive issues here and important people, who, even if they're clean, might not like the associations. You remember who was in those photographs from your side: Bellido and Spinola, to name two.'

'It's ten years old, anyway,' said Calderón, idealism instantly doused.

'That's not so long to hold a grudge,' said Falcón, and the two men looked at him as if he might be holding several simultaneously.

Falcón gave a report on his conversation with Consuelo Jiménez and handed over the print-out of the address book, mentioning that the killer had stolen Raúl Jiménez's mobile. Calderón ran his finger down the list. Ramírez yawned and lit another cigarette.

'So what you're saying,' said Calderón, 'is that despite that terrible scenario the killer left in the apartment, despite all the interviews and statements so far . . . we actually have no definite leads?'

'We still have Sra Consuelo Jiménez as the prime suspect. She is the only one with defined motive and she has the means to execute it. Eloisa Gómez is a possible accomplice to a murderer acting on his own.'

'Or not,' said Calderón. 'The killer could still be paid for by Sra Jiménez and, if that's the case, I'm sure she wouldn't want to draw attention to herself by giving the killer his own key. She would have told him to find his own way in.'

'And he'd use the prostitute or the lifting gear?' asked Ramírez. 'I know what I'd do.'

'If he used the girl to get in why would he film her?' asked Calderón. 'That doesn't make sense. It makes more sense the other way round – to show us how brilliant he is.'

'There's possibilities and improbabilities in both scenarios,' said Falcón.

'Do you both have Sra Jiménez down as a serious candidate for having her husband killed?'

Ramírez said yes, Falcón no.

'Which way do *you* want to take the case, Inspector Jefe?'

Falcón cracked his knuckles one by one. Calderón winced. Falcón didn't want to have to come clean just yet about what his instinct was telling him. He needed more time to think. There were enough extraordinary things about this case already without him suggesting that they take a look at what had happened to Raúl Jiménez in the late 1960s. But he was the leader and as such he had to have the ideas.

'We should work on both scenarios and on Raúl Jiménez's address list,' he said. 'I think we have to maintain a presence in and around the building to try to find a witness who will corroborate one theory of the killer's entry and possibly give us a description. We need to interview the removals company. And we should keep the pressure up on both Consuelo Jiménez and Eloisa Gómez.'

There was no argument from Calderón.

They were driving back to the Jefatura on Blas Infante. Ramírez was at the wheel. As they crossed the river to the Plaza de Cuba, the advertisement for Cruzcampo beer triggered a sudden parched quality to the Inspector's throat. He wouldn't mind one, he thought, but not with Falcón. He wanted to drink with somebody more convivial than Falcón.

'What do you think, Inspector Jefe?' he asked, jerking Falcón out of his reflection on how awkward his first meeting with the young judge had been.

'I think more or less what I said to Juez Calderón.'

'No, no, I don't think so,' said Ramírez, tapping the steering wheel. 'I know you, Inspector Jefe.'

That turned Falcón in his seat. The idea that Ramírez had the first idea on how his mind worked was nearly laughable to him.

'Tell me, Inspector,' he said.

'You were telling him things while you were thinking something else,' replied Ramírez. 'I mean, you know that going through that address book is going to be as big a waste of time as, say, interviewing those kids that Sra Jiménez fired.'

'I don't know that,' said Falcón. 'And *you* know that the basics have to be done. We have to be seen to be thorough.'

'But you don't think there's a connection, do you?'

'I've an open mind.'

'This is the work of a psychopath and you know it, Inspector Jefe.'

'If I was a psychopath and I enjoyed killing people, I wouldn't choose an apartment on the sixth floor of the Edificio del Presidente with all the complications it entailed.'

'He likes to show off.'

'He's studied these people. He's got to know his target. He's been specific,' said Falcón. 'He will have seen them visiting their new house. He will have seen the removals people coming to the apartment . . .'

'We need to talk to *them* first thing tomorrow,' said Ramírez. 'Missing overalls, that sort of thing.'

'It's *Viernes Santo* tomorrow,' said Falcón. Good Friday.

Ramírez pulled into the car park at the back of the Jefatura.

'Motive,' he said, getting out of the car. 'Why are you taking the bitch out of the frame?'

'The bitch?'

'Those boys I spoke to, the ones who were glad to get away from Consuelo Jiménez, they didn't have a good word to say about her personally, but professionally, they said she was brilliant.'

'And that's unusual in Seville?' said Falcón.

'It is for that kind of woman, the wife of a rich husband. Normally they don't like to get their hands dirty and they'll only talk to the Marqués y Marquesa de No Sé Que. But Sra Jiménez, apparently, did everything.'

'Like?'

'She washed salad, chopped vegetables, cooked *revueltos*, waited at table, went to the market, paid the wages and kept the books, and she did the talking and the greeting, too.'

'So what's your point?'

'She loved that business. She made it *her* business. The new place they opened in La Macarena – that was *her* idea. She made all the drawings, supervised the building of the interiors, decorated it, found the right staff – everything. The only thing she didn't touch was the menu, because she knows that people go there for the menu. Simple, classic Sevillano dishes done to perfection.'

'You sound as if you've been there?'

'Best salmorejo in Seville. Best pan de casa in Seville. Best jamón, best revueltos, best chuletillas ... best everything. And reasonable, too. Not exclusive either, although they always keep a table for the toreros and other idiots.'

Ramírez shouldered through the door at the back of the Jefatura, held it open for Falcón and followed him up the stairs.

'Where are you taking me on this?' asked Falcón.

'How do you think she'd react, say, if her husband decided to sell the business?' asked Ramírez, which stopped Falcón mid step. 'I didn't bring it up in front of Calderón, because I've only got those two boys' word for it.'

'Now I'm glad it was *you* who talked to them,' said Falcón. 'What did I just say about the basics?'

'You still won't get me to work through that address book,' said Ramírez.

'So these boys saw Raúl Jiménez talking to somebody?'

'Have you heard of a restaurant chain called Cinco Bellotas run by a guy called Joaquín López? He's young, dynamic and he's got good backing. He's one of the few people in Seville who could buy and run Raúl Jiménez's restaurants tomorrow.'

'Any connection between him and Sra Jiménez?'

'I don't know.'

'That's a very elaborate plan. Elaborate *and* gruesome,' said Falcón, continuing up the stairs, toeing the outer door to his office. 'Ask yourself this question, Inspector: Who could she possibly have found, and what kind of payment would it have taken, to persuade someone to do all that preliminary filming, get into an apartment like that and torture an old man to death?'

'Depends how badly she wants it,' said Ramírez. 'There's no innocence there, if you ask me.'

The two men looked out of the window of Falcón's office at the diminishing ranks of cars in the darkening evening.

'And, look, the other thing,' said Falcón, 'whatever the killer showed Raúl Jiménez was for real. He didn't want to see it, which was why the killer had to cut...'

Ramírez nodded, sighed, his brainwork done for the day. He lit a cigarette without thinking or remembering that Falcón detested smoking in his office.

'So what *is* your angle, Inspector Jefe?'

Falcón found that his focus had shortened. He was no longer staring out over the emptying car park but was looking at his own reflection in the glass. He seemed hollow-eyed, vacant, unseeing, even sinister.

'The killer was forcing him to see,' he said.

'But what?'

'We've all got something that we're ashamed of, something that when we think of it we shudder with embarrassment or something worse than embarrassment.'

Ramírez stiffened beside him, the man solidifying, his carapace suddenly there, impenetrable. Nobody tinkered inside Ramírez's works. Falcón checked him in the glass, decided to make it easier for the Sevillano.

'You know, like when you were a kid, making a fool of yourself with a girl, or perhaps being cowardly, failing to protect somebody who was your friend, or a moral weakness – not standing up for something you believed in because you could get beaten up. These sorts of things, but transferred to an adult life with adult implications.'

Ramírez looked down at his tie, which was about as introspective as he'd ever been.

'Do you mean the sort of things that Comisario Lobo warned you about?'

This struck Falcón as brilliantly deflective. Corruption – the manageable stain. Machine wash, rinse and spin. Forgotten. It's only money. All part of the game.

'No,' he said.

Ramírez drifted towards the door, announced that he was packing it in for the day. Falcón dismissed him via the glass.

He was suddenly exhausted. The massive day settled on his

shoulders. He closed his eyes and instead of the thought of dinner, a glass of wine and sleep, he found his mind still turning, spiralling around the question:

What could be so terrible?

8

Javier Falcón sat in the study of the large eighteenth-century house that had belonged to his father. The room was on the ground floor and looked out through an arched colonnade on to a central patio, in the middle of which was a fountain of a bronze boy up on one toe with one leg trailing and an urn over his shoulder. When the fountain spouted, water came out of the urn. Falcón only ran it in summer when the trickle of water could delude him into thinking he was cool.

He was alone in the house. The housekeeper, Encarnación, who had been his father's housekeeper, left at 7 p.m. which meant that he never saw her. The only evidence of her presence was the occasional note and her habit, annoying to him, of moving things around. The plant pots on the patio would suddenly be arranged in a different corner, small pieces of furniture would be removed to reappear in different rooms, effigies of the Virgen del Rocío would occupy previously vacant niches. His wife, his ex-wife, had been a great promoter of change, too.

'We could make this room your snooker room,' she'd said. 'We could put a humidor there for your cigars.'

'But I don't smoke.'

'I think it would be nice.'

'And I don't play snooker.'

'You should try.'

These stupid conversations drifted back to him as he sat at his desk with his magnifying glass. Not the ridiculous antique Sherlock Holmes affair his wife had bought him for a birthday, which was too absurd for the Inspector Jefe del Grupo de Homicidios. This was a magnifying glass mounted on a perspex box that also shed light on to whatever he was observing.

He was going through the photographs he'd taken from Raúl Jiménez's desk. In front of him, leaning against a framed photograph of his mother holding him as a baby, flanked by his then seven-year-old brother Paco and five-year-old sister Manuela, were two other photographs side by side. The first was another shot of his mother, who was sitting on the beach with the wind in her hair, wearing a swimsuit and holding a bathing cap covered with rubber white-petalled flowers. It was her favourite informal photograph. On the back was written *Tangier, June 1952*. She had been twenty-five years old and it was impossible to believe, looking at her there, full of vitality, that she only had nine more years to live.

The second photograph was of his father – black hair swept back, a small pencil moustache, his nose too big for his young face, the mouth of a sensualist and the eyes. Even in black and white, the eyes were extraordinary. They looked as if they were used to seeing clearly over great distances and any received light would glow in the irises, which were green but turned to amber close to the pupil. In his eighties, after the first heart attack had weakened him, those green eyes still managed to hold the light in them. They were the eyes you'd expect an artist of his stature to have – observant, piercing and numinous. In the shot his father was wearing a white dinner jacket and a black bow tie. On the back was written *New Year's Eve, Tangier, 1953*.

Falcón worked his way through the Jiménez photographs, furious at the poor quality of the prints. He wondered why the hell he was doing this. He had a habit of working tangentially, but this was absurd. There was no connection to the case. What difference would it make if he did see either of his parents in these photographs? What if they were in Tangier at the same time as Raúl and Gumersinda Jiménez? So were 40,000 other Spaniards. As he built the argument against his illogical muddling so his fascination grew and it occurred to him briefly that he might just be getting old.

The yacht photographs, which were just shots of Raúl Jiménez's new toy, didn't interest him until he came to one of the harbour full of boats and people partying on the decks. Jiménez and his wife and children were in the foreground. They looked happy. His wife was waving with the two kids over her knees giggling. Falcón shifted the magnifying glass up and along through the other boats lined up behind Jiménez's. He stopped, slid back to a couple on the deck and dismissed the likeness. He carried on and then returned to the couple and realized why he'd dismissed them. It was his father and he was leaning on the ship's rail of a yacht, much larger than Raúl's. He was with a woman whose face he could not see properly but who had blonde hair. They were kissing. It was a quick, private moment that the Jiménez photographer had inadvertently caught. He checked the back. *Tangier, August 1958*. Pilar, his mother, would still have been alive. He looked at the blonde woman more closely and was stunned to find that it was Mercedes, his father's second wife. He felt nauseous and pushed the magnifying glass away. He pressed his palms into his eyes. That's what happened when you went off on a tangent . . . you came across unexpected truths. It was the whole reason he did it.

The phone rang – his sister on a mobile in a packed bar.

'I knew I'd find you at home if you weren't at work,' said Manuela. 'What are you doing, little brother?'

'I'm looking through some old photographs.'

'Hey! Come on, grandpa, you've got to learn to live a little. We're here in La Tienda for the next half-hour, come and have a cervecita with us. Then we're going to dinner at El Cairo. You can come there too, if you bring your walking stick.'

'I'll join you for the cervecita.'

'You do that, little brother. And one thing. One very important condition . . .'

'Yes, Manuela?'

'You're not allowed to say the word "Inés". OK?'

She hung up. He shook his head at the dead phone. Manuela's bad psychology. He put on his jacket, straightened his tie, checked his pockets and found Raúl Jiménez's son's address and telephone number. It was Viernes Santo tomorrow. The holiday. He tried the number just on the off chance. José Manuel Jiménez picked up the phone. Falcón introduced himself and offered his condolences.

'I've already been informed,' he said, about to put down the phone.

'I just wanted to talk to you about –'

'I can't speak to you now.'

'Perhaps we could meet tomorrow . . . for a short talk. It would be important for background detail.'

'I really don't see . . .'

'I would come to Madrid, of course.'

'There's nothing to be said. I haven't seen my father in years.'

'That's the point. I'm not interested in now.'

'There's really nothing.'

'Think about it overnight. I'll call again in the morning. It won't take long and it would be a great help.'

Jiménez stammered and hung up. Falcón knew the man was a lawyer but he hadn't come across as one; too uncertain and unconfident. He turned off the lamp and went out on to the patio. He breathed in the cool night air and the near silence, as the workings of the city arrived at a faint roar in this dark and hollow centre of the house. He stretched, opened his chest and arms, and saw among the arches of the gallery above the patio what Eloisa Gómez would have called, 'the shadows move'. He sprinted up the stairs, digging in his pocket for the key to open the wrought-iron barred door at the top. He strode the length of the gallery to the next wrought-iron door, which led to another stretch of arches outside his father's old studio. It was empty. He moved back to the arch where he thought he'd seen the movement and looked down into the patio. The water in the fountain, flat and black as a pupil, stared up to the sky. Just tired, he thought, and squeezed his eyes shut.

He left the house, stepped out through a small door cut into the massive wooden-and-brass riveted gates, which were the entrance to his oversized home on Calle Bailén. Too big for him, he knew it, and too grand for his position, but each time he thought of selling it he quickly foundered on what it would entail. First of all, he would have to do what he should have done as instructed by his father's will – clear out the studio and incinerate everything. Burn the lot, right down to the last rough sketch. He couldn't do it. He hadn't done it. He hadn't even been back into the studio since his father died nearly two years ago. He hadn't even unlocked that last wrought-iron door in the gallery.

His father's lawyer had died three months after the reading of the will, and Paco and Manuela didn't give a damn. They were too engrossed in their own inheritance – Paco's bull-breeding *finca* at Las Cortecillas on the way up to the Sierra de Aracena and Manuela's holiday villa in El Puerto de Santa María. They hadn't had the same relationship with their father that he'd had. He'd spoken to him almost every day since the first heart attack and, once he'd started working in Seville, if they didn't go out for lunch on Sunday they would at least meet for a fino just to get him out of the house. They'd nearly recaptured that same level of intimacy as when he'd been a boy in the early 1970s. He was the only child left after Manuela had decamped to Madrid to study veterinary science and Paco was installing himself on the farm after his recovery from a severe goring in the leg which he'd suffered as a *novillero* in La Maestranza bullring in Seville. The injury had ended any hope of a career as a torero.

Falcón headed down the narrow, cobbled street canyons to the bar on Calle Gravina. It was a converted *mercería*, still with the old scales on the counter. People were spilling out on to the street with their beers. Manuela was with her boyfriend deep in the crowd. Falcón squeezed through. Men he barely knew gave him *un abrazo* as he went past, strange women kissed him – Manuela's friends. His sister kissed him and hugged him to her gym-worked body. Alejandro, her boyfriend, whom she'd met on the rowing machines at the club, handed Javier a beer.

'My little brother,' she said, as she'd always said since they were small, 'you look tired. More dead bodies?'

'Only one.'

'Not another gruesome drug slaying?' she said, lighting one of her foul menthol cigarettes, which she thought were better for her.

'Gruesome, yes, but not drugs this time. More complicated.'

'I don't know how you do it.'

'There can't be many of your friends who could imagine that someone as beautiful and sophisticated as Manuela Falcón could have been up to her shoulder dragging out stillborn calves.'

'Oh, I don't do that any more.'

'I can't see you cutting poodles' toenails.'

'You must talk to Paco,' she said, ignoring him. 'He's very stressed, you know.'

'The Feria's his busiest time of year.'

'No, no, not that,' she whispered. 'It's the *vacas locas*. He's worried his herd has been infected with BSE. I'm testing the whole lot for him, off the record.'

Falcón sipped his beer, ate a slice of sweet and melting *jamón Ibérico de bellota*.

'If they bring in official testing,' she continued, 'and they find one animal with the disease, he has to slaughter the whole herd, even the ones with 120-year-old bloodlines.'

'That's stressful.'

'His leg's bad. It always is when he's stressed. He can hardly walk some days.'

Alejandro put a plate of cheese in front of them and Javier instinctively turned his face away.

'He doesn't like cheese,' explained Manuela, and the plate was removed.

'Your name came up today at work,' said Falcón.

'That can't be good.'

'You vaccinated a dog for someone. It was a bill.'

'Whose dog?'

'I hope he paid you.'

'You wouldn't have found a signed receipt if he hadn't.'

'Raúl Jiménez.'

'Yes, a very nice Weimeraner. It was a present for his kids . . . they're moving to a new house. He was due to collect today.'

Falcón stared at her. Manuela blinked at her beer, put it down. This happened rarely, that real murder slipped into a social situation. Normally he would entertain, if asked, with tales of detection, his idiosyncratic approach, his attention to detail. He never told how it really was – always laborious, at times very tedious and interspersed with moments of horror.

'I worry about you, little brother,' she said.

'I'm in no danger.'

'I mean . . . this work. It does things to you.'

'What?'

'I don't know, I suppose you have to be callous to survive.'

'Callous?' he said. 'Me? I investigate murder. I investigate the reasons why these moments of aberration occur. Why, in the heart of such reasonable times, such heights of civilization, we can still break down and fail as human beings. It's not like I'm putting down pets or slaughtering whole herds of cattle.'

'I didn't know you were so sensitive about it.'

They were so close he could smell the menthol from the cigarettes on her breath, even over the sweat and perfume in the bar. This was how it was with Manuela. She was provocative and it was why her boyfriends, selected for looks and wallet, never lasted. She couldn't keep up the fluttering femininity.

'*Hija*,' he said, not wanting this, 'I've had a long day.'

'Wasn't that what you said was one of Inés's accusations?'

'You said the forbidden word, not me.'

Manuela looked up, smiled, shrugged.

'You hoped I'd been paid for vaccinating that poor man's dog. It struck me as hard-hearted, that's all. But perhaps you were just being . . . phlegmatic.'

'It was a small joke in bad taste,' he said, and then surprised himself by lying. 'I didn't know the dog was a present for the kids.'

Alejandro stuck his magnificent jaw line in between them. Manuela laughed for no reason at all, other than it was early days and she was still keen to make her man feel good about himself.

They talked about *los toros*, the only topic they had in common. Manuela enthused over her favourite torero, José Tomás, who was, unusually for her, not one of the great beauties of the *plaza* but a man she admired for always being able to bring some tranquillity to the *faena*. He never rushed, he never shuffled his feet, he would always bring the bull on with the face of the *muleta*, never the corner, so the bull would always pass as dangerously close to him as possible. Inevitably he would be hit and when this happened he always picked himself up and walked slowly back to the bull.

'I saw him on television in Mexico once. He was hit by the bull and it tore his trouser leg open. The blood was running down his calf. He looked pale and sick, but he stood up, got his balance, waved his men away and went back to the bull. And, the camera showed it, there was so much blood running down his leg that it was filling his shoe and squirting out with every step. He lined the bull up and put the sword in to the hilt. They carried him straight out to the infirmary. *Que hombre, que torero.*'

'Your cousin, Pepe,' said Alejandro, who'd heard that story too many times, 'Pepe Leal. Will he get a chance in the Feria?'

'He's not our cousin,' said Manuela, forgetting her role for a moment. 'He's the son of our sister-in-law's brother.'

Alejandro shrugged. He was ingratiating himself with Javier. He knew that Javier was Pepe's confidant and that, when work permitted, he would go to the plaza on the morning of the *corrida* to make the bull selection for the young torero.

'Not this year,' said Javier. 'He did very well up in Olivenza in March. They gave him an ear from each of his bulls and they'll invite him back for the Feria de San Juan in Badajoz, but they still don't think he's big enough for the Feria de Abril. He can only sit around and hope for someone to drop out.'

He felt sorry for the boy, Pepe, just nineteen years old, a great talent, whose manager could never quite get him into the first category plazas. It was nothing to do with ability, only style.

'Fashion will change,' said Manuela, who knew that Javier felt responsible for the boy.

'He's convinced he's too old to get anywhere now,' said Javier. 'He looks at El Juli, who seems to have been with us for decades and who's only a couple of years older than him and he loses heart.'

Alejandro ordered three more beers from the barman. Manuela was giving Javier her raised eyebrow.

'What?' he asked.

'You,' she said. 'You and Pepe.'

'Forget it.'

'Remember what the guy wrote in *6 Toros* last year.'

'He was an idiot.'

'You're closer to Pepe than his own father. All that business he does in South America and he won't even go and see his son when he's performing in Mexico.'

'You're being sentimental, like that journalist was,' said Javier. 'I only ever help Pepe with his bulls.'

'You're proud of him in a way that his father isn't.'

'You're not being fair,' he said, and then to change the subject: 'I came across a photograph of Papá today . . .'

'You need to find yourself a woman, Javier,' she said. 'It won't do, you going through all the old albums.'

'This was a shot I found in Raúl Jiménez's study. He was in Tangier around the same time. Papá didn't know he was being photographed.'

'Was he doing something unforgivable?'

'It was dated August 1958 and he was kissing a woman . . .'

'Don't tell me . . . she wasn't Mamá?'

'That's right.'

'And you were shocked?'

'Yes, I was,' he said. 'It was Mercedes.'

'Papá was no angel, Javier.'

'Wasn't Mercedes still married then?'

'I don't know,' said Manuela, waving it all away with her cigarette. 'That was Tangier in those days. Everybody was as high as a kite and fucking everybody else.'

'Can you try and remember? You were older. I wasn't even four years old.'

'What does it matter?'

'I just think it might help.'

'With Raúl Jiménez's murder?'

'No, no, I don't think so. It's personal. I just want to sort it out, that's all.'

'You know, Javier,' she said, 'maybe you shouldn't be living in that big house all on your own.'

'I did try to live there with somebody else, who we can't mention.'

'That's the point. Old houses are crowded and women don't like sharing their living space unless they choose to.'

'I like it there. I feel in the centre of things.'

'You don't go out into "the centre of things" though, do you? You don't know anywhere that isn't between Calle Bailén and the Jefatura. And the house is far too big for you.'

'As it was for Papá?'

'You should get yourself an apartment like mine . . . with air conditioning.'

'Air conditioning?' said Javier. 'Yes, maybe that would help. Clear the air. Don't the latest models have a button on the side that says "past reconditioned"?'

'You always were a strange little boy,' she said. 'Maybe Papá should have let you become an artist.'

'That would have solved everything, because I'd have been so broke I'd have had to sell the place as soon as he died.'

The rest of Manuela and Alejandro's friends arrived and Javier drained his beer. He excused himself from dinner through a barrage of fake protest. Work, he said, over and over again, which few of them understood as they were well cushioned from the hard edges of daily toil.

At home he ate some mussels in tomato sauce, cold. Something left for him by Encarnación, who knew that he couldn't be eating properly without a woman in the house. He drank a glass of cheap white wine and mopped the sauce up with some hard white bread. He wasn't thinking and yet his head seemed to be full of a sense of rushing. He thought it was his mind unwinding after the day, until he realized it was more of a rewind, like a tape, a fast rewind. Inés. Divorce. Separation. 'You have no heart.' Moving to this house. His father dying . . .

He stopped it. There was an audible thump in his head. He went to bed with too much happening in his body. He slammed into a wall of sleep and had his first dream, that he could remember, for some considerable time. It was simple. He was a fish. He thought he was a big fish, but he could not see himself. He *was* fish; aware only of the water rushing past him and a scintilla in his eye, which he closed on, which instinct told him he should close on. He was fast. So fast that he never saw what he instinctively pursued. He just took it in and moved on. Only . . . after a moment he felt a tug, felt the first rip of his insides, and he burst to the surface.

Awake, he looked around himself, astonished to find that he was in bed. He pressed his abdomen. Those mussels, had they been all right?

9

Friday, 13th April 2001, Javier Falcón's house, Calle Bailén, Seville

He was up early; the jitteriness in his stomach had gone. He spent an hour on the exercise bike, setting himself some arduous terrain on the computer. The concentration required to break through the pain barrier helped him map out his day. This was no holiday for him.

He took a taxi to the Estación de Santa Justa, and drank a *café solo* in the station café. The AVE, the high-speed train to Madrid, left at 9.30 a.m. He waited until 9.00 a.m. and called José Manuel Jiménez, who answered the phone as if poised for it to ring.

'*Diga.*'

Falcón introduced himself again and asked for an appointment.

'I've got nothing to tell you, Inspector Jefe. Nothing that would help. My father and I haven't spoken for well over thirty years.'

'Really?'

'Very little has passed between us.'

'I'd like to talk to you about that but not over the phone,' he said, and Jiménez didn't respond. 'I can be with you by one o'clock and be finished before lunch.'

'It's really not convenient.'

Falcón found himself surprisingly desperate to talk to this man, but it had to be out of police time. He went in harder.

'I'm conducting a murder investigation, Sr Jiménez. Murder is always inconvenient.'

'I cannot shed any light on your case, Inspector Jefe.'

'I have to know his background.'

'Ask his wife.'

'What does she know about his life before 1989?'

'Why do you have to go back so far?'

This was ludicrous, this battle to speak to the man. It made him more determined.

'I have a curious but successful way of working, Sr Jiménez,' he said, just to keep him on the phone. 'What about your sister . . . do you ever see her?'

The ether hissed for an eternity.

'Call me back in ten minutes,' he said, and hung up.

Falcón paced the station concourse thinking of a new strategy for ten minutes' time. When he called him back he had a chain of questions lined up like a cartridge belt.

'I'll expect you at one o'clock,' said Jiménez, and hung up.

He bought a ticket and boarded the train. By midday the AVE had delivered him to the Estación de Atocha in central Madrid. He took the metro to Esperanza, which seemed auspicious, and it was a short walk to the Jiménez apartment from there.

José Manuel Jiménez let him into the hall. He was shorter than Falcón but more powerfully built. He held his head as if ducking under a beam or carrying a load on his shoulders. As he spoke his eyes darted about under cover of some heavy, dark eyebrows, which his wife was not keeping under control. The effect, rather than being furtive, was deferential. He took Falcón's coat and led him down a parquet-floored corridor, away from the kitchen and voices of family, to his study. He walked leaning forwards, as if dragging a sled.

The study had several overlaid Moroccan rugs that covered the parquet floor up to an English-style walnut desk. Lining the walls to the window were the bound books of a lawyer's workplace. Coffee was offered and accepted. In the minutes he was left alone, Falcón inspected the family photographs sitting on top of a glass-fronted cupboard. He recognized Gumersinda with her two young children. There were none of Raúl. There were none of the daughter beyond twelve years old. The other photographs were of José Manuel Jiménez's family through the ages culminating in two graduation photographs of a boy and a girl.

Jiménez came back with the coffee. They manoeuvred around each other as Falcón found his way back to his seat and Jiménez got behind his desk. He clasped his hands; his biceps and shoulders swelled under his green tweed jacket.

'Amongst some old shots of your father's I came across one of my own father,' said Falcón, going for the tangential approach.

'My father was a restaurateur, I'm sure he had lots of photographs of his customers.'

So he knew that much about his father.

'This was not amongst the celebrity photographs . . .'

'Is your father a celebrity?'

It was a chink he had not wanted opened, but maybe, as Consuelo Jiménez had shown, revealing something of oneself could lead to surprising revelations from others.

'My father was the painter Francisco Falcón, but that was not why –'

'Then I'm not surprised he wasn't on my father's wall,' Jiménez cut in. 'My father had the cultural awareness of a peasant, which was what he was.'

'I noticed he smoked Celtas with the filters broken off.'

'He used to smoke Celtas *cortas*, which were unfiltered but better than the dry dung he told us he had to smoke after the Civil War.'

'Where was he a peasant?'

'His parents had land near Almería, which they worked. They were killed in the Civil War and lost it all. After their deaths my father drifted. That's all I know. It's probably why money was always important to him.'

'Didn't your mother . . . ?'

'I doubt she knew. If she did, she didn't tell us. I really don't think she knew anything about his life before she met him and my father wasn't going tell her parents until he'd got her.'

'They met in Tangier?'

'Yes, her family moved there in the early forties. Her father was a lawyer. He was there, like everybody else, to make money after the Civil War had left Spain in ruins. She was just a girl, eight years old maybe. My father appeared on the scene a bit later . . . some time in 1945, I think. He fell for her the moment he first saw her.'

'She was still young wasn't she? Thirteen years old?'

'And my father was twenty-two. It was a curious relationship, which her parents were not happy about. They made her wait until she was seventeen before they let her get married.'

'Was it just the age difference?'

'She was their only child,' said Jiménez. 'And I doubt they were impressed by his lack of family background. They must have seen what base metal he was. He was flashy, too.'

'He was rich by then?'

'He made a lot of money over there and he enjoyed spending it.'

'How did he make his money?'

'Smuggling, probably. Whatever it was, I'm sure it wasn't legal. Later he got into currency dealing. He even had his own bank at one stage – not that it meant anything. He got into property and construction, too.'

'How do you know all this?' asked Falcón. 'You were barely ten by the time you left and I doubt he told you very much.'

'I pieced it all together, Inspector Jefe. That's the way my mind works. It was my way of making sense of what happened.'

Silence came into the room like news of a death. Falcón was willing him to continue, but Jiménez had his lips drawn tight over his teeth, steeling himself.

'You were born in 1950,' said Falcón, nudging him on.

'Nine months to the day after they were married.'

'And your sister?'

'Two years later. There were some complications in her birth. I know they nearly lost her and it left my mother very weak. They wanted to have lots of children, but my mother wasn't capable after that. It affected my sister, too.'

'How?'

'She was a very sweet-natured girl. She was always caring for things . . . animals, especially stray cats, of which there were plenty in Tangier. There wasn't anything you could . . . she was just . . .' he faltered, his hands kneaded the air, forcing the words out. 'She was just simple, that's all. Not stupid . . . just uncomplicated. Not like other children.'

'Did your mother ever recover her strength?'

'Yes, yes, she did, she recovered her strength completely, She . . .' Jiménez trailed off, stared up at the ceiling. 'She even became pregnant again. It was a very difficult time. My father had to leave Tangier, but my mother could not be moved.'

'When was this?'

'The end of 1958. He took my sister and I stayed.'

'Where did he go?'

'He rented a house in a village up in the hills above Algeciras.'

'Was he on the run?'

'Not from the authorities.'

'A bad business deal?'

'I never found that out,' he said.

'And your mother?'

'She had the baby. A boy. My father mysteriously appeared on the night of the birth. He'd come over secretly. He was worried that something would go wrong, like the last time, and she wouldn't survive the birth. He was . . .'

Jiménez frowned, as if he'd come up against something beyond his comprehension. He blinked against the interfering tears.

'This is very difficult ground, Inspector Jefe,' he said. 'I thought that when my father died I would be pleased. It would be a relief and a release from . . . It would signify the end of all these unfinished thoughts.'

'Unfinished thoughts, Sr Jiménez?'

'Thoughts that have no ending. Thoughts that are interminable because they have no resolution. Thoughts that leave you forever hanging in the balance.'

Although these words were recognizable as language, their meaning was obscure and yet Falcón, without knowing why, understood something of the man's torment. Hints prodded his own mind – his father's death, the things left unsaid, the studio uninvestigated.

'It may just be our natural state,' said Falcón. 'That in coming from complicated beings who are unknowable, we will always be the carriers of the unresolved and further compound it with our own irresolvable questions, which we in turn hand on. Perhaps it is better to be uncomplicated like your sister. To be uncluttered by the baggage of previous generations.'

Jiménez drilled him with animal eyes from under the brush of his brow. He fed on the words from Falcón's mouth. He pulled himself up, cleared the intensity from his face.

'The only problem there . . .' he said, '. . . in my sister's case, is that her lack of complexity gave her no system, no potential for reordering the chaos after the cataclysm hit our family. She lost her tenuous link with a structured existence and thereafter floated in space. Yes, I think that's what her madness is like . . . an astronaut disconnected from his ship, spinning in a massive void.'

'I think you've run ahead of me.'

'I have,' he said, 'and I know why.'

'Perhaps we should go back to your father fearing that your mother might not survive the birth.'

'What I was thinking then, what I was confronting was the surprising memory, in view of later events, that my father was profoundly in love with my mother. It is something that even now I have a great difficulty in admitting. As a boy, when my mother died, I could never believe that of him. I thought he had set about breaking her.'

'And how did you come to that conclusion?'

'Psychoanalysis, Inspector Jefe,' he said. 'I never thought I would be a candidate for that quackery. I'm a lawyer. I have an organized mind. But when you're desperate, and I mean full of despair, so that all you see is your own life collapsing around you, then you admit it to yourself. You say: "I'm nuts and I'm going to have to talk it out."'

Jiménez levelled this explanation directly at Falcón, as if he'd seen something in him that needed attention.

'So what happened to your mother and the baby?' asked Falcón.

'My mother needed some days to recover. I remember that time very well. We weren't allowed out of the house. Servants were told to say nobody was at home. Food came in secretly from neighbours' houses. Some armed men, who normally guarded the construction sites, were installed across the street. My father paced the floor like a caged panther, stopping only to look through a crack in the shutter if he heard something in the street. The tension and the boredom were there in equal measure. It was the start of the family madness.'

'And you never found out what it was your father was afraid of?'

'At the time I was a kid, I didn't care. I just wanted to avoid being bored. Later . . . much later, I thought it was important to find out what it could have been that had driven my father to such lengths. So, thirty years after the event, I thought the only person to ask would be him. It was the last time we spoke on a personal level. And this is the magic of the human brain.'

'What?' asked Falcón, jumping in his seat, as if he'd missed the vital moment.

'If we have something in there that we don't like we bypass it. Like a river that's tired of flowing around the same loop again and again, it just cuts through and joins up with the stretch of river beyond the loop. The loop becomes a small disconnected lake, a reservoir of memory which due to lack of supply eventually dries up.'

'He forgot about it?'

'He denied it. As far as he was concerned it had never happened. He looked at me as if I might be insane.'

'Even with your mother dead and your sister in San Juan de Dios?'

'It was 1995 by then. He was married to Consuelo. He was in a different life. The past could have been as distant to him as . . . a previous existence.'

'Were you surprised by Consuelo?'

'Her appearance?' he said. 'My God, I was stunned. It made my flesh creep. I burnt the photograph he sent of their wedding.'

'So you got no help from your father?'

'Only that what I thought I needed to know was unimportant. There was nothing in my father's world, as far as I could see, that he could have possibly placed more value on than the life of a child. The admission was in his silence, in his flat denial, in the whole expression of his life . . . this marriage to his wife's lookalike . . .'

'Wouldn't that have been torture?'

Jiménez gave a derisive snort.

'If you could call the comfort of a beautiful woman a punishment . . . then, yes.'

'You think he wiped the slate clean and started a new life?'

'My father was an instinctive animal. The passages of his mind were not those of a normal human being. To be as successful a businessman as he – and I know because I work for some very success-ful men myself – you can't think like ordinary people . . . and he didn't.'

'You've lost me again. Maybe you're thinking too fast.'

Jiménez leaned across the table, jaw set.

'Don't believe for one moment that I don't know what I'm doing,' he said. 'I have never spoken about these things before to anyone, other than the man who teased apart the knot in my brain. And you know why? Because I wouldn't dream of infecting my wife's peace of mind with such terrible things. They would blacken our home and we'd be left stumbling around in the dark.'

'I'm sorry,' said Falcón.

Jiménez held up his hand in apology, realized he'd been too grave. He sat up and opened his shoulders.

'We left Tangier at night. No suitcases, just the clothes we stood up in and my mother's wedding dress and jewellery. Everyone at the port had been prepaid. We didn't show any documents. There was a moment when it looked as if we were going to be stopped, but more money appeared and we got on the boat and sailed away. We picked up my sister in the village above Algeciras and started our lives as gypsies.

'There was never any sense of danger. My father never again paced

95

the floors, but as soon as his instinct told him to move on . . . we moved on. We normally went to large towns or cities. We spent some time here in Madrid, but my father detested Madrid. I think Madrid made him feel provincial, reminded him of who he was.

'We arrived in Almería at the beginning of 1964. My father was running a couple of coasters from Algeciras to Cartagena, but he got a chance to build a hotel on the front in Almería so we moved there. My father seemed to like the idea of settling down. He must have thought that five or six years running was enough, that the world moves on, that fat grudges waste away without the nourishment of revenge. He was wrong. This is why I thought it was important to know what he'd done to make the people he'd offended so implacable that they would never stop trying to track him down. And I have to admit it would still interest me, even though I've tamed my fascination with the irrelevance of it.'

'Why?'

'I think it would help me to gauge what a monster he was.'

Falcón shuddered, split by the contradictory emotions of Raúl Jiménez being a monster and a memory of his own father playing at being one. What terrible slavering faces he pulled as he devoured him. His father had no inhibition because there was little in his world that demanded personal control and several times Javier had worn a toothmark embedded in his back for days.

'Are you all right, Inspector Jefe?'

He hoped he hadn't been pulling one of his father's huge-tongued, gargoyle faces.

'Unfinished thoughts,' he said.

'Where were we?'

'Almería, 1964,' said Falcón. 'You didn't mention how your mother took all this moving around.'

'As far as her health was concerned, she was fine. If she was unhappy she didn't show it to us or to him. There was no such thing as wives having a say in those days, anyway. She just got on with things.'

'Your father was building the hotel?'

'I should tell you about Marta at this stage. You remember what I said about how she loved to care for things?'

'Cats.'

'Yes, cats. Once we left Tangier she transferred all that on to Arturo. My mother could have left Arturo's upbringing to Marta.

She did everything for him. He was her life. It's curious, isn't it? Marta never had dolls. They were bought for her, but she never took to them. She was more fascinated by living things. Strange, don't you think, for someone so uncomplicated?'

'Perhaps she didn't have a developed imagination.'

'Possibly. Imagination is a complex thing, but then so is life.'

'She probably wasn't reading anything into it.'

'I used to wonder what went through her mind.'

'And you don't any more?'

'She barely said a word for the first twenty years. Then something remarkable happened. Over the years the staff have changed there. It's a sign of the times that not many young people want to become mental health workers and so those jobs are being filled by immigrants. In Marta's case there was a Moroccan boy who came in with a kitten he'd found and something must have clicked in her. She became animated. It must have brought back the early days, the houseboys and the cats.'

'She spoke?'

'Not words. She articulated something, nothing intelligible. She hadn't used her vocal cords for decades. It was the start of something though. There's been little progress since then. She doesn't "say" anything to me when I go there. Maybe I'm too powerful a reminder of the original trauma.'

'Did her doctors know what that trauma was?'

'Not until three years ago, and not the full story.'

'Three years ago?'

'When I could even approach talking about it myself. They'd been asking me who Arturo was. She'd got that far. And I referred them back to my father, who denied that there had been anybody of that name in family circles, which was not true. My mother's father was called Arturo. Did I tell you they died?'

'No.'

'The year before Arturo was born, both my mother's parents died within three months of each other. She had cancer. He had a heart attack. I think it must have been why my mother was prepared to risk having another.'

'What did you tell Marta's doctors?'

'My psychoanalyst clarified everything for them later in a letter, but at that stage I told them he was a younger brother who'd died.'

'Which he had done,' said Falcón, 'hadn't he?'

'I suppose in your line of work you are quite conversant with the nature of pure evil,' said Jiménez.

'I've come across bad things and mad things, but I'm not sure that I've ever come across "the nature of pure evil". Everything that I've investigated has been criminal and therefore comprehensible. Once you start talking about evil then we are on metaphysical ground.'

'And that,' said Jiménez, 'is beyond the remit of the Inspector Jefe del Grupo de Homicidios de Sevilla?'

'I'm not a priest,' said Falcón. 'Had I been, it might have helped, because your father's murder was the most shocking of my career. When I saw his face and realized what had been done to him I was aware of being in the presence of something very powerful. I am normally quite dispassionate in my work, but this affected me. It's not something I would want my superior officers to know about.'

Jiménez sat sideways in his chair, one leg crossed over the other. He flexed his hand open and shut. Falcón thought he might want to know what had happened to Raúl, but didn't want to ask.

'The evil mind has a deep understanding of human nature,' said Jiménez, after some moments. 'It is a mind quite happy pottering about amongst revenge and betrayal, nurturing them. It knows instinctively where and how to strike and reach the very heart of . . . things. They didn't kill my father, which would probably have been just. They didn't rape and murder my mother or my sister or me, which would have been unjust and cruel. They did the one thing that they knew would successfully tear my father's family apart. They took Arturo. They just took him one day and we never heard from him or them ever again.'

Jiménez blinked rapidly, lost in the vast wasteland of his incomprehension.

'You mean they kidnapped him?'

'On the way to her school Marta would always take Arturo to his. On the way back she would pick him up. One day he wasn't there and he wasn't at home either. We scoured the town while my mother called my father at the site. He was six years old. Still a baby really. And they took him.'

Jiménez stared up at his family photographs as if their richness was tainted by this poisonous memory. His bottom lip trembled. His Adam's apple leapt in his throat.

'Didn't the police get anywhere?' asked Falcón.

'No,' said Jiménez, the word coming out like a ghost's breath.

'Normally when a child goes missing . . .'

'They got nowhere, Inspector Jefe, for the simple reason that they were given no information.'

'I don't understand.'

Jiménez leaned across the desk, which creaked; his eyes bulged from his head.

'My father reported the abduction, told them it was a mystery, and within twenty-four hours we had left Almería,' said Jiménez. 'I don't know whether it was because he was terrified that these people might strike again or whether it was his way of avoiding difficult questions from the authorities, or both. But we left Almería. We spent two weeks in a hotel in Malaga. I was with Marta, who retreated into herself and never spoke another word. My mother and father were next door and the screaming . . . the tears . . . My God, it was terrible. Then he moved us all to Seville. We rented some apartment in Triana and then moved into the Plaza de Cuba later in the year. My father had to go back to Almería a few times to wrap up his business and make an appearance in front of the authorities, and that was the end of Arturo.'

'But what did he say to you, the family? How did he explain it and his bizarre reaction?'

'He didn't explain it. He just used his volcanic anger to make us understand that we should all forget Arturo . . . that Arturo did not exist.'

'And the kidnappers – are you saying there were no demands . . . ?'

'You haven't understood, Inspector Jefe,' said Jiménez, pushing his pleading hands across the table. 'There *were* no demands. That was their price. Arturo was their price.'

'You're right. I don't understand. I don't understand any of it.'

'Then you are in our club. My dead mother, my mad sister, me, and now you,' said Jiménez. 'In that move between Almería and Seville we lost all trace of Arturo. No evidence of him arrived with us. All photos, his clothes, toys, even his bed. My father rewrote family history and left Arturo out. By the time we moved into the apartment in Plaza de Cuba we were like the living dead. My mother stared out of the window all day, looking in the street below, jumping at the glass whenever a small boy appeared. My sister maintained her silence and had to be taken out of the school she'd just been put into. I stayed away from there as much as I could. I lost myself . . .

with new friends, who would never know me as the boy who'd had a younger brother.'

'Lost yourself?'

'I think that's what happened to me. I had a strange inability to recall anything before I was fifteen. Most people have memories as far back as three or four, some even as far back as babies in their prams. I had nothing distinct, just vague hints, shadowy forms of what I'd been . . . until a few years ago.'

Falcón tried to remember his first memory and couldn't get much beyond breakfast yesterday.

'And you have no idea why your father made this devastating decision?'

'I assume it was something criminal. A serious investigation into Arturo's abduction would have necessitated major revelations, which presumably would have ruined my father . . . probably put him in prison. It obviously had something to do with that ugly business in Tangier. There may have been a moral angle to it as well, appalling behaviour of some sort, which might have turned his wife against him. I don't know. Whatever, my father must have reasoned it out in his own peculiar way, that Arturo would have been in North Africa or certainly in a ship bound for North Africa within hours of his abduction. He must have weighed it up, in his monstrous mind, that the police would have no chance, that *he* would have no chance.

'The kidnappers' message was clear. This is the price for what you've done. And now this is your choice: come after him and ruin yourself or accept this heavy price and continue. Don't you think that the *perfection* of this terrible choice is in the nature of pure evil? They were saying, Do you want to embrace good or evil? If you are a good man you will come after your son, you will do everything in your power and it will ruin you utterly. You will end up living in exile or prison. Your family will be destroyed. And . . . this is the horror of it, Inspector Jefe, *still you will not get Arturo back.* Yes, that was it. That's what I worked out. They forced him to embrace evil and, having done it, he had to resort to the devil's means to survive. He persuaded himself and us that Arturo did not exist. He stamped him out and us with him. He forced us to cope with the loss in *his* way and he destroyed everything. His wife and his family. And this must have been his final calculation: given that Arturo is lost, that my family will be destroyed whatever I do, then what would *I* prefer?'

Jiménez held up a hand, weighed it, lifted it high and said:

'The feathery lightness of moral goodness?'

He brought the other hand up and sent it crashing to the desk: 'Or the golden weight of power, position and wealth?'

Silence while both men contemplated the unevenness of those scales.

'I thought,' said Falcón, through the leathery hush of the book-lined room, 'that we'd outgrown the age of tragedy, an age where there could be tragic figures. We no longer have kings or great warriors who can fall from such heights to such depths. Nowadays we find ourselves admiring screen actors, sportsmen or businessmen, who somehow lack the stuff of tragedy and yet . . . your father. He strikes me as that rare beast . . . the modern tragic figure.'

'I just wish the play had not been my life,' said Jiménez.

Falcón stood to leave and saw his coffee cold and undrunk on the edge of the desk. He shook Jiménez's hand for longer than usual to show his appreciation.

'That was why I had to call you back,' said Jiménez. 'I had to speak to my analyst.'

'To ask permission?'

'To see if he thought I was ready. He seemed to think it was a good idea that the only other person to hear my family story should be a policeman.'

'To act on it, you mean?'

'Because you would be bound by confidentiality,' said the lawyer seriously.

'Would you prefer that I didn't talk to Consuelo about any of this?'

'Would it serve any purpose other than to frighten her to death?'

'She has had three children with your father.'

'I couldn't believe it when I heard.'

'How *did* you hear?'

'My father dropped me a line whenever one appeared.'

'She had to force him into it. It was a condition of their marriage.'

'That's understandable.'

'She also told me that he was obsessively security conscious. He installed a very serious door in the apartment and made it his business to lock it every night.'

Jiménez stared down at his desk.

'She told me something else which should interest you . . .'

Jiménez's head came up on a very tired neck. There was a trace of fear in his eyes. He didn't want to hear anything that might demand more revision of his newly constructed view of events. Falcón shrugged to let him off the hook.

'Tell me,' he said.

'First, she believed her gregarious restaurateur husband, with his collection of smiling photos, to be a man in the grip of abject misery.'

'So it did get him in the end,' said Jiménez, with no satisfaction. 'But he probably didn't know what *it* was.'

'The second thing was a detail of the will. He left some money to his favourite charity, Nuevo Futuro – *Los Niños de la Calle.*'

Jiménez shook his head, in sadness or denial of the fact, it was difficult to tell. He came round to Falcón's side of the desk and opened the door. He walked his sled-dragging walk down the corridor. Had he walked differently before his analysis? thought Falcón. Maybe he'd been stooped then, as under a weight, and now at least the baggage was behind him. Jiménez produced Falcón's coat, helped him into it. A single question rocked in the balance of Falcón's mind. To ask it or not?

'Has it ever occurred to you,' said Falcón, 'that Arturo might still be alive? Forty-two years old he'd be by now.'

'It used to,' he said. 'But it's been better for me since I achieved a sense of finality.'

10

Even this AVE, the late one, which wouldn't get into Seville until after midnight, was full. As the train shot through the Castillian night, Falcón brushed the crumbs of a bocadillo de chorizo from his lap and stared out of the window through the transparent reflection of the passenger opposite him. Thoughts trickled through his mind, which was tired but still racing from the intrusions he'd made into the Jiménez family.

He'd left José Manuel Jiménez at 3 p.m., having asked if he'd mind him visiting Marta at the San Juan de Dios mental institution in Ciempozuelos, forty kilometres south of the city. The lawyer warned him that it wasn't likely to be a productive meeting but agreed to phone ahead so that he'd be expected. Jiménez had been right, but not for the reasons he'd thought. Marta had had a fall.

Falcón came across her in the surgery having a couple of stitches put in her eyebrow. She was ashen, which he supposed could have been her normal colouring. Her hair was black and white, wound up and pinned in a bun. Her eyes were set deep in her head and their surrounds were charcoal grey with large purple quarter-circles that reached the top of her cheekbones. It could have been bruising from the fall, but had a more permanent look to it.

A Moroccan male nurse was sitting with her, holding her hand and murmuring in a mixture of Spanish and Arabic, while a female junior doctor stitched the eyebrow which had bled profusely, spattering the hospital-issue clothing. Throughout the operation she held on to something attached to a gold chain round her neck. Falcón assumed it was a cross, but on the one occasion that she released it he saw there was a gold locket and a small key.

She was in a wheelchair. He accompanied the nurse as he pushed her back to the ward, which contained five other women. Four were silent while the fifth maintained a constant murmur of what sounded like prayer but was in fact a stream of obscenities. The Moroccan parked Marta and went to the woman, held her hand, rubbed her back. She quietened.

'She always becomes agitated at the sight of blood,' he explained.

The Moroccan's name was Ahmed. He had a degree in psychology from Casablanca University. His good nature and openness iced over visibly when Falcón showed him his police ID.

'But what are you doing *here*?' asked Ahmed. 'These people don't go out. They're permanent residents, barely capable of the simplest of things. Beyond the gates is as good as another planet to them.'

Falcón looked down on Marta's salt-and-pepper head, the white pad over her eyebrow, and an immense sadness broke inside his chest. Here was the real casualty of the Jiménez story.

'Does she understand anything of what we say?' he asked.

'It depends,' he said. 'If you talked about C-A-T-S, she might react.'

'What about A-R-T-U-R-O?'

Ahmed's face settled into a bland wariness, which Falcón had seen before in immigrants under police questioning. The blandness was to minimize any irritation in the officer, the wariness to combat intrusive questioning. It was an attitude that might have worked with Moroccan police, but it annoyed Falcón.

'Her father has been murdered,' he said quietly.

Marta coughed once, twice and the third was followed by a stream of vomit, which pooled in her lap and dripped to the floor.

'She's in shock from her fall,' said Ahmed, and moved away.

Falcón sat on the bed, his face level with Marta's. Vomit clung to some hairs on her chin. She was panting and not looking at him. Her hand still held the locket. Ahmed returned with new clothes and cleaning equipment on a trolley. He screened Marta off. Falcón sat across the room to wait. Under her bed was a small, padlocked metal trunk.

The screens were pulled back and Marta reappeared in new clothes. Falcón walked with Ahmed as he pushed his trolley.

'Have you ever talked to her about Arturo?'

'It's not my job. I'm qualified, but only in my own country. Here I am a nurse. Only the doctor talks to her about Arturo.'

'Have you been present?'

'I have not been in attendance, but I have been there.'

104

'What's her reaction to the name?'

Ahmed performed his cleaning tasks on automatic.

'She becomes very upset. She brings her fingers to her mouth and makes a noise, a kind of desperate pleading noise.'

'Does she articulate anything?'

'She is not articulate.'

'But you spend more time with her, maybe you understand her better than the doctor.'

'She says: "It wasn't me. It wasn't my fault."'

'Do you know who Arturo is?'

'I haven't seen her case notes and nobody has seen fit to inform me.'

'Who is her doctor?'

'Dra Azucena Cuevas. She is on holiday until next week.'

'What about the kitten? Wasn't it you who brought in the kitten and she started . . . ?'

'There are no cats allowed on the ward.'

'The locket round her neck, and the key – is that the key to the trunk under her bed? Do you know what she keeps in there?'

'These people don't have very much, Inspector Jefe. If I see something private, I leave it for them. It's all they have apart from . . . life. And it's amazing how long you survive if that is all you have.'

That was Ahmed. A perfectly intelligent, reasonable and caring individual, but not an expansive one, not in front of authority. He had irritated Falcón. He tried to picture him as the blackness ripped past the window of the AVE, just as he had done José Manuel Jiménez, whose tormented features were pin-sharp in his mind. He failed because Ahmed had done what all immigrants seek to do. He'd blended in. He didn't stand out. He'd merged with his drab, grey surroundings and disappeared into modern Spanish society.

The trickle of these thoughts stopped as he found that the transparent reflection of the woman opposite was returning his look. He enjoyed this: to stare at his leisure as if he was doing nothing more than admiring the hurtling night. The flickering of sex started up in him. He had been celibate since Inés had left. Their sex had been nearly riotous in the early days. It made him pull at his collar to even think of it. Eating outside on the patio and Inés suddenly coming round to his side of the table and straddling him, tugging at his trousers, pushing his hands up her dress. Where had all that gone?

How had marriage snuffed that out so quickly? By the end she wouldn't let him look at her dressing. 'You have no heart, Javier Falcón.' What was she talking about? Did he watch blue movies? Did he fuck prostitutes while watching blue movies? Would he stamp out the existence of his own child? And yet . . . Raúl Jiménez still had, yes, the comfort of a beautiful woman. Consuelo, his consolation.

The woman opposite was no longer meeting his eye in the glass. He turned to her real face. There was a small horror there, a minor pity as if she'd perceived the complications of a mid-forties man and wanted none of it. She dived into her handbag, would have liked it to swallow her whole, but it was a little Balenciaga number with room for a lipstick, two condoms and some folding money. He turned back to the glass. A small light hovered in the blackness, remote, with no other in sight.

He slumped back exhausted from the endless cycles of thought, not of his investigation but of his failed marriage. That always induced some internal collapse as soon as he came up against the wall of Inés's words: 'No tienes corazón, Javier Falcón.' It even rhymed.

It was the new chemistry in his brain, he decided later, that had given him his first new thought about Inés, or rather a realization about an old thought. He wasn't going to be able to move on, he wasn't going to be able to flirt with a woman in a railway carriage until he'd proved to himself that Inés's words were wrong, that they did not apply. It hit him harder than he'd expected. There was even a jolt of adrenalin, which should have meant fear, except that all he was doing was sitting in the AVE roaming around his own head, which contained the uncomfortable notion that she might be right.

He drifted into sleep, a man in a silver bullet train speeding through the dark to an unknown destination. He had the dream again of being the fish; of flashing through the water with fear driving his tail as the visceral tug slowly tore through him. He came awake thumping his head into the seat. The carriage was empty, the train in the station, crowds of passengers pouring past his window.

He went home and watched a movie without taking anything in. He turned off the television and collapsed unfed and unsettled into his bed. He dipped in and out of sleep, not wanting to have the dream again but not wanting to be awake with an anxious world outside his walls. Four o'clock brought him round into a permanent dark wakefulness and he worried about the new chemicals in his brain, which might alter the balance of his mind, while the wooden beams in his vast house groaned like other less fortunate inmates in a distant part of the asylum.

Saturday, 14th April 2001

He got up at 6 a.m. unrested, his nerves jangling like keys on a gaoler's ring so that he actually started thinking about keys in the house and where they were, the ones that would open his father's studio. He went to the desk in the study and found a whole drawer full of keys. How could there be so many doors? He took the drawer up to the wrought-iron gate that locked off the part of the gallery in front of his father's studio. He tried them all, but none of them worked and he walked off, leaving the drawer there on the floor, the keys spread out.

He showered, dressed, went out, bought a newspaper, the *ABC*, and drank a *café solo*. He checked the death notices. Raúl Jiménez was being buried today at eleven o'clock in the Cementerio de San Fernando. He drove to the office, checked the voice mail on his mobile, which was all from Ramírez.

There was a full turnout of all six officers from the Grupo de Homicidios, which was not usual for a Saturday before Easter. He briefed them on the outcome of the discussion with Calderón and put Pérez and Fernández into the Feria ground opposite the Edificio del Presidente, Baena in the streets around the apartment block, and Serrano on working up a list of laboratories and medical suppliers who might have had an unusual sale of chloroform or missing instruments. The four men left. Ramírez stayed, arms folded, leaning against the window.

'Any further thoughts, Inspector Jefe?' he asked.

'Did we get a statement from Marciano Ruíz?'

Ramírez nodded at the desk, said there was nothing new in it. Falcón read it through only to avoid having to tell Ramírez about his trip to Madrid and the Jiménez family horrors. It had to have more relevance to the murder or Ramírez would start undermining him, and he'd find other officers looking at him sadly as the guy who'd started a murder inquiry by going back to an incident of thirty-six years ago.

'I went to see Eloisa Gómez yesterday afternoon,' said Ramírez.

'Did you get anything out of her?'

'She didn't offer me a free blow job, if that's what you mean.'

'Not after what you did to her yesterday,' said Falcón. 'Did she crack?'

'She's not going to talk to me even if she did do it, and now she's scared.'

'You were getting on so well,' said Falcón. 'I thought you were going to ask her home.'

'Maybe I should have been more patient,' said Ramírez. 'But, you know, I really thought she'd let him in and a hard verbal shock might do the trick.'

'We'll start the day with Mudanzas Triana,' said Falcón, moving along. 'Then we'll go to the Jiménez funeral with a video camera and film the mourners. We'll check those mourners off against the address list and follow up with interviews. We'll build a picture of his life.'

'What about Eloisa Gómez?'

'Pérez can pull her in again this afternoon. That'll be nearly forty-eight hours since she was with Raúl Jiménez. If she was an accomplice, the killer will have made contact by then and that might have changed her mental landscape.'

'Or her entire landscape,' said Ramírez. 'For the worse.'

Ramírez picked up the video camera and drove them to Mudanzas Triana, who were on the Avenida Santa Cecilia. They spoke to the boss, Ignacio Bravo, who listened to their theoretical scenario with unmoving eyes behind puffy lids while smoking one Ducados lit from another.

'First of all, it's impossible,' he said. 'My workers are –'

'They signed a statement,' said Ramírez, dead bored, handing it over.

Bravo read the document, flicking ash in the vague direction of a miniature tyre that enclosed an ashtray.

'They will be fired,' he said.

'Talk us through your arrangement with Sr and Sra Jiménez,' said Falcón. 'You can start with why they wanted to move during Semana Santa, which must be the busiest time of year for a restaurant.'

'And not cheap for removals. Our rates double. I explained it all to her, Inspector Jefe. But we couldn't do it the next week when her restaurants were closed because we're all booked up . . . as is everybody else. So she paid her money. She didn't care.'

'When did you first take a look at the job?'

'I went there last week to see the layout, the quantity of large furniture, the number of packing cases needed, all that stuff. I called her the next day to tell her it would be a two-day job and gave her a quote.'

'A two-day job?' said Ramírez. 'So when did you start?'

'Tuesday.'

'Which would make it a three-day job.'

'Sr Jiménez called to say he didn't want his study moved until Thursday. I told him it would cost even more than double and that we could do the job in the time. He insisted. I don't argue the point with rich people; I just make sure they pay. They're the worst . . .'

He trailed off when he saw the look from the policemen.

'How many people knew about the change from the original arrangement?' asked Falcón.

'I see what you're getting at,' he said, unable to get comfortable. 'Of course, everybody had to know. It involved changing all the jobs around. You don't think that one of my men is the murderer?'

'What's intriguing us,' said Falcón, leaving Bravo's suspicion to hang in the air, 'is that, if our scenario is correct, the murderer must have known about the change in the arrangement. He must have known that Sr Jiménez was going to stay an extra night and be on his own. He could only know that from Sr Jiménez himself or from here. When did you confirm the job with Sra Jiménez?'

'Wednesday, 4th April,' he said, flicking through his diary.

'When did Sr Jiménez make the change?'

'Friday, 6th April.'

'Had you already assigned a work team for the job?'

'I did that on the Wednesday.'

'How do you do that?'

'I call my secretary, who informs the depot foreman, who writes it up on a whiteboard downstairs.'

Falcón asked to speak to the secretary. Bravo called her in: a small, dark nervous woman in her fifties. They asked what she'd said to the foreman.

'I told him that there'd been a change, that Sr Jiménez didn't want the study to be touched until Thursday morning and that a small bed should be left in the kids' room.'

'What did the foreman say?'

'The foreman made a coarse remark about what the bed would be used for.'

'What does he do with that information?'

'He puts it up on the whiteboard in red to show that it's a change,' she said. 'And he posts the comments about the study and bed in a separate column.'

'He also types it on to their worksheets,' said Bravo, 'so there's two ways they can't forget. They're not very gifted people in the removals business.'

The three men went down into the depot and looked at the whiteboard, which contained all the information for all jobs in April and May but with the Jiménez job still open. The foreman came out. The secretary was right, he looked the sort who kickstarted the day with a couple of brandies.

'So everybody in this depot would know of the change to the Jiménez job?' said Falcón.

'Without a doubt,' said the foreman.

'What's the security like here?' asked Ramírez.

'We don't store anything here, so it's minimal,' said Bravo. 'One man, one dog.'

'During the day?'

Bravo shook his head.

'No cameras either?'

'It's not necessary.'

'So you can just walk in off the street through the back there from Calle Maestro Arrieta?'

'If you wanted to.'

'Any overalls gone missing?' asked Ramírez.

Nothing had gone missing, nothing had been reported. The overalls were all standard issue with MUDANZAS TRIANA stencilled on the back. It wasn't a difficult thing to copy.

'Anybody been in here who shouldn't?' asked Ramírez.

'Just people looking for work.'

'People?'

'Two or three guys a week come in here and I tell them the same thing. We don't recruit people off the street.'

'What about the last two weeks?'

'A few more than usual trying to get some money together for Easter and the Feria.'

'Twenty?'

'More like ten.'

'What did they look like?'

'Well, fortunately they were all short and fat, otherwise I'd have a job recalling them all for you.'

'Look, funny guy,' said Ramírez, getting his finger out, 'somebody came in here, picked up some information about the job you were doing in the Edificio del Presidente and used it to get himself into an apartment there and torture an old man to death. So try a little harder for us.'

'You didn't say he was tortured to death,' said Bravo.

'I still don't remember,' said the foreman.

'Maybe they were immigrants,' said Ramírez.

'Some of them might have been.'

'Moroccans, maybe, who work for no money.'

'We don't employ –' started Bravo.

'We heard you the first time,' said Ramírez. 'I didn't believe you then. So, look, if you want a quiet life with no visits from Immigration, then start thinking, start remembering who's been in here since last Friday and if you saw anyone taking a particular interest in that whiteboard.'

'Because,' said Falcón, nodding at the foreman, 'you're the only person we've met who's probably seen this killer, talked to him.'

'And you know . . . that's something the killer might start thinking, too,' said Ramírez. '*Buen-as.*'

11

Saturday, 14th April 2001

'He was right – Sr Bravo,' said Ramírez. 'It's too obvious a connection but the killer could be one of his workers.'

'But only if the second scenario, where Eloisa Gómez lets the killer into the apartment, is the correct one,' said Falcón. 'If he got in using the lifting gear he'd have been missing from work in the afternoon. We're going to have to interview every worker and put more pressure on the girl.'

'You know what I don't like about this guy?' said Ramírez. 'Our killer?'

Falcón didn't answer, stared out of the window at the different bars and cafés flashing past on Calle San Jacinto as they headed back up to the river through Triana. He was suddenly depressed by the way his investigation was coming down to the sort of minutiae of everyday life encountered in removals companies.

'He's lucky,' finished Ramírez. 'He's very lucky, Inspector Jefe.'

'Let's hope he's relying on it,' said Falcón, savage and morose. He was jittery from the coffee on an empty stomach and flat from lack of sleep and still no break in the case. His men on the street in Los Remedios hadn't come up with anybody, not one person, who even remembered seeing the removals truck and the lifting gear.

'What does that mean, Inspector Jefe?'

'People who rely on their luck always rely on it until well after it has run out. Like gamblers,' said Falcón. 'They're ultimately stupid people.'

'Now you're implying something, Inspector Jefe.'

'Am I? I don't think so.'

'You don't think he's finished, do you? This killer.'

'I don't know.'

'You think he wants to test his luck some more . . . to see how far he can go.'

Falcón didn't like this about Ramírez. The good cop in him who never stopped, who constantly observed, picked over words, levered up sentences. And now he was doing it to him.

'You talk about "he",' said Falcón, a diversionary tactic, 'but we haven't even got that far.'

Ramírez grinned as they crossed the Puente de Isabel II and headed north along the east bank of the river towards San Jerónimo and the cemetery.

'You know we're wasting our time here, don't you, Inspector Jefe?'

'No, I don't. Where do you think we're going to get our break? We haven't got it in any of the obvious places – on the body, in the apartment, in the Edificio del Presidente, outside it, in the removals company – none of these places.'

'You know I called you yesterday?' said Ramirez, changing tack.

'I didn't pick up any messages until this morning.'

'It was just that I was thinking you were right, Inspector Jefe,' said Ramírez.

Falcón looked across at him slowly, nothing furtive, as if he was just taking in the view of the '92 Expo site, La Isla Mágica looking totally mundane across the sluggish, grey river. Ramírez never thought anybody was right, least of all his Inspector Jefe.

'As you said, it's too elaborate. The method,' said Ramírez.

'For the motive to have been something as ordinary as business, you mean?'

'Yes.'

It took a fraction of a second for a number of subliminal observations to coalesce in Falcón's mind. Ramírez had been more agreeable today than ever before. He hadn't undermined him at Mudanzas Triana. He'd dealt with the foreman, who was much more his type. He'd called him four times on a public holiday. He'd revealed that he'd been to see Eloisa Gómez and admitted that his impatience had sealed off possibly valuable information. He'd said that he, Javier Falcón, had been right.

'You know the procedure,' said Falcón. 'We're not allowed to do nothing. We had very little to offer Juez Calderón apart from Consuelo Jiménez and Eloisa Gómez. The former is a complex and sophisticated individual with opportunity and means, the latter had the opportunity but won't talk to us. Our job is to develop leads and, when they don't present themselves through the evidence, we either have to gradually and humanely sweat them out of people or dig for them . . . sometimes in barren places like cemeteries and address books.'

'But you doubt that those sources will have any bearing on the case?'

'There's doubt, of course, but I'll do it because it might throw up something that could indirectly develop a lead.'

'Such as?'

'What you talked about the other night. What was the guy's name – Cinco Bellotas?'

'Joaquín Lopez.'

'The boys that Sra Jiménez fired . . . they saw the two men talking. We don't know what that was about. It could have an implication, it could be totally innocent. We have to look at it.'

'But you're still thinking that this is the work of a disturbed mind?'

'Undisturbed minds can become disturbed if their whole way of life is threatened.'

'But all the filming, getting into the apartment, hiding there for twelve hours . . .'

'We still don't know that he did that. I'm more inclined to think that "he" formed a relationship with the girl, that "he" got the necessary information from Mudanzas Triana and put the two together to get into the apartment.'

'But what about the horror show that he put Jiménez through?'

'None of this is beyond imagination,' said Falcón, doubting himself as he said it. 'It's not unimaginable, is it?'

'It is to me.'

This was true, thought Falcón, and Marta Jiménez flashed through his mind with her vomity chin and padded eyebrow. Ramírez was uncomplicated. He would always be an Inspector because his imagination only ever allowed him to aspire to being the post above. His horizons were limited.

'What do you think he showed him, Inspector?'

Ramírez braked for a traffic light, gripped the wheel, fixed his eyes on the car in front, waiting for him to move. He tried to jog his mind into unvisited lateral grooves.

'The stuff of horror,' said Falcón, 'is not necessarily the truly terrible.'

'Go on,' said Ramírez, thinking him a strange beast, but glad to be relieved from creative duty.

'Look at us now at the height of our civilization . . . I mean, we can laugh at cannibalism, for God's sake. There's nothing that can frighten us . . . we've seen it all, except . . .'

The lights changed, Ramírez stalled the car, horns honked.

'Except what?'

'That which we've decided we don't know.'

'Isn't that unimaginable?'

'I mean the things that we know about ourselves. The very private, deeply hidden stuff that we show no one and that we firmly deny ever happened because we would not be able to live with the knowledge.'

'I don't understand what you're talking about,' said Ramírez. 'How can you know something without knowing it? It's fucking ridiculous.'

'When my father moved to Seville in the sixties he became friendly with the local priest who used to walk past his door on the way to the church at the end of Calle Bailén. My father didn't go to church or believe in God, but they used the same café and, over years of argument, became friends. One time at three in the morning my father was working in his studio and he heard someone shouting in the street: "Eh! *Cabrón!* You were sent to me, weren't you, Francisco *Cabrón?*" It was the priest, who was not tranquil any more but angry and nearly mad. His cassock was torn apart, his hair was wild and he was drinking brandy from the bottle. My father let him in and he stormed around the patio raging against himself and his useless life. That morning he'd been giving communion and it had suddenly come to him.'

'He lost his faith,' said Ramírez. 'They're always doing that. They get it back.'

'It was worse than that. He told my father that he'd never had any faith. His whole church career had started because of a lie. There'd been a girl who hadn't returned his love. It seemed that he'd gone into the Church to spite her and all he'd ended up doing was spiting himself. For more than forty years the priest had known this . . . but without knowing it. He was a good priest, but it didn't matter because there was one flaw in the edifice of his life, the tiny lie on which it was all based.'

'What happened to him?' asked Ramírez.

'He hanged himself the next day,' said Falcón. 'What do you do if you're a priest and you've spent your whole life teaching the pursuit of truth in God's word?'

'My God,' said Ramírez, 'but you don't have to kill yourself. You don't have to take life so seriously.'

'That's why my father told me the story,' said Falcón. 'I'd said I wanted to be an artist . . . just like him. He told me to be careful because art is about the pursuit of truth too, whether it be personal or universal.'

'I get it,' said Ramírez, hitting the steering wheel, laughing.

'You get it now,' said Falcón. 'What we know without knowing it.'

'Fuck that! I know why you became a cop,' he said, roaring.

'Tell me.'

'The pursuit of truth. Fuck me, that's brilliant,' said Ramírez. 'We're all fucking artists now.'

Had that been it? No. Because when he'd got over the idea of being an artist, come to terms with his father's doubts about his talent, he'd told him that he would become an art historian instead and his father had laughed in his face. 'Art historians are just policemen working with pictures. They hunt for clues. They fill their lives with speculation and conjecture and nine times out of ten they get it all wrong. Art history is for failures,' he'd said. 'Not just failed artists, but failed human beings, too.' The reserves of derision his father had for these people . . . So he became a cop. No, that wasn't quite it either. He went to Madrid University and studied English (the only race, including the Spanish, his father had any time for) and he developed a taste for American *noir* movies of the 1940s. Then he became a cop.

He had a sense of rush, as in shooting to the surface from sleep, except he was awake with his thoughts flashing past him, bright and fast like a shoal of sardine. He shook his head, shuddered back into real life, the seats of the car, plastic, glass, other solid, man-made things.

'Did Serrano come back with anything on the chloroform and surgical instruments?' he asked, steadying himself with words.

'Nothing, so far.'

They pulled up at the cemetery. Ramírez reached back for the video camera, Falcón hovered on the pavement, surveyed the large crowd, the wall of flowers outside the chapel, the blue sky nearly making the scene cheerful. Consuelo Jiménez was in the middle of the herd, her three children bewildered amongst the forest of adult legs. Falcón had been that high, too, at a funeral.

They must have had the blessing. The coffin was being loaded into the car from the chapel. The driver pulled away to the gates, the mourners gathered behind and began a slow procession up the cypress-lined avenue into the heart of the cemetery. Beyond the box hedges were the mausoleums and monuments, a huge bronze of the torero Francisco Rivera in his suit of lights, an imaginary bull forever thundering past him, one hand holding a broken sword, the other an imaginary cape.

The car arrived at Jesús de la Pasión. They unloaded the coffin and took it up to the granite mausoleum where they positioned it opposite the only other occupant – his first wife. Consuelo Jiménez received condolences from those she'd missed earlier. Falcón checked inside the mausoleum. The shelf below the first wife wasn't quite empty. There was a small urn in the corner, too small to contain ashes. He shone his pen torch in there and read the small silver plaque: *Arturo Manolo Jiménez Bautista*. Maybe that was José Manuel's 'finality'.

Falcón rejoined the mourners, gave his condolences and strolled back to the entrance. Ramírez was off amongst the graves with the videocam.

'Of course, you knew him, didn't you?' said a voice close to Falcón's ear, a hand gripping his elbow.

Ramón Salgado's dog-sad face crept into his peripheral vision. Here was one of those people for whom his father maintained a savage derision. Not to his face, of course, because while Salgado was an art historian he was better known as the dealer who had made his father famous. He still had a list of very wealthy clients and, right up to his father's first heart attack, regularly sent these clients to Calle Bailén, so that they could be relieved of those useless blocks of cash that cluttered their bank accounts.

'No, I didn't know him,' said Falcón, summoning up the usual coolness he felt for this man. 'Should I have done?'

Falcón held out his hand, Salgado used both hands to clasp it. He pulled back. Salgado put a hand through his long, pretentious hair, whose white silveriness kinked into curls over the collar of his dark-blue suit. 'Salgado . . . even his dandruff glitters,' his father used to say.

'No, no perhaps you wouldn't have met him, come to think of it,' said Salgado. 'He never went to the house. That's right. I remember now. He always sent Consuelo on her own.'

'Sent her?'

'Whenever he opened a new restaurant, he always had to have a Falcón in it. You know, synonymous with Seville and all that.'

'But why did he have to *send* her?'

'I think perhaps he knew about your father's practices and, being the very important businessman that he was, wasn't prepared to put up with the ... er ... rather, how shall I put it? Sardonic, yes, sardonic ... relieving process.'

He meant, of course, the utterly contemptuous ripping off of clients that his father used to indulge in with such obvious pleasure.

They set off towards the cemetery gates. The pink rims of Salgado's sagging eyes made him look as if he'd just mopped up after crying. Javier had always thought that he must have been much heavier than the stick he was now, and that this weight, when he'd lost it, had dragged the gravity-bound skin of his face into swags below his eyes and jaw line. It was his father who'd said that he looked like a bloodhound, but at least he didn't drool. This was a veiled compliment. His father had loathed reverence, unless if came from a beautiful woman or someone whose talent he admired.

'How did you know him?'

'As you know, I live in El Porvenir. When he opened that restaurant of his, I was one of his first clients.'

'You didn't know him before?'

They were walking briskly and Salgado's long limbs had a tendency to flail. His foot caught the side of Falcón's and he would have been sent sprawling if Falcón hadn't saved him.

'My God, thank you, Javier. I don't want to fall at my age, break a hip and end up housebound and growing vague.'

'You're fine, Ramón.'

'No, no, it's a great fear of mine. One silly mistake and a few months later I'll be a lonely old fool gaping in a dark corner of some unvisited home.'

'Don't be silly, Ramón.'

'It's happened to my sister. I'm going to San Sebastián next week to bring her down to Madrid. She's had it. Fell over, knocked her head, broke her knee and had to go into a home. I can't go all the way up there every month so I'm bringing her further south. Terrible. Anyway, look, why not let's go and have a fino?'

Falcón patted him on the shoulder. He didn't want to spend any time with Salgado, but he was feeling sorry for him now, which had probably been his intention.

'I'm working.'

'On a Saturday afternoon?'

'That's why I'm here.'

'Ah, yes, I forgot,' said Salgado, looking around him, mourners passing on both sides. 'You'll have your work cut out just drawing up the list of his enemies, let alone talking to them all.'

'Will I?' said Falcón, knowing Salgado's powers of exaggeration.

'A powerful businessman like that doesn't go to his grave without dragging a few along with him.'

'Murder is a substantial step.'

'Not for the people he used to deal with.'

'And who *are* these people?'

'Let's not talk about this at the cemetery gates, Javier.'

Falcón had a quick word with Ramírez and got into Salgado's large Mercedes. They drove to Calle Betis down by the river, between the bridges, where Salgado parked up on the pavement shunting an old Seat forward half a metre to fit himself in. They walked along the pavement, which was some metres above the river, until Salgado stopped and made a show of breathing in the Sevillian air, which at this point was not at its sweetest.

'*Sevilla!*' he said, happy now that he was assured of company. '*La puta del Moro* – that's what your father called it. Don't you remember, Javier?'

'I remember, Ramón,' he said, depressed now that he'd volunteered to expose himself to what he was sure was going to be some of Salgado's famous wheedling.

'I miss him, Javier. I miss him very much. He had such a penetrating eye, you know. He said to me once: "There are two smells that make Seville, Ramón, and my trick is – no, my great open secret is that now, at the end of my life, I only paint one of them, which is why I always sell." He was playing, of course. I know that. These scenes of Seville he painted were nothing to him. They were his little game, now that his reputation was assured. I said: "So now the great Francisco Falcón can paint smells. What do you dip your brush in?" And he replied, "Only the orange blossom, Ramón, never the horseshit." I laughed, Javier, and I thought that was the end of it, but after a long pause he added: "I've spent most of my life painting the latter." What do you think of that, Javier?'

'Let's go and have a manzanilla,' said Falcón.

They crossed the road and went into La Bodega de la Albariza and stood at one of the large black barrels, ordered the manzanilla and a plate of olives, which came with capers and pickled garlic, white as teeth. They sipped the pale sherry, which Falcón preferred to fino because of the sea zest in the grapes down at Sanlúcar de Barrameda.

'Tell me about Raúl Jiménez's enemies,' said Falcón, before Salgado leapt into another pool of reminiscence.

'It's all happening again as we speak, as we sip our manzanilla. It's all happening just as it did back in 1992,' he said, enjoying being oblique as he held the complete attention of Javier Falcón. 'I feel it. Here I am at seventy years of age and I'm making more money than I have done in my life.'

'Business is good,' said Javier, on the edge of boredom.

'This is off the record, isn't it?' Salgado said. 'You know, I shouldn't . . .'

'There's no record, Ramón,' said Falcón, showing his empty hands.

'It's illegal, of course . . .'

'As long as it's not criminal.'

'Ah, yes, a fine distinction, Javier. Your father said you were the bright one. "They all think it's Manuela," he used to say, "but Javier's the one who sees things clearly."'

'The anticipation's killing me, Ramón.'

'La Gran Limpeza,' said Salgado. The Big Cleaning.

'What are they washing?'

'Money, of course. What else gets that dirty? They don't call it "black money" for nothing.'

'Where does it come from?'

'I don't ever ask that question.'

'Drug money?'

'Let's just call it "undeclared".'

'OK. So they clean it. Why do they clean it?'

'Why do they clean it now, should be your question.'

'All right, I'll ask that.'

'Next year the euro arrives and it's the end of the peseta. You have to declare your pesetas to get your euros. If they're black, that could be uncomfortable.'

'What do they do with them?'

'Buy art, amongst other things, and property,' said Salgado. 'Try buying an apartment in Seville at the moment.'

'I'm not in the market.'

'And art?'

'*Tampoco.*'

'Have you got round to cleaning out your father's studio yet?'

There it was. The question. Falcón couldn't believe he'd fallen for Salgado's pathetic act in the cemetery. This was what Salgado slipped in to every conversation they ever had, which was why he didn't want to spend any time with him. Now the wheedling would start, unless he came down hard or just changed the subject.

'There's a lot of black money in the restaurant business, isn't there, Ramón?'

'Why do you think he was moving house?' said Salgado.

'That's almost interesting.'

'Nobody ever bought a painting from your father with a cheque,' said Salgado. 'And you're right about the restaurant business, especially tourist restaurants serving reasonable meals paid for in cash with no invoices. Hardly any of that money reaches the books that the taxman sees.'

'So that's what's happening now . . . What about back in 1992?'

'That's all been and gone. I was just being illustrative.'

'I wasn't here, but I heard there was a lot of corruption.'

'Yes, yes, yes, but it was ten years ago.'

'You sound as if you've got something to hide, Ramón. You weren't . . . ?'

'Me?' he said, outraged. 'An art dealer? If you think I had any opportunity to cash in on Expo '92, you're mad.'

'Do you know *anything*, Ramón? I mean, are we gathered here just for you to air your generalities or do you have something specific that will help me find Raúl Jiménez's murderer? What about all these people who come to your shows? I bet they talk about "real" things, once they've stopped talking all that shit about the pictures.'

'"All that shit about the pictures"? Javier, I'm surprised at you, of all people.'

We're getting to it now, thought Falcón. This is a trade. Information for what Salgado wants more than anything else: the chance to rummage through my father's studio. It wasn't about money either. It was the prestige. It would be the crowning moment of this man's inglorious life to mount one final exhibition of the unseen work of the great Francisco Falcón. The collectors who would come. The Americans. The museum curators. Suddenly he would be the centre again, as he had been forty years ago.

Falcón bit into a large, fleshy olive. Salgado nipped the bud off a caper and twiddled the stalk in his fingers.

'Is this information cast iron, Ramón?'

'I've overheard some things to which others have added, unaware of what I already know. Over the years I have built a picture. A *tableau vivant*.'

'And does this picture have a title?'

'*Orange Blossom and Horseshit* – I think that would be an apposite title.'

'And you'd give me a print of this outstanding work if I were to give you access to my father's studio and what . . . ? Let you put on a show of his . . . ?'

'*Oh, no, no, no, que no*, Javier, *hombre*. I would never demand such a thing. Of course, it would be very nice to have a nostalgic trip around his abstract landscapes, but it's all passé now. If he had some hidden nudes like the one in the Prado, the two in the Guggenheim and the one that Barbara Hutton donated to MOMA, then that would be a different matter. But you and I know . . .'

'Then I'm puzzled, Ramón.'

'I just want to spend a day alone in his studio,' he said, nipping off another caper. 'You can lock me in. You can search me when I come out. All I ask is a day amongst his paintbrushes, his rolls of canvas, his stretchers and oils.'

Falcón stared at the old man, his glass of manzanilla halfway to his mouth, trying to see inside, the inner workings, the springs and cogs. Salgado turned his glass round by the stem, making a circular mark on the wooden slats of the barrel top. He looked sad, because that was how he always looked. And he was impenetrable, his urbanity as good as armour plate.

'I'm going to have to think about this, Ramón,' he said. 'It's not exactly a normal piece of business.'

12

Falcón and Ramírez sat in the interview room at the Jefatura with the videocam plugged into the television while a younger policeman, who knew about these things, made it all work. Ramírez asked after the old guy in the cemetery.

'Ramón Salgado. He was my father's dealer.'

'He didn't look as if he could have lifted Jiménez out of his chair,' said Ramírez, 'or shinned up a ladder.'

'He's also an art historian, who gives occasional unattended lectures at the university. He has a gallery on Calle Zaragoza close to the Plaza Nueva. Some influential people still go there, including Sra Jiménez and her husband.'

'He looked like he knew how to get money out of people.'

'We talked about black money in the restaurant business. He even touched on Expo '92, which I don't think he'd meant to, and there was an offer of information.'

'But he didn't tell you anything?'

Falcón felt the touch of that probe again.

'I know Ramón Salgado,' said Falcón. 'On the face of it he's a successful businessman – money, big car, house in El Porvenir, influential clients – but in his own eyes he's a failure. He's never committed himself like the artists he represents. He lectures to empty theatres. He's written two books with no academic or commercial success.'

'So, what did he want?' said Ramírez.

'Something personal . . . to do with my father, in return for information. I don't want to give it to him and get gossip back.'

'There's a huge market for gossip,' said Ramírez.

'You've never been to an art opening, have you, Inspector? It's full of people pretending to know more than they do, who think that only *they* can see the truth in the work and then . . . they try to put it into words.'

'That's bullshit, not gossip.'

'They're people who want to be where "it" is happening. They want to touch "it". They want to tell you about "it".'

'What's "it"?' asked Ramírez.

'Genius,' said Falcón.

'Rich people are never content with what they've got, are they?' said Ramírez. 'Even the guys in the *barrio* who've made it aren't happy with that. They want to come back and ram their success down your throat all night and still be friends at the end of it all.'

'My father never understood it either and he was a rich man himself,' said Falcón. 'He despised it.'

'What?' asked Ramírez, thinking they were still talking about genius.

'Acquisitiveness.'

'Oh, I'm sure he did,' said Ramírez sarcastically, reaching for his cigarettes, knowing that old man Falcón had a left a fortune in property he'd 'acquired'. If he despised acquisitiveness then the old *cabrón* despised himself.

The equipment was finally ready. They turned to the screen. The white noise slammed into the first image: the silence of the cemetery, the cypress shadows striping the path, the mourners gathered around the mausoleum.

Falcón's mind drifted over thoughts of Salgado, his father, the uninvestigated studio and the odd request. It was Salgado who'd made the breakthrough for his father, which was why special contempt was reserved for him in private. Salgado had created the show in Madrid, which saw the sale of the first Falcón nude back in the early sixties. The European art world had gone crazy. The house in Calle Bailén was bought on the strength of it.

On the back of that bright but parochial renown, Salgado had put on a show in New York. There was talk of a set-up, that the painting had already been promised to the Woolworth heiress and 'Queen' of Tangier, Barbara Hutton, and that the 'show' was just that, a way of creating excitement about the Francisco Falcón name. Whatever happened, it worked. Barbara Hutton did buy the painting and the show was attended by a glittering array of New York socialites. The name Falcón was on everybody's lips. The next two New York shows were huge successes and for a few short weeks in the mid sixties Francisco Falcón was almost as a big a name as Picasso.

Some of this success was due to the talents of Ramón Salgado, who knew from the outset the limit of his client's work. The fact was – and it gave rise to much bitterness, anger and frustration in his father – there were only four Falcón nudes. They were all painted in the space of a year in the early sixties in Tangier. By the time his father had moved to Spain that particular vein of genius had dried up. He never recaptured the unique, mysteriously forbidden qualities of those four abstracts. His father used to talk to him about Gaugin. How Gaugin was nothing until he saw those South Sea Island women. They touched off his genius. He saw them, he saw *into* them. Take him away from that and he'd have ended up in France painting doors. That's what had happened to Francisco Falcón. His first wife died, as did his second, and he'd left Tangier. Critics said that the nudes had been painted with a knowing innocence, which gave them their untouchable presence, and that perhaps it was the trauma of those final years in Tangier that broke the flow. His losses closed off access to the purity of that innocence. He never even attempted to paint another abstract nude.

Something caught Falcón's eye. A black speck had flashed against white on the screen.

'What was that?'

Ramírez jolted in his seat. He was barely watching the damn thing, too. The whole business a waste of time as far as he was concerned.

'I saw something,' said Falcón. 'Something in the background. Top right. Can we rewind it?'

Ramírez hovered around the screen like a bluebottle over dung. His large and imprecise finger stabbed at the machine and the figures started sprinting backwards. Another stab and they moved at a more dignified pace.

It was after the ceremony at the mausoleum. The mourners were drifting away. Falcón watched the background – the sawteeth of family mausoleum roofs, the flat lines of the high ossuary blocks where poorer individuals' bones lay. The camera started a slow pan from left to right.

'Was that it again?' asked Falcón, not sure now that he was concentrating.

'I didn't see anything,' said Ramírez, stifling a yawn.

'Get that guy back in here and let's freeze the picture.'

Ramírez brought the young policeman back in and he replayed the sequence frame by frame.

'There,' said Falcón, 'top right, against the white mausoleum.'

'*Joder*,' said Ramírez. 'Do you think that's him?'

'You caught him just at the end of that pan.'

'Eight frames,' said the young policeman. 'That's one-third of a second. I don't know how you saw that.'

'I didn't see it,' said Falcón. 'It just caught my eye.'

'He's filming the mourners,' said Ramírez.

'He must have seen you with your camera and fallen back behind the mausoleum wall,' said Falcón. 'But that, I'm pretty sure, is one-third of a second of our killer.'

They watched the video three times over and got nothing more out of it. They went to the computer department and found an operator still working. He digitalized the tape images and fed the eight frames into the computer, sectioned out the vital element and blew it up to screen size. There was some distortion but not so much that they couldn't see how careful this person was being about his appearance. He wore a black baseball cap with no brand mark. The peak was turned to ten o'clock so that he could get the camera cleanly to his eye. He wore gloves and had a roll-neck jumper up over his mouth and nose. He was kneeling and his dark coat was flush with the ground.

'We can't even tell what sex "he" is,' said Falcón.

'I can clean these images up for you,' said the operator. 'It'll take me the weekend, but I can do it for you.'

They took a print-out of the frame and went back to Falcón's office.

'So, what was he doing there?' said Falcón, sitting at his desk. 'Was he filming someone in particular or just the scene in general?'

'The end of his work,' said Ramírez. 'The bastard dead and buried. That's my guess.'

'Would he take that sort of a risk just for personal satisfaction?'

'Not such a risk. We don't normally film mourners at a victim's funeral,' said Ramírez.

'It could be the end of *that* piece of work and the start of the next,' said Falcón.

'Wasn't that what you were implying before we went to the cemetery?'

'I don't remember implying anything.'

'You said that undisturbed minds can become disturbed. Isn't that the same thing?'

'A madman with a malignant motive,' said Falcón. 'Or a motiveless madman who's malign.'

Ramírez looked behind him to see if someone more intelligent had just entered the room.

'It's the point, though, isn't it?' said Falcón. 'We still don't know enough to break off any line of inquiry.'

He stuck the print-out up on the wall.

'It's like that game in kids' magazines,' said Ramírez, slumping back in his chair. 'You have to guess the identity of a pop star from an eye or a nose or a mouth. My kids think that I should be good at it because I'm a policeman, but they don't seem to understand that I don't know who any of these people are. Who the hell is Ricky Martin?'

'Son of Dean?' said Falcón, with no idea.

'Who the fuck is *Dean* Martin?'

It set Falcón off. Hysteria broke. Maybe it was the disturbed nights with strange dreams. He laughed madly and silently. Tears brimmed and he dashed them away. He writhed in his seat as wave after wave engulfed him. Ramírez looked at him like a lawyer with an unreliable client who has to take the stand.

Ramírez called the men in the field, listened to their reports. Nothing. He left for lunch. Falcón pulled himself together and went home still stunned by his outburst, the fact that it had happened to him, that loss of self-control. He ate something Encarnación had left on the cooker without registering what it was. He went to bed, hoping for an hour's sleep. He woke at 9 p.m. in the pitch black of his bedroom. He jerked out of sleep as if someone had tugged at a knot in his stomach. He'd seen drunks do the same, coming to in the cells as if plugged straight back into the mains of life. He was groggy and his tongue was coated with something nasty. His limbs were stiff and his joints creaking.

He stood under the shower and let the water pummel the mess out of him. His head and insides were like a blender with cutlery fed into it, all smashed and mangled. He went to his dressing room and put on a pair of grey trousers and a white shirt that crackled as he shrugged it over his shoulders. When he looked at himself in the mirror he couldn't stand the sight of himself. His shirt. He hated the whiteness of it. He couldn't bear the . . . non-colour. He tore it off, shuddered at his loathing of it, hurled it across the room. He went up close to the mirror, inspected his face, pressed the soft skin beneath the eyes, saw it wrinkle but not return to its former smoothness. Age. Is the inside wrinkling like the outside? Are small creases forming in the brain so that I go to bed liking white shirts and wake up hating them?

He put on a green shirt.

Back in the bedroom he had a sudden memory flash as he looked at the rucked-up dark-blue sheets of the bed. Inés had always wanted white, but he couldn't sleep in white sheets. There it was again, that anti-white tendency. They'd settled on light blue. Falcón had a curious perception of himself as an eccentric, as his father had described some of the English collectors he'd known. No, that was a neat lie slipped in there by his ego. He saw himself as Inés must have seen him – an old man with ways and habits, except forty-five was not old. When he was fifteen, forty-year-olds were old. They all wore suits and hats and moustaches. Now that he was thinking about it, he realized that he wore suits all the time; even at weekends he wore a jacket and tie. Inés had tried to get him into light sweaters, jeans, those long-sleeved knit shirts done up to the neck, even collarless shirts which were impossible for him to wear. The lack of structure. He liked a shirt and tie because it held him together, made him feel enclosed. He hated looseness and bagginess. He liked made-to-measure suits. He liked the sensation of a shell that a good suit gave him. He enjoyed its protection.

Protection from what?

There was that hurtling sensation again. This time, rather than shudder out of it, he tried to examine it. It was like film fast-forward, but that wasn't quite right because there was no progress – quite the opposite. Not regression, but stasis. Yes, that was it. He was standing still while his past caught up with him. The idea there and then gone like debris flashing past a window. And where did that come from? Debris flashing past . . . The dream came back to him from the sleep that he'd thought had been dreamless, which was why he'd woken with a start. He knew where the dream had come from. He'd read an account of the aftermath of the PanAm flight 103 crash over Lockerbie in Scotland. A man had woken up in his house to find a row of passengers, still in their seats, in his garden and . . . they all had their fingers crossed. That pitiful detail had driven the horror of the bombed plane into Falcón's mind; it had stayed with him and now the memory had resurfaced. The noise. The vital, vital debris flying past the window – bits of turbine, wing trim – and then thrown out into the yawning night, hurtling through the thin blackness, the mind incapable, only instinct fighting back to less dangerous times, the roller coaster, Magic Mountain, Oh, we'll be all right, fingers crossed. The unseen ground rushing to meet them. The blacker black. The unstarred kind. Oh God, the whole world upside down. We were never meant for this. What use 'Brace! Brace!' now? This really is economy class. And we'll be *so* late. All those thoughts – wild philosophizing, persuasive little jokes, the craving for normality – as we're rushing towards it, dying to meet it.

But he hadn't. He'd woken up. There'd been no impact. His mother had told him – his first mother or his second mother? – one of them had told him that as long as you didn't hit the ground in a dream you'd be all right. Ridiculous. You're in bed. The things you'll believe.

He knelt down and tied up his shoelaces, knotted them tight, enclasped his feet so that they were sure and steady, reliable. This was not a time for stumbling about, slopping around in the yellow leather babouches he'd bought because they reminded him of his father, which was what he'd worn as he worked – barefoot or babouches, never anything else.

It was exasperating, this constant resurfacing.

He went out of the room into the arched gallery overlooking the patio. It was warm. The air breathing around the pillars was as soft as a young girl come to kiss him. He sucked in the exotic air that suddenly filled his head with the scent of possibility. The black pupil of the still water in the fountain in the patio looked up at the night. He shivered. All these houses look in on themselves, he thought. I'm walled in. The sides encroach. I have to get out. I have to get out of myself.

He started down the stairs but turned back to the gallery, to his father's studio. The drawer of keys had gone. Encarnación. Strange, he thought, with a name like that and I so rarely see her. Here she is, supposedly endlessly assuming bodily form, but she never appears. I only see evidence of her activity. He walked to the gate because he could see now that a key had been left in the lock and hanging from a piece of string, another key. He stroked his palms with the tips of his fingers. Damp. His hands had always been dry and cool. Inés had remarked on it. When they were lovers he used to be able to just run his hands down her hot back and it would make her press her stomach into the bed, push her bottom up to him, offer her sex to him. Those cool, dry hands on her skin. By the end of their marriage she was calling him the fishmonger. 'Don't touch me with those blocks of ice!'

He turned the key. One, two and a half. The latch clicked open. The door swung noiselessly. Who had oiled those hinges? The fantastic Encarnación? His heart pounded as if he knew something was about to happen. He took the key from the lock, closed the wrought-iron gate.

At this end of the gallery his father had put bars over the openings of the arches, obsessed with security as he always was. Falcón walked the length of it, the flat black water of the fountain rippling in his vision. He paced back to the door in the middle, the heavy mahogany door with its prominent panels jutting out, saying 'Do not enter' or perhaps even more demanding: 'Do not enter unprepared'.

The second key slid into the lock, turned easily. It was all encouraging. He pushed on the heavy door, the first resistance. It opened on an absurd creak, like a vampire's coffin. He giggled. Nervous as Leda when she saw that swan bracing its wings. One of his father's little jokes about women who trembled under the surge of his charisma. He fumbled for the switch.

A huge empty wall spattered with paint came up under the halogen glare of the lights. The end where his father used to work. Five metres by four metres of worked-on wall. The vestiges of four canvas squares seemed to float under the dribbles and slashes of paint. One end of the wall closest to the window was almost totally black, thick with paint as if he'd worked there on ideas crowded with pending doom. There was a predominance of red over the rest of the wall, which was not a colour that had featured much in any of his work since the Tangier nudes – voluptuous lines laid over blocks of Moroccan colour – touareg blue, desert ochre, burnt amber, terracotta and then the reds, the whole range of blood reds from capillary crimson, to vein vermilion, to deep arterial amaranthine. They all said it was in the reds. The life flow. But he hadn't used red since Tangier. The paintings he made of details of Seville rarely used red. The abstract landscapes were green and grey, brown and black and always suffused with a mysterious light from an unknown source. Light which the *ABC* critic called 'numinous' and *El País*, 'Disney'. 'You can't teach people to see,' his father had said. 'They will only see what they want to. The mind is always interfering with vision. You should know that, Javier, in your job. Witnesses who've seen things so clearly, but once put under cross-examination are found hardly to have been there. You'd learn more from a blind man. Remember *Twelve Angry Men*? Yes. But why "angry"? Because people believe deeply in the veracity of their own vision. If you can't rely on your own eyes, whose can you?'

In remembering these words Falcón had stopped in mid stride, as ridiculous as those mime artists down Calle Sierpes. His mind turned and spun around the crux, a truth that would enable him to see into the mind of Raúl Jiménez's killer. The one who would make his victim see, who would force him through the mind's interference, to see an unacceptable truth. But he didn't reach it and came round as surprised as an anaesthetized patient given time out from the world.

He circled the notched tables covered with jars and clay pots stuffed with sheaves of brushes all dried hard, crisp with encrusted paint. Underneath the tables there were cardboard boxes and piles of books, catalogues and magazines, obscure art periodicals and reams of paper, rolls of canvas, sheets of hardboard. It would take him half a day just to carry the stuff downstairs, let alone look through it all. But that was the point. He was not supposed to look through it. It was to be taken away and incinerated. Not dumped but destroyed beyond recognition.

Falcón ran his hands through his hair again and again, maddened by what he was about to embark on, aware that the reason he'd come in here was specifically to disobey his father's wishes. He'd been avoiding this moment since his father's death, needing to get further from the end of that era so that he could start on his own. His own era? Did ordinary men like him even have their own era?

He crouched down and pulled out a single magazine from a pile. It was a *New Yorker*, his father a great fan of the cartoons, the more surreal the better. He'd particularly enjoyed a drawing of a chess pawn standing next to a desert cactus with the caption: 'Queen's pawn to Albuquerque, New Mexico.' The dazzling brilliance of its meaninglessness – he'd thought it such a perfect attitude to life, perhaps because his own had been brought close to meaninglessness by the loss of his dazzling genius.

The memories crowded, jostled for a ticket.

A row about Hemingway. Why Hemingway had shot himself in

1961, the year that his mother had died. A man who had achieved so much and had killed himself because he couldn't stand not being able to do it any more. Javier had been sixteen when they talked about it.

Javier: 'Why couldn't he just retire? The guy was over sixty. Why didn't he just hang up his pencil case, settle himself into a lounger in the Cuban sunshine and drink a few *mojitos*?'

Father: 'Because he was sure that what he'd lost could be refound. Should be refound.'

Javier: 'Well, that alone should have kept him occupied. Hunt the treasure . . . that's a game everybody enjoys.'

Father: 'It's not a *game*, Javier. This is not a game.'

Javier: 'His place in literature was assured. He had the Nobel Prize. With *The Old Man and the Sea* his work was done. There was nothing more to be said. Why try to say more if there's . . . ?'

Father: 'Because he had it and he lost it. It's like losing a child . . . you never get over what could have been.'

Javier: 'And look at you, Papá. You're no different and yet . . .'

Father: 'Let's not talk about me.'

Falcón threw down the magazine at his crassness remembered. He pulled out a box, flipped open its flaps. All this stuff. The accumulation of a lifetime's rubbish, even more so with an artist who would hold on to anything that might precipitate a new idea. He walked the book-lined walls at the side and back of the room. 'Should I burn these, too?' he asked himself. 'Is that what you want me to be – a book burner? Throw them all from the gallery into the patio and have a bonfire of words and pictures? You cannot have meant me to do this.' The persuasiveness of the guilty mind that was about to transgress.

The wall on the street side had four floor-to-ceiling windows, which his father had installed to maximize natural light. Each window was encased in a steel lattice that could be slid back. The room no less than a fortress.

He arrived back in front of his father's work wall and went through a door in the corner, which was windowless and lit by a single unshaded bulb. Four racks of vertical slots had been built along one wall. Stretched canvasses and other material leaned in them. A plans chest occupied most of the opposite wall. It was piled high with boxes, almost to the ceiling. It smelt musty, stale and, after the long winter, damp. He went to the racks and pulled out a sheet of paper at random. It was a charcoal outline of one of the Tangier nudes. He pulled out another sheet. A pencil drawing of the same nude. Another and another sheet, each one a reworking of the same nude, a development of a detail, an examination of an angle. He went to the canvasses. The same Tangier nude painted again and again, sometimes big, sometimes small but always the same nude. Falcón searched the other racks and found that the four racks in which his father had arranged the work corresponded to each of the four Falcón nudes. Each rack contained hundreds of drawings and charcoals, oils and acrylics.

A tremendous sadness suddenly overwhelmed him. This work, the wall of racks in this dimly lit room, was what was left of his father's attempt to refind his genius, to get it down right, even once more, even if it was just a tiny detail, to have it again. There was pain on the back of that surge of sadness, because Falcón could see, even in the pathetic light from the cheap bulb, that not one of these pieces contained anything of the exceptional qualities of the originals. Everything was in its place, but there was no life, no leap, no surge, no flow. This was mediocre. His abstract landscapes were better than this. His cupolas and windows, doors and buttresses, even they were better than this. He would burn these; he would burn them without a second thought.

He climbed up on a stool and lifted down one of the boxes from the plans chest. Heavy. More books. He flipped open the box, rooted through them, some leather-bound, others cloth, some by writers from the sixties and seventies, others classics. He opened a cover and found the personal dedication. They were gifts from admirers: aristocrats, ministers, theatre directors, poets. He tore open another box of carefully packed porcelain. Another box contained silverware. Cigars – unsmoked. Cigarette cases. Wood carvings. Figurines. His father loathed china figurines. Three boxes full of them. The early ones in newspaper from the seventies, the later stuff in bubblewrap. He realized what he was looking at. This was homage paid to his father. These were the small gifts bestowed on him when he attended public occasions. They were small expressions of gratitude for his genius.

More memories. Going away with his father. He rarely paid for a meal or a hotel room, which were always festooned with flowers. If they stayed in a private house the locals would silently leave offerings of fruit and vegetables to show their appreciation of a visit from the great man.

'This is how it is,' his father would say. 'Greatness is constantly rewarded. If I were a footballer or a torero it would be no different. Genius is the thing – with foot, cape, pen or brush, it doesn't matter, and yet . . . what is it? Great artists paint lacklustre paintings, brilliant toreros make terrible messes of great bulls, magnificent authors write bad books, sublime footballers can play like shit. So what is this . . . this *fickle* genius?'

Yes, he would get angry with it, hold up his hand with thumb and forefinger pinched together so that the ends turned white and Javier thought he might be about to say that genius was nothing.

'Genius is an interstice.'

'A what?'

'A crack. A tiny opening to which, if you are blessed, you may put your eye and see the essence of it all.'

'I don't understand.'

'You wouldn't, Javier, because you are blessed with normality. The interstice for a footballer is in that moment when he knows, without being conscious of it, exactly where the ball is going to be, how he should run at it, where he should place his feet, where the goalkeeper is, the precise moment he should strike the ball. Calculations that are seemingly impossible become fantastically simple. The movement is effortless, the timing sublime, the action so . . . slow. Have you noticed that? Have you noticed the silence in these moments? Or do you only remember the roar as the ball caresses the net?'

Another one of those endless conversations with his father. Falcón shook his head to rid himself of it. He went through all the boxes, vaguely uneasy at his father's methodical organization. His father had usually worked in a great miasma of paint, hashish, music and, in Seville, mostly at night and yet in this storeroom he was the bean counter. And as if to confirm this fact he opened a box that was full to the top of money. He didn't have to count it because there was a note on top that told him it contained eighty-five million pesetas. A huge sum of money, one that could have bought a small palace or a luxury apartment. He recalled Salgado's talk of black money. Was this to be destroyed, too?

The last box contained more books, leather-bound but untooled and untitled. The spines were smooth, too. He flicked one open at random. The pages were covered in his father's immaculate hand-writing. A single line jumped out at him:

I am so close.

He snapped the book shut and reopened it at the first page, which was inscribed: *Seville 1970–* . Journals. His father had kept diaries, which he'd never known about. Sweat popped out of his forehead again and he smeared it away. His hands were damp. He went back to the box to see what order they were in and realized he was holding the last one. He flipped through the pages to December 1972 and the last words of the journal:

I am so bored now. I think I will stop.

Down the side of the books he found an envelope addressed 'To Javier'. Hairs bristled on his neck. He slit it open with a trembling finger. The date on the letter was 28th October 1999. The day before he died, three days after his final will.

Dear Javier,

If you are reading this letter, then you are considering disobeying the instructions and my specific wishes laid down in my last will and testament of 25th October 1999, which, in case you have forgotten, states in unambiguous language that the contents of my studio are to be completely destroyed.

Yes, there is a loophole in this for you, Javier, with your logical policeman's brain. You may have decided that this offers the opportunity to inspect, appreciate, read and sniff over my belongings prior to destroying them. You know me better than any of my children. We have talked together in a way, with an intimacy, that I never achieved with either Paco or Manuela. You know what this means. You know why I have done this and left it in your hands.

For a start neither Paco nor Manuela could burn 85,000,000 pesetas, but you will, Javier. I know you will, because you know where this money comes from and, more important, you are incorruptible.

You may think that my profound trust in you gives you the right to read these journals. Of course, I can do nothing to prevent you and that is right, but I should warn you that what you'll find in them could be destructive as well. I will not be responsible for this. You must decide.

The journals are incomplete. Detective work will be required. You are perfect for this task. Do not take it up lightly though, Javier, especially if you are strong, happy and invigorated by your present life. This is a small history of pain and it will become yours. The only way to avoid it is not to start.

Your loving father,
Francisco Falcón

Saturday, 14th April 2001, Falcón's house, Calle Bailén, Seville

Falcón put the letter back in the envelope, tucked it in the box. He slashed out the lights in the two rooms, sensed the darkness gulping back his father's work, hungry for it. He locked up the gates and left the house, wanting to walk off these developments, pace them out.

The gardens in front of the Museo de Bellas Artes were beginning to fill up with young people smoking joints and swigging from litre bottles of Cruzcampo. It was still early at 11 p.m.; in a few more hours the dark trees would roar with the noise of a massive open party. He set off from there away from the centre, away from anywhere he might be known.

A rhythm settled in him, one that demanded no thought, only the feel of the cobbles through the soles of his shoes. The words of his father's letter rattled through him as endless as a freight train thudding over points in the track. He knew that he would do it, that he could not resist reading the journals.

After half an hour he found he was on Calle Jesús del Gran Poder – a big name for an unprepossessing street. He cut through to the Alameda, where the girls were out in amongst the trees, the parked cars and the open space where the flea market was held every Sunday morning. Music thumped from the clubs and bars on the far side. A girl stretching her spandex miniskirt over her bottom approached and asked him what he was looking for. Her face was black and white in the yellow street lighting, the breasts forced up into a graphic cleavage, a fishnet top, a bare, round stomach. Her lips were glossy black, her tongue came out probing as a sea creature from a rock. He was mesmerized. She made some suggestions, which surprised Falcón by working. He *would* like some sex. It had never occurred to him to buy it. She had his attention now, using all the tricks. His insides were all stirred up, but in the wrong position, the wrong colour – black tripe – seething like the coils of a snake, monstrous and silent, feeding ideas into his mind, terrible ideas that he didn't know he could have. He was appalled but gripped by the live excitement of it. He had to wrench himself away.

'I'm a policeman,' he said stiffly. 'I'm looking for Eloisa Gómez.'

She sulked and nodded him to a group standing out in the square. He walked out from under the trees, disturbed to find that he could no longer be certain about himself. Unpredictability was seeping into his nature. He had to remind himself that he was good, a force for the good, because the snapshot he'd just seen of the dark side of his nature showed it to be teeming with life. As he walked the rough ground of the Alameda he conceived the insane notion that he could become afraid of himself, of what he had inside him that he didn't know. Wasn't that what the killer had done to Raúl Jiménez, shown him what he dreaded every day of his life?

He reached the group of women standing opposite the entrance to Calle Vulcano, where more girls stood in the light of the road, their thigh-high boots silhouetted. Fantasy women, who with their every action tell men that they can do whatever they want, except kiss this mouth. The group parted without a word and waited for him to speak because they knew he wasn't a punter. He asked for Eloisa Gómez. A short, fat girl with stiff, dyed-black hair and a swollen face said she wasn't around. She hadn't been seen since she took a call from a client the previous night.

'Is that unusual, for her not to come back here?' he asked, and they shrugged.

'You must be a cop,' said one of the girls. 'Are you with that *cabrón* who came here last night?'

'I'm a homicide cop,' said Falcón. 'She was with a client Wednesday night, Thursday morning. After she left he was murdered.'

'Too bad.'

He brought up Eloisa's number on his mobile, punched it in. There was no reply; he left a message, giving his number, telling her to call. They made him feel like a zoo animal, waiting to see if he'd do something interesting, until a blonde girl at the back said: 'You want a blow job, we'll give you the usual police discount.' They laughed.

He headed up Calle Vulcano past the fantasy girls to Calle Mata and then east on to Calle Relator. He was remembering the last time he'd been in this area, which must have been with his father because he never came here for a drink or a *tapa*. There were craftsmen in this part of town. Yes, a frame maker, and there was a copyist, too, a dangerous type, dark-skinned, who his father said was a heroin user. What was his name? A nickname. The first and only time he'd met him he'd come to the door in nothing but a pair of black satin briefs. He was thin with the musculature of a wild animal. Big teeth. He'd been shocked by him, by the way he didn't bother to dress and discussed business with his father with a hand inside the front of his briefs.

He crossed Calle Feria to an old church with a Latin name – Omnium Santorum – which stood next to a covered market. It was dark and quiet so that when his mobile rang it startled him.

'*Diga,*' he said.

Silence apart from the ethereal hiss.

'*Diga,*' he said, again, harder.

The voice when it came was calm, soft and male.

'Where are you now?'

'Who is this?' said Falcón, irritated by people who didn't announce themselves.

'Are we close?' said the voice, and those three words transfixed him, bent him over in the middle, as if crouching would make him hear better.

'I don't know, are we?'

'Closer than you think,' said the voice, and the phone went dead.

Falcón whirled around, checked every doorway and street corner, the dark alley between the church and the market. He ran, looking down the side streets. A couple with a small dog crossed the road to avoid him. He must have seemed quite mad, dancing with the shadows like a boxer gone sloppy in the head.

He stopped and stared into the pavement, fidgeted through the two possible scenarios. If the killer didn't know Eloisa Gómez before, he had got her number from Jiménez's mobile phone, which he stole from the apartment. He called her last night and now he must have got *her* mobile phone because he's picked up my number from the message I've just left, which means . . . Guilt settled in his chest. He's killed her. And if he did know her before . . . it didn't change the outcome.

We messed that up badly, he thought. He broke into a run, arrived in the Alameda in a sweat and out of breath. The women circled him.

'Where does Eloisa Gómez live?' he asked. 'And does anybody know where she went after she got that call last night?'

The fat girl took him on a hobbling run to a house on Calle Joaquín Costa, past groups huddled in vacant lots and doorways, crouched over tinfoil, sucking on empty biro tubes, waiting for the spear-tailed moment of the dragon chase. She unlocked the door of a broken-down old building with grasses and flowers growing out of the cracks in the plaster. There was no light in the stairwell and the wooden stairs stank of urine. The girl pointed to a door on the first landing. He hammered on it. No answer. She brought a spare key from her room. Inside there was no Eloisa, only a brand-new large, cuddly panda on the punched-out sofa.

'That's for her niece,' said the girl. 'Her sister lives in Cádiz.'

The panda sat with its arms out in a stiff embrace, its eyes stupid and sad. Falcón momentarily contemplated his own loneliness in the face of that dumb toy. He called Eloisa Gómez's number again and got the voice mail.

'Where is she?' he asked.

He gave the girl his card, told her the usual things. She took it with a trembling hand. She knew what it all meant.

His failure made him angry. He left the Alameda and went up Calle Amor de Dios. He walked with apparent purpose, but aimlessly turned left and right down the disorganized streets until he hit the stink of cats. The walls closed in before opening up to a church called Divina Enfermera. Divine Nurse? The tarmac was all torn up in great chunks of black cake and piled in the Plaza San Martín. He had been here with his father on the way to the copyist. They'd passed the Divine Nurse and his father had a made a dirty joke and shown him the divine nurses at work. Sixty-five-year-old women sitting outside their houses, legs apart, crow black above their dimpled thighs. His father had appalled him by endlessly negotiating a blow job until Javier couldn't bear it any longer and ran to the end of the street and stood below a tiled advertisement for Amontillado fino and manzanilla *pasada*.

The street names slipped past him until he came out in San Juan de Palma, which was packed with people spilling out of the Cervezería Plazoleta and drinking beer around the two palm trees that disappeared above the lights. It was so easy to feel alone in this city. He walked on past the home of the Duquesa de Alba. He'd been in there once, standing below the tumbling towers of bougainvillea, drinking nectar with high society. Is this how tramps feel inside? I'm becoming a vagrant from myself.

A breeze cooled the patina of sweat on his forehead. He didn't think he was thinking and yet words drifted up from nowhere, unbidden. Male menopause. Forty-five. Ripe for it. More crap from Manuela's magazines. No. This is just straight, unadulterated age. The creeping onset has been noted by mind and body. Age is just the disintegration of possibility and the assertion of probability with the odds shortening every day – Francisco Falcón, June 1996.

He ran. Took off as if he had a chance of getting away from what was developing in his head. People stepped aside from his pounding feet. Those with a stronger herd instinct joined him, as if he might know where he was going. The fools, the damned fools. By the time he reached Calle Matahacas there were twenty people with him and it was then that he saw the crowd materializing out of the darkness and felt the deep silence that Sevillanos reserve for two things – *La Virgen* and *los toros*.

At the end of the street in Escuelas Pías, above a heaving sea of black heads, the candlelit Virgin appeared. Her bowed head, her white, bejewelled robes, her tear-splashed cheek swirled in the updraught of burnt incense. Awe lapped at her feet from the packed humanity below as her *paso* swayed and rocked in the darkness.

The people behind Falcón shunted him forward towards the astonishing vision of beauty, which both amazed and repelled him, awed and terrified him. The crowd in front thickened. Small women, waist high to him, murmured prayers and kissed their rosaries. He was trapped now in this bizarre parallel world. The Alameda with its whores and grunt-driven clients, its junkies chasing spear-tailed oblivion was running a different life, one with blood and dirt in it. One that was well outside this high, cathedral silence with this mortifying beauty that moved on a tide of reverence and adulation.

Can we all be the same species?

The question came to him from nowhere, but it made him think that it was possible for good and evil to reside in the same place, the same person. Even himself. Panic tightened in him. He had to get out of this crowd and the only way was forward.

The Virgin stopped and sank into the dark. The candlelight wavered across her face, caught the crystalline tears, the mournful eyes. He had to get past her; he had to get past this terrible emblem of loss, this gorgeous example to the world of its barbaric capacity.

He fought past the penitent women, the quiet mothers, the father with a sleeping child on his shoulders. He couldn't bear it.

They hit him. They thumped his back as he crashed through. He shouldered their derision. He hit the barrier, scrambled underneath it and ran between the silent nazarenos dressed in black with high coned hats, indiscernible from the night. Their eyes were on him. Their sinister eyes in their hooded faces – the silent orders more demanding than the others. He ran through the files of barefoot men, away from the floating Virgin. He was desperate.

The crowds thinned and he was able to vault the barrier, but he didn't slow down until he'd broken into Calle Cabeza del Rey Don Pedro and only then did he realize in the quiet of the street that he was talking out loud to himself. He tried to listen to what he was saying, which was even madder. He moved on, brought himself under control and slipped down an alleyway into Calle Abades and stopped dead in the street because alone there, looking back at the building she'd just left, was his ex-wife, Inés. She was laughing; laughing so hard that she threw her head and long hair forward and gripped her own thighs. She was facing the light shed from the door of the Bar Abades and Falcón knew she wasn't drunk, because she didn't like alcohol. He knew that she was laughing because she was happy.

The doors of the bar opened and a group came out. Inés took hold of an arm from one of the group and they headed down the street away from him. She was wearing very high heels, as always, and she walked with a sureness of foot that was breathtaking on the uneven cobbles. Getting his own feet to move was more problematic. The moment had opened up a yawning black ravine down his middle. On one side his earlier, happier married life and on the other his present, solitary, darkening self. And in the middle? The gulf, the rift, the bottomless pit of those terrible falling dreams where the only cure is the jolt awake into more relentless reality.

He followed her. He listened to her gaiety. There were jokes being told about judges and defence lawyers. It was a relief to find that these were work colleagues, but each peal of recognizable laughter from Inés rammed into him and stuck there with a bull's weight behind it. Her joy was nearly unbearable beside his own brand-new torment. And when the flint of his imagination hit the circular saw of his suspicions, screeching sparks flew in his head.

On Avenida de la Constitución the group called for taxis. He watched from the shadows to see who she was travelling with. Four of them got into one taxi. He watched her ankle, the triangle of strap from her shoe, disappear behind the closing door. He watched, derelict, as the red taillights pulled away into the traffic.

He walked down to the river, sticking to the main avenues, no appetite for the narrow streets of El Arenal, the tourists and their relaxed jollity. He crossed the black, gleaming river on the Puente San Telmo and stopped halfway, struck by the advertising on the apartment blocks on the Plaza de Cuba – Tio Pepe, Airtel, Cruzcampo, Fino San Patricio – sherry, phones and beer. This is Spain now – all our needs covered.

The river rippled and slopped underfoot. Raúl Jiménez's first wife came to mind. The torture of not knowing had been too much for a mother to bear. He wondered if she did it from where he was standing and remembered that Consuelo Jiménez had said she'd gone down to the bank one night and thrown herself away. He imagined her floating downstream, the edges of water creeping up her face, the corners of her eyes and mouth, until they met and the blackness she so craved closed over her.

His mobile rang. The stupidity of its ring welcome amongst his morbid ramblings. He put it to his ear, heard the hiss of ether and knew it was him.

'*Diga*,' he said quietly.

No answer.

He waited, not breaking the spell with superfluous words this time.

'You are thinking, Inspector Jefe, that this is your investigation, but you should know that I have a story to tell and, whether you like it or not, you will let me tell it. *Hasta luego*.'

Sunday, 15th April 2001, Falcón's house, Calle Bailén, Seville

Falcón came round with his heart thumping in his chest, still operating at the heightened speed of an adrenalin-fired pace. He checked his pulse – ninety. He swung his legs out of bed, exhausted before he'd even started. His face was hot and his hair full of sweat as if he'd been running all night, or rather morning. He hadn't got to bed until four o'clock. He hadn't wanted to come home.

He did an hour on the exercise bike and persuaded himself that he felt better. He showered and dressed. The world outside at this remove seemed dead. He drank coffee, ate toast rubbed with garlic and olive oil. His father's breakfast. He went up to the studio and arranged the journals in date order, noting the quality of the books became poorer as the years progressed – the paper thinner, the bindings no longer stitched but glued and that all cracked, with loose pages. The handwriting changed, too. The first books were scarcely recognizable as his father's. The letters cramped, the spacing uneven, the lines drifting downwards and the accents and tildas seemingly shaken up in a cup and dashed over the page. It was unconfident, unstable, close to mad. Thereafter the hand was more even but was not transformed into the beautiful script that Javier knew until he arrived back in Spain in the sixties.

It was here that the gap occurred. One diary ended during the summer of 1959 in Tangier and the next started in May 1965 in Seville. Everything had happened in those years. His mother and stepmother had died. His father had painted the Falcón nudes, become famous and left Morocco. It was the vital book, but how was he supposed to use his police skills to find it?

It was close to one o'clock and he was due for lunch at his brother Paco's finca in Las Cortecillas, which was over an hour's drive away. He wanted to make a start on the journals but knew he'd have to stop almost immediately. He would read the opening entry and leave it at that – a taster, a *pincho* before the *gran plato*.

19th March 1932, Dar Riffen, Morocco
Today I am seventeen and Oscar has given me this present of an empty book, which he has told me I must fill. It has been nearly a year since what I now refer to as 'the incident' occurred and I have begun to think that if I do not set things down as I think of them I will forget who I used to be. Although, after ten months of the Legion's training and brutal discipline, I am already unsure. To get through the days in barracks it is best not to think. To get through the days out in the field it is best not to think. In action I can't think, it all happens too fast. I sleep with only one dream, which I don't want to think about. So, I don't think. I tell Oscar this and he says: 'You don't think therefore you are not.' Whatever that means. He tells me this book will change that. I hope I am not too late. Already the life before 'the incident' has lost its definition. It is all irrelevant now. My education means nothing except that I can read and write, which is a lot more than the *tontos* in my company. My old friendships mean less. My family has forgotten me, is dead to me. Who am I? My name is Francisco Luis González Falcón. On my first day in the legion the Captain told us we were *novios de la muerte*. He was right. I am a bridegroom of death, but not in the way he meant it.

His mobile rang, his sister Manuela reminding him to pick her up. She started to complain about how Paco was going to make her work for her lunch and Javier sympathized but didn't listen. How the minutiae impinged.

They drove out of the city in brilliant sunshine and headed north on the road to Mérida. As they came out on to the rolling plains, the swaying grasses, Javier relaxed. The pressures of the city, the intensity of its narrow streets, the crush of people, the hordes of tourists, the deepening complexity of his investigation were all behind him. He'd never envied Paco's love of the simple life, the space, the bulls roaming the pasture, but now, since Raúl Jiménez's murder, the city, rather than provoking fascination, was inducing fear. It wasn't the first time he'd run into a night-time procession of the candlelit Virgin. He'd even run into one after leaving a crime scene and been totally unmoved. He had never identified with the city's mad Mariolatry. But twice in two days he'd been left shattered by what was, in effect, a mannequin on a float, and last night he'd panicked completely. The need to get away from it, or rather get past it, had come from instinct. There had been nothing rational at work. He shook his head and settled back as they eased through the blinding white village of Pajanosas.

As soon as they arrived at the finca Manuela changed out of her red Elena Brunelli linen suit into her veterinary overalls. Paco shouldered a gun and packed three tranquillizer darts. They all got into a Land Rover and went looking for one of Paco's *retintos*, which had a horn wound in its side from a fight with another bull.

They found the bull on its own under a holm oak. He was fully grown and was already sold for this year's Feria. Paco loaded a dart and shot the bull in the haunch. The bull set off at a trot through the trees. They followed in the vehicle until the bull settled into the grasses in a sunlit clearing, confused by the lack of force in its hind legs. They got out and, as they neared, its head came up, still with some vestiges of strength in the vast hump of neck muscle. The primitive eye took them in and for a moment Javier saw inside the bull's head. There was no fear there, only an immense intuition of its own power, which was being slowly consumed by the effects of the tranquillizer.

The bull's head sank back into the grass. Manuela cleaned the wound, put in a couple of stitches, gave an antibiotic jab and took a blood sample. Paco talked non-stop and held the bull's horn, thumbed its smooth, sharp tip and watched out for other bulls that might attack. Javier, patting the haunch of the dazed animal, had a sudden wish for that sense of self that the bull had momentarily shown him. Complexity made humans so fragile. If only we could be as concentrated as the bull, so conscious of its power, rather than having to see to our constant, pathetic needs.

Manuela injected the beast with a stimulant and they retreated to the Land Rover. The head came up and the bull immediately began to gather its forces, instinct telling it that it was vulnerable on the ground. It stood, centred its strength and forced itself to move. The back legs performed a skipping hop as it disappeared into the trees.

'Fantastic bull,' said Paco. 'He'll be all right for the Feria, won't he, Manuela?'

'He'll still have that wound, but he'll show them who he is,' she said.

'You watch him, Javier. Monday, 23rd April he'll be in La Maestranza and there's nobody, not even José Tomás, who'll get the better of that bull,' said Paco. 'Pepe heard anything yet?'

'Nothing.'

'He'll get his chance. Somebody will get done between now and the Feria, the numbers dictate it.'

They had lunch of roast lamb, which Paco had baked in a brick bread-oven he'd restored on the property. There was a whole crowd there for lunch, with the parents-in-law, uncles, aunts, Paco's wife and the four children. Javier forgot himself amongst family and drank a lot of red wine, more than usual. They all slept afterwards. Manuela had to wake Javier, who was sleeping as still as a fallen idol.

It was just getting dark as they walked out to the car and Javier was still groggy. Paco had his arm round his shoulders. They stood around saying a prolonged goodbye.

'Did either of you know that Papá was in the Legion?' asked Javier.

'What Legion?' said Paco.

'El Tercio de Extranjeros in Morocco in the thirties.'

'I didn't know,' said Paco.

'Hah!' said Manuela. 'You've been clearing out the studio. I wondered when you'd get round to that, little brother.'

'I'm just reading some journals he left, that's all.'

'He never talked about any of that . . . the Civil War,' said Paco. 'I don't remember him ever talking about a life before Tangier.'

'He mentioned an incident, too . . .' said Javier, 'something that happened when he was sixteen that made him leave home.'

His brother and sister shook their heads.

'You *will* tell us, little brother, if you come across another one of his nudes that he might have let slip down the back of a chest or something. I mean, that wouldn't be quite fair, would it?'

'There's hundreds of them. Take your pick.'

'Hundreds?'

'Hundreds of each one.'

'I'm not talking about copies,' said Manuela.

'Nor am I . . . they're all "originals", all painted by him.'

'Explain yourself, little brother.'

'He painted them over and over again, trying to get back to . . . I don't know, the secrets of the original work. They're all worthless, and he knew it, which was why he wanted them destroyed.'

'If Papá painted them, they can't be worthless,' said Manuela.

'They're not even signed.'

'We can fix that,' said Manuela. 'What was the name of that dreadful person he used . . . ? some heroin addict. He lived near the Alameda.'

The two brothers stared at her, Javier remembering his father's words from the letter. Manuela glared back.

'Heh! *Que cabrones sois,*' she said, putting on her filthiest Andaluz accent. They laughed.

Javier didn't bother to ask them why they were all calling themselves Falcón, which would have been his father's mother's maiden name, rather than González, which should have been the family name. The diaries would clear that up. Paco and Manuela knew nothing.

Manuela drove back to Seville, Javier wedged in the corner by the door. As the unseen city drew closer the tension coiled inside him, dread leaked into his guts. The orange glow appeared in the sky and he retreated into his head, the narrow alleys of his thinking, the dark dead ends of unfinished thoughts, the crowded avenidas of half-remembered things.

Back at the house on Calle Bailén he went straight to the kitchen and drank from a bottle of chilled water in the fridge. The doorbell rang. It was 9.30 p.m. Nobody ever came to see him at this time.

He opened the front door to find Sra Jiménez standing two metres back from it, as if about to change her mind.

'I was just picking up my luggage from the Hotel Colón,' she said. 'I remembered the house wasn't far. I thought I'd see if you were in.'

A remarkable coincidence, given his recent arrival.

He let her in. Her hair was different, less structured than before. She was wearing a black linen jacket, a black skirt and some red satin mules with kitten heels, which took the grieving edge off the mourning widow. She led the way to the patio. He followed her bare heels and legs whose muscles sprang with each step.

'You know the house,' said Falcón.

'I only ever saw the patio and the room where he showed his work,' she said. 'You don't seem to have changed anything.'

'Even the paintings are still there,' he said, 'hanging as they were

148

when he last showed. Encarnación keeps them dusted. I should take them down . . . get things organized.'

'I'm surprised your wife didn't do all that.'

'She tried,' said Falcón. 'I wasn't quite ready at the time, you know, to strip the house completely of his presence.'

'He did have a formidable presence.'

'Yes, some people found him intimidating, but I wouldn't have thought you would, Sra Jiménez.'

'Your wife though, perhaps she was a little overawed . . . or overwhelmed. You know, a woman likes to make a house her own and feels thwarted if . . .'

'Would you like to take a look?' he said, moving across the patio, not wanting her to intrude further into his private life.

Her heels clicked sexily on the old marble flagstones around the fountain. Falcón opened up the glass doors into the room, turned on the light, waved her in and noticed the instant shock on her face.

'Something the matter?' asked Falcón.

Consuelo Jiménez walked slowly round the room taking in each painting, from the domes and buttresses of the Iglesia de San Salvador to the pillared Hercules of the Alameda.

'They're all here,' she said, looking at him, amazed.

'What?'

'The three paintings I bought from your father.'

'Ah,' said Falcón, economical with his embarrassment.

'He told me they were originals.'

'They were . . . at the time of selling.'

'I don't understand,' she said, gripping her jacket at the waist, annoyed now.

'Tell me, Sra Jiménez, when my father sold you the paintings . . . you had some drinks and *tapas* on the patio and then, what? He took you by the elbow and brought you in here. Did he whisper on your shoulder: "Everything in this room is for sale except . . . that one"?'

'That's *exactly* what he said.'

'And you fell for that three times?'

'Of course not. That's what he said the first time . . .'

'But that was precisely the painting you ended up buying?'

She ignored him.

'The next time he said: "This one is too expensive for you."'

'And the time after that?'

'"The frame is all wrong on this one . . . I wouldn't sell it to you."'

'And each time you bought the painting he told you that you shouldn't or couldn't buy.'

She stamped her foot, very angry in her retrospective humiliation.

'Don't be too upset, Sra Jiménez,' said Falcón. 'Nobody else owns the paintings you have in your possession. He wasn't stupid or careless. It was just a little game he liked to play.'

'I'd like an explanation,' she said, and Javier was glad he wasn't one of her employees.

'I can only tell you what happened. I was never very sure of his motive,' said Javier. 'I didn't go to any of the parties. I'd sit in my room reading my American crime novels. When the guests had gone, my father, who was normally drunk at this stage, would burst into my room, whether I was asleep or not, shouting "Javier!" and shaking a wad of cash in my face. His takings for the night. If I was asleep I'd grunt something encouraging. If I was awake I'd nod over the top of my book. Then he'd go straight up to the studio and paint the exact painting he'd just sold. By morning it would be framed and hanging on the wall.'

'What an extraordinary person,' she said, disgusted.

'I actually watched him paint that one of the cathedral roof. Do you know how long it took him?'

She looked at the painting, a fantastically complicated series of flying buttresses, walls and domes all laid down with a cubist energy.

'Seventeen and a half minutes,' said Javier. 'He asked me to time him. He was drunk *and* stoned at the time.'

'But what's the point of it?'

'A one hundred per cent profit on the night.'

'But why should such a man . . . ? I mean, it's just too ridiculous. They were expensive, but I don't think I paid more than a million for any of them. What was he playing at? Did he need this money or something?'

Silence while a warm wind did a turn of the patio.

'Would you like your money back?' he asked.

Her head turned slowly from the painting, eyes fixed on him.

'He didn't spend it,' said Falcón. 'Not a peseta of it. He didn't even bank it. It's all in a detergent box upstairs in his studio.'

'And what does it all mean, Don Javier?'

'It means . . . that maybe you shouldn't be so angry with him because the game he was playing was ultimately against himself.'

'Can I smoke?'

'Of course. Come out on to the patio, I'll give you a drink.'

'A whisky, if you have it. I need something strong after that.'

They sat on some wrought-iron chairs at a mosaic-covered table under a single wall lamp in the cloister of the patio. They sipped the whisky. Falcón asked after her children. She replied with her mind elsewhere.

'I went to Madrid on Friday,' he said. 'I went to see your husband's eldest son.'

'You're very thorough, Don Javier,' she said. 'I'm not used to such rigour after so many years of living with the natives.'

'I'm especially rigorous when fascinated.'

She crossed her legs, flexed her toes under the red satin band of the mule, which was pointed in his direction. She seemed like someone who would know what to do in bed and be quite demanding, but rewarding with it. Salacious thoughts followed his idle theorizing and he saw her kneeling with her black skirt rucked up over her haunches, looking back over her shoulder at him. He shook his head, not used to these uncontrolled ideas rampaging through his mind. He made a conscious effort to subdue any recklessness, concentrated on the ice in his glass.

'You wanted to know why Gumersinda killed herself,' she said.

'I was interested in your husband's abject misery, as you called it, which must have been Gumersinda's state, too, when she died. I wanted to know what could have caused such devastation.'

'Are all policemen like you?'

'We're like people . . . each one of us is different,' said Falcón.

'Did you find out?'

Throughout the account of his conversation with José Manuel, Consuelo Jiménez's jaunty sexiness disappeared. The shoe, which had been so close to his knee, was withdrawn and joined its partner on the marble flagstones of the patio floor. Only the padded shoulders of her jacket had any shape by the time he'd finished. Falcón poured more whisky.

'*Los Niños de la Calle*,' he said.

'I was thinking that, too,' she said.

'His obsession with security.'

'I would have had to have found out what Raúl had done. I wouldn't have been able to leave it. I'd have to know that to understand him . . . his motives.'

'What if you had to give up your entire life to the task?'

She lit another cigarette.

'Do you think this has any bearing on the murder?'

'I asked him whether he thought Arturo might still be alive,' said Falcón.

'And had returned to take his revenge?' said Sra Jiménez. 'That's absurd. I'm sure they killed the poor boy.'

'Why? I'm just as sure they would make use of him . . . knotting carpets or whatever.'

'Like a slave?' she said. 'And what if he escaped?'

'Have you ever been to somewhere like Fez?' he asked. 'Think of Seville, with most of its major buildings removed, all its squares and greenery torn out, and then compress it all so that the streets are narrower, the houses almost touching overhead and finally stew it, so that everything is falling apart. Multiply that by a hundred, subtract a thousand years from today's date and that is Fez. You could go into the Medina as a child and come out an old man without having walked each street. If he ever managed to escape and found his way out of the Medina without being caught, where could he go? Who is he? Where are his papers? He belongs nowhere and to nobody.'

Consuelo shrank from that terrible possibility.

'So is that who you're looking for now?'

'Senior policemen, I mean people with budgets to run a police force, have an aversion to fantasy. I would have to do a lot better than produce a record of my conversation with José Manuel to persuade them to start that kind of a manhunt,' said Falcón. 'We have to be more plodding, less inventive, because everything we do ends up going before a judge and they loathe fiction in their courts.'

'So what *are* you going to do?'

'Look through your husband's life and see what comes up,' he said. 'You could help.'

'Would that get me off the suspects list?'

'Not until we find the murderer,' he said. 'But it might save me a lot of time trying to find my way around a seventy-eight-year life.'

'I can only help with the last ten.'

'Well, that includes a time when he was in the public eye . . . Expo '92.'

'The building committee,' she said.

'There's also that interesting phenomenon of "black" pesetas wanting to become "white" euros.'

'I'm sure you already know about the restaurant business.'

'I'm not interested in a little tax fraud, Doña Consuelo. That's not my department. I have to look at things with more dramatic possibilities. Stuff, for instance, that would require a great deal of trust and where perhaps trust was broken and fortunes lost, lives ruined, leaving powerful motives for revenge.'

'Is that why you're a homicide cop?' she asked, getting to her feet.

He didn't answer, walked her to the door, tried not to listen to her kitten heels tapping out Morse code for S-E-X on the marble.

'Who introduced you to my father?' he asked; a diversionary tactic.

'Raúl was given an invitation so he sent me. I'd worked in a gallery and he assumed I knew what I was doing.'

'Is that how you met Ramón Salgado?'

She missed a beat.

'His gallery sent out the invitations. It was Ramón who opened the door, made the introductions.'

'Was it Ramón Salgado who told you of your remarkable resemblance to Gumersinda?'

She blinked as if she hadn't remembered that drop of information leaking out of her. Falcón opened the door, which led out into the short cobbled access street lined with orange trees that led down to Calle Bailén.

'Yes, it was,' she said. 'Coming here tonight brought it all back. I rang the bell and heard him talking to the people he'd just let in so that he was turned away from me when he opened the door. When our eyes connected I could tell he was completely floored. I think he might have even started to call me Gumersinda, but that might be my memory exaggerating the moment. Still, by the time we got to the drinks he'd told me, which meant that I drank too much whisky and blabbed away like an idiot to your father, whom I'd spent half my life dying to meet.'

'So Ramón and your husband knew each other from the Tangier days?'

Another thing she hadn't remembered saying.

'I'm not sure,' she said.

They shook hands. He looked at her legs as she walked down to Calle Bailén. He shut the door and went straight up to the studio.

Extracts from the Journals of Francisco Falcón

20th March 1932, Dar Riffen, Morocco
Oscar (I don't know if this is his real name, but it's the one he uses) is
not only my NCO but my teacher, too. He was a teacher in 'real life' as
he calls it. That is all I know about him. Los brutos (my comrades), tell
me that Oscar is here because he's a child molester. They cannot know
this for certain because it is one of the precepts of the Legion that you
don't have to reveal your past. Los brutos, of course, take great delight in
revealing their past to me. Most are murderers, some are rapists and
murderers. Oscar says they are flesh, blood and bone with some primitive
strings attached inside, which allow them to walk upright, communicate,
defecate and kill people. Los brutos are suspicious of Oscar only because
they fear and distrust even the rudiments of intelligence. (I hide to write
in this book or Oscar lets me use his room.) But los brutos respect him
too. He's beaten every one of them at some time or another.

Oscar took me on as his pupil and charge when he caught me drawing
in the barracks. He had a couple of los brutos hold me and tore the paper
from my hands and found that he was looking at himself in all his
brutal intelligence. I was paralysed with fear. He grabbed me by the
collar and hauled me off to his room, followed by shouts from los brutos
egging him on. He threw me against the wall so that I collapsed winded.
He looked at the drawing again, got down on his haunches, put his face
up to mine and looked into my head with his steel-blue eyes. 'Who are
you?' he asked, which was strange. I knew better than to answer with
my name and shut up. He told me the drawing was good and that he
would be my teacher but that he had a reputation to maintain. So I still
got beaten.

17th October 1932, Dar Riffen
I admitted to Oscar that I've only made two entries in this book since he
gave it to me. He is furious. I tell him I have nothing to report. All we
do is go on endless exercises followed by bouts of drinking and fighting.

He reminds me that this journal should not just be an account of the external but an examination of the internal. I have no idea how to approach this internal thing he is talking about. 'You have to write about who you are,' he says. I show him my first entry. He says, 'Because you have no family does not mean you have ceased to exist. They are only a reference, now you must find your own context.' I write this down with no idea of its meaning. He tells me that a French philosopher said: 'I think therefore I am.' I ask: 'What is thinking?' There is a long pause in which for some reason I imagine a train moving through a vast landscape. I tell him this and he says, 'Well, it's a start.'

23rd March 1933, Dar Riffen
I have just completed my first major work, which is the entire company individually caricatured riding their own camel, which has taken on some of their characteristics. I mount them on boards and hang them in the barracks so that they all seem to be in a caravan heading for the Dar Riffen arch, which instead of the usual legionnaire's motto reads: legionarios a beber, legionarios a joder. All the officers come in and ask to see it. Oscar tears down my cartoon arch, saying: 'You don't want to be court-martialled and shot for a silly drawing.' Now I am never short of cigarettes.

12th November 1934, Dar Riffen
We have just welcomed back Colonel Yagüe and the Legion, who have been in Asturias to put down the miners' rebellion . . . Oscar is grim. There was no resistance and, having relieved Oviedo and Gijón, los brutos 'demonstrated a lack of discipline and were not restrained by command'. This means that they killed, raped and mutilated without fear of punishment. Somehow in this conversation Oscar reveals that he is German and bores me by saying how German soldiers would never have behaved like this. His empty boots seem to be screaming in the corner of the room. 'This is the beginning of a catastrophe,' he says. I don't see it like that and can only get excited by the gory stories told and retold. Apparently I still haven't learnt how to think. I've noticed, in all the history I've read, under Oscar's pointing finger, just how many times the thinkers are taken away and shot, hanged or beheaded.

17th April 1935, Dar Riffen
My second major work – Colonel Yagüe wants me to paint his portrait. Oscar gives me some advice: 'Nobody likes the truth unless it happens to

coincide with their own version of it.' It's only when I have Colonel Yagüe sitting in front of me that I realize the real nature of the task. He's a bull of a man, with thick round spectacles, grey receding hair, heavy jowls and a half-smile that's nearly friendly until you see the cruelty in it. I sit him so that none of the damaging profile is showing. I ask if he wants to retain the glasses and he tells me that if he doesn't he will look like a newly born puppy. I see a coat on a chair with a fur collar. I ask him to wear it and tell him it will frame his face and give him an adventurous, heroic look. He puts it on. We are going to like each other.

1st May 1935, Dar Riffen, Morocco
The portrait is a triumph. There is a small private unveiling ceremony with a select band of officers. Colonel Yagüe is delighted by the reaction. The fur collar was inspired. I thinned his face down and gave him a jutting chin so that he looked defiant, resilient, dependable but bold and enterprising, too. In the background I have the massed ranks of legionnaires marching through the arch, which reads as it should: Legionarios a luchar, legionarios a morir. *Oscar tells me: 'I see we have had a convergence of delusion.' Colonel Yagüe does not hang the painting. He could not be seen to be more grand or ambitious than his superiors.*

14th July 1936, Dar Riffen
Summer manoeuvres finish with a parade taken by General Romerales and General Gómez Morato, our two most senior commanders of the Army of Africa. Oscar, who has a nose for these things, says that something is going to happen. His evidence is that during the banquet after the parade, even before the dessert course was served, there were shouts of 'Café!' which was clearly not a demand for coffee. It stands for Camaradas! Arriba! Falange Española! *and is evidence of Colonel Yagüe at work. He's a falangist, who Oscar believes loathes General Gómez Morato. I don't know how he informs himself of this and he says that all I had to do was look at the officers who came to the private unveiling ceremony of my portrait of Colonel Yagüe.*

We are locked away in our barracks with no knowledge of what is going on across the straits. Oscar finds a newspaper, El Sol, *in which there's an article about the shooting of an officer called Lt José Castillo outside his home in Madrid only a month after the man was married. 'The Falange did that,' says Oscar. I am puzzled. I don't know where* we stand. I ask Oscar who we should support and he tells me: 'Our commanding officer, unless you want to get shot.' At least there are no difficult decisions to be made on that score, although Oscar alarms me by adding: 'Whoever that might be.'

Later in the evening he calls me in. He's very excited. He's been listening to the radio. Spain is in a state of shock. Calvo Sotelo has been shot. I couldn't care less, having never heard the name before. Oscar cuffs me round the head. Sotelo is the monarchist leader and a prominent figure on the right. His murder will have terrible consequences. I ask who killed him and Oscar bats an imaginary ball from hand to hand saying: 'Tit-tat, tit-tat.

'Except that the left have gone too far this time,' he says. 'This will not be seen as personal because of Calvo Sotelo's position. This is a political killing and now, I can guarantee it, there will be civil war.' I ask him where he stands in all of this and he holds out his hands, the palms criss-crossed with a thousand creases so that I think I must draw them. 'Before you,' he says and I leave him none the wiser.

19th July 1936, Ceuta
Colonel Yagüe marched us out of the barracks at 9 p.m. and by midnight we had control of the port of Ceuta. Not a shot was fired at us or by us. We were disappointed to meet no resistance as on the march we'd all been spoiling for a fight. By morning we were told that Melilla, Tetuán, Ceuta and Larache were all under military control and that General Franco was on his way to take over command.

We march back to the barracks at Dar Riffen in the early morning. General Franco arrives at the barracks in the afternoon and we are all on parade to meet him. We surprise ourselves by going mad without knowing why. Colonel Yagüe makes a speech which starts with the words: 'Here they are, just as you left them . . .' and we see that the general is very moved. We roar, 'Franco! Franco!' and he announces a pay rise of one peseta a day. We all erupt again.

6th August 1936, Seville
My first time on Spanish soil. We were one of the first detachments across the straits by boat and were disappointed not to be airlifted. They put us on trucks and we drove straight up the middle of completely empty roads to Seville. Our orders are to head north under Colonel Yagüe to Mérida. We've been told that anyone who resists us is a communist and, as such, against Spain, and that they are to be dealt

with in the most severe manner and shown no mercy. The word is that the opposition is 'shitting in its pants' at the thought of the Army of Africa. Our reputation from the Asturias miners' rising travels before us. The effect of these orders, shot through with their bloodthirsty emotion, is like electricity through our ranks. We were already fired up and now we are invincible and righteous, too.

10th August 1936, near Mérida
The advance has been relentless (300 km in four days) and we have quickly learnt that the news of the terror we inspire travels at the speed of sound. We call it castigo, punishment. When we have quelled any resistance, we move through the towns and villages with knives and machetes. It is the cold steel that terrifies. It is not impersonal like bullets.

At El Real de la Jara the people fled into the hills only to be rounded up by the Moors of the Regulares who did such terrible things to them that we met no resistance until we reached Almendralejo. There a madness seized us and we killed everybody left in the town. Hundreds of corpses, men and women, littered the streets. The stench in the heat was soon unbearable and we left the stunned houses, lifeless under a pall of smoke from the burning roofs. Oscar presses me 'to write it all down', but I am too exhausted for anything after the demands of the day.

11th August 1936, Mérida
Officers joke that they are giving the peasants 'agrarian reform'.

One of the Moors from the Regulares shows us his flyblown and stinking collection of men's testicles. They castrate victims as a rite of battle. This is too much for Oscar, who puts it in a report to our Captain and the practice is soon banned.

15th August 1936, Badajoz
The 4th Bandera stormed the Puerta de la Trinidad. They went in singing and took heavy machine-gun fire full in the face, which drove them back for a moment. They breached the gates at the second attempt and we went in after them, stumbling over their dead bodies. Once inside it was street-to-street fighting all the way to the centre. In the afternoon anybody suspected of resistance was herded into the bullring near the cathedral. There was a lot of weeping and wailing, but we were savage after our losses in the initial assault. Shots rang out until nightfall. The Regulares searched the town, house to house, looking for

anybody with a weapon or even a recoil bruise on their shoulder. After
the indiscipline of Asturias, Oscar is determined that we will not lose
control and go on an orgy of looting and raping like the other companies
in the bandera and the Regulares. The men are disgruntled until Oscar
brings in some cases of drink, mixed bottles stolen from a bar. We pour
aguardiente, anís and red wine into the same glass and this drink
becomes known to us as the Earthquake.

22nd September 1936, Maqueda
I know now what it is to be battle-hardened. Before they were just words
attached to veterans. Now I realize that it is a mental state which
endures. It comes from making multiple decisions under extreme
pressure, from the complete suppression of fear, from seeing men die
around you daily, from the conquering of exhaustion, from the acceptance
of the inevitability of battle.

29th September 1936, Toledo
The attack was launched at midday on 27th September. Before the
assault we were marched past the mutilated corpses of two executed
nationalists a couple of kilometres outside town. The order came down
from the colonels: 'You know what to do.' The fighting was fierce and
the Regulares took a beating in the initial storming of the town. Just as
we were expecting to have to pull back and regroup the leftists gave up
and ran for it. There was some street fighting. The Moors were
particularly savage that afternoon, hacking away at prisoners with their
machetes until the steep cobbled streets of the town were literally running
with blood. Grenades were thrown into the San Juan Hospital and as
the Regulares approached a seminary, in which a group of anarchists
were holed up, it burst into flames.

30th September 1936, Toledo
Oscar has found out that the republicans left the El Grecos in the city
and has arranged through our Captain for us to see them. In the end we
see seven of the Apostle paintings but not the famous Burial of Count
Orgaz. I am mesmerized and quite unable to unravel his technique, how
he seems to achieve an inner light that shines through the flesh and
blood, even the robes, of the apostles. After the roar of battle, the
mutilations, the blood-spattered streets, we find peace in front of those
paintings and I know now that I want to become an artist.

20th November 1936, Ciudad Universitaria de Madrid
This war has reached a new level. We have been bombing our own
capital with explosives and incendiaries for more than a week. We were
camped out by the railway tracks on the west side of the River
Manzanares, with our every attempt to get across being easily driven
back. Then suddenly we were over it and running up to the university,
unopposed and amazed. We couldn't think what had happened – another
loss of nerve at the vital moment or the usual republican fiasco of one
unit retreating before the replacement had arrived. The fight that ensued
indicated the latter. We've taken the School of Architecture but have
been driven back from the hall of Philosophy and Letters. We are
fighting International Brigades of German, French, Italians and
Belgians. The buildings ring with German communist songs and the
'Internationale'. Oscar says these brigades are all made up of writers,
poets, composers and artists. They even name their battalions after
literary martyrs. I ask him why artists exclusively support the left and he
gives one of his usual enigmatic replies: 'It's in their nature.' And I, as
always, have to ask him what he means. Our pupil/teacher relationship
has never changed.

'They are creative,' he says. 'They want to change things. They don't
like the old order of monarchy, the church, the military and the
landowners. They believe in the power of the common man and his right
to be equal. To bring this about they have to destroy all the old
institutions.'

'And replace them with what?' I ask.

'Exactly,' says Oscar. 'They will replace them with a different order
. . . one that they like with no kings or priests, no businessmen or
farmers. You should think about that, Francisco, if you want to be an
artist. Great art changes the way we look at things. Think of
Impressionism. They laughed at Monet's blurred vision. Think of
Cubism. They assumed that after Braque was shot in the head and had
to be trepanned, he lost his mind. Think of Picasso's Les Demoiselles
d'Avignon *– call them women? And what do you think General Yagüe*
hangs on his wall? Or General Varela?'

'You're playing with me now,' I say.

An attack starts and we crawl to the window and shoot down on the
men running out of Philosophy and Letters (we're in Agriculture).
There's a large explosion in the Clinical Hospital (we find out later that
a bomb was sent up in the lift to the Regulares). We decide to retreat
from Agriculture and go back to the French Institute's Casa de

Velázquez, which is full of the dead bodies of a company of Poles. As we zig-zag back, Oscar shouts to me that General Yagüe will probably go to his grave wrapped in the canvas of my heroic painting. Bullets rip across the wooden doors of the building and we change course and dive through the windows on to the soft landing of the dead Poles. We fire back through the windows until the attack loses heart.

'Think about it,' says Oscar. 'Here we are at the front line, not just of a civil war, but of the whole of cultural Spain, maybe even civilized Europe. What do you want to paint in the future? Yagüe on horseback? The Archbishop of Seville at his toilet? Or do you want to redefine the female form? See perfection in a line of landscape? Find truth in a urinal?'

We make for the back of the building and sprint across behind the Santa Cristina hospital to the Clinical Hospital to support the Regulares. We find the shattered lift in the rubble of its shaft and run up the stairs. In one of the laboratories there are six dead Regulares with no evidence of bullet wounds or bomb blast. On the floor a fire smokes and there is the smell of roast meat. There are animals in cages all around and we realize that the Moors have cooked and eaten some of them. Oscar shakes his head at the bizarre scene. We go up on to the roof and survey the terrain. I ask Oscar what he wants out of all this and he just says that he doesn't belong anywhere. He's an outsider.

'It's you that matters,' he says, 'you're young. You have to decide. Look . . . if you want to cross over, don't worry about me, I won't shoot you in the back. And I'll put it in my report that you went over for artistic reasons.'

This is what I hate about Oscar, he's always trying to prod me into thinking, into making decisions.

25th November 1936, outskirts of Madrid
We have pulled out of the direct assault on Madrid. That vital month we spent in the relief of Toledo gave the republicans time to organize themselves. We could keep hammering away but it would cost us too much. The strategy has changed now. We are going to overrun the outlying country and lay siege. We are an army that swings from the most advanced techniques (aerial bombing) to the mediaeval (siege) . . .

In the space of six weeks the two armies seem to have become more equal. The leftists now have Russian tanks and planes and men from all over the world are fighting in their International Brigades. They have the supply ports of the Mediterranean – Barcelona, Tarragona, Valencia.

Oscar had always said it would be over by Christmas, now he thinks it will take years.

18th February 1937, near Vaciamadrid
We have been shoved off the Madrid–Valencia road, which is what we expected when we first took it. The Russian fighters strafed us mercilessly. We are in a stalemate now and can only wait to see how it goes in the north. We have time and good supplies of cigarettes and coffee. Oscar has made a chess set out of empty cartridges and we play, or rather he teaches me how to lose gracefully. We have conversations so that I can practise my basic German, which he is also teaching me.

'Why are you a Nationalist?' he asks, moving out a pawn.
'Why are you?' I counter, meeting his pawn with mine.
'I'm not Spanish,' he says, covering the pawn with his knight. 'I don't have to decide.'
'Nor am I,' I say, supporting my pawn with another. 'I'm African.'
'Your parents are Spanish.'
'But I was born in Tetuán.'
'And this allows you to be apolitical?'
'It means I have no foundation for political belief.'
'Your father – was he a rightist?'
'I have no father.'
'But was he?'
No answer from me.
'What was his work?'
'He owned a hotel.'
'Then he was of the right,' says Oscar. 'Did he go to Mass?'
'Only to drink the wine.'
'Then that is your foundation. You learn politics at the dinner table.'
'And your father?'
'He was a doctor.'
'Difficult,' I say. 'Did he go to Mass?'
'We don't have Mass.'
'Even more difficult.'
'He was a socialist,' says Oscar.
'Then you are surely in the wrong place.'
'I shot him on 27th October 1923.'
I look up, but he continues to study the chessboard.
'You're dead in three moves,' he says.

23rd November 1937, Cogolludo, near Guadalajara
Our bandera has been broken up and we have been distributed around
the rest of the army. We think we have been positioned here for a new
attempt on the capital. Oscar is not speaking to me because here I record
my first win on that most arduous of fronts – the chessboard.

15th December 1937, Cogolludo
The leftists have surprised us by mounting an offensive on Teruel just as
we were preparing to overrun the capital and spend Christmas on the
Gran Via. We only know that Teruel is the coldest place in Spain and
that 4,000 Nationalists are besieged inside the town.

31st December 1937, near Teruel
Brutally cold: –18°C. Blizzard. Snow a metre thick. I hate it. I write
this with difficulty and only to take my mind off the terrible conditions.
The counterattack has ground to a halt but we continue to shell the
town, which is no more than snow-covered rubble. We stop when the
visibility drops to zero.

8th February 1938, Teruel
We started an attack yesterday, trying to force an encirclement. The
fighting is fierce and Oscar is hit in the stomach and we have to carry
him back to the rear. I have taken over his role as NCO.

10th February 1938, Teruel
I found Oscar in the field hospital and even with the morphine he's in
terrible pain. He knows he will not survive the wound. He has left me
his books and chess set and has given me strict instructions to burn his
journals without reading them. He is sobbing with pain and as he kisses
me I feel his warm tears on my face.

23rd February 1938, Teruel
We buried Oscar this morning. Later I burnt his diaries. I obeyed his
instructions and dropped the first book into the fire without opening it.
As it burned I could not resist looking through the pages of the next book
which were all about a love he could not seem to bear. He never
mentioned the girl by name, which did not surprise me as we never
talked on a personal level except when he told me he'd shot his father. In
the third book he began using imaginary dialogues, which were easier to
digest than his stolid prose. It was with a jolt that I saw my own words

163

and came to the electrifying conclusion that I was the inconsiderate lover. This was further confirmed when, enraged by some unconscious remark of mine, he referred to me as Die Künstlerin. *I burnt the rest without reading it.*

I sit now writing with a candle clenched between my knees. It occurs to me that all Oscar's urging me to write down my thoughts was in the desperate hope that I would reveal myself to him. He must have been disappointed by my endless remarks on military manoeuvres.

I feel no disgust even though Oscar was physically repellent. I am sad to have lost my teacher and friend, the man who was more of a father to me than my own. I am lonely again without his brute appearance, his snapping mind, his sure military guidance. I am having incomprehensible thoughts. Something has been disturbed in me which I can only recognize as some shapeless need. I do not understand it. It refuses to be defined.

15th April 1938, Lérida
I was knocked unconscious for some hours and have been brought to the hospital here, which I have to be reminded we captured nearly two weeks ago. I have made no entries since Oscar's funeral. I am furious with myself because I cannot remember whether I made any progress with my thoughts. This 'need' I wrote about is a blank in my brain. Events have been reasserting themselves. The relentless advance after we put the republicans to flight at Teruel. Crossing the River Ebro and taking Fraga. Even the assault on Lérida takes some shape. But however much I squeeze my mind I cannot recover what I was thinking of, what it was that Oscar's diaries had levered open. I am bereft without knowing why.

18th November 1938, Ribarroya
This is the last republican bridgehead. They are all now beyond the Ebro and the situation has returned to what it was in July except that now the snow falls and more than 20,000 men have lost their lives in the mountains. I remember all those chess games I played with Oscar before I learnt a subtler insight. I was always the attacker and Oscar the defender who, having read my undisguised plans, would then become the fierce counterattacker and wipe me off the board. It has been so with our armies. The republicans attack and in doing so reveal the concentration of their forces and the paucity of their aims. We defend, marshal our response and drive them back to a position where they are weaker than

they were before. As Oscar told me: 'It is always easier to react than to be original. You'll find the same holds for art as in life.'

26th January 1939, Barcelona
Yesterday we came into the empty city behind unopposed tanks. We'd crossed the Llobregat River the day before and could already smell the desperation that hung above the collapsing republican will. There was no sense of triumph. We were exhausted to the point of not even knowing if we were glad to be alive. By evening we were in control and it was then that our supporters felt safe enough to venture out into the streets to rejoice and, of course, to take their revenge on the defeated. We did not stop them.

15

Monday, 16th April 2001, Falcón's house, Calle Bailén, Seville

Another 20,000-volt wake-up call, as if he'd had a heart attack and been defibrillated back to life. His watch told him it was six o'clock, which meant that he'd had an hour and a half of sleep, or rather not sleep, more like death. The brain, a strange organ that kept him awake with a torment of thoughts about his father, the Civil War, art, death ... and then, just as he was about to give up on the possibility of ever sleeping again – shut down. No dreams. No rest. But a respite. The brain, unable to stand any more of the endless babble, had brought down the shutter.

He dragged himself, heart pounding, to the exercise bike and started working out until he had the sensation of being pursued to the point of glancing over his shoulder. He stopped, dismounted, wondered if this was bad for him, psychologically – the expending of vast amounts of energy to go nowhere. Agitated stasis. He needed it though, to lull himself out of the cyclical thinking. Cyclical? That was it. He was just doing with his body what he was doing with his mind. He ran down to the river and up to the Torre del Oro and back. He saw no one.

He was the first in the office, having driven through silent streets. He sat at his desk, desolate amongst the spartan furniture and the piled concrete silence of the Jefatura. Ramírez turned up at 8.30 and Falcón greeted him with the news of Eloisa Gómez's disappearance. He checked the incident room, but there had been very little activity. Seville was too worn out after a week of passionate Mariolatry and bacchanalia to lift a phone.

Ramírez produced the envelope he'd picked up from the computer room. All eight of the images of the disappearing cameraman from the cemetery were there and the operator had sharpened up the two best examples, but they still didn't help. There was no visible eye, the nose was in shadow from the peaked baseball cap and the jaw line was obscured by the collar of the coat. There was visible skin, but its colour and texture was unclear. The computer operator had shown the pictures to a CCTV expert who'd ventured the opinion that the killer was male, between twenty and forty years old.

'It's not going to help us,' said Ramírez, 'but it'll be something for Juez Calderón to feast on. Our first sighting of the killer . . . better than no sighting at all.'

'But who *is* he?' asked Falcón, surprising Ramírez with his sudden savagery. 'Is he acting alone? Is he being paid? What is his motive?'

'Are we even sure now that he was unknown to his victim?' asked Ramírez, taking up Falcón's tone.

'*I'm* sure. I wouldn't like to have to prove it in court, but I'm certain that he got his information from Mudanzas Triana, he used Eloisa Gómez to get into the flat, and he waited until the maid arrived to get out. And it was all done to confuse us.'

'Then I think we should bring Consuelo Jiménez in and sweat her about the sighting . . . see if she breaks down under pressure,' said Ramírez. 'She is the only one close to the victim, with all the necessary information and a defined motive.'

'At this point I want to work *with* Consuelo Jiménez rather than against her. I'm meeting her at midday to sort through all her husband's business associates, divide them into those with and without motive.'

'Doesn't that put her in control of our investigation, Inspector Jefe?'

'Not quite . . . because we'll be doing our own digging. You came up with Joaquín López of Cinco Bellotas. He's worth an interview. Pérez can go down to the town hall and get the names of any companies who had contact with the Expo '92 Building Committee. Fernández will go down to the licensing department and pull names from there and then he can go on to the health and fire departments and only when we've been through everything, right down to the people who come in to the restaurants to sell flowers to customers who are forgetting to be romantic, will we leave Sra Jiménez alone. So we work with her, but she will feel the pressure.'

'What about the local hoods?'

'If there'd been something wrong there, one of the restaurants would have been burnt down, not the owner tortured and killed. But we still put out our feelers.'

'Drugs?' said Ramírez. 'Seeing as we're dealing with extreme behaviour, psychopathic violence.'

'Talk to Narcotics. See if Raúl Jiménez or anyone associated with him has ever been under any kind of surveillance.'

The rest of the squad arrived over the next quarter of an hour and Falcón briefed them, showed them the images from the video tape and fired them up to do a long, hard day's boring work. He asked Serrano about the chloroform and surgical instruments; nothing so far from the hospitals, who were still checking their stocks, and he was working his way around the labs. He sent Baena down to Mudanzas Triana to interview the workers specifically to find out what they were doing on Saturday morning at the time of the Jiménez funeral. They left and he took a long call from Juez Calderón in which he covered the same ground, and another from Comisario Lobo. Normally this endless repetition would have annoyed him, but today both Calderón and Lobo had terminated the calls. After that he tore into his paperwork, which he never did on a Monday morning, especially during an investigation. He left early for his meeting with Consuelo Jiménez.

They started by watching the video of the mourners at the funeral. Sra Jiménez named them all and gave their relationship to her husband. There was no one unusual in the crowd. They reconstructed Raúl Jiménez's last twenty-four hours and then his last week. The meetings, the lunches, the parties, the discussions with builders, a landscape gardener, an air-conditioning engineer. She supplied a list of companies whom they'd dealt with over the last six years – those who'd pitched for business, those who'd failed, those who'd been dropped. It was difficult to believe, after what Ramón Salgado had said, that Raúl Jiménez's only possible enemies were butchers, fishmongers and florists who'd lost business supplying his restaurants. Consuelo Jiménez's glances at her expensive watch grew more frequent and Falcón moved in with the important question.

'We've covered everything except the Expo '92 Building Committee,' he said. 'Can I see the files on that?'

'What files?' she said.

'Your husband's records.'

'Not here,' she said, calling in the secretary, 'and not in the apartment.'

The secretary was asked the same question and gave a well-rehearsed answer, looking at her audience as if she was going to get a pay rise. Sra Jiménez started to rush him, invoked her children.

Falcón sat in his chair as she gathered her things and stood by the door, drumming her handbag with her fingernails.

'This has been very useful,' he said, and meant it, because her calculated visit to him last night and her selective co-operation this morning had shown him the first possibility that her determination had developed, via ambition, into ruthlessness.

He went home for lunch. Encarnación had left him a large pot of *fabada Asturiana*. Beans, *chorizo*, *morcilla*. He wasn't hungry but he hoped that the heavy dish and the two glasses of wine would put him to sleep. He lay down with his mind full of doubt that he was running his investigation properly. His stomach made old plumbing noises. His legs twitched. More agitated stasis. He begged for sleep but it didn't come. He called Ramón Salgado and, when he got through, remembered that he'd gone to San Sebastián to bring his sister down to Madrid.

His hands were moist on the steering wheel as he drove to the office, his guts roiled with the fat from the fabada, his tongue was gloved in suede. His mind would not settle on one thought and take it through to its conclusion. Desperation, like rancid fat, slipped into the stew and turned the whole mix. He pulled over on República de Argentina and called his doctor, who couldn't see him until morning. He had a whole night to get through and was appalled by the notion and yet he saw how ridiculous it was, too. He remembered how he'd been five days ago, how wonderful it had been to be stable. Tears pricked his eyeballs. He pressed his forehead to the steering wheel. What was going on?

He got out of the car, wiped his eyes and shook himself. He went into the nearest bar and ordered something he never drank – brandy. That's what they always had in the movies. The great nerve settler. The barman sent names past his head – Soberano, Fundador. He asked for anything and a *café solo* to disguise his breath.

The brandy tore his lungs apart and he had to catch his breath. He fingered the coffee cup and was spooked by the thought that the hand resting on the stainless steel bar was not his own. He shook it, flexed it, touched his face. The barman checked him as he wiped a row of glasses.

'Another?' he asked.

Falcón nodded, unable to believe what he was doing. The amber liquid trickled into the glass. He longed for the barman's steadiness, just to be able to hold a bottle over a glass rim without it spinning out of control. He shot the second brandy, scalded his mouth on the coffee, slapped a note on the bar and left.

In the car park of the Jefatura he calmed himself down, slowed his thoughts by vicing his head in his hands. The light in his office was on. Ramírez had his back to the window and was reading a file and commenting to somebody sitting by the desk.

People frowned at him as he went up the stairs. He veered into the toilet and checked himself in the mirror. His hair was up like a rough sea, his face flushed and his eyes pink. His shirt collar was outside the lapel of his jacket and his tie loose from his neck. The shell was cracking up. He patted his face with cold water, had a sudden urge from his guts and locked himself in a stall. Food poisoning. Maybe this was all food poisoning, he thought desperately. Encarnación's fabada gone off.

The main door to the toilets opened. He heard Ramírez.

'. . . for all I know, he's fucking her as well.'

'The Inspector Jefe?' said Pérez, incredulous.

'He's probably desperate after his divorce.'

Then silence as they realized one of the stalls was occupied.

They left. Falcón washed his hands, reasserted the authority in his dress, combed his hair.

The two men were in his office. On the desk was the report from the Policía Científica.

'Anything in this?' he asked.

'Nothing to help us,' said Ramírez.

'What did Joaquín López have to say?'

'He was very interesting, especially about the wife,' said Ramírez, unable to disguise his antipathy for Sra Jiménez. 'It seems that Sr López was much further on in his negotiations than I thought. All the discussions had taken place and the money was agreed. The lawyers were already drawing up the contract.'

'And then he met Consuelo Jiménez . . .' said Falcón.

'Exactly . . . he met the wife,' said Ramírez. 'And she didn't know about the deal.'

'I should think Raúl Jiménez thought it was his business to sell,' said Falcón.

'He did. And it was. But both he and Joaquín López had underestimated her influence. They had a lunch so that they could meet. Sr López was impressed by the way the restaurants were run. The décor, all the stuff that the wife does.'

'I hope he didn't offer her a job.'

'He was thinking about it. The point of the lunch was to see if she liked the idea of continuing to run the restaurants or if suddenly not being the wife of the owner was going to make a difference.'

'And the lunch was a disaster?'

'She completely froze him out. Joaquín López said that everything had happened before the lunch. The whole thing had been decided. Raúl Jiménez was like a whipped dog next to the wife. Sr López didn't even have to make the call afterwards – he knew the deal was off.'

'And what's your reading of this development?' asked Falcón.

'I think she had him done,' said Ramírez. 'You might think this is an elaborate way of going about it, but that's just the point. The wife has made a success out of paying attention to the details. She thinks things through from beginning to end. Nothing is left to chance, whether it's making sure the kitchens are getting the right produce or planning her husband's murder.'

'You know what?' said Falcón. 'I agree. I think she's capable.'

Ramírez's chest expanded. He went to the window and looked out over the car park as if it had become his kingdom.

'But there might be another dimension,' added Falcón. 'On the surface, she and I had a good, co-operative meeting this afternoon, except she told me very little. And when I asked for her husband's records from his time on the Building Committee for Expo '92 she denied there were any such files and got the secretary to do the same.'

'That's crazy,' said Pérez. 'There has to be something.'

'Another thing: Raúl Jiménez is a very successful businessman. He comes from Andalucian peasant stock and by his son's account he was a ruthless operator. So ruthless that thirty-six years ago his youngest son was kidnapped as an act of revenge. He barely co-operated with the police. He moved his family out of the town. And then he systematically stamped out any memory of his child. He did this because he was faced with the choice of losing everything or losing everything except his wealth and status.'

'I'm not sure of your point, Inspector Jefe,' said Ramírez.

'What stopped Raúl Jiménez selling those restaurants?' asked Falcón.

'The wife.'

'She didn't murder him, did she?' said Falcón. 'But given Raúl Jiménez's reputation you'd have thought she'd have to.'

'She threatened to expose him,' said Pérez.

'Over a kidnapped child thirty-six years ago?' said Ramírez. '*Joder.*'

'She didn't know that then. I only told her that after I'd spoken to José Manuel Jiménez.'

'So what did she have on him?'

'Something to do with Expo '92,' said Falcón. 'I think she must have found his papers and uncovered a level of corruption unsurpassed in Spanish commercial history.'

'But why hide them now?'

'Because she's got what she wants. The restaurants,' said Falcón. 'All her husband's papers can do now is jeopardize her position. If he was found to be corrupt it could have an effect on the business. She could lose the lot.'

'Then his death was very convenient,' said Ramírez.

'Wouldn't it have been more logical for Sr Jiménez to murder his wife?' said Pérez. 'Then he could have sold his restaurants and avoided any scandal.'

'Murder takes place when logic breaks down,' said Ramírez, looking at Pérez as if he was a traitor to the cause.

'Let's run a background check on Consuelo Jiménez . . . official and unofficial,' said Falcón. 'She talked about an art gallery she worked for in Madrid and an affair with the son of a duke which ended in an abortion back in 1984.'

'She's clean, according to the police computer,' said Ramírez. 'I have some contacts in Madrid who are checking her name out in a different way to see if there's any connection with drugs or vice.'

'What about the Building Committee?' said Falcón, and Pérez humped a box up on to his desk. He started lifting out sheaves of paper.

'These are the names and addresses of all companies involved in any building project of any size leading up to the opening of Expo '92. This is a list of all companies involved in building projects outside the Expo site which were either wholly or partially funded by the state. Most of this is residential development in places like Santiponce and Camas. This is a list of all the companies who were responsible for projects within the pavilions: designers, lighting and sound people, air conditioning, flooring contractors . . .'

'What are you telling me, Sub Inspector?' asked Falcón.

'This little book is a directory of all the people who were involved in working for or supplying the pavilions, restaurants, bars, shops . . .'

Ramírez loomed into frame, gripping the edge of his desk.

'Look, Inspector Jefe, we know what went on. Everybody got fat from this. But it was ten years ago and we know how the layers of confusion pile up after a matter of days, hours even. And what are we looking for? The guy who didn't make a fortune? Where's he going to be? The guy who was ripped off? Where do we look for him? Is he even going to be in these lists of companies and people? And if he is, where do we start? Glass suppliers? Marble quarries? Tile factories? It would be a huge task for a specially designed anti-corruption squad, let alone the six of us in the Grupo de Homicidios. There has to be a hot lead to get us into doing this level of work.'

Falcón clicked his knuckles one by one. It was a good speech, but it didn't sound like Ramírez. It was succinct for a start and Ramírez didn't have that kind of objective brain. He was a subjective, reactive type. Pulling Consuelo Jiménez in and sweating her was more his approach.

'So both of you think that we should develop this investigation by building a case against Consuelo Jiménez?'

Ramírez nodded. Pérez shrugged.

'She's tough,' said Falcón, 'and I don't think we've got enough on her to make her feel even slightly uncomfortable. We're going to have to dig.'

'What about surveillance?' asked Ramírez.

'I can't justify that sort of expense yet,' said Falcón. 'I'd need more on her. The lover motive is dead and the Joaquín López motive still isn't strong enough, although it's worth running it past Juez Calderón.'

'Sr López has offered his help in any way.'

'I'm sure he has.'

'What if they find something in Madrid . . . will you put her under surveillance then?'

'If she's been implicated in murder before, then yes. If it's shop-lifting, no.'

'To really nail her we have to show a connection between her and the cameraman in the graveyard,' said Pérez, which didn't advance the conversation.

'What was he doing there? Ask yourself that first,' said Falcón. 'His job was done. If he's operating under instructions, why film the funeral?'

'Maybe he's been making a little blackmail movie,' said Pérez.

'That is stretching credibility, Sub Inspector.'

'Is the disappearance of Eloisa Gómez stretching credibility, too?' asked Ramírez. 'The wife saw her on that video we were watching after they'd taken the body away.'

'I think that's something between the killer and Eloisa . . .'

'The wife might not have liked the idea of an accomplice out there,' said Pérez.

'Think about why he's playing these games with Eloisa Gómez's mobile phone,' said Falcón. 'Why say that line about having a story to tell?'

'What line was that?' asked Ramírez.

'I told you.'

'You told us about "Are we close?" and "Closer than you think", said Ramírez, 'but "a story to tell" – no, you didn't mention that.'

Falcón was amazed and embarrassed. It worried him that his memory was so shot through with holes. The brandy. He told them what had happened out on the bridge.

'It's a distraction,' said Ramírez.

'Insane,' said Pérez.

'It's obscure on its own, but taken in conjunction with the man appearing at the funeral with his camera it could mean that he's going to act again,' said Falcón. 'We have to keep an open mind. We can't close down any possibilities to concentrate solely on Consuelo Jiménez.'

Ramírez started some agitated pacing around the room. Falcón dismissed the two men but called Pérez back.

'I want you to do a couple of things with these lists,' said Falcón. 'Take the first two you gave me and find out which of those companies still exist. Then find all the names of the directors, executive and non-executive, in all these companies between 1990 and 1992. That's all, then we drop it.'

16

Falcón couldn't stand to be alone, which for a private man was a bizarre revelation. As soon as Pérez left the office he became anxious, frightened that something would happen in his head. He couldn't rely on himself. He felt like an old person who'd noticed the first signs of dementia – moments of confusion, memory lapses, the inability to recognize simple things – and sensed the imminent free fall to total dislocation from life. Other people gave him context, reminded him of his old confidence. He couldn't concentrate on the report from the Policía Científica. Panic rose in his chest and he had to walk it back down.

He became so desperate at the thought of his loneliness after work, the survival of a whole night before his doctor's appointment, that he called the British Institute and reintroduced himself into the conversational English classes he had enrolled in the year before and failed to attend. This was how he found himself sitting in the middle of a class in a state of appalled fascination as the Scottish teacher told the students about some recent laser treatment on her eyes. Lasers in the eye? He couldn't even think about it.

After class he went out for a drink and tapas with some of the other students. He found strangers comforting. They didn't know him. They couldn't judge his own strangeness. He would have to avoid his sister, her friends. This was his new life and that was how he thought of it already after only a few days.

He got home at 1 a.m., exhausted. It was a tiredness he'd never encountered before. A deep structural fatigue, like an ancient bridge that had shouldered epochs of traffic and strained against relentless tons of water. His legs quivered, his joints creaked and yet inside his head, whoever it was inside his head, was as alert as a night animal.

He hauled himself up to the bedroom like a butcher's boy with a carcass on his back.

The sheets were as cool as lotion as he crawled naked into bed for the first time since he was a boy. His eyelids rolled shut, heavy as boulders.

And still sleep did not come.

Ghastly images surfaced. Horror faces that were inconceivable except, there they were, in his mind. Every time his brain keeled over into the dark, they came and jolted him back. He writhed in the sheets, turned the light on, jammed his fists into his eyes. He wouldn't have minded tearing them out if he could have guaranteed to blind the mind's eye, too. The mind's eye. He hated that expression. His father had hated it. That's why *he* hated it. Pretentious and inaccurate. Tears came. *Madre mía*, what is this? Huge wracking sobs lifted his shoulders off the bed.

He threw off the covers, staggered out of the room blinded by tears. He tried to pull himself together in the gallery, march it off. He held on to the balustrade and looked into the patio, saw the black pupil in the centre of the fountain staring up and thought he'd just hop over the ledge, dive on to the marble flagstones below, dash his brains out in a last cacophonous roar and then silence. Peace at last.

The idea was too compelling. He pushed himself away from it, stumbled down the stairs and into the study. He opened the drinks cabinet, which was full of whisky, his father's preferred drink. He pulled the cork out of the first bottle that came to hand and drank heavily from the neck. It smelt and tasted like wet charcoal but had the burn of a glowing ember.

A full-length mirror gave him a terrible update on his appearance – naked, quivering, genitals shrivelled, tear-stained face, both hands locked round the bottle as if it was going to get him ashore. Because that's where he felt himself to be, out in some mountainous sea with no hope of landfall. He drank more of the liquid asphalt and sank to his knees. He was still crying, if that was what it could be called, this huge retching of the body, as if it was trying to sick up something bigger than itself. He drank again from the bottle of molten tar until it was all gone. He fell back, the bottle toppled and rolled. The label flashed away from him. He belched an essence of bitumen and slithered into a glittering darkness as if he was being laid down in a new black road.

He came to steamrollered, all joints dislocated, bones crushed, face distorted. He was lying in a pool of his own urine, shivering with the cold. It was first light outside. His legs stung. He swabbed the floor and went upstairs and collapsed in the shower, grovelling in the tray. He was still drunk and his teeth seemed as large as cobblestones.

Still dripping, he made it to bed and scratched the covers over himself. He slept and dreamt the fish dream. It was nearly beautiful to be flashing through the blue-green water, but the freedom of perfect instinct was disturbed by the terrible wrench, the visceral tug that was pulling him inside out.

Tuesday, 17th April 2001, Falcón's house, Calle Bailén, Seville

The savage light stepped into his head. Steel tips flashed and sparked in his dark cranium. His organs were as delicate as bone china. He gasped at the ecstatic pain of the drunk.

An hour and half later, scrubbed, shaved, dressed and combed through, he lowered himself into a chair in front of his doctor, hesitant as a man with elephant haemorrhoids that ran from nose to tail.

'Javier . . .' said the doctor, instantly running out of words.

'I know Dr Fernando, I know,' said Falcón.

Dr Fernando Valera was the son of his father's doctor and was ten years older than Falcón although the last week seemed to have evened up their ages. The two men knew each other well, both were *aficionados de los toros*.

'I saw you across a crowd of people at the Estación de Santa Justa on Friday,' said Dr Fernando. 'You looked quite normal then. What's been going on?'

The softness of the doctor's voice made Falcón emotional and he had to fight back the silly tears at the thought that he'd finally arrived in a haven where somebody cared. He gave the doctor a rundown of his physical symptoms – the anxiety, the panic, the pounding heart, the sleeplessness. The doctor probed with questions about his work. The Raúl Jiménez case was mentioned, which the doctor had read about. Falcón admitted it was at the sight of the man's face that he'd noticed the chemical change.

'I can't tell you the details, but it had something to do with the man's eyes.'

'Ah, yes, you're very sensitive about eyes . . . as your father was.'

'Was he? I don't remember that.'

'I suppose it's quite natural for an artist to worry about his eyes, but in the last ten years of his life your father became obsessed – yes, that's the word: obsessed with blindness.'

'The idea of it?'

'No, no, becoming blind. He was certain it would happen to him.'

'I didn't know.'

'My father tried to tease him out of it, told him if he wasn't careful he'd go hysterically blind. Francisco was appalled at the idea,' said Dr Fernando. 'Anyway . . . Javier . . . we are here to talk about you. To me you are suffering the classic symptoms of stress.'

'I don't get stress. I've been at this job for twenty years and I never suffered from stress.'

'You're forty-five.'

'I *do* remember that.'

'This is when the body begins to realize its weaknesses. Body and mind. The pressures in the mind create symptoms in the body. I see it all the time.'

'Even in Seville?'

'Maybe more so in *Sevilla la maravilla*. It's quite a pressure to be happy all the time because . . . it's expected of you. We're not immune to modern life just because we live in the most beautiful city in Spain. We tell ourselves we should be happy . . . we have no excuse. We are surrounded by people who appear to be happy, people who clap their hands and dance in the streets, people who sing for the pure joy of singing . . . and you think they don't suffer? You think that they are somehow excluded from the battle of the human condition – death, infirmity, lost love, poverty, crime and all the rest of it? We're all half mad.'

Falcón wondered whether this was intended to make him feel better about being crazy.

'I was beginning to think I was wholly mad,' he said.

'You are under very particular pressures. You face the momentary breakdowns in our civilization, when the condition has become intolerable and the wire has snapped. You face the consequences of that. This is not an easy job. Perhaps you should talk to somebody about this . . . somebody who has an understanding of the work.'

'The police psychologist?'

'That's what they're there for.'

'Inside an hour everybody would know that Javier Falcón was cracking up.'

'Aren't these appointments confidential?'

'They get out. It's like living in a barracks or a school in the Jefatura. Everybody knows you're splitting up with a girlfriend before you do.'

'You speak from painful experience, Javier.'

'In my case it was even worse, Inés being a *fiscal*, and a very noticeable and unreserved one . . . perhaps we shouldn't get started on Inés, Dr Fernando.'

'So you won't see the police psychologist?'

'I want something more private. I don't mind paying for it. You're right, maybe talking it out might help.'

'It's not so easy to get a private consultation. There are also many different approaches to the science of the mind. Some people perceive it as a purely clinical condition, a chemical imbalance to be rebalanced by the introduction of drugs. Others use drugs and a theoretical approach based on say, Jung or Freud, amongst others.'

'You will have to advise me.'

'I can only tell you that so-and-so is a good psychologist, this one works exclusively with a psychopharmacologist, this one is a serious Freudian. You might not like their approaches. You know, "What does my relationship with my *caca* when I was a kid have to do with my adult problems?" It doesn't mean they are bad at their work.'

'You still think I should go to the police psychologist?'

'There's the added advantage of availability.'

'So now you're going to tell me that in the *ciudad de alegría, Sevilla la maravilla*, there isn't a single available mind doctor? *¡Somos todos chiflados!*'

'We all suffer,' said Dr Fernando. 'The Spanish, not just the Sevillanos, rise above their problems through . . . *la fiesta*. We talk, we sing, we dance, we drink, we laugh and party night after night. This is our way of dealing with the pain. Our next-door neighbours, the Portuguese, are very different.'

'Their natural condition is to be depressed,' said Falcón. 'They've given in to the human condition.'

'I don't think so. They're melancholic by nature, like our Galicians. They have the Atlantic to confront every day, after all. But they are great sensualists, too. There's a country that would commit suicide if you cancelled lunch. They love to eat and drink and enjoy the beauty of things.'

'Yes,' said Javier, getting interested. 'And what about the British? My father so admired the British. How do they cope with life? They're so reserved and inhibited.'

'Well, to us they are, but amongst themselves . . . I believe they have this expression: "to take the piss".'

'That's right,' said Javier, 'they never take things too seriously. They make fun of everything. Nothing is sacrosanct. The famous British sense of humour. And the French?'

'Sex. Love. And all that leads up to it. *La Table.*'

'The Germans?'

'*Ordnung.*'

'The Italians?'

'*La Moda.*'

'The Belgians?'

'Mussels,' said Dr Fernando, and they both laughed. 'I don't know any Belgians.'

'And the Americans?'

'They are more complicated.'

'They all have their own personal analysts.'

'Yes, well, it's not so easy to be leaders of the modern world with the right to the pursuit of happiness written into the constitution,' said Dr Fernando. 'And they're a mixture: Northern Europeans, Hispanics, Blacks, Orientals. And maybe that's it, they've lost touch with their traditional safety valves.'

'It's a good theory. You should write a thesis.'

'You're enjoying yourself, Javier.'

'Yes, I am,' he said, looking up, as if trying to remember why he was here.

'Perhaps you should get out more. Work less. Be more sociable.'

'I'd still like you to find someone for me to talk to,' said Falcón, the weight back on his shoulders.

Dr Valera nodded and wrote out a prescription for some mild anti-anxiety pills called Orfidal and something to help him sleep.

'One thing is certain, Javier,' he said, giving him the paper. 'Alcohol will not resolve any of your problems.'

Falcón picked up the prescription on República de Argentina and swallowed an Orfidal with his own spit. Ramírez was waiting for him in the office with a package addressed to Inspector Jefe Javier Falcón, with a Madrid postmark on it.

'It's been X-rayed,' said Ramírez. 'It's a video cassette.'

'Take it down to Forensics and get them to check it.'

'Something else that might be interesting. I sent Fernández down to Mudanzas Triana yesterday to help Baena with the interviews. He got friendly with the foreman. One of the things that came out was that Raúl Jiménez used Mudanzas Triana because they'd moved him before. They're holding stuff in store for him from his last two moves.'

'His wife said he moved into the Edificio del Presidente in the mid eighties.'

'From a house in El Porvenir.'

'And before that he was in the Plaza de Cuba.'

'Which he moved out of in 1967.'

'When his first wife died.'

'When they put his name into the computer at Mudanzas Triana they found he still had stuff in the warehouse. They asked if he wanted it moved into the new home. He said no, and he was very emphatic. They offered to dump it for him because it was costing him money. Again he said no.'

Ramírez left with the package. Falcón's hand hovered over the phone. He sat back and thought about the quality of that information. The Orfidal was working. He was calm and concentrated in his thinking, although he was aware that he might be suffering a paranoid tendency – to believe that Ramírez was diverting his attention with tantalizing but fruitless information. He had two options: the first was to apply for a search warrant, which would mean filing documentary proof that he thought that events of thirty-six years ago had a bearing on the case. The second was to ask Consuelo Jiménez for access, but she'd already blocked him on the Building Committee's files.

The phone made him jump in his seat. Juez Calderón was asking for a meeting. He'd just had an unusual visit from Magistrado Juez Decano de Sevilla Alfredo Spinola. They agreed to meet before lunch at the Edificio de los Juzgados.

Ramírez returned with the 'clean' video cassette from the Policía Científica. There was a printed card with the cassette which read:

'Sight Lesson No.1. See 4 and 6.' The title of the cassette was *Cara o Culo I.*

'Wasn't this the title on the empty slipcase in Raúl Jiménez's apartment?' asked Ramírez.

'The killer must have taken it,' said Falcón. 'And . . . Sight Lesson?'

They went to the interrogation room, where the video was still set up. Ramírez slipped in the cassette. Tinny music started up and bad graphics. There followed a series of sketches, each one five or ten minutes long, in which quite normal situations such as a drinks party, dinner in a restaurant, a poolside barbecue, disintegrated into improbable orgies of group sex. Falcón was instantly flattened by boredom. The music and false ecstasy irritated him and his palms began to moisten again. The Orfidal wore off. He breathed deeply to maintain calm. Ramírez leaned forward, playing with his ring. He made comments to himself throughout and whistled occasionally. Falcón came out of his torpor only once during the last sketch, which he thought had been the one playing on the TV when Raúl Jiménez was with Eloisa Gómez.

'I don't know how you can tell that,' said Ramírez.

'It's just shapes on a screen.'

Ramírez grinned. The cassette finished.

'What's this "Sight Lesson"?' he asked. 'If this was playing on the night Jiménez died, so what?

'That was the last sketch of six. We were asked to look at four and six.'

'We've done that.'

'So it's got nothing to do with the fact that it was playing on the night of the murder.'

'Sight lesson?' murmured Ramírez.

'He's teaching us,' said Falcón. 'He sees things that nobody else sees.'

'He's not teaching me anything,' said Ramírez. 'I know all that stuff backwards.'

'Maybe that's the point. What do you look at when you watch a pornographic movie?'

'You look at them doing it.'

'That's why they're called "skin flicks" in the States, because that's all you look at. The skin. The surface. The action.'

'What else *is* there?'

'Maybe he's saying that there's more to this than meets the eye.

It's not just genitals and penetration. We forget that the performers are real people with faces and lives,' said Falcón. 'Let's watch that last sketch and just look at the faces this time.'

Ramírez rewound the tape. Falcón turned the sound down to zero. They stood closer.

'Have you seen the way these people are dressed?' said Falcón.

'It's got to be twenty years old, this movie,' said Ramírez. 'Look at those shirt collars – I remember them.'

Falcón concentrated on the faces and, as he moved from one to the next, taking in the eyes and mouths, he wondered what was driving these people to do this. Was the money enough to abandon morality, innocence and intimacy? He moved from a pair of vacant eyes to a mouth with gritted teeth, from a slack and lifeless face to a sneering lip, and shuddered under the slow weight of the small, unfolding tragedy. Did these people even know each other? Perhaps they'd just met that morning and by the afternoon . . .

One of the girls had dark, curly hair. She never looked at the camera. She either stared straight ahead or looked down on the surface of the table she was leaning on, as if it was only a matter of time before she was on the other side of this experience. One hand was balled into a fist of bleak determination. He realized that if the camera's focus had been pulled close-up on the faces while a voice-over unravelled the lives of the participants, the movie could have had documentary possibilities. Did these people have partners outside this temporary world? Would it be possible to have sex with seven or eight strangers and then go back home for dinner with a boyfriend or girlfriend? Did they have to give up on life to be able to do this work?

A wave of sadness collapsed in his chest.

'Seen anything?' asked Ramírez.

'Nothing relevant,' said Falcón. 'I don't know what we're looking for.'

'Is this *tío* laughing at us?'

'This is his game and we play it because we learn something about him every time. Let's go to number four.'

Ramírez rewound the tape, set it to 'play'. It opened on a party in an apartment. The doorbell rang. The camera followed a girl in tight shorts and a halter-neck top down a corridor. She opened the door and let in two men and two women. Ramírez put his big finger to the screen.

'Look at her,' he said.

It was the girl with the curly dark hair and the balled fist, who never looked at the camera.

'That's a wig,' said Ramírez.

The camera followed the group down the corridor to the party, which was now unaccountably out of control with everybody naked and performing. The four new arrivals, rather than running screaming from the apartment, joined in.

'There she is again,' said Ramírez.

This time she was stripped to the waist and sitting on the sofa looking up at a man's bulging trouser front. The camera went in close as the girl's hands reached for the man's fly.

'You know who that is?' said Ramírez.

'Incredible.'

'It is, isn't it?' said Ramírez, his satisfaction palpable. 'She's younger and sort of fatter, but that is very definitely Sra Consuelo Jiménez.'

17

Tuesday, 17th April 2001, Jefatura, Calle Blas Infante, Seville

They were back in the office. Falcón behind his desk staring at the cassette while Ramírez stood tapping his ring finger against the window, looking out over the car park as if he had the whole lot to sell before the end of the week.

'At least we know she's not a virgin,' said Ramírez.

'You know what this does?' said Falcón, batting the cassette across the desk. 'It does exactly what it's meant to do. It confuses everything.'

'It was supposed to teach us something. It was a sight lesson,' said Ramírez, straightening himself up, shaking his head at the cars, a really impossible task.

'How does this make you feel about the case you're building against Consuelo Jiménez?'

'I don't know,' he said, turning his back to the window. 'In one way it supports it and in another it destroys it.'

'That's the point,' said Falcón. 'It shows she's capable of stepping outside the boundaries. But why should the killer, supposedly paid for and instructed by her . . . why should he send us the tape?'

'Unless he didn't send it.'

'Look – *Sight* Lesson number one: Raúl Jiménez with his eyelids cut off. Who else could it be? It's too knowledgeable.'

Ramírez walked across the room, wagging his ring finger.

'You said it was designed to confuse, yes?' he said. 'Sra Jiménez is under pressure. You've spoken to her at length almost every day since the murder.'

'You think she sent it herself or had it sent?'

'Look at our reaction. We cannot believe that she would be prepared to expose herself to that extent. But think about it. She appeared in a pornographic movie twenty years ago. Big deal. She probably had her reasons. Cash shortage being the most likely. I mean, what do you want to do? Work as a chambermaid for a decade or suck a few cocks? The only way this movie would have an impact on her life is if we sent it to her friends in Seville with a red circle around her head and "Consuelo Jiménez" flashing on the screen, and if you haven't got a budget for surveillance, then you certainly haven't got a budget for that.'

Ramírez couldn't help himself. That crude, irrepressible pugnacity always found a way out.

'Maybe there's another level to this sight lesson,' said Falcón. 'I thought this was the sketch that was playing when the killer filmed Raúl Jiménez with Eloisa Gómez. What does that say about Raúl Jiménez . . . if he knew who he was watching?'

'He's very strange.'

Falcón contemplated the binary tracks of the human brain, the endless choices. This way or that? What was driving the instinct to always choose the wrong way, so that instead of lying in bed with your wife, reflecting on the joy of marriage and children, you find yourself screwing a whore in your study while looking at your wife performing on the screen? Raúl Jiménez had an instinct for worthlessness.

'If you take into consideration the likeness of Consuelo Jiménez to the dead wife . . . it's almost impossible to imagine what was going on in the man's head,' said Falcón.

'Guilt,' said Ramírez.

'Guilt requires perception.'

'Beats me,' said Ramírez, easily bored. 'What are we going to do with this?'

'Confront Consuelo Jiménez with it . . . see how she reacts.'

'I'm game for that.'

'We're also due to meet Juez Calderón before lunch,' said Falcón. 'I don't think two policemen leaning on Consuelo Jiménez about her unfortunate past is going to be productive. I want you to prepare the material for the meeting with Juez Calderón. You could also tell Baena, if he's still down at Mudanzas Triana, to see if they'll let him have a look at Raúl Jiménez's stuff or at least give him an inventory.'

Ramírez's colour darkened with some tight internal rage. He didn't like having his machinations turned on him and he didn't want to be excluded from the humiliation of Consuelo Jiménez. Falcón called her. She agreed to see him and asked him to come before lunch was served in the restaurants.

He took another Orfidal in the toilet, amazed at how effective the first had been, tempted to spend the rest of his life on them. He drove through the subdued city and thought that his doctor might be right, that this was just stress. We live in an age of constant mild anxiety. Because there are no longer any defining events of world upheaval we focus our concentration on the minutiae of everyday life, engross ourselves in work and activity to suppress the anxiety that goes with relative peace. Yes, that's it, he thought, I'll take these pills for a few more weeks, crack this case and take a holiday.

There were a couple of spaces at the back of the Edificio de los Juzgados. He parked up and set off through the Jardines de Murillo into the *barrio* Santa Cruz. He slowed down as the doctor's words came back to him ... the most beautiful city in Spain ... and he looked around himself as if for the first time. The sky overhead beyond the clear, rinsed air and the high palms was nothing short of cerulean. The Andalucian sun shone above the green leaves of the plane trees casting patterns of light and shade on the smooth cobbles below. Towers of magenta bougainvillea, spectacular after the rains, tumbled down the white and ochre buildings. The bright blood-red of geraniums nodded through the black balustrades of the wrought-iron balconies. The smell of coffee and baking bread loafed in the quiet streets. The cavernous cool of narrow alleyways broke out into the warmth of open squares where the golden stone of ancient churches settled in silence.

He walked under the high plane trees of the Plaza Alfalfa and regretted the business that he was on – the pain and the embarrassment at odds with the full flush of the day. The secretary showed him in to Consuelo Jiménez's office. She sat right up to the desk, with her hands flat on the leather inlay, padded shoulders braced. Falcón sank into a chair, his stomach still fluttering with gaiety. These pills. Like a man listening to his favourite music under headphones he had to stop himself from roaring it out.

He handed her the video cassette in a plastic evidence bag. She turned it over and flinched at the title. He told her he'd received it in the post that morning and about the sight lesson card.

'This is one of my husband's dirty movies, isn't it?'

'It was playing while the killer filmed your husband having sex with the prostitute in his study. The card accompanying it told us to look at sections four and six very closely.'

'Very good, Inspector Jefe, and what happened?'

'You have no idea of the contents of this video?'

'I'm not interested in pornography. I abhor it.'

'From the clothes of the actors and actresses in this film we estimate it to be about twenty years old.'

'*Clothes* in a dirty movie . . . that's novel.'

'Only initially.'

'Come on, Inspector Jefe, if there's been a development then let's have it out and talk it over.'

'The two sections we were instructed to view by the sight lesson card feature you, Sra Jiménez, as a young woman.'

Silence. Long enough for a new ice age to have formed.

'Why do you think . . . ?' started Falcón.

'*What* are you talking about, Inspector Jefe?'

The vicious edge to her voice shredded his confidence and the possibility loomed in his mind that they had been mistaken, that Ramírez had misjudged, that it hadn't been her and the furniture in the office was rushing past him as he crashed headlong into the most embarrassing moment of his professional career.

'I was wondering,' he said, steadying himself, 'why anybody would want to send us this film.'

'Why do you think you can come into my office with this disgusting notion . . . ?'

'Do you have a video player?'

'Come with me,' she said, snatching up the bag.

They left the office and went down the corridor to a small room with a two-seater sofa, a chair and a TV/Video. Falcón struggled into a latex glove with his hands now running with sweat. The film was preset to start at the fourth section. He decided to avoid maximum embarrassment by just playing the first moments where the four people are let into the apartment. He froze the frame on her as she came in the door. She scoffed at it, holding her blonde hair out to him. He let the video play on until the camera closed in on her unmistakable face. He tried to freeze the frame but the video would not obey. The young Consuelo unzipped the man's trousers and fished out his penis and that was when Consuelo Jiménez, puce in the face, barged him out of the way, stopped the video, and tore it out of the player.

'*That* is evidence,' said Falcón.

She smashed the cassette to the ground, impaled it with her heel. The plastic casing cracked and she tried to shake it off but it was as tenacious as dog shit. She kicked her shoe off, ripped the cassette off the heel and dashed it against the wall where it splintered and fell into pieces. Falcón rushed at it with the evidence bag and shovelled in the remains. She was on him, hitting him about the head and back, screaming and livid, the language worse than he'd heard even in the drug dens of the Poligono San Pablo. He turned on her, grabbed her by the shoulders, shouted into her face and she broke down on his shoulder and wept into the material of his suit.

He sat her down on the sofa. She buried her face in the arm. Falcón's mind split into two worlds; was this pretence or real? She came round slowly, face destroyed. He sat in the chair to distance himself.

'Yes,' she said, 'that *was* me.'

'A hard time?'

'A very bad moment,' she said, reducing the hours it must have taken to a flashing fraction.

'Money problems?'

'Everything problems,' she said, staring into the abyss of the inevitability of intrusion. 'I volunteered the details of my second abortion, paid for by my lover. This was the prelude to my first abortion, financed by me. Return flight to London, hotel and hospital. It was a lot of money to raise in two months without any help.'

She shuddered, put her hand to her mouth as if she might be sick.

'It's not the kind of thing anybody would want to have to remember,' she said. 'That a pregnant woman had to do that sort of thing to earn the money to terminate a foetus. It's just completely disgusting to me.'

This was a big lesson, this Sight Lesson No.1. Perhaps it would have been good for Ramírez to have seen this, because this fits with the profile of the killer. He knows things. He finds the shame or the horror in people's pasts and shows it to them, forces them to relive it.

'How would anybody know about this?' asked Falcón. 'Did anybody know about it?'

'I'd already edited it out of my own life. I can't remember a thing about it. I did something that had to be done and when it was over I dispatched it to the deepest abyss. I can barely remember who I knew at that time. I came back from London and set about changing everything.'

'The father?'

'You mean the man who did *not* become a father,' she said. 'He was a mechanic at a garage my father managed. When I told him, he ran. I never saw him again.'

'How would anybody know about this?'

'They wouldn't,' she said. 'It was the first time in my life I'd encountered true loneliness. I did everything on my own. I didn't even tell my sister.'

'How did you find the clinic in London?' he asked, the sordid checking of the facts inevitable.

'My doctor gave me an address in Madrid of a woman who had all the details.'

'And raising the money . . . how did you find yourself in that world?'

'They were people who knew about that address, too,' she said. 'It was no coincidence that I should meet a girl in a café on the same afternoon, who made a proposal to me that would supply precisely the right amount of money.'

'Did you see her again?'

'Never.'

'And the other performers?' he asked, and she shook her head.

'You know, given the racket they were involved in, they were surprisingly good people. What we were doing was depraved and the atmosphere on the set should have been horrible, but we smoked a few joints and it was all very friendly. They were humane and sympathetic. I was probably lucky. I've met more abusive people in the restaurant business. And the sex . . . the sex was really nothing. The most difficult thing was for the men to maintain an erection because it was all so uncharged . . . unsexy.'

Falcón squirmed as the question he didn't want to ask formed in his head. He shelved it. Too distasteful.

'You said you changed everything when you came back to Spain.'

'The night before the operation I was staying in a cheap hotel in Victoria. I went walking to take my mind off the next day. I wanted to lose myself. I went up to Hyde Park Corner, down Piccadilly into Shepherd's Market and Berkeley Square. I drifted into Albemarle Street and found myself outside an art gallery. There was an opening of an exhibition. I watched the people as they came and left. They were beautifully dressed, sophisticated and completely urbane. None of those women would have got themselves pregnant by a garage mechanic. I decided that they were my people and I would consort with them and become them.

'When I got back to Madrid I worked hard and bought some nice clothes and went to see a gallery owner who said I was unsuitable, that I didn't know the first thing about art. He humiliated me. He took me around the paintings and let me reveal my ignorance. Then he asked me about the frames. Frames? What did I care about frames? He told me to learn how to type and threw me out.'

She was mesmerizing Falcón, fixing him with a look of pure grit. Her fist was balled on the arm of the chair, just as it had been in the film.

'I studied art history. Not formally – I couldn't afford that. I worked at it in my spare time. I went to meet frame makers. I met artists, unknowns, but ones who knew what they were talking about. I worked in a shop selling art materials. I learnt everything. I met more established artists . . . and that was how I got the job in the gallery. And when I got it I went back to the guy who turned me down. He didn't remember me. While we were talking Manolo Rivera came in . . . do you know him?'

'Not personally.'

'Well, he came in and kissed me and said *hola* and the gallery owner offered me a job on the spot. It gave me great pleasure to turn him down.'

'Did your husband know any of this?'

'Only you, Inspector Jefe,' she said. 'Intimacy is easier with those that don't share your bed. And . . . I think we recognize each other, don't we, Don Javier?'

Falcón blinked at her, not sure where she was leading him.

'We look as if we're on the inside,' she said, 'but we're not. We're on the outside looking in, just like your father.'

'But not your husband,' he said, to change the subject.

'Raúl? Raúl was lost,' she said. 'If that was what he was watching when he was with his puta, what does that tell you about him?'

'Ramírez said it was guilt.'

'Ramírez isn't as stupid as he looks,' she said, '. . . just macho.'

'You don't think your husband knew it was you?' said Falcón.

'I can't believe he did. I didn't get a credit.'

'He saw the likeness, though.'

She nodded.

'Do you think that, for Raúl, to see someone who looked like his first wife . . .'

'. . . behaving like a puta,' she added for him.

'. . . somehow assuaged his feelings of guilt?'

She shrugged, stood up, smoothed her skirt, said she had to go for lunch.

He walked back to the Edificio de los Juzgados, the day gone grey again, the leaves of the palm trees clacking in the breeze as the clouds reasserted themselves. Ramírez was waiting for him outside the Edificio de los Juzgados with a thick file under his arm. They went through security. He pulled a sheet of paper from the file: an inventory of Raúl Jimenez's possessions in the Mudanzas Triana warehouse.

On the way up to Juez Calderón's office he read through the inventory, which included a complete home movie kit, an 8mm camera, film canisters, projector and screen. The Juez was waiting for them, standing at his desk, hands planted as if he was thinking about bulldozing them straight back out into the hall.

18

Tuesday, 17th April 2001, Edificio de los Juzgados, Seville

Falcón and Ramírez turned off their mobiles and sat down in front of Calderón, who maintained his businesslike stance until they were comfortable. He lowered himself into his seat as if he was making a tremendous effort to contain his anger.

'Proceed,' he said, and steepled his fingers. 'Let's start with the latest on the prime suspect.'

'We have had a major development in that respect,' said Falcón, and Ramírez on cue slid the two 'cleaned' blow-ups of the suspected killer out of the file and handed them to Calderón. 'We believe that this is our murderer.'

Calderón's eyes widened as the two sheets came across the desk but regained their grimness when he saw that neither shot was conclusive. Falcón kept up a running commentary on how they'd come across the sighting. His voice seemed disembodied to him, as if he'd become non-human, a robotic word-generator. The bone-deep tiredness was separating him from himself. More phrases toppled from his mouth: '. . . believed to be male in the age range twenty to forty years old . . .' '. . . a further development . . .' '. . . a pornographic video . . .' '. . . confused our perception of the prime suspect . . .' He stopped only when Calderón put his hand up and read the report on the blue movie. The hand dropped. Falcón's tape started up again, and he wondered how many words a human uttered in a lifetime. 'The prostitute Eloisa Gómez . . .' '. . . missing since last Friday night . . .' '. . . contact has been made . . .' '. . . stolen mobile . . .' '. . . feared murdered . . .' All this so long ago and yet so recent, he thought. And the investigation into Raúl Jiménez's private life – the abduction of the boy, the wife's suicide, the daughter's madness, the son's neurosis – a different century, which of course it was. Everything is from a different century now. A great tranche of history has been set adrift, so that we can begin a new accumulation of wrongs without reference . . .

'Inspector Jefe,' said Calderón, 'your speculation on history is not germane to this investigation.'

'It isn't?' he said, and from his sudden fear that he'd been caught leaking came what he hoped was inspiration. 'Motive is always historical, unless it's psychotic. The only question is: how far back do we have to go? Last month, when Raúl Jiménez tried to sell his restaurant business to Joaquín López? The last decade, when he was presiding over the Expo '92 Building Committee? Or thirty-six years ago, when his son was abducted.'

'Let's concentrate on what we have before us,' said Calderón. 'You are an Inspector Jefe with five men under you; there's a limit to what you can achieve with those resources. You have pursued the available leads. You have achieved things – this sighting, for instance. But the most important thing is the apparent audacity of the killer and his inclination to communicate with you. As you have said, in being bold he is making mistakes, which in the case of the funeral was nearly fatal for him. He is sending things to you. He is talking to you.'

'In the light of Consuelo Jiménez's reaction to the pornographic movie, are you proposing that we drop our prime suspect?' asked Ramírez. 'And wait for the killer to talk to us?'

'No, Inspector, Consuelo Jiménez provides a focus for the investigation. She is all we've got. We believe the killer was not known to the victim. At the moment there are two people with possible motives: Joaquín López of the Cinco Bellotas chain, whose motive is very weak; and Consuelo Jiménez, whose motive is a classic, almost a stereotype. Given her reaction to the video, as described by the Inspector Jefe, she is looking less likely, but this does not take her completely out of the frame. She has done enough to make you believe her capable of at least being ruthless. She seems to have been rather disgusted by her husband's sexual interests and his business infidelity. She has not done enough to make me believe that she couldn't possibly have hired someone to carry out this gruesome business. And, if she did hire him, and he has now killed his accomplice, it may be that she has made a poor choice, because he seems to be off the leash.'

'Do you think we should attempt to communicate with him?' asked Falcón.

'And what are we going to say to this *tío*?' asked Ramírez.

'Let's profile him . . . now,' said Calderón.

'I've already said he's bold and playful,' said Falcón. 'I'd like to add creative. He's into film, the idea of the eye, sight and vision. He's interested in the way we look at things. How clearly we do or don't see them – the sight lesson.'

'There's going to be more of those,' said Calderón.

'He's also interested in the way we present ourselves to the world and how at odds this is with our secret lives and possibly our secret history.'

'He does his research,' said Ramírez, 'filming the Familia Jiménez, discovering the change in the move at Mudanzas Triana.'

'He must have charm, maybe good looks and an understanding of the unfortunates of this world if he's capable of persuading Eloisa Gómez to be an accomplice,' said Falcón. 'A woman like her really doesn't need visits from the police and she must have known she was going to get them, even if he told her he was just going to steal a few things.'

'What does he do?' asked Calderón. 'There's money coming from somewhere. He has access to camera, video and computer equipment.'

'He went to Madrid to post the pornographic movie,' said Ramírez. 'He wouldn't leave that in the hands of just anybody. He has time.'

'Anybody who's obsessed has time,' said Falcón. 'He could be working in the film industry, that would give him access to the equipment and if he was working freelance he'd have the time and the money.'

'The Médico Forense said he showed some surgical skills.'

'All sorts of people are good with their hands,' said Calderón. 'You said he's obsessed, Inspector Jefe.'

'The second time he called me he left me in no doubt that he had a story to tell and that he was going to tell it in his way. There was anger and perhaps bitterness.'

'So we could unsettle him by interfering,' said Calderón. 'We might force a mistake by making him angrier.'

'You know what creative people hate more than anything else?' said Falcón. 'Criticism from people that they think are unworthy to judge. Believe me, I know – I've seen my father's rage.'

'But his work,' said Ramírez, 'this work . . . what can you say about it?'

'We could talk to him about his mistakes,' said Falcón. 'Tell him about the chloroform rag, the sighting in the cemetery. How unprofessional he's been.'

Calderón nodded. Falcón took out his mobile with clammy hands. There were two messages. The first was a text message, which he instinctively played because he was rarely sent them.

'He's beaten us to it,' he said, and handed Calderón the mobile. The text message was a riddle in the form of a poem.

> *Cuando su amor es ciego*
> *No arde más su fuego.*
> *Jamás abrirá los ojos*
> *Ni hablará con los locos.*
> *En paz yacen sus hombros*
> *Donde se agitan las sombras.*
> *Ahora ella duerme en la oscuridad*
> *Con su fiel amante de la celebridad.*

The lover is blind, her fire burns no more. Never again will she open her eyes nor speak to madmen. Her shoulders lie in peace where the shadows move. Now she sleeps in darkness with her faithful lover of celebrity.

'You can tell him his poetry is shit, that should annoy him,' said Calderón, handing back the mobile.

'He's killed her,' said Falcón. 'And he's telling us that he's put the body in the Jiménez mausoleum in the San Fernando Cemetery.'

'Call him,' said Calderón. 'Tell him.'

Falcón pulled up Eloisa Gómez's number from the mobile memory and punched it in. No reply. The three men left the building, got into Falcón's car and drove along the river to the cemetery. They ran up the cypress-lined avenue to Jesús de la Pasión, Falcón trying Eloisa Gómez's number all the way. As they neared the Jiménez mausoleum they heard a mobile ringing from inside. Falcón terminated the call and the ringing stopped.

The mausoleum door opened to a push. The stench indicated that putrefaction had already started. Eloisa Gómez was lying on her back on the shelf underneath Raúl Jiménez's coffin. Her mobile was on her stomach and tucked underneath it was an envelope on which was written: Sight Lesson No.2. Her skirt was rucked up, revealing black underwear and a suspender belt to which only one stocking top was attached. The other leg was bare.

Her head lay in darkness at the back of the small mausoleum. Falcón took out a pen torch and played it over her body. Her arms were crossed over her chest, each hand demurely covering a breast. There was a burn mark and deep bruising at her neck. Her face still bore the make-up of her trade. Over each eyelid there was a coin and he could tell by the way the coins had sunk into the sockets that her eyes were missing. It threw him back against the coffin of the dead wife, the pen torch fell from his grip. He crabbed his way out of there and staggered down the steps, shaking himself down, shuddering.

Ramírez was calling the Jefatura incident room, telling them to send a patrol car and the Policía Científica but not to bother with the Juez de Guardia because the Juez de Instrucción was already present.

'What's it like in there?' said Calderón, seeing the horror in Falcón's face.

'She's dead,' he said, 'and her eyeballs have been removed.'

'*Joder*,' said Calderón, visibly shocked.

'Sight lesson number two is under the mobile on her stomach. We'll have to wait for the forensics to come before we go any further.'

Falcón walked away, took some deep breaths. He did a cursory check around the mausoleum and came back to Calderón.

'We were talking about this guy's creativity earlier,' he said. 'This smacks of improvisation. Somehow I don't think this was part of the plan. This is just to show us how clever he can be. I think it's important for him that we know this.'

'But if she was an accomplice he must have known he was going to have to deal with her?' said Calderón.

'Like this? I know it sounds ridiculous, but do you know how difficult it is to get a body into a cemetery? You can't just walk in with one over your shoulder. Look at these walls. The gates are shut at night. It's a difficult business. And if she wasn't his accomplice, he's gone to the trouble of tracking her down, killing her, disposing of her body in this intricate way and . . . I think we'll find out . . . introducing her into his theme.'

'His theme?'

'Sight, vision, illusion, reality.'

'You think he's operating alone?'

'There are still some doubts in me about Consuelo Jiménez, but I respect what you said about giving the investigation focus, because without her we're in an open sea. My instinct tells me he's operating alone, but there's an outside chance he was hired by Consuelo Jiménez, that he's done his job and developed a taste for the work, and I mean The Work. I think this is like a work of art for him.'

'So now you think he's an artist?'

'*He* thinks he's an artist with all his sight lessons and his poetry and "I've got a story to tell".'

'If she wasn't his accomplice,' said Calderón, 'and she was just in the apartment in his film, and he decided he had to deal with her, how did he track her down?'

'The girls in the Alameda said that Raúl Jiménez called twice because Eloisa Gómez wasn't there the first time and he was specifically interested in her. So the killer, if he was in the apartment at the time, would have overheard the name. He also stole Raúl Jiménez's mobile. He has her number. But listen . . . this is interesting. There's a line in the poem he sent us: "*Donde se agitan las sombras.*" Where the shadows move. That was Eloisa's line – it's what girls like her have to look out for.'

'Then he's spoken to her,' said Calderón. 'He's formed some kind of relationship with her.'

'And *that* is unusual between a prostitute and a client.'

'So he *did* know her.'

'If she was seeing somebody privately I'm surprised her girlfriends didn't know about it,' said Falcón. 'But then . . . I think we mishandled her first interview and we're police, after all. They don't like us. They don't feel inclined to talk to us.'

'Do you think, Inspector Jefe,' said Calderón, nearly momentous, 'that we have a serial killer on our hands?'

'We have a multiple murderer and, with the killing of Eloisa Gómez, I think we have something close to a random act, although, as I said, I think we'll find that she's become part of his theme, so it depends how you define random. The planning and motivation that went into the Raúl Jiménez killing were absent from this murder. Where there had been logic, method and technique, now we have pure inspiration.'

'So you think that he will kill again?'

'I do . . . but I don't think it will be random. I think it will fit into the structure of his work. And something fitted with Eloisa Gómez. She's said something, apart from *Donde se agitan las sombras*, which has worked within the warped structure of this killer's mind.

'If you think about it, these girls, they scratch out their living in some dark and dangerous places. They see aspects of human nature on a daily basis that rarely cross the path of normal people. They need insight to survive their sometimes frightening liaisons. A lot of killers prey on prostitutes. For some men the only thing that these girls arouse is all that is weak in themselves and it makes them angry. Raúl Jiménez seemed like a harmless, wealthy guy indulging himself, only we know there was some very perverse wiring in his head.'

'Well, her instinct worked with him,' said Calderón. 'But it failed dramatically with the killer.'

'He got inside her head. He touched her. She talked to him. Prostitutes survive with their clients by keeping their distance. Intimacy is fatal.'

'That's a world you wouldn't want to live in . . . where intimacy is fatal,' said Calderón, and Falcón, who had not made a professional friendship since he'd worked in Barcelona, knew that he liked him.

A patrol car eased up the main avenue of the cemetery, blue lights flashing between the black granite and white marble. Calderón lit a cigarette, smoked it with distaste. Falcón took out his mobile and checked the second message he'd forgotten about in the excitement of the first. It was Dr Fernando Valera telling him he'd arranged an appointment for him with a psychologist and giving an address in Tabladilla.

Felipe and Jorge, the same forensics on the Raúl Jiménez killing, turned up and they all stood around waiting for the Médico Forense. She arrived some minutes later, a woman in her thirties with long dark hair, which she stuffed into a white plastic cap. Her inspection of the body took less than fifteen minutes. She came out of the mausoleum, casually handed Falcón's dropped pen torch to a patrolman and gave her report to Juez Calderón. She put the time of death at some time early on Saturday morning and, as rigor mortis was fully developed, she reckoned that the body had been there since the weekend. Cause of death was by strangulation and, given the nature of the burn mark, probably done with the missing stocking. The depth of the marks around the front of the neck would indicate that the killer had tackled her from behind and used the girl's own weight to kill her. She was not prepared to make a comment about the eyes until she had the girl back in the Instituto.

Felipe and Jorge moved in, dusted the mobile and envelope, which were clean. They opened the envelope, dusted the card inside, also clean. They handed it over to Falcón with raised eyebrows.

¿Por qué tienen que morir aquellos a quienes les encanta el amor?

Why do they have to die, those that love to love?
And on the reverse side was the answer:

Porque tienen el don de la vista perfecta.

Because they have the gift of perfect sight.

Falcón read it out loud and then slipped it into the evidence bag. The Médico Forense conferred with Calderón and the secretaria, who took down notes. Ramírez repeated the sight lesson.

'I don't know what that means,' he said. 'I understand it, but . . . do you know what that means, Inspector Jefe?'

'Well . . . maybe it's ironic,' said Falcón. 'A prostitute does not love to love.'

He changed his mind almost as soon as he'd said it. The sad-eyed, stiffly embracing panda in Eloisa Gómez's bedroom came to mind, along with the thought that maybe the killer had reached that far in.

'And the gift of perfect sight?'

'Maybe as you said, Inspector Jefe,' said Calderón, returning to the conversation, 'these girls see things very clearly.'

'The stocking,' said Falcón. 'The single stocking that was removed . . .'

'He probably put her under the chloroform to get that off her,' said Ramírez.

'Yes, that was probably it,' said Falcón, disappointed by the likely mundanity. He was imagining some breakthrough between the killer and Eloisa Gómez, that they'd achieved some intimacy, until, at the onset of sex, with all its psychological leaking, the killer's true nature was revealed.

'Where was she killed?' said Calderón. 'It has to have been local, doesn't it?'

'And he has to have had transport, too,' said Ramírez.

'Or they could have come here together and then he killed her and hid the body. There must be a lot of gardening rubbish here,' said Falcón, and told Ramírez to get a shot of the girl sent down and run it past the *portero* to see if he recognized her. 'We're going to have to search this cemetery, too.'

Ramírez spoke into his mobile and surveyed the hectares of crosses and mausoleums that stretched off in all directions to the distant palm trees and cypresses at the walls of the cemetery. Falcón looked over the garish flower arrangements, the endless names, the ranks of the dead reaching off up to the blue sky and the high cirrus.

An ambulance crawled up the main avenue at a respectful pace, the blank windscreen made it seem unpeopled, impersonal.

'I'll speak to Comisario Lobo and get some manpower released to search this cemetery,' said Falcón, and Ramírez nodded, pulled a cigarette from the pack with his lips and lit it.

'The eyes,' said Calderón. 'Do you think he removed the eyes here as well?'

'I have it on the authority of a jealous husband I gaoled some years ago in Barcelona that it's not so difficult to do,' said Falcón. 'He did it to his wife who was having an affair. He said they just popped out under his thumbs like a couple of bird's eggs.'

Falcón shuddered at himself retelling the story and the forensics came over to give their report.

'He killed her outside the mausoleum and dragged her in,' said Felipe. 'It was too narrow for him to carry her inside so he had to drag her up the steps and lift her in. Her skirt's all rucked up at the back, the remaining stocking is badly laddered and the back of the bare leg is grazed. We've found plenty of strands of material in the shelving where he's scraped his coat, but there's no blood, saliva or sperm. No discernible footprints either. We did find this in the victim's hair though, which might help you find the killing place –'

Jorge handed over a bag containing rose and chrysanthemum petals, grass and leaves.

'Gardening detritus,' said Felipe and the forensics left.

Calderón signed off the levantamiento del cadaver. The ambulancemen lifted the body into a bag, zipped it up and stretchered it away. The ambulance reversed back down Jesús de la Pasión to the main avenue and, lights flashing, drew stunned glances from a straggle of mourners, baffled by the sight of it in this place. Lobo gave Falcón a squad of fifteen men to search the cemetery. Calderón rejoined him.

'This line, "where the shadows move",' he said. 'If that's what you were afraid of, would you go to a cemetery . . . with anyone, let alone a client? It doesn't make sense.'

'Unless you consider how difficult it is to get a dead body over one of those walls,' said Falcón. 'I think he'd brought her in close . . . close enough to open the door for him to Jiménez's flat and close enough to go to a cemetery with him.'

'The girl was killed Saturday morning,' said Ramírez, coming back from his mobile conversation, 'and we know the killer was here later that day because he was seen at the funeral.'

'Maybe he didn't know where the Jiménez mausoleum was,' said Falcón, 'but he was filming too, so he had a double reason for being here.'

'The grass clippings,' said Calderón.

'If he killed her here, he buried her under the grass clippings, probably assuming that nobody would be taking away gardening detritus on a weekend. If he killed her elsewhere and got the body over the wall, he'd have had to bring her here in a car and he probably didn't want to leave his car parked outside the cemetery walls for too long.'

'This flash of inspiration you were talking about has given him a lot of trouble,' said Calderón.

'It's important to him thematically, and he wants to show us his talent,' said Falcón.

Calderón went back to the Edificio de los Juzgados in a taxi. Falcón and Ramírez had the cemetery emptied and closed off for the rest of the day. Lobo came up with another twelve men and by six o'clock they'd moved through the whole cemetery. A black stocking had been found hanging from the handle of the broken sword of the bronze statue of the torero, Francisco Rivera. A large quantity of dead flowers, grass clippings and leaves were found in a skip close to a rusted metal gate in the wall at the rear of the cemetery. The wall backed on to a factory. A narrow, overgrown passage ran down its entire length. Leaning up against the wall between the factory and the cemetery were some old metal doors and a ladder of the sort used in the cemetery to climb up the high ossuary blocks. The grass in the passage had been trodden down. The passage was only visible to the security guards patrolling the industrial zone if they actually went down it on foot. The skip butted up against the wall. It would have been possible for the killer to have lifted the very small Eloisa Gómez up and over the wall and to have heaved her into the skip.

'That's the second time he's done this to us,' said Falcón.

'Confused us about the killing scenario?' said Ramírez.

'Yes, it's one of his talents . . . to slow the whole process down,' said Falcón.

'We're always having to do double the work,' said Ramírez.

'It's something my father used to say about genius . . . they make everything around them look so slow.'

By 6.30 p.m. Falcón and Ramírez were in the Alameda but found none of Eloisa's group in the square. They went to her room in Calle Joaquín Costa. Falcón knocked on the door of the fat girl, who kept the key to Eloisa's room. She came to the door in a blue towelling dressing gown and pink furry slippers. Her eyes were puffy with sleep but she was instantly alert when she saw the two policemen. Falcón asked for the key and told her to start thinking about the last time she'd seen her friend and to get the other girls to do the same. She didn't have to ask what had happened and handed him the key.

The door opened on the stupid panda. The two men looked around at the pitiful accumulation of a small, hard life. Ramírez nosed amongst the cheap bric-a-brac on the dressing table.

'What are we doing here?' he asked.

'Just looking.'

'Do you think he's been here?'

'Too risky,' said Falcón. 'We need the address and telephone number of her sister. The panda's for her niece.'

Ramírez looked from the panda to his boss and had a vision of Falcón as lost and pathetic, diminished and unconnected.

'I won one of those for my daughter at the Feria last year,' said Ramírez, nodding at the silent guest. 'She loves it.'

'Strange how cuddly toys bring out that instinct,' said Falcón.

Ramírez backed away from any potential intimacy.

'Not such perfect sight,' said Ramírez, looking down on a pair of contact lenses on the bedside table.

'She knew him before,' said Falcón, 'I'm sure of it. Think of all that filming he did to make *La Familia Jiménez*. He'd have seen him going back to the same girl again and again. He'd have wanted to know why.'

'She probably gave the best blow job in town,' said Ramírez crudely.

'There's got to be a reason for it.'

'She looked very young,' said Ramírez. 'Maybe he liked that.'

'His son said he fell for his first wife when she was thirteen.'

'Whatever, Inspector Jefe,' said Ramírez. 'This is all conjecture.'

'What else have we got to structure our ideas?' said Falcón. 'We don't need any more clues with the trail he's leaving.'

'We've still got a prime suspect, according to Juez Calderón,' said Ramírez.

'I haven't forgotten her, Inspector.'

'If she's hired someone and unleashed a madman she might be persuaded that she's not so safe herself,' said Ramírez. 'I still think we should sweat her.'

The girls from Eloisa's group filed past the door on their way to the fat girl's room. Ramírez found Eloisa's address book. They went down the hall to where the girls slouched in the smoke-filled room.

Falcón talked them through what had happened. The only noise was from the click and rasp of cheap lighters and the drawing in of smoke. He asked if there was anybody that Eloisa was seeing outside the business and there was some derisive laughter. He pressed them to think about it and they all said they didn't have to. There was nobody except the sister in Cádiz. He roamed their faces. They had the look of refugees about them. Refugees from life, stuck on the borders of civilization, remote from comfort. He told them they could leave. The fat girl remained.

'There was somebody,' she said, once they'd all left. 'Not a regular, but she saw him more than once. She said he was different.'

'Why didn't you mention this before?' asked Falcón.

'Because I thought she'd got away. That's what she said she was going to do.'

'Start from the beginning,' said Falcón.

'She said he didn't want to have sex with her. He only wanted to talk.'

'One of those,' said Ramírez, and Falcón stabbed him silent with a look.

'He told her he was a writer. He was doing something for a film.'

'What did they talk about?'

'He asked her everything about her life. There was no detail he wasn't interested in. He was particularly interested in what he called "crossing borders".'

'Do you know what he meant by that?'

'The first time she had sex. The first time she had sex for money. The first time she permitted certain things to be done to her. The first time she got pregnant. The first abortion. The first time she was hit. The first time a man pulled a knife on her. The first time a man pushed a gun into her . . . cut her. Those borders.'

'And they only talked?'

'He paid her for sex but they only talked,' she said. 'And by the end they just talked.'

'Did she say what he looked like?' asked Falcón. 'Where he was from? How he spoke? Did he have a name?'

'She called him Sergio.'

'Was it him she went to see on Friday night?'

She shrugged.

'Did you ever see him?'

She shook her head.

'She must have described him.'

'We're careful what we tell each other . . . it can come back on us,' she said. 'She only told me that he was *guapo*. Maybe she talked to her sister more.'

'So you think, if she was going to run away with him, that she had feelings for him?'

'She said that no man had ever spoken to her like he did.'

'Did he talk about himself to her?'

'If he did, she didn't tell me anything.'

'What do you know about Sergio . . . other than a name?'

'I know that he'd done a very dangerous thing,' she said. 'He'd given Eloisa hope.'

'Hope?' said Ramírez, as if this had no weight with him at all.

'Look around you,' said the fat girl. 'Imagine what hope does to you, if you live like this.'

Falcón and Ramírez were back at the Jefatura by 8 p.m. having searched and sealed off Eloisa Gómez's room. They'd found nothing. They went through the address book on Eloisa's retrieved mobile and found no reference to Sergio. Falcón left Ramírez with the paperwork while he went to Tabladilla to keep his appointment with the psychologist. He parked across the street from the building and paced up and down the length of his car, eyeing the plaques on the outside of the door, reluctant to initiate the consultation.

A memory of his father getting mechanics to tinker about inside the engine of the Jaguar, even when it was working perfectly, came back to him. He always said it was "just in case something was about to go wrong". Madness. The point was that Falcón did need some tinkering, but what would happen? What terrible black thread would be teased out of his tightknit brain? Would it all unravel? He saw himself dazed and slack-jawed, staring up at two white-coated assistants as they eased his arms into a surgical gown. Just one small cut and you'll be set adrift from your past. He was already out of control, he saw that, thinking about open brain surgery when all this was going to be was a talk. He wiped his damp palms together, sandwiched a handkerchief between them and crossed the street.

The stairs were either interminable or he was making them so and he had to drive himself through the door at the top. A girl sat behind a desk.

'*Hola*, Sr Falcón,' she said, cheerful, used to dealing with broken minds. 'This is your first time, isn't it?'

She had blonde hair and thick pouting lips. She held out a form for him to fill in. He didn't take it. On the wall beyond the girl was one of his father's paintings of the doorway to the Iglesia Omnium Santorum. Checking the room he found another – one of the larger, less successful abstract landscapes.

'Sr Falcón,' said the girl, standing now, skirt hem at the level of the desk.

He knew he would not be able to stand this. He would not be able to sit in front of someone and discuss his father's life and work and have the man nosing about inside his head, looking for the crimps and creases in the texture of his thoughts and ironing them out. He left without a word. It was the easiest thing he'd done in years. He just walked away.

A ghastly turbulence started up in his chest as he got into the car, but it passed as he drove back home with the windows down. He walked to the British Institute and sat at the back of the class and half listened through a session of conditionals. I would be feeling better now if I had been to the shrink. I'd be singing my madness out on the couch if I hadn't lost my nerve. It would help if I could talk to someone.

He looked around the students in the class. Pedro. Juan. Sergio.

Lola. Sergio? His thoughts grew strange and large in his head. Sergio. We might as well call this madman Sergio. He can talk. He sees things clearly. He gets inside and turns things over. He'd talked to Eloisa, given her hope and taken her hopeless life from her. Why don't I talk to him? He's telling me his story, why don't I tell him mine? Let him wrench these horrible creatures from my brain.

'Javier?' said the teacher.

'I'd like to apologize if I've been talking out loud.'

Falcón laughed to himself, grinned at the way the larger world outside had been diminished by the high-vaulted gothics of his own mind. He could live in here for years and, as soon as he'd thought it, he threw himself out, like a heretic from a cathedral. He delved into the machinery of language. It was so easy to fit words together, so relaxing. It was only the meaning that bled into the spaces around them that troubled.

He attached himself to some other students and went for a drink. They walked to the Bar Barbiana in the Calle Albareda. They drank beer, ate tapas – *atún encebollado, tortillitas de camarones.* The students didn't belong with the clientele of this bar who were, as they were saying, *muy pijo* – upper class – probably with fincas in the country, until Lola looked embarrassed and they changed the subject because they thought Falcón was *muy pija* in his suit and tie.

They split up before Javier was ready to go home. Was he ever ready to go home these days? His house was a prison, his room a cell, the bed a rack on which he was stretched out every night. He walked around town, stood close to groups in well-lit bars, put his beer down amongst theirs, until they noticed him and sealed him off.

He ended the night under the high palms and the deeper darkness of the massive rubber trees in the Plaza del Museo de las Bellas Artes. The *botellón* was in full swing, the air full of hashish, clinking glass and the low roar of humans at their leisure.

Extracts from the Journals of Francisco Falcón

30th June 1941, Ceuta
Pablito came into my room this afternoon, lay down on my bed, rolled a
cigarette on his chest and lit it. He has something to tell me. I know this
but I always ignore him. I was drawing a Berber woman I'd seen in the
market that morning. Pablito's nonchalance bristled on the bed. He
smoked like a cow would, always chewing.

'We're going to Russia,' he said. 'To hit the Reds. Kick them up the
ass on their own soil.'

I put down my pencil and turned to him.

'General Orgaz volunteered us. Colonel Esperanza has been asked to
form a regiment. A battalion is going to be made up out of the Legion,
the Regulares and the Flechas, here in Ceuta.'

That's how I remember Pablito's little announcement. Banal. I'm so
bored I'm going along with it. So little has happened in the last few
years I forgot I had this journal. My diary is in my drawings. I'm
unused to writing. Four pages cover two years. Isn't this the rhythm of
life? Periods of change, followed by long periods of getting used to the
change until you feel compelled to change again. Boredom is my only
motive. It's probably Pablito's, too, but he dresses it up in
anti-communist rhetoric. He doesn't know the first thing about
communism.

8th July 1941, Ceuta
There was a good turnout in the port to see us off. General Orgaz
stirred us all up. If we didn't suspect it before, we know it now – we're a
political device. (Am I sounding like Oscar now?) The uniform says
something about what's going on in Madrid: we're wearing the red
berets of the Carlists, the blue shirts of the Falange and the khaki
trousers of the Legion. Royalists, fascists and military all satisfied and
implicated.

The Germans have been at the Pyrenees for months. Rumour had it that they were going to send a strike force to take Gibraltar, which sounded too much like invasion. We're being sent to Russia to make the Germans feel better about Spain, to make it look as if we're on their side. The newspaper tells us that Stalin is the real enemy, but no mention of us entering the war. Games are being played and we are in the middle. I have a feeling of doom about this whole expedition, but beyond the harbour walls we pick up a school of dolphin, who escort us most of the way to Algeciras, which I take to be a good omen.

10th July 1941, Seville
We've been put in the Pineda barracks at the southern end of the city. We had a night on the town. We didn't pay for a single drink. The last time some of our number were here they were hacking men to death on the streets of Triana. Now we're the heroes, sent to keep communism at bay. Five years is an eon in human relations.

   Despite the brutal heat, I like Seville. The dark, cool bars. The people with short memories and a need to express joy. I think this is a place to live in.

18th July 1941, Grafenwöhr, Germany
We changed trains at Hendaye in southern France. The French shook their fists and hurled rocks at the carriages as we passed through. At our first stop in Germany, Karlsruhe station was full of people cheering and singing 'Deutschland, Deutschland über alles'. *They covered the train in flowers. Now we're somewhere northeast of Nürnberg. Weather grey. New recruits and most of the* guripas *already depressed, missing home. Us veterans depressed because we've just been told that the División Azul, as we're called, is not going to be motorized but horsedrawn.*

8th August 1941, Grafenwöhr
Pablito has a black eye and a cut lip. He doesn't like the Germans any more than the communists he hasn't yet met. The men, the guripas, like wearing their blue shirts and red berets instead of the regulation German uniform. A fight broke out in the Rathskeller in town. 'They tell us we don't know how to take care of our weapons,' says Pablito. 'But the real reason is that we're fucking all their women and the girls have never had it so good.' I don't know if we'll ever fit in with our new allies. The food stinks worse than the latrines, their tobacco smokes like hay and there is no wine. While Colonel Esperanza has taken delivery of

a Studebaker President, we have been supplied with 6,000 horses from Serbia. It should take us two months just to get the animals trained, but we're moving up to the front at the end of the month. Pablito's heard that we're going to march on Moscow, but I see the way the Germans look at us. They put a high value on discipline, obedience, command and neatness. Our secret weapon is our passion. But it is too secret for them to see. Only in battle will they understand the flame that burns inside every guripa. One shout of 'A mí la legión!' and the whole floor will rise up and ram the Russians back to Siberia.

27th August 1941, somewhere in Poland
Our reputation with local women precedes us. We've been forbidden to have anything to do with Jewish women, who we recognize by the yellow star they have to wear, or the Polish women (panienkas). We heard that 10 Company of 262 marched with blown-up condoms attached to their rifles as a protest.

2nd September 1941, Grodno
First signs of battle on the march to Grodno . . . outskirts of the town have been levelled. The centre is full of rubble, which the Jews have been put to work cleaning up. They are exhausted as their rations are meagre. Pablito's attitude to the Germans is hardening by the day. He now finds them sinister. We're to be toughened up by being marched to the front. Pablito has fallen for a blonde, green-eyed panienka called Anna.

12th September 1941, Ozmiana
Colonel Esperanza's Studebaker has taken a beating on the roads. It won't be long before he's marching like the rest of us. A black Mercedes pulled up alongside the other day and General Muñoz Grandes got out and had lunch with us. Pablito and the guripas were in an uproar. He inspires us, as he is one of the few commanders who understand what it's like to be an ordinary soldier.

16th September 1941, Minsk
Pablito says there's a compound outside town where the Russian prisoners are kept. They're given no food. The locals throw what they can over the fence and are shot at for their trouble. Pablito is happy – his panienka has turned up in Minsk. I'm happy because the chickpeas and olive oil arrived yesterday.
   Already cold. Autumn chill in the air.

9th October 1941, Novo Sokol'niki
We're stalled outside Velikje Luki – rail lines blown up by partisans. We forage in town and end up roasting dead horses over charcoal pits in the rail yard, singing songs, drinking potato vodka. Pablito, lovesick for Anna, sings very well. Flamenco on the steppe.

10th October 1941, Dno
Off-loaded here on to different gauge trains. Old woman hanging from a lamppost. Partisan. Guripas shocked. 'What is this war?' one of them asks, as if he didn't know what had happened in his own country three years ago.
  Next stop Novgorod and the front. We're on combat pay from now on. Reds rule the skies. Supplies low. Few spares. Partisans. No Pablito – he didn't show up for evening Mass.

11 October 1941, Dno
Occupation measures in force here so I have to accompany the German patrol on a house-to-house search for Pablito. We don't find him. In one house I'm astonished to see Anna, his panienka, working with some Russian civilians. I can't think how she could have got so far. Outside in the street I tell the German NCO and two men go in and haul her out. The other women start screaming and the Germans beat them down with rifle butts. They force Anna to her knees in the street and ask about Pablito. She denies everything but knows why she's been chosen. The NCO, a colossal brute, takes his glove off and gives her four savage slaps to her face that leave her head hanging like a torn doll. They take her to a burnt-out building across the street. Anna's scarf comes loose and her blonde hair falls down. The men murmur. The NCO has a face like tank armour plates. The grey afternoon turns bleaker. The temperature drops. More questions asked, more denials follow. They strip her naked. She is blue white underneath. She sobs from the cold and fear. They twist her arms up behind her back and lift her off the floor. She screams. The NCO asks for a bayonet and uses the blade to flick her hardened nipples and that does it. The terror of cold steel. She tells how she was forced to lead Pablito into a trap for the partisans. They let her dress again. The patrol takes all the women away. I return and make my report to Major Pérez Pérez.

12th October 1941, Dno
In the morning Lt Martínez orders me to put together an eleven-man
firing squad. Two male communist partisans and Pablito's panienka
have been delivered to us for execution. We put them against the wall in
the freight yard. The girl cannot stand and there are no posts to tie her
to. Lt Martínez tells the two men to hold her up between them. They
arrange themselves like a family photograph. Lt. Martínez walks back to
our line and shouts 'Carguen!', 'Apunten', and on the word 'Fuego' she
looks up. I shoot her in the mouth.

A patrol found Pablito later that day, hanging by some wire from a
tree. He'd been stripped naked, his eyes had been gouged out and his
genitals cut off. We had a funeral Mass for him, our first casualty.
Pablito, the anti-communist, who died without firing a shot.

13th October 1941, Podberez'e
We left the train under heavy artillery fire and deployed south of the
town along the river Volkhov. There's thick forest behind us, full of
partisans. Across the Volkhov are the Russians. Thick mud all around,
known as the rasputitsa, *difficult to move. Frost at night.*

30th October 1941, Sitno
We've been withdrawn after a fierce week and some bad losses. This war
is less understandable by the moment. We attacked Dubrovka the other
day. We thought to outflank the Russian defences and come at them
from behind. As soon as we reformed south of the town we were hit by
artillery and in getting out of the sector found ourselves in a minefield.
What was a minefield doing there? There were bodies everywhere.
García with his left leg missing and holding his crotch, shouting, 'A mí
la Legión!' We closed ranks and attacked the Russians. We went mad
when we got to them and would have hacked them all to death if we had
not been so exhausted. Lt Martínez tells us that the Russian units all
have political officers whose job it is to maintain discipline. They sow
mines behind their front-line troops to stop them from retreating. Who
are we fighting here? Not the local people. As soon as we take prisoners
they become as useful to us as our own men.

1st November 1941, Sitno
I know heat. I understand heat. I've seen what it does to men. I've seen
men die from drinking water. But cold, I don't know cold. The landscape
has hardened around us. The trees are brittle with frost. The ground

beneath the drifting powdery snow is like iron. Our boots ring against it.
A pick makes no impression. We have to use explosives to dig ourselves
in. My piss turns instantly to ice as it hits the ground. And our Russian
prisoners tell us that it is not yet cold.

8th November 1941
There's ice on the Volkhov. It's difficult to believe that it will freeze
one-metre solid and completely change the strategy of this little war.
Already soldiers can cross the river on planks. They tried to move horses
as well, but one came off the planks and fell through the ice. In its
frenzy it tore the reins from its handler, who watched as the terrified
animal tried to clamber out. It was surprising how short a time it took
for such a large beast to succumb to the cold. Within a minute its back
legs ceased to operate. In two minutes its forelegs were still. By afternoon
ice had formed around its middle and the animal was frozen solid, still
with the terror moment alive in its eyes. It has become a monument to
horror. No sculptor could have done better given the task by some mad
municipality. The guripas new to the front can't take their eyes off it.
Some look back to the west bank of the river and realize that civilization
is behind them and that beyond the Ice Horse there won't be the expected
glory, the passionate cause, but rather a blood-slackening sight of the
coldest chamber of the human heart.

9th November 1941
In Nikltkino I came across a scene from the Middle Ages. A Russian
prisoner with a hammer was moving among the ranks of his dead
comrades, breaking their fingers, which still clutched their weapons. None
of them wore boots. They'd all been stolen. With the fingers and arms
broken and the weapons removed, their furs and quilted jackets can be
taken. I now look like the Wolf Man and have recently acquired a
bearskin hat. The front is now extended to include Otonskii and Posad.

18th November 1941, Dubrovka
The Russians have counterattacked the limits of our new front. Posad hit
with everything – mortar, anti-tank and artillery. We got it the next
day, followed by a full charge from the Reds. They started with a
resounding 'Urrah!' and something else which, when they got closer, we
heard as: 'Ispanskii kaput!' Our artillery broke them up; we mowed
down the rest like wheat – which was how the Russians charged,
standing upright, never crouched. Perhaps they thought it unmanly.

They regrouped and hit us again at night and we met them on the snow-covered plain under the slow-falling flares, the woods black behind them. Unreal. The night so silent before the mayhem. We threw grenades and followed up with a bayonet charge. The Reds dispersed. As they merged back into the woods we heard our new recruits, who'd just experienced their first charge, shout after them: 'Otro toro! Otro toro!'

5th December 1941
I am back at the front after a flesh wound sent me to the field hospital. I never want to see that place again. Not even the cold could suppress the stench; rather it has frozen it into my nostrils permanently.

The cold has reached a new dimension: −35°C. When men die from heat they go mad, they start jabbering, their brain in a rage. In the cold a man just drifts away. One moment he is there, perhaps even drawing on a cigarette and the next he is gone. Men are dying from the cerebral fluid freezing in their heads under their steel helmets. I'm glad of my fur hat. With the drop in temperature the Russians have started talking to us in Spanish, using Republicans to translate. They promise warmth, food and entertainment. We tell them to fuck their whore mothers.

28th December 1941
Christmas Eve in profound cold. The men recite poetry and sing about Spain – the heat, the pine trees, mother's cooking and women. The Russians are ruthless and attack on Christmas Day. The numbers they throw at us are appalling. We've heard of their punishment battalions. Political undesirables are sent to run at our guns. They fall three or four deep and the real soldiers come running over the top of them, using the bodies as a ramp. We are in the most Godless place on earth with barely any daylight and death all around. Atrocity reported in Udarnik in the north of our sector – guripas found nailed to the ground by icepicks. Our rage peters out with the cold and hunger.

18th January 1942, Novgorod
The Russians smell our weakness and, just when we think it is so cold that we'll never move again, they attack. We're sent to Teremets to help the Germans. We try to dissuade the endless waves of Russians by using some of our old African tricks. We strip prisoners of all useful clothing, cut off their trigger fingers, split their noses, cut off an ear and send them back. It has no effect. The next day they're running at

us again with clubs and bayonets. I was lucky to get out of Teremets alive and only made it back because I was sent to the rear with a broken leg.

17th June 1942, Riga
Complications set in with the leg after a bout of pneumonia. I was too weak to move and missed the return battalion in the spring. They reset the leg. I caught typhus. The wound wouldn't heal. I hardly knew what was happening to me for five months. I had a visit from the new commander of 269, Lt Col Cabrera, who has asked me to go back up to the front with the newly manned 'Tía Bernarda', as my unit is nicknamed. The war has gone better for the Germans recently and they are back in control of all territory west of the Volkhov and are beginning to turn the screw on Leningrad.

9th February 1943
A Ukrainian deserter came over today and told us more than we wanted to know about what was happening in Kolpino. Huge numbers of batteries were being brought up behind the town, hundreds of trucks unloading shells. The enemy were ready to attack tomorrow. After all this waiting we didn't believe him, but he showed us his clean underwear and that was enough. The Russians always issue clean underwear before an attack. It means you're going to die, but you can do it with dignity. It was why he had deserted. But why, with all that firepower behind him, did he come over to us, who are about to receive it? Vodka does something to the Slavic brain.

The big Kolpino guns started lobbing shells at our positions south. The infantry blew up their minefields in front of their lines. Our own pathetic artillery started up and the Russian got the psychology just right . . . they didn't even dignify it with a reply.

Night came at five in the afternoon. The cold crept inside our bones. We're all scared, but the inevitability brings out the determination. The Reds' tank engines started up in unison with a deafening roar. The motors run all night, the Russians worried they'll freeze.

'Tomorrow the bulls will run,' says one of the sergeants. I go out to check the sentries. The cold makes them slack. As I chat to the men, the pine trees in front of the peat bogs bristle where thousands of soldiers rush through the woods to take up their positions for tomorrow's attack.

10th February 1943
Nothing the Ukrainian deserter told us prepared us for this. At 6.45 the
Kolpino guns opened fire on us. One thousand pieces of artillery fired at
once. The devastation, in a matter of minutes, was as complete as after
an earthquake. Whole hillsides came away, erupted, as if under volcanic
pressure. The frost-brittle pine trees burst into flame. The snow around
us instantly melted. Heavily fortified positions behind us disappeared into
smoking earth. We were cut off. No phones and no visibility as the air
filled with black smoke and the stink of peat. We crouched under a
torrent of earth, planks, barbed wire, lumps of ice and then the limbs.
Arms, legs, helmeted heads, a half-roasted torso. It was the opening
statement. It said: 'You will not survive.'

Some of the men were sobbing, but not through fear, just unable to
contain their shock. We waited. The inevitable Urrah! *and the Reds*
charged. They hurled themselves into our minefields and after ten metres
they were all down. The next wave followed. Another ten metres and
they were all down. As they reached the edge of the minefield we opened
fire and mowed down line after line of them. The corpses were five deep
and still they came. We blasted away, our machine-gun barrels glowing
dull red even in the deep cold of the morning.

The Reds sent their new KV-1 tanks towards their objective – the
Sinevino heights. Our 37mm shells bounced off the armour.

We were cut off to our left and rear. They pounded our position. Our
Captain was hit in the arm. The smaller T-34 tanks smashed through
our line, infantry behind, which we mowed down, blood streaking across
their white capes. They hit us with anti-tank and mortar until we
couldn't think. We had no machine guns by the end of it. No automatic
rifles. Any Russian who got close enough was dragged in and stabbed.
More mortar fire. I wanted to laugh, our position was so desperate. The
Captain was hit in the leg. He hopped around, exhorting us to stand
firm. 'Arriba España! Viva la muerte!' *We were stupid with battle.*
Our faces were all blackened, apart from the eye sockets, which were
white. We slept where we stood. The Captain started a final rousing
speech: 'Spain is proud of you. I am proud of you, it is completely my
privilege to have commanded you in today's battle . . .' He was
interrupted by twenty Russian rifles pointing down into our trench.

12th February 1943, Sablino
The first question from the Reds was: 'Who's got a watch?' Our two
remaining officers had their watches taken. Four of our wounded were

bayonetted where they lay. They marched us down the Moscow–
Leningrad road. The scene of devastation was so immense, the Russian
casualties so thick on the ground, that it was understandable that every
Red we met should be blind drunk. Some of our guards drifted off to
various drinking parties on the way. As we reached the river two of the
Russians escorted the Captain away for interrogation. That left four men
to take us to the barbed-wire corral at Ian Izhora. We didn't fancy a
night out in the open. We talked it through in Spanish and at the signal
hit them. A single punch to the throat of the guard nearest me and I
was off the log road and running for the peat bog, zig-zagging over the
ground. Their aim was wild. We made it to an old anti-tank ditch and
ran along it to where our own lines had been. We saw only drunk and
sleeping Russians. We made it back to the main road where we heard
the words, 'Alto! ¿Quién vive?' We replied, 'España', and fell into
waiting arms.

13th February 1943
What I saw a few days ago has diminished me. I am less human after
what I have seen and done. Glory in battle is a thing of the past.
Individual heroics disappear in the miasma of modern warfare, where
thundering machines annihilate and vaporize. One is brave and should
feel glorious to have even entered the arena. I have and I have survived,
and I have never felt more lonely. Even after I ran away from home I
was never as lonely as I am now. I know no one and no one knows me. I
am cold, but from the inside out. In my wolf-fur coat and bearskin hat
I am a lone animal, with no pack, out on the snow plain where the
horizon has merged with the landscape so that there is no beginning and
no end. I am tired with a tiredness that crushes my bones, so that I only
wish to sleep with dreams as white as the snow and in a cold that I know
will carry me away painlessly.

9th September 1943
I haven't written a word since Krasni Bor and now that I read it back I
know why. I am gathered under Return Battalion 14 and that gives me
the strength to face the page again. Today the Russians told us that the
Italians had capitulated. They put up a poster in huge red letters:
'Españoles, Italia se ha capitulada! Pasares a nosotros.' Some
guripas slipped under the wire and tore down the sign and put up their
own: 'No somos Italianos.' For once the Germans agreed.
  My mind is set on home, except I have no home. All I want is to go

back to Spain, to sit in the dry heat of Andalusia with a glass of tinto. I decide that I will go to Seville and Seville will be my home.

14th September 1943
We marched away from the front to Volosovo, about 60 km. I expected to be happy, most of the guripas were singing. I am still plagued by fatigue. I hoped that moving away from the front would help, but my spirit has darkened and I can barely speak. I sweat at night, my pillow is sodden even though it is not hot. I never slip into sleep. My dropping off is a series of jolts, of body spasms that start in my middle and crack up into my head like a bullwhip. My left hand shakes and has a tendency to go spastic. I wake up with the feeling that my hands are not my own and I am terrified from the first moment.

I look back through my drawings and it is not the Leningrad skyline with the dome of St Isaac's Cathedral and the Admiralty spire, nor is it the portraits of my comrades and the Russian prisoners that move me. It is the winter landscapes. Sheets of white paper with the vague smudges of buildings, izbas or pine trees. They are an abstraction of a mental state. A frozen wilderness in which even the certainties have only a wavering presence. I show one to another veteran of the Russian front and he looks at it for some time and I think he's seen in it what I have, but he hands it back with the words: 'That's a funny-looking wolf.' I am perplexed by this, but eventually it amuses me and it gives me my first glimmer of hope since February.

7th October 1943, Madrid
Today I officially left the Legion after twelve years service. I have a kit bag and a satchel of my books and drawings. I have enough money to last me a year. I am going to Andalucía, to the autumnal light, the piercing blue skies and the sensual heat. I will draw and paint for a year and see what comes of it. I am going to drink wine and learn to be lazy.

Because of the American blockade there's very little fuel for public transport. I will have to walk to Toledo.

19

Wednesday, 18th April 2001, Falcón's house, Calle Bailén, Seville

The disasters of sleep – all that free falling and spitting out mouthfuls of teeth and examinations not reached in time and cars with no brakes and precipices with crumbling edges – how do we survive them all? We should die of fright night after night. Falcón came hurtling into the enveloping darkness with these thoughts plummeting down the lift shaft of his mind. Was he surviving them, his own personal disasters? He only survived them by banishing sleep, crashing out of his falling empire and into the cracked glass of his own world.

He went for a run by the dark river. Dawn broke and on the way back he stopped to watch a rowing eight. The hull of the shell sliced through the water, dipping with each lurch of power from the harmonious crew. He wanted to be out there with them, part of their unconsciously brilliant machine. He thought about his own team, its lack of cohesion, its fragmented efforts, and his leadership. He was out of touch, had lost control, was failing to communicate direction to the investigation. He braced himself, dropped to the ground and throughout his fifty press-ups told the cobbles that today would be different.

The Jefatura was silent. He was early again. He glanced down Ramírez's report. The portero did not remember seeing Eloisa Gómez going into the cemetery, which was not surprising. Serrano had completed his check of all hospitals and medical suppliers and there were no records of thefts or unusual sales. He read through Eloisa Gómez's autopsy. The Médico Forense had revised her time of death to later on Saturday morning, around 9 a.m. The contents of her stomach revealed a partially digested meal of *solomillo*, pork fillet, which must have been consumed after midnight. There was also a practically undigested snack of what was probably *chocolate y churros.* The alcohol content in her blood showed that she'd been drinking most of the night. Falcón imagined the killer taking Eloisa out as if she was his girlfriend, treating her to an expensive dinner, taking her to a bar or club and then the classic early-morning snack – and then what? Back to my place? Maybe he hadn't chloroformed her but rolled the stocking off her leg, kissing her thigh, her knee, her foot. Then, just as she'd fallen back on the bed to be loved properly, perhaps even for the first time, she'd sensed something and opened her eyes to find his face over her, the black stocking a taut, dark crack between his two fists and his eyes intent with the relish of a live throat struggling and quivering under his restraining hands.

Except that he had chloroformed her. There were traces. Falcón moved on from the stomach and blood analysis. The vagina and anus showed signs of recent sexual activity. There were traces of spermicide, but no semen in the vagina and an oil-based lubricant in the anus, which was distended from frequent penetration. Falcón's mind slipped again and he saw Eloisa Gómez servicing her clients in the backs of cars and in her room until she got the call, the call she'd been waiting for all day. The call she'd been thinking of as her disembodied voice sobbed and whimpered under the bestial intrusions of her trade. The call that touched her so lightly, the words like a feather on a child's ear, and it moved her, turned her, flipped her stomach over her heart. Such a gross seduction of some- one who would start when the shadows moved, could only have been pulled off by another who had made a study of human nature with his own very specific purposes in mind. In his own way the killer was as brutally demanding as any client.

The only interesting thing to be derived from the report was that it looked as if the killer had taken Eloisa Gómez to the cemetery on Saturday morning, probably when it first opened, and had killed her there.

Ramírez arrived with the rest of the group at 8.30 a.m. They were briefed on the latest developments and given the profile of the killer, who would now be referred to as 'Sergio'. If the killer had strangled the girl in the cemetery on Saturday morning then it was clear that he'd returned at night to put her in the Jiménez mausoleum. This would mean that he probably had transport and also accommodation in Seville. This galvanized the group. The idea that he was local made it somehow personal. Fernández, Baena and Serrano would take the area in and around the cemetery and try to find someone who'd seen Eloisa Gómez there on Saturday morning. The killer may have parked his car in the vicinity when he came back to deal with the body, so the security people in the industrial zone would have to be interviewed, given that the narrow passage at the back of the cemetery was the likely way in for Sergio.

A different strategy was going to be used on Sra Jiménez. Ramírez would ask to look at the packing cases held in the Mudanzas Triana warehouse and also date all the different shots in the *Familia Jiménez* video, to see if there was a pattern to Sergio's filming.

Sub-Inspector Pérez provided the list of directors of major building contractors still existing who had been involved in the development of the Expo '92 site. Falcón sent him down to Mudanzas Triana to continue Baena's work interviewing the employees. He wanted to know if any odd people had been seen in the depot and to find out about the storage warehouse, who ran it and who had access to it.

Alone, Falcón looked down the list of building companies and counted forty-seven. He consulted Pérez's original list and found that only one company had ceased to exist since the completion of the Expo site – MCA Consultores S.A.

Falcón went to the Chamber of Commerce and looked up MCA, whose activities were described as building security consultants, giving advice on structure, design and materials in high-traffic buildings. He flicked through three years of accounts in which the company had generated between 400 million and 600 million pesetas a year until its closure at the end of 1992. An address was given on República de Argentina. The directors of the company leapt off the page: Ramón Salgado, Eduardo Carvajal, Marta Jiménez and Firmin León. He wondered what Ramón Salgado knew about building security – about as much as Raúl Jiménez's incapacitated daughter, Marta. At least Comisario León had a job that was vaguely connected, but it did not persuade Falcón that this wasn't just a shell company channelling funds to Raúl Jiménez and his valued friends. And Eduardo Carvajal . . . why did that name mean something to him?

He photocopied the documents and went back to the Jefatura. As he pulled into the car park he remembered that Carvajal's name had come up in a case that was still being talked about when he'd arrived from Madrid to take up his new post. The police computer revealed that Eduardo Carvajal had been part of a convicted paedophile ring but had never faced trial. He'd been killed in a car crash on the Costa del Sol in 1998. He called Comisario Lobo for a meeting.

Before going up he took his messages, which included one from the Cádiz Police, saying they were bringing Eloisa Gómez's sister up for the identification of the body and another from his doctor, asking why he'd failed to keep his appointment. He called Dr Valera and told him about his father's paintings in the waiting room.

'Has it occurred to you, Javier, that this is something you should talk about?'

'No,' he said, 'but if it did, then I would not want to talk to somebody who . . .'

'Who what?' said Valera.

'Who thinks he knows my father.'

'You have to credit these people with more intelligence . . .'

'Do I?' said Falcón. 'You never went to his openings, Dr Fernando.'

'This might be difficult,' said Valera. 'He was a very famous man.'

'But not everybody is interested in art.'

They hung up. Falcón went up to see Lobo, who took the photocopies and pored over them like a man about to feast on small children. He asked how Falcón had come across the documents.

'Of all the companies directly involved in the building of Expo '92, this was the only one that had ceased to exist. I asked Sub-Inspector Pérez –'

'You know Pérez and Ramírez have been friends for years?' Lobo interrupted.

'I've noticed they talk.'

'How relevant is this to the investigation?'

'With the killing of Eloisa Gómez I think this case has taken a different turn,' said Falcón. 'The soured business relationship may have been an initial motive but now, I think, this killer is operating on his own.'

'I've heard Ramírez has other ideas and Juez Calderón, too.'

'I've sent Inspector Ramírez round to see Sra Jiménez on his own. He'll apply a different kind of pressure to me. We'll see if he's satisfied or not,' said Falcón. 'As for Juez Calderón, I think he's open-minded. He has a practical, rather than obsessive, attitude to our prime suspect.'

'You think Ramírez obsessive?'

'Sra Jiménez is just the kind of woman that Inspector Ramírez despises. I think she represents a change in the order of things that he is not yet ready for.'

Lobo nodded, went back to the documents.

'Who on this list could you talk to privately?' he asked.

'Ramón Salgado, but he's away until the end of the week. I've been trying to talk to him since we met at the funeral. He offered me some inside information on Raúl Jiménez.'

'What sort of information?'

'Untrustworthiness in their exclusive world.'

'Any reason why he should be believed?' asked Lobo. 'He must at the very least be a friend of Raúl Jiménez to be on this list.'

'I have my doubts about him.'

'And what does this information cost you?'

'Access to my father's studio,' said Falcón, and remembered an exchange with Consuelo Jiménez. 'They know each other, Salgado and Sra Jiménez. She has been reticent about their relationship. She says they met at one of my father's evenings, but they might go even further back than that. She was in the art world in Madrid and Salgado circulated in that world, too.'

'I think you have to speak to Salgado, but face to face,' said Lobo. 'And these documents are between us . . . you understand?'

Lobo made eye contact and slipped the papers into his drawer. Falcón took it as a dismissal.

'I had no idea how political your appointment would become,' said Lobo, to the back of Falcón's head. 'The forces are ranged against us now. We are smaller but have the advantage of being more intelligent. We must not cross the moral line, though. I hope your arrangement with Salgado is as you say.'

Falcón went straight to the toilet and took an Orfidal with a cupped hand of water.

Eloisa Gómez's sister, Gloria, looked only marginally older than her sibling, but she had none of her confidence. She sat in the passenger seat, pressed up against the door, arms folded across her chest, as they made their way through the traffic to the Instituto Anatómico Forense. She had a sharp, foxy face that had no small talk in it. She was held in, closed and alone in a world where nobody was to be trusted.

'Did you know what your sister did for a living?' asked Falcón.

'Yes.'

'Did she talk about it?' he asked, and Gloria misunderstood.

'We did the same work . . . for a while,' she said. 'Until I got pregnant.'

'I meant more recently,' said Falcón. 'Did she talk about what was going on in her life?'

Silence. A sideways look told him that he did not have her confidence. He started again.

'This person who killed Eloisa murdered one of her clients as well. It's possible he will kill again. We know that Eloisa knew him. He passed himself off as a writer. They became friends and perhaps even something more than that. I think Eloisa had begun to see him as a way out of this life . . .'

'He *was* that,' she said flatly, which silenced Falcón, so that she added, 'When a girl got *SIDA* we pointed to the *SALIDA*.'

'She said his name was . . .'

'Sergio,' filled in Gloria.

'Did she talk about Sergio?'

'I told her to forget Sergio. I told her he was a fantasy and to be careful of him.'

'Why?'

'Because he was giving her hope and that makes you see things differently. You start believing in possibilities. You overlook things. You make mistakes.'

'You were right.'

'This is what happens when you trust someone –' she said, and lifted her hair at the neck to show the shiny, fossilized skin of a serious burn. 'It goes all the way down my back.'

'So you got out?'

'I had a choice: the work or poverty. I chose poverty over pain and death.'

'But this didn't persuade Eloisa?'

'Nothing had ever happened to her,' said Gloria. 'A knife had been pulled on her, sure. Somebody pointed a gun at her head once. She'd been slapped around, but she didn't carry any scars. I knew, though, as soon as she started talking about Sergio, that he'd singled her out.'

She unfolded her arms and they hung limp at her sides as if she was utterly defeated by life, as if all there was to add to the sum total of her experiences was the guilt of the survivor.

'What did she tell you about Sergio?' he asked, before she sank without trace.

'She said he was guapo. They're always guapo. She said he was like us.'

'Like *you?*' asked Falcón.

'Eloisa and I used to call ourselves *las forasteras,*' she said. 'The outsiders. We called our clients *los otros.* The others . . . but she said *he* wasn't.'

'And what made her say that?'

'Everything she said about him made *me* think that he was one of los otros. He was educated, well dressed, he had a car and an apartment.'

'She didn't talk about what type of car and which apartment?'

'He wasn't stupid,' she said. 'Los otros were always stupid. In that respect he was different.'

'So what had happened to Sergio to make him un forastero?'

'She thought he might be a foreigner or have foreign blood in him. He looked Spanish. He dressed Spanish. He spoke Spanish. But he was different.'

'North African?'

'She didn't say that and Eloisa never liked those people. She never went with them. She would not have been drawn to him if he had that look. She thought he had perhaps been away a long time or had a mixed education.'

They arrived at the Instituto. It was silent and empty. They viewed the body behind the glass. The eyes had somehow been filled out. Gloria Gómez put her hands up to the glass and pressed her forehead to it. Distress creaked out of her like suffering furniture.

'Are either of your parents still alive?' he asked the back of her head, whose hair was thinning already, her cheap coat split on the shoulder. She rolled her forehead from side to side on the glass.

'Would Eloisa have had any reason to go to the San Fernando Cemetery?'

Gloria turned her back to her dead sister.

'She went there whenever she could,' said Gloria. 'Her daughter is buried there.'

'Her daughter?'

'She had a little girl when she was fifteen. She died at three months.'

They drove back to the Jefatura in silence. Falcón made one last effort in the car park to see if Eloisa had mentioned anything about Sergio's appearance.

'She said he had beautiful hands,' was all he could get out of her.

The phone was ringing as he came into his office. It was Dr Fernando Valera telling him that he'd solved his problem, that he'd found a clinical psychologist who he could guarantee was not interested in art. Falcón was in no mood to discuss it.

'Her name is Alicia Aguado. She'll see you in her house, Javier,' said the doctor, giving him an address in Calle Vidrio. 'Clinical psychology is a very rigorous training and she's combined it with some . . . unusual techniques of her own. She's very good. I know how difficult it is to initiate these things, but I want you to see this woman. You're already desperate. It's important.'

He hung up thinking how everybody was seeing his desperation, smelling it, Sergio, too. Ramírez came in and sat with his feet stretched out.

'Did Sra Jiménez crack?' asked Falcón.

Ramírez brushed something imaginary from his tie as if he was about to share a sexual confidence – no, a triumph.

'I bet she wears expensive underwear,' he said. 'And thongs in summer.'

'I see she's won you over,' said Falcón.

'I've called Pérez at the Mudanzas Triana warehouse and told him to pick up the packing case with the home-movie kit in it,' said Ramírez. 'She released it, no problem at all. But you might be interested in what she added as I was leaving.'

Falcón wound him on with his finger.

'She said: "You take that case and only that case. If you look in any of the others you can be sure that none of it will be admissible as evidence."'

Falcón asked him to repeat himself, which he did. He picked it up more clearly the second time – Ramírez was lying and badly, too. He doubted that Consuelo Jiménez would be so unsubtle.

'What about dating the takes from the *Familia Jiménez* tape?'

'She said she would look at it but she was very busy at the moment and that she wouldn't be able to get down to it until after the Feria.'

'Helpful.'

'It's difficult when you're so bereft,' said Ramírez.

20

Falcón sat at home, his fork hovering over his untouched lunch, thinking not about Ramírez but Comisario León, who had not reached his position without considerable political talent. If León was keeping in touch with his investigation via Ramírez and allowing this pressure to be applied to Consuelo Jiménez, who presumably knew nothing about MCA, what did that mean, given that the Comisario had been a director of the consultancy? Falcón put his fork down as a wave of paranoia shuddered through him like nausea. They were going to take him out at the first opportunity. While the details of MCA stayed dormant, Comisario León was happy for them to keep knocking at Consuelo Jiménez's heavy door. If they leaked, he was finished.

They reconvened after lunch to watch some of Raúl Jiménez's old home movies. Pérez, who'd brought them up from Mudanzas Triana, joined the session. He'd also reported that the warehouse had a single entrance and that all the long-term storage was in one area at the back of the building. Each client had a locked cage for cases and furniture. All the packing cases were sealed with tape. The tape dated back to the time when the cases were stored, so if somebody had opened them it would be obvious. Raúl Jiménez's cases were amongst the oldest pieces stored in the warehouse. All Mudanzas Triana personnel had access to the warehouse but only the warehouse manager had the keys to the storage cages. Nobody could access the cages without him being present. The keys were kept in a locked safe in his office. The warehouse was patrolled at night by two security guards with dogs. In the last forty years there had been four reported break-ins with nothing significant stolen as each break-in had been interrupted.

Falcón was glad that Pérez sat in on the session to react to the brunt of Ramírez's comments. He hadn't expected to become so emotionally engaged by the black-and-white flickering images of Raúl Jiménez's earlier and happier life. Never before, in the dark of the cinema, had he been so moved. Fiction hadn't been able to do this to him. He'd always seen through the contrivance, withdrawn from the imperative engagement and never shed a single sentimental tear.

Now, having come to know the protagonists in the most personal way, he watched in the darkness as José Manuel and Marta played on the beach while the uncomplicated waves folded on to the shore. Raúl's wife, Gumersinda, walked into frame, turned and held out her arms. Running after her into the frame came the toddling Arturo. He reached her outstretched arms and she clasped his small chest in her hands and lifted him high above her head, so that his legs dangled and he looked down on her smiling face with pure and wild delight. As the toddler was taken skywards Falcón's stomach flipped. He remembered that feeling and had to pinch at the tears, shudder under the weight of the tragedy that had torn this family apart.

He couldn't understand his emotional intensity over this family. He'd come into contact with other families ravaged by murder or rape, drug addiction or extreme violence. Why was the Jiménez family so different? He had to talk about this before his desperation turned from leaking to free flow. Alicia Aguado . . . would she work?

The lights came up in the room. Ramírez and Pérez turned in their chairs to look at their superior.

'There's reels of this stuff,' said Ramírez. 'What exactly are we doing here, Inspector Jefe?'

'We're adding to the profile of our killer,' he said. 'We have a physical idea of him from the blow-ups we've taken from the video shot in the cemetery. We have been told he is guapo and he has beautiful hands. Physically he is taking shape. Mentally: we've talked about his creativity and his playfulness. We know he is interested in film. We know that he has made a study of the Jiménez family . . .'

He found himself drying up. Why were they looking at these movies?

'The box in which these films were stored was sealed,' said Pérez, reiterating his report. 'These canisters haven't seen the light of day since they were put in there.'

'But what a day that was,' said Falcón, like a drowning man

clutching at passing reeds. 'The day he expunged his youngest son's memory from his mind.'

'But what does it add to the profile?' asked Ramírez.

'I was thinking of those terrible self-inflicted injuries,' said Falcón. 'Before Jiménez did that to himself he was refusing to watch something on the television. Then he had his eyelids cut off and what did he see? What would have induced Raúl Jiménez to do that to himself?'

'If somebody cut my eyelids off . . .' started Pérez.

'You saw the boy, the tiny helpless boy,' said Falcón. 'You heard him shrieking and whooping in his mother's arms . . . Don't you think . . . ?'

He stopped. The two men were looking hard at him, their faces blank and uncomprehending.

'But, Inspector Jefe,' said Pérez, 'there was no soundtrack.'

'I know, Sub-Inspector . . .' started Falcón, but he hadn't known and his mind was suddenly shot through with a colourless panic and he couldn't even remember his colleague's name. He couldn't think of another word to follow the one he'd just said. He'd become the dried actor he most feared: the one playing himself in his own life.

He came to as if the bubble he'd been encased in had burst and real life had streamed back up to him again. The men had moved away and were dismantling the screen. Falcón was surprised to find it close to 9 p.m. He had to get out, but he had a need to salvage something from this situation first. He went to the door.

'You file the report on these films, Sub-Inspector . . .' he said, that name still eluding him. 'And when you do it I want you to use your imagination. I want you to think about who was holding the camera and the mental state of the man at the time.'

'Yes, Inspector Jefe,' said Pérez. 'But you've always told me to report the facts and not attempt to interpret them.'

'Do your best,' he said and left.

He tried to dry swallow an Orfidal, but it got stuck in the clag of his mouth and he had to go to the bathroom and scoop water to his lips and over his hot face. He dabbed himself dry and found he didn't recognize his own eyes in the mirror. They were somebody else's, these pink-rimmed, filmy things, sunken in their sockets, flinching in his skull. He was losing his authority. Nobody would respect these eyes.

He got out of the Jefatura into the cool night air, drove back home and walked to Dra Alicia Aguado's small house in Calle Vidrio, arriving there shortly before his 10 p.m. appointment. He paced the pavement outside the newly renovated house, nervous as an actor before an audition, until he couldn't stand it any longer and rang the bell. She let him in and called him up a dark stairway to the light.

In the consulting room Falcón noticed that there was nothing on the light-blue walls and no bric-a-brac. In fact, the only furniture was a sofa and a double seat in the shape of an 'S'.

The room was narrow, the house feeling small and contained, making his own place seem absurd. It was clearly a well-managed and comfortable head to reside in. Whereas his own sprawling, multi-roomed, cavernous, storeyed, balconied, baroque, Byzantine madness was like a boarded-up asylum, where a single inmate had hidden until it had all gone quiet . . .

Alicia Aguado had short black hair, a pale face and no trace of make-up. She held out her hand but did not look directly at him. As their hands touched she said:

'Dr Valera didn't tell you I was partially sighted,' she said.

'He only guaranteed that you would not be interested in art.'

'I wish I could be, but I've had this condition since I was twelve years old.'

'What is the condition?'

'Retinitis pigmentosa.'

'I've never heard of it,' said Falcón.

'I have abnormal pigment cells, which for no definable reason begin to stick together on the retina in clumps,' she said. 'The first symptom is night blindness and the last, much later, is complete blindness.'

Javier was paralysed by this exchange. He held on to her hand, which she slowly extracted and showed him to the S-shaped chair.

'I have to explain a few things about my method,' she said, sitting next to him but facing him on the specifically designed seat. 'I cannot see your face clearly and we communicate so much through our faces. As you may know, we are hard-wired for facial recognition at birth. This means that I have to use other ways of registering your feelings. It's a method similar to a Chinese doctor's, which relies on pulse. So we sit in this strange seat, you rest your arm in the middle, I hold on to your wrist and you talk. Your voice will be recorded by a tape within the arm. Are you happy with all that?'

Falcón nodded, lulled by the woman's calm authority, her placid face, her green and unseeing eyes.

'Part of my method is that I will rarely instigate conversation. The idea is that you talk and I listen. All I may do is to try to direct your thoughts or prompt you if you reach a dead end. I will, however, set you off.'

She turned a switch on the side of the chair that started the tape. She took Falcón's wrist in an expert but gentle grip.

'Dr Valera has told me that you're suffering the symptoms of stress. I can tell that you are anxious now. He says that the change in your mental stability started at the beginning of an investigation into a particularly brutal murder. He has also mentioned your father and your reluctance to be treated by someone who might know your father's work. Can you think why the first incident should – What was that?'

'What?'

'That word, "incident", it provoked a strong reaction in you.'

'It's a word that appears in my father's journals, which I've just started reading. It refers to something that happened when he was sixteen which made him leave home. He never says what it was.'

Now that he'd seen the efficacy of her method he had to suppress his desire to twist his wrist out of her grip. Alicia Aguado not only seemed tuned in to the human anatomy but also to the writhing of its soul.

'Do you think that was why he wrote his journal?' she asked.

'You mean to resolve this "incident"?' said Falcón. 'I don't think that was his intention. I don't think he would have even started if one of his comrades hadn't given him a book to write in.'

'These people are sent sometimes.'

'Like this killer has been sent to me?'

Silence, while she let that sink in.

'Everything said in this room is confidential and that includes police information. The tapes are locked in a safe,' she said. 'I want you to tell me what started it.'

He told her about Raúl Jiménez's face. How the killer wanted Jiménez to look at something, which he'd refused to do. Falcón spared no detail in the description of how it must have felt to come round with no eyelids and how this, combined with the horror of what the killer was showing, had driven Raúl Jiménez to appalling self-mutilation. He believed that his breakdown had started on seeing that face, because in it he saw the pain and terror of someone who had been forced to confront their deepest horrors.

'Do you think the murderer sees himself in a professional capacity?' she asked. 'As a psychologist or psychoanalyst?'

'Ah!' said Falcón. 'You mean do *I* see him like that?'

'Do you?'

Silence, until Alicia Aguado decided to move things along.

'Some connection has been made by you between this murder case and your father.'

He told her about the photographs of Tangier he'd found in Raúl Jiménez's study.

'We lived there too, at the same time,' he said. 'I thought I might find my father in the photos.'

'Was that all?'

Javier flexed his hand, uncomfortable at the information flowing through his wrist.

'I thought I might find a picture of my mother, too,' he said. 'She died in Tangier in 1961 when I was five years old.'

'Did you find her?' asked Alicia, after some time.

'No, I didn't,' he said. 'What I found in the background of one of the shots was my father kissing the woman who eventually became my second mother . . . I mean, his second wife. The date on the back was before my mother died.'

'Infidelity is not so unusual,' she said.

'My sister would agree with you. She said he was "no angel".'

'Has this had an effect on how you see your father?'

Falcón found himself actively thinking. For the first time in his life he was actually searching the narrow cobbled streets of his mind. Sweat broke from his forehead. He wiped it away.

'Your father died two years ago. Were you close to him?'

'I thought I was close to him. I was his favourite. I . . . I . . . now I'm confused.'

He told her about the will, his father's expressed wishes for the destruction of his studio and how he was disobeying him by reading the journals.

'Do you think that strange?' she asked. 'Famous men normally want to leave something for posterity.'

'There was a warning letter which told me it could be a painful journey.'

'Then why are you doing this?'

Falcón hit a cul-de-sac in his mind, a flat white wall of panic. His silence deepened.

'What did you say it was that so appalled you about the murder victim?' she asked.

'That he was being forced to see . . .'

'Remember who you were looking for in the victim's photographs?'

'My mother.'

'Why?'

'I don't know.'

In the silence that followed Alicia stood, put the kettle on and made some herbal tea. She fumbled for some Chinese teacups. She poured the tea, took his wrist again.

'Are you interested in photography?' she asked.

'I was until recently,' said Falcón. 'I even have my own dark room in the house. I like black-and-white photography. I like to develop my own pictures.'

'How do you look at a photograph?' she asked. 'What do you see?'

'I see a memory.'

He told her about the home movies he'd seen that afternoon, how they'd made him weep.

'Did you go to the beach much as a child?' she asked.

'Oh, yes, in Tangier the beach was right there next to the town . . . I mean, *in* the town almost. We went every afternoon in summer. My brother and sister, my mother, the maid and I. Sometimes it would just be my mother and I.'

'You and your mother.'

'Are you asking me where my father was?'

She didn't respond.

'My father was working. He had a studio. It overlooked the beach. I went there sometimes. He used to watch over us though, I know that.'

'Watch over you?'

'He had a pair of binoculars. He let me use them sometimes. He helped me find them . . . my mother, Manuela and Paco on the beach. He said it was our secret. "It's how I keep an eye on you."'

'Keeping an eye on you?' she said.

'You mean, it sounds as if he was spying on us,' said Falcón. 'That doesn't make sense. Why should a man spy on his own family?'

'In these family movies you saw today, did you ever see the father?'

'No, he was behind the camera.'

233

She asked him why he was watching these movies and he explained the whole Raúl Jiménez story. She listened, fascinated, only stopping him to change the tape halfway through.

'But why are you watching these movies?' she asked again, at the end of it all.

'I've just told you,' he said. 'I've just spent nearly half an hour . . .'

He stopped and thought for long, endlessly complex minutes.

'I told you that I see photographs as memory,' he said. 'I'm entranced by them because I have a problem with memory. I told you that we used to go to the beach as a family, but I didn't really remember it. I didn't see it. It's not something inside me that I recall. I've invented it to fill the gaps. I know we did go to the beach, but I can't remember it as if it's my own. Am I making sense?'

'Perfect sense.'

'I want these movies and photographs to jog my memory,' he said. 'When I was talking to José Manuel Jiménez about his family tragedy he told me he had problems recalling his childhood. It made me try to remember *my* earliest memory and I panicked, because I knew it wasn't there.'

'Now you can answer my earlier question, about why you're reading the journals,' she said.

'Yes, yes,' he said, as if something had clicked, 'I'm disobeying him, because I think the journals might have the secrets to my memory.'

The tape clicked off. Distant city sounds filled the room. He waited for her to change the tape but she made no move.

'That's all for today,' she said.

'But I've only just begun.'

'I know,' she said. 'But we're not going to disentangle you in a single session. This is a long process. There are no short cuts.'

'But we're just . . . we've just started touching on things.'

'That's right. It's been a good first session,' she said. 'I want you to do some thinking. I want you to ask yourself if you see any similarities between the Jiménez family and your own.'

'Both families have the same number of children . . . I was the youngest . . .'

'We're not talking about it now.'

'But I need to make progress.'

'You've done that, but there's only so much reality that the human mind can take. You have to get used to it first.'

'Reality?'

'That's what we're striving for.'

'But what are we in now, if it's not reality?' he said, panicked by this thought. 'I have more daily doses of reality than anybody I know. I'm a homicide detective. Life and death is my business. You don't get more *real* than that.'

'But that's not the reality we're talking about.'

'Explain.'

'The session is over.'

'Just explain that one thing to me.'

'I'll give you a physical analogy,' she said.

'Whatever . . . I have to know this.'

'Ten years ago I broke a wine glass and, as I was cleaning it up, a tiny sliver got into my thumb. I couldn't get it out and because of the nerves there the doctor didn't want to touch it. Over the years it hurt occasionally, nothing more, and all the time the body was protecting itself from that glass. It formed layers of skin around it until it was like a small pea. Then one day the body rejected it. The pea came to the surface and, with the aid of some magnesium sulphate, popped out of my thumb.'

'And that's your explanation of the kind of reality we're talking about?' he said.

'Slivers of glass can enter the mind, too,' she said, and just the concept nauseated him. 'Sometimes these slivers of glass are too painful to deal with. We push them to the back of our mind. We think we can forget them. Our mind even protects itself from them by scarfing these slivers in layers . . . I mean, lies. And so we distance ourselves from the sliver until one day something happens and, for no reason at all, it heads for the surface of our conscious mind. The difference between the mental and the physical is that we can't apply magnesium sulphate to draw the sliver of glass into consciousness.'

He stood and paced the room. Those tiny slivers of glass rising to the surface had triggered some minor terror. It was as if he could feel them crackling in his head like . . . like an ice field. Was that another physical analogy?

'You're frightened,' she said, 'which is normal. None of this is easy. It demands great courage. But the rewards are enormous. The reward is eventually a real peace of mind and the restarting of all possibilities.'

He walked down the stairwell, away from the light of Alicia's door and into the dark of the street, turning over that last line, coming to terms with the fact that she was thinking that he'd reached the point at which the end of possibilities would become a probability.

He hit the street and walked quickly alongside a group of young people heading into the centre of town. Most of the streets were empty, still hung over after the ecstasy and excess of Semana Santa. The bars were still shut, not opening until tomorrow when the Sevillanos would finally get back into the stride of their normal living pace. Falcón found himself in squares which would normally be full of people, even in mid week, but which were nearly silent and dark, with only disjointed voices, as if it was much later, and the street cleaners were out discussing last night's football. His mind was empty of the usual crush of everyday life, where nothing is thought about and each action begets the next.

The disjointed voices fell silent. He had no desire to go home. He would tramp about like this for some hours. He compared the Jiménez family to his own. Yes, his family had been torn apart, too. No, torn apart was too strong. His mother's sudden death had not broken them up, but it had damaged them, like the hairline cracks on pottery glaze. He remembered his father's stricken face, as he'd looked from Paco, to Manuela, to Javier. And he somehow saw his own gaping and fragmented face, as he gasped at the theft of his whole world. The thoughts started up a terrible welling of black ghastliness, so that he quickened his pace over the satin cobbles.

Better times came to mind. The sunny return of Mercedes. The woman who would become his father's second wife. Javier had instantly fallen for her. And now this memory was tarnished by that photograph he'd found in Raúl Jiménez's apartment: his father consorting with Mercedes before his mother was dead. That rucked up something worse and he jogged across the Plaza Nueva, the trunks and branches of the trees gloved in fairy lights. Christmas every day now. He stared blankly into the spot-lit perfection of MaxMara, the pristine clothes on the eternally perfect mannequins. He prayed for a less complicated life, where he didn't have these thoughts and emotions that flayed his insides, leaving him looking almost the same from the outside, but raw and internally bleeding like a bomb-blast victim.

Sweat popped out of his forehead as he walked, half trotted, down Calle Zaragoza, and something like hunger opened out in his stomach, so he thought about going to El Cairo and having a *tapa* of *merluza rellena de gambas*. He preferred the *sangre encebollada*, but blood and onions on a night like this required a stronger stomach. He passed Ramón Salgado's gallery with only a single lit piece of sculpture in the window. Further on was a classic Sevillano house, which had been converted into a café with an expensive restaurant above, peopled by businessmen and lawyers with their wives and girlfriends.

Back-lit, standing in the doorway on the top step, being helped into her coat, was Inés. Her hair was up and she only wore it like that when she wanted to be attractive and sexy, never for work. He didn't see the man she was with as they stepped into the darkness of the street, joined arms and headed towards Reyes Católicos. There was no one else. This was a dinner for two. He stopped dead as Inés glanced behind her and then her high heels tickled the cobbles as she broke into a momentary skipping run to catch up. He followed them from across the street. The earlier hunger and the beginnings of exhaustion were forgotten now as the mind fell on new fuel.

They crossed Reyes Católicos and walked past the bar, La Tienda, which was closed. They cut across Calle Bailén and went behind the museum and out on to the Plaza del Museo, so that he had to hang back until they disappeared down Calle San Vicente. He waited and then followed, but by then the street was empty. He walked up and down the first hundred metres wondering if he'd imagined it all or that maybe the man had an apartment here, in this street, barely a kilometre from his own house.

He retreated home, broken as an entire army; the hunger was gone and the exhaustion of defeat had taken over. He showered, but only the day's grime left him. He took a sleeping pill and crept under the covers. He stared at the endlessly receding ceiling, mesmerized as he could be by the white flashes in the middle of the road unrolling in the flare of the headlights. He thought he should resist, that it was dangerous to fall asleep at the wheel. Confusion distorted his sense of place. He reached forward with a hand, expecting everything to career out of control, for the frame of his vision to suddenly include a barrier, a bank and a life-ending tree to crash into. He flew into sleep as if through an empty windscreen, into the night.

Extracts from the Journals of Francisco Falcón

12th October 1943, Triana, Seville
An army truck gave me a lift from Toledo all the way to Seville, which
was lucky. The country is on its knees, with no petrol and little food.
There's not much on the roads, apart from occasional carts drawn by
emaciated horses or mules.

I've taken a room run by a fat Moorish-looking woman with long
black hair down to the small of her back, which she winds up into a bun.
She has black eyes as dull as charcoal and she sweats constantly, as if on
the brink of collapse. Her breasts have parted company and live in
isolation on either side of her ribcage. She has a belly as big as a
drinker's, which sways under her black skirts as she walks. Her ankles
are purple and swollen and she catches her breath in pain as she moves
from room to room. I would like to draw and paint her, preferably
naked, but she has a male companion, who is as thin as a village dog
and carries a knife, which I hear him whetting lovingly every morning
before he goes out. The room has a chest of drawers, none of which opens,
and a bed with a picture of the Virgin above it. I take it because it has a
patio outside, which only the landlady uses to dry her washing. I dump
my bags and go out to buy materials and drink.

25th October 1943, Triana, Seville
It must be the soldier in me but I've settled into a routine although I do
not get up early any more. Nothing happens in this city until after
10 a.m. I walk to the Bodega Salinas on the Calle San Jacinto, drink a
coffee and smoke a cigarette. I use this bar because the owner, Manolo,
keeps the best barrels of tinto from which he fills my five-litre bottles. He
also sells me a homemade aguardiente, which I buy by the litre. I go back
to my room and work until 3 in the afternoon. The only interruption is
by the water seller. At 3 I eat lunch in the bar with a jug of tinto, refill
my bottle and return to my room to sleep until 6 p.m. I work again

until 10, have dinner and stay on at Manolo's, drinking with the crooks and idiots who gather there.

29th October 1943, Triana, Seville
In the Bodega Salinas yesterday one of the other customers known only by the name of Tarzan (after the film Tarzan the Ape Man*) comes to sit at my table. He has a tremendous belly and a face like a cluster of potatoes (Johnny Weismuller would be appalled). His eyes are closed up and puffy. He sits down and everybody is listening.*

'So,' he says, putting a meaty forearm on the table, 'where do you get that look from?'

'What look is that?' I ask, puzzled by the question.

There's nothing aggressive about Tarzan, despite his pummelled face. He wears a black hat that he never removes but slips to the back of his head occasionally in order to scratch the front.

'A look that says you don't belong here,' he replies calmly, but I sense those puffy eyes looking through their slits as if down a rifle barrel.

'I'm not sure what you mean.'

'You're not from Seville. You are not Andaluz.'

'I come from Morocco, Tetuán and Ceuta,' I say, but this doesn't satisfy.

'You look at us and make notes. You have old eyes in a young head.'

'I am an artist,' I say. 'I make notes to remind myself of things that I have seen.'

'What have you seen?' he asks.

I realize now that these people do not think I am who I say I am. They think I'm Guardia Civil (who are always from out of town) or worse.

'I was a soldier,' I say, avoiding the word Legion. 'I've been in Russia with the División Azul.'

'Where?' asks a bandy-legged guy, who is a picador of some repute.

'Dubrovka, Teremets and Krasni Bor,' I say.

'I was in Shevelevo,' he says, and we shake hands.

Everybody is relieved. Why they should think a member of the secret police would sit openly in a bar making notes on them (the densest group of dullards in Southern Spain) I have no idea.

15th December 1943, Triana, Seville
A young man, perhaps twenty years old, comes into the bar. He calls himself Raúl and they all know him and like him. He's been in Madrid

239

working, but all he can talk about that first night is going to Tangier,
where there is real money to be made. They humour him and tell him
he should talk to El Marroquí, which is my new name. R. sits at my
table and tells me of the fortunes to be made from smuggling out of
Tangier. I tell him I have plenty of money and that I'm only interested
in becoming an artist. He tells me that there's lots to be made out of
American cigarettes, but there's money in everything because of the
American blockade of Spanish ports. His only worry is that now that
the Blue Division has been pulled out of Russia this might relax the
American attitude to Franco and they'll lift the blockade. I sit up at this
because I realize that he is not just an idiot with pesetas on his mind but
someone who understands the real situation. I offer him a drink; his
company is more lively than the usual Bodega Salinas customer. I learn
that the free port status of Tangier means that all these goods can come
in and be freely traded, with no duty or tax. The companies who buy
and sell these goods also don't have to pay any taxes. Everything is very
cheap. All you have to do is buy it, ship it across the straits and you can
sell it at a premium. This all sounds fine except he has no money to buy
and no ship to transport the goods. This he waves away as uninteresting
detail. 'You start by working for others,' he says. 'You see how the
business operates and then you fit yourself in.'

'Where there's money,' he says, fixing me with his young
inexperienced eyes, 'there's danger.'

I wonder why he addresses this to me and he just says that danger
means that premiums are always paid.

R. went to Madrid to work in construction but the owner of the
building ran out of money. He then bought his way into a shoeshine
syndicate. Only rich people have their shoes shined. He realized that rich
people are rich only because they have superior knowledge. He listened to
them and their talk was of Tangier, where the administration is both
Spanish and corrupt and will stay that way for the foreseeable future. R.
has it all worked out. I have to remind him that I don't need money. He
disagrees vehemently and tells me just how little even well-known artists
make from their work. At the end of the evening we are quite drunk
and he asks if he may sleep on my floor. He is cheerful and lively so I
agree on the condition that he leaves before I start work.

21st December 1943
I've been robbed. R. and I came back from the Bodega Salinas, unlocked
my room and found that someone had got in via the patio and stolen

everything except my notebooks, drawings and paintings. My clothes, paints and even the Virgin above the bed have gone. The last is the worse loss because all my money was in the backing. I have only what is in my pocket. I tell the landlady what has happened. I am angry and I imply something about the only other user of the patio. She flies at me and between us we put our relationship beyond repair. Later we find broken pots in the patio and R. points to where somebody must have got in over the wall and used the pots, which were nailed into the stucco, to climb in and out.

22nd December 1943
The fat Moorish bitch is unforgiving and has appeared with her whipped cur of a husband and some other resident bandits to persuade us to leave. With my training I'm tempted to tear them to pieces but then I'd have the Guardia Civil to contend with and gaol. R. and I leave. He works on me relentlessly and now we are heading south on foot to Algeciras.

27th December 1943
I thought some of the Russians were poverty-stricken, primitive people, but the villages we've been through have revealed that this part of Spain is locked in some Dark Age with no hope and insanity a constant companion. It is not unusual to see people howling at the moon. In searching for food in one village R. came across a boy chained with a metal collar to a wall. His eyes were all pupil and in looking into them R. saw nothing to indicate there was anything human residing there.

5th January 1944, Algeciras
We have arrived here half-starved and in rags after an attack by some wild dogs who were hungrier than us. I killed three with my bare hands before the pack ran off leaving us torn and bleeding. R., who has always been respectful, now holds me in something like awe. There is a shrewdness about this boy that makes me feel uncomfortable.

7th January 1944, Algeciras
Spain in this state is no country for anyone. Africa is so close, visible and near across the straits. I can smell it and surprise myself by how much I want it again.

   R. has come back saying that he's found a contrabandista *who has offered us two months work, food and lodging on the boat with a guarantee to drop us in Tangier with $10 each in our pockets. If it* *works we can renegotiate terms after the two-month trial period. I ask him what we have to do, but it is not a detail that interests him. He likes to do the deal. He produces two cigarettes, which shuts me up. I wonder why I've put myself so completely in his hands until I remember all those other legionnaires who left and came back to Dar Riffen, unable to stomach the outside world.*

R. tells me something about himself as if to bind me to him. His tone is matter of fact. He recounts how a truckload of anarchists came into his village in 1936 and demanded from the mayor all the fascists. The mayor told them that they had all fled. The anarchists returned two days later with a list of names. Among the names were Raúl's parents. The anarchists took them off into the ravine and shot them all. 'Almost everybody I knew was shot that afternoon,' he said. He was twelve years old.

10th January 1944, Algeciras
The contrabandista's boat is an old fishing vessel about 15 metres long and 3 or 4 metres wide. It has one large hold aft with all the accommodation in the fore. There's a small wheelhouse with two cracked panes of glass; underneath is the engine, which is where we find Armando. He is thickset with black hair and a dirty, stubbled face. His eyes are brown and soft but he has a thin-lipped mouth with a taut smile. I don't dislike him, especially when he makes up a stew of beans, tomatoes, garlic and chorizo. He tells us there are clothes in one of the cabins that will fit us better than anything of his would. We eat and drink and I feel fat and sleepy but remember to ask A. whose clothes we are wearing. They belonged to the last crew who were shot and killed by some Italians. R. asks him how he got away and he says bluntly: 'I killed the Italians.'

After the crumbling and sordid Algeciras, Tangier is prosperous. The port is full of ships and all the cranes are working. The dockside is massed with Moroccans, either huddled under the pointed hoods of their burnouses or crouching under the weight of some cargo. Trucks and cars crawl amidst the jostle of humanity; many of them are large American automobiles. Above the port, in a commanding position, is the Hotel Continental. Other hotels line the Avenida de España – the Biarritz, the Cecil, the Mendez. I blanche at the possibility that my father has moved here to take advantage of the boom.

R. jumps about the foredeck, whooping for joy. A. looks at me with dead eyes and asks what this is all about. I tell him that R. has the same nose for money that a dog has for a bitch on heat. A. rubs his chin, which rasps against his rope-hardened hands. I would like to draw those hands . . . and his face, where the sensual and the brutal meet.

Once we have moored up A. has a private talk with R. who disappears. A. smokes a pipe; he gives me a paper and tobacco to roll a cigarette. He puffs away and says: 'You're the best crew I've ever had.' I tell him that we haven't done anything yet. 'But you will,' he says. 'R. will be the trader and you'll do the killing.' Those words chill my guts. Is that all he could see when he looked into my face? I realize that R. has been talking.

11th January 1944
We sailed last night. R. was back within a few hours, followed by an American and two Moroccans wheeling a barrow with two 200-litre drums of diesel. The fuel was cheaper than any A. had ever bought. R. and A. talked some more prices and by nine we were loading sacks of chickpeas and flour and 8 drums of gasoline. R. offers to do the books and A. says: 'What books?' R. can read and write but his real gift is with numbers. He did the books for his parents from the age of eleven. 'When they went to market they bought this and sold that. I wrote it down. After six months I could tell them where they were making money and losing it.' This market was in the next village. 'Now you know why your parents were shot by the anarchists,' I say. This had never occurred to him.

13th January 1944
We held off the coast before going into the small fishing village of Salobreña under cover of darkness. A. signals from off shore and, on receiving the right reply, moves in. While we're waiting A. lets me have a look at his only firearm, a shotgun with engraved silver above the trigger guard. 'A work of art to kill with,' I say. I'm only nervous that I have to do this work with just two shots, but he assures me that the shot spread is very discouraging for those on the margins. They go off to do the business and I guard the ship. They come back half an hour later arguing. The buyers would not accept R.'s inflated price. A. is furious that he has to sail to another port and find another buyer. R. tells him to be patient, they will be back to talk to us again. A. paces the deck. R. smokes. At 3 a.m. R. tells A. to start the engines. As R. prepares to cast off four men come running towards us. I patrol the deck with the shotgun. Money changes hands. We unload and leave before dawn.

15th January 1944
R. shows A. that if he'd accepted the price offered at Salobreña he would
have broken even and if he'd paid his usual price for diesel he'd have
made a loss. R. works on him about the type of cargo he is shipping. It's
too heavy and not profitable enough for a small ship. He says we should
be doing cigarettes. 'Cigarettes are the new money. You buy everything
with cigarettes. Francs, Reichsmarks, Lire mean nothing.' A. whitens at
the idea. The Italians are running that show and he doesn't want to get
involved. R. points to me and says: 'He's a trained soldier. He was with
the Legion. He's been to Russia. There's no Italian who could match
him.' R. has done his homework. I didn't tell him any of that. A. looks
at me and I say: 'I'm not doing it with a shotgun. If you want to run
cigarettes we need at least a sub-machine-gun.' R. laughs at me. 'One
sub-machine-gun!' he says. 'That American who sold us the diesel and
gasoline . . . he can get you anything you want. A howitzer, a Sherman
tank, a B-17 bomber – although he said that might take a little longer
to arrange.'

29th January 1944
The Allies landed in Anzio last week and R. is nervous that his precious
market is going to be destroyed by the end of the war. I tell him the
Allies still have plenty of work to do and that the Germans will not
give up territory easily. R. is desperate to get his own boat already and I
point out that we still haven't earned our first $10, let alone enough
money to put down on even a rowing boat. R. insists that A. teach him
everything about the boat and the sea – how to read a chart, plot a
course, read a compass and navigate by the stars. I sit in on these
tutorials as well.

20th February 1944
A. has been having his own way and we've been making regular trips
with chickpeas, flour and gasoline until R. pulls off a strange deal to run
a cargo of black pepper up to Corsica for a very low freight. The shipper
is a German who's come down from Casablanca and bought this cargo
from a Jew in the town. I can't think what the Corsicans want with all
this black pepper and, when the German realizes that I speak his
language and fought in Russia, he confides in me that they will transship
it and it will end up in Germany in a munitions factory.

24th February 1944

We have put into Corsica and R. is delighted to have made contact with both Germans and Corsicans. It now seems that we will be putting into Corsica in the future with cargoes of cigarettes and the Corsicans will have the problem of putting them into Marseilles or Genoa. As he points out to A., we make more money for less risk. A. cannot give him credit for this simple piece of business. He is king because he has the boat and does not realize how important R.'s intelligence is to making his stupid boat work profitably.

I have a conversation with A. about the difference between peasants and fishermen: Fishermen are always humble in the presence of the sea. The sea's might draws them together. They will always help each other out. Peasants have only their land. It makes them small-minded and possessive. They are never humble, only suspicious. They are taciturn because anything said may give their neighbour an advantage. Their nature is to protect and expand. If a peasant sees his neighbour stumble and fall it fills his mind with possibilities. He finishes with the statement: 'I am a fisherman and your friend R. is a peasant.'

R. maddens me with his endless dreaming about his own boat.

1st March 1944

We dropped off our cargo with the Corsicans and put into Naples with an empty ship for R. to find an Italian to do business with. He's learnt from the Corsicans that permission is required. A. won't go ashore and I realize how much the incident with the Italians shook him up.

12th March 1944

R. was determined to show A. how much money can be made from a well-organized Italian deal. Our boat is filled with Lucky Strikes. We hardly have room to sleep for the cartons and boxes, even loose packets. A. is nervous. All his money is in this one run. We slip into the Gulf of Naples at night and hang in the chill blackness of a very calm sea, waiting. R. comes to me in the cabin where I cradle the sub-machine-gun. He tells me to be ready, to stay out of sight and at the first hint of trouble I am not to question anything but to kill everybody. 'But I thought we had permission,' I say. 'Sometimes you have to prove yourself first to get that permission. Nothing is certain with these people.' I ask him why he hasn't told A. that, and he said: 'All men have to think for themselves. If you leave it to others you're taking a risk.'

I check that all four magazines are full and click one into the breach of the gun. The water slaps against the side of the boat. After some minutes there's the bubbling of an approaching engine. I put out my cigarette and go up to the wheelhouse and crouch below the cracked panes of glass. I sense that something has changed in R., but the approaching boat is on us before I have time to think this through. A light comes on as it pulls alongside. The old tyre buffers squeak and squeal as the boats kiss together. I hear an Italian voice, singsong and unthreatening. I put an eye over the window ledge. A. and R. are standing at the rail about three metres in front of me. The Italian understands Spanish. Two men slip over the rail aft and make their way round to the dark side of the wheelhouse. I know that this is not right. I hear the two men on the other side of the wall, their clothing brushing against the slats. Is this the first hint of trouble? I hear a shout and don't think but put a short burst through the wheelhouse wall. I run out and jump the rail into the Italian's boat. There's no one on the deck of our boat. I lope around the aft of the Italian ship. The engine suddenly throttles up and I put a short burst in to the wheelhouse, killing two men. I pull the throttle back. The boat idles and drifts away from ours. I listen and check the deck and then go below. The cabin is empty. The door to the hold opens on to a diesel-smelling blackness. I find a torch in the cabin. I put my back to the bulwark and hold the torch out. Nothing. No shot. A boy, no older than seventeen, is huddled in the corner of the hold. I find only a small knife on him. He is shaking with fear. I pull him up on to the deck. The white hull of A.'s boat is still visible in the rippling darkness. A light comes on in the wheelhouse and the engine starts up. R. is at the wheel. The Italian boy is on his knees praying. I tell him to shut up, but he has found his rhythm. R. throws me a line. 'All dead?' he asks. I point to the boy at my feet. R. nods and says: 'It's better to kill him.' The boy wails. R., who I now notice is soaking wet, gives me a handgun.

'I need more of a reason than that to kill him,' I say.

'He's seen everything,' says R.

'Maybe it's time for you to get your hands dirty,' I say.

'Mine already are,' he says.

The gun is in my hand. I pull the weeping boy over to the side of the boat. His head lolls off the side. His crying is strangled in his throat. I shoot him behind the ear. I hand R. the gun thinking, This is what I am capable of.

The same hand that pulled the trigger is now guiding the words out of the pen and I am no closer to understanding how this hand can be the instrument of creation and destruction.

We take the boats up to Corsica and drop the bodies overboard on the way. I am in the Italian boat and pull alongside. It's going to take two men to shift each body. We come to A. and I say that we should honour him with a prayer. R. shrugs. I say what we used to say over a fallen comrade in the Legion. I call out his name and make my own response, which is: 'Present!' As we ease him over the side, I see that he's been hit twice, in the shoulder and the back of the head.

We offload the cigarettes and drydock both boats in Ajaccio. We remodel and repaint both boats using the money from the cigarettes. R. disappears for a day and comes back with papers for both boats in each of our names. We sail to Cartagena and register the boats under the Spanish Flag and change the boat names. We have had no time to talk about what has happened and as the time lengthens away from the incident, and all memory of A. disappears, I see that one of R.'s talents is for shutting the door. His link to me is that he has entrusted me with the only memory of importance to him, which is the death of his parents. I think it was then that he decided memory was something that interfered, rather than clarified and, in offering only nostalgia as recompense for a lack of belonging, had no value.

14th March 1944
A conversation with R. goes like this:
  Me: What happened with the Italians?
  R.: You saw, you were there.
  Me: I didn't see what started it.
  R.: Then why did you open fire?
  Me: The two guys who came aboard our boat should not have been there. I opened fire at the first hint of trouble . . . as ordered.
  R.: Was that all?
  Me: I heard a shout . . . like a signal.
  R.: The Italian had a gun. I shouted. He shot A. I jumped in the water. I heard that burst from your sub-machine-gun and the Italians did, too. They made a run for it.
  Me: A. was shot twice.
  R.: What do you mean?
  Me: He was hit in the shoulder and the back of the head.
  R.: I was in the water. Maybe the Italian fired twice.
  Me: Where did you get that handgun?
  R.: Why are you interrogating me?
  Me: I want to know what happened. You said you got your hands

dirty. You said sometimes you have to prove yourself first before you get permission.

Long pause in which I decide I will never know what goes on inside R.'s head.

R.: The handgun belonged to one of the Italians you shot.

At least he replied, even if it was a lie.

23rd March 1944

Some more information about what I now call Opera Night. I go to the American in Tangier to get another magazine for the sub-machine-gun and ask for some more bullets for the handgun he sold to R. He gives me a box of .45 calibre shells without question. He also tells me in passing that the best thing the Allies did for business was to hand over the running of Naples to Vito Genovese. I don't know this name. The American tells me he's a gangster with the Camorra, which I find out later is the Naples version of the Sicilian Mafia.

There has been a change in R. since we embarked on this business. He is not as likable as before. His charm is now turned on and off as required. It occurs to me that R. has been let loose in the world with the single, burning memory of the shooting of his parents. My unthinking remark that they had been killed precisely because of his acumen must have run through him like a white-hot bayonet. The guilt I have induced has made him ruthless and savage. He has made me his partner. I don't know why, because now he doesn't seem to need one.

30th March 1944, Tangier

R. has given me my pay of $100. He tells me to keep the money in dollars and only change what I need into pesetas. I tell him I'm going back to being an artist and he says that I have learnt nothing.

Me: It's what I have to do.

R.: I respect that. (He doesn't at all)

Me: As you said, we have to think for ourselves.

R.: Forgive me, but what you are doing is not thinking.

Me: I want to see how far I can take it.

R.: Do you think that talent has anything to do with success in the world of art?

Me: It helps.

R.: Then you're a fool.

Me: You don't think van Gogh and Gaugin and Picasso and Cézanne had any talent . . . do you know who I'm talking about even?

R.: The fool always thinks that everybody else is foolish. Of course I know who they are. Those men have genius.

Me: And I don't?

He shrugs.

Me: And when did you become an art expert?

He shrugs again and nods at a few people. We are sitting outside the Café de Paris in the Place de France.

Me: How does a peasant boy from some dusty pueblo outside Almería get to know the first thing about art?

R.: How does an ex-legionnaire get to be a genius? El Marroquí? Is that how you will sign your work?

Me: Genius is not selective.

R.: But who decides? Were Gaugin and van Gogh celebrated in their time?

Me: What makes you think I want to become celebrated?

He says nothing but looks at me with intensity and I realize that I am sitting in front of someone who has found his milieu, a man who is utterly confident in his substance and who has seen something in me that I haven't seen in myself.

R.: Why do you keep those journals? Why are you writing out your life?

Me: I only write down what happens and what occurs to me.

R.: But why?

Me: This is not for public consumption.

R.: What is it for?

Me: It is a record, just like your books of accounts.

R.: They just remind you of where you are in the world?

Me: That's right.

R.: You don't think people will read them and think, 'What an extraordinary man!'?

I do think this sometimes but I say nothing to him.

R.: Any man of substance has to have some vanity.

1st April 1944

We have our first rest so that R. can work out how the banks operate. We stay in the Residencial Almería. All nationalities are here and a lot of single women working in the hundreds of companies that have set up here since the beginning of the war.

R. enjoys his money. He has had a suit made for himself by a French Jew in the Petit Soco. He wears this suit to visit the banks. He dines at a restaurant run by a Spanish family in the Grand Hôtel Villa de France. *After he's eaten he takes a short walk down to the Rue Hollande and then back up the hill to the Hotel El Minzah, where he takes his coffee and brandy. His vanity is that he likes to think himself wealthy. It works, because he makes contacts and does business in these places, which are full of black marketeers looking for people like R. to run their goods into Europe.*

I like to sit outside in the sunshine by the Café Central in the medina and watch the chaos of the Soco Chico. At night I find myself drawn to the sleaziness of the port. There's a Spanish bar called La Mar Chica with sawdust on the floor and an old slut from Malaga who dances passable flamenco. She smells bad, as if her whole biology is faulty and in sweating she is actually purging her system of all its ills.

26th June 1944
Since the Allies invaded Normandy we have been working non-stop. R. found a drunken Scot who needs money to pay off gambling debts so we're the new owners of the Highland Queen. *A Spaniard, Miguel, who used to work the fishing boats out of Almuñecar, will run the new vessel.*

3rd November 1944
Sitting off Naples at first light we are attacked. They go for the Highland Queen, *which has drifted away. By the time I draw near they have M. on the deck with a gun to his head. I do not understand their language. R. radios for me to open fire, which I do and they all drop to the deck, including M. The pirates' own boat steams away and I use a British Lee Enfield .303, which is very accurate over distance, to shoot the man at the wheel. They are Greeks. We tow the two boats into Naples. M. has a messy wound in his right leg and we have to leave him there. Our fleet becomes four.*

15th November 1944, Tangier
R. is working on renting warehouse space in the port and outside in the city. My role is security, which means having trusted men who will prevent outsiders getting in and insiders from stealing. He tells me that people are afraid of me. I'm surprised. They have heard how I dealt with the Greeks. I realize that it is R. who is creating this myth around me and I am powerless to stop it.

17th February 1945, Tangier
R. has acquired warehousing. I go direct to the Legion in Ceuta and recruit veterans who know me. I return with twelve men.

8th May 1945, Tangier
The war ended today. The town has gone wild. Everybody is drunk except me and my legionnaires. The suburbs of the city have been filling up with Berbers, Riffians and Tanjawis who have been drawn from the barren mountains and set up homes in chabolas made from crates and pallets. They have nothing to lose and will steal anything. We have to be severe. The beatings have not deterred them. If we catch them now we cut off an ear, again and we split their noses or cut off a thumb and forefinger. If they come back after that we throw them off the cliffs on the outside of town.

8th September 1945, Tangier
The Spanish administration is withdrawing from Tangier. R. is momentarily frightened but it seems the city will return to its previous international status and business will not be affected.

1st October 1945, Tangier
We have decided to buy property. I have found the perfect house off the Petit Soco, a labyrinthine affair built around a central courtyard in which there is a large fig tree. Light comes from the most surprising places. R. thinks it is the house of a madman. His house is just inside the medina gates off the Grand Soco where a lot of other Spanish live. He alarms me by constantly talking about the thirteen-year-old daughter of a Spanish lawyer, who lives opposite. The father of the girl miraculously becomes our lawyer and it is he who draws up the contracts for buying the property. I pay $1,500 and R. $2,200 and we don't have to borrow a cent.

7th October 1945, Tangier
I am painting again. I draw the house and paint it in abstractions of dark and light. Occasionally patterns emerge within these black-and-white structures. I think of the Russian work and realize where this monochromatic obsession comes from.

26th December 1945, Tangier
During our Christmas Eve dinner R. asks if I want to get married. 'To you?' I ask and we laugh so hard that the truth gradually becomes

painfully apparent. He is a massive presence in my life. (Me less so in his.) He controls my every move. We are partners but he pays my expenses, instructs me on security measures, and makes all the plans. I am eight years older than him. I was thirty this year. It must be the Legion, that life . . . I need structure in order to perform. I am not my own man . . . except here when I retreat to my courtyard.

This house is like my head, which, given that (as R. said) it is the house of a madman, is revealing. I occupy new rooms. One with a very high ceiling and, at the top, a window with Moorish latticework. I sit on a carpet and smoke hashish and watch, completely fascinated, as the pattern cast on the wall moves with the sun.

P., the barman at the Café Central in the Petit Soco, pointed out a 'fellow Spanish artist' the other day who looked worse off than some of those living in the chabolas on the edge of town. His name is Antonio Fuentes. He paints, but he doesn't sell and he doesn't show. I don't see the point and try to discuss this with him but he's impenetrable. P. introduces me to an American musician – Paul Bowles. We speak in Arabic as my English is poor and his Spanish worse. He talks about majoun, *a sort of hashish jam I have heard of but never tried. P. makes it and we buy some.*

5th January 1946, Tangier
It is cold and wet. The weather has been too bad to take the boats out. R. shows me the present he has bought for the young daughter of our lawyer – a doll carved out of bone. It is extraordinarily delicate but a little macabre. Later we see the girl crossing the street with her parents, heading for the medina and the Spanish cathedral. She is very beautiful but still a girl. Her breasts are small bumps and the line of her body totally straight from armpit to thigh. I don't see what is stirring him until he reveals another thing to me from his earlier life. She reminds him of a girl from his village whose parents were shot on the same day as his own. This girl though, would not leave her parents and could not be prised away from them, not even by her own father. In exasperation the anarchists shot her, too. What does this say about R.'s infatuation with the lawyer's daughter? She stirs in him that which he values most.

25th January 1946, Tangier
I have some majoun. I spread it on bread and eat it in the strange room with the high ceiling. I wash it down with some mint tea. Hardly has my glass hit the tray than I fall back in a relaxed stupor. After some

minutes I feel my body come tingling alive from hair ends to toe calluses.
I float upwards to within a foot of the ceiling and look out of the latticed
window, which has a view across the rooftops of the medina to the walls
and the grey sea beyond. A watery sunshine plays the shadow of the
window across my shirt. I flap my arms and legs, concerned to be 7
metres from the ground with no visible support. I close my eyes and
relax. I feel colder than I've ever been, even in Russia. I open my eyes to
see the whitewashed ceiling and, growing out of that white expanse,
small patches of black, which prove to be clusters of frozen dead bodies,
and I become very afraid. I will myself out of this state but it persists for
hours. I wake up in the dark. This morning I see mildew patches on the
ceiling from the winter rains. The small clusters. The spores. The living
dead.

21

Thursday, 19th April 2001, Jefatura, Calle Blas Infante, Seville

As Falcón was thinking that this Raúl from his father's journals could be nobody other than Raúl Jiménez, he called Ramón Salgado to be told that his schedule was unchanged. He was going to have an early dinner in Madrid, take the AVE, and would not be back home before 1 a.m. on Friday. He also had a meeting in the morning. His secretary, Greta, suggested lunch, which was longer than Falcón wanted to spend with Salgado, but then it would be entertaining to see the old dealer's face as MCA Consultores was introduced into the mix.

The Jefatura was silent as he sat back working through his memory, trying to find an instance when the name Raúl Jiménez had been mentioned by his father. In 1961 when his mother had died his father had been exclusively painting. There was no business that he could remember. And while he'd been in Seville, no Raúl Jiménez had come to the house. It was also surprising that his father did not appear on the Jiménez wall of celebrities. They must have fallen out.

As he rocked back on his swivel chair he glanced at the group's reports. There'd been a sighting of a grey hatchback around the small industrial zone at the back of the cemetery. One of the security men had it down as a Golf, the other as a Seat. The number plates had been too dirty to read although one had seen the initial letters SE, which made it a Seville plate. Serrano's report mentioned that only cars behaving suspiciously were noted and this grey hatchback had cruised slowly around the factories that butted up against the cemetery.

Pérez's report on Mudanzas Triana was expert and in depth. There was even a diagram of the warehouse floor plan with the location of the Jiménez storage cage. Extensive interviews with the foreman, Sr Bravo and the other workers showed that it was unlikely that the killer would have had time to do all the filming for *Familia Jiménez* whilst holding down this kind of job. On the day that Betis lost 4–0 to Sevilla all regular personnel were out on jobs. On the morning of Raúl Jiménez's funeral they were, again, all working. There was a list of casual labour employed over the last year and finally an admission that some of these were illegal. Only a small percentage gave addresses. Pérez's report on the home movies consisted of two lines of the bare facts.

Fernández had shown Eloisa Gómez's picture around all the mourners he'd come across in the cemetery. None remembered her. The gardeners did not work on Saturday or Sundays. The area for garden detritus was cordoned off by thick bushes. Fernández thought that Eloisa Gómez could easily have been killed and hidden on the Saturday morning. The cemetery gates opened at 8.30 a.m. on a Saturday, but few people turned up before 10.00 a.m.

After going through the reports Falcón worked on a series of questions, designed to break Consuelo Jiménez's resolve if she was maintaining any.

The group arrived. Falcón updated them all on the slow progress and assigned the cemetery and industrial zone to the same three men. He asked Ramírez to leave and told Pérez that he wasn't convinced that he had the enthusiasm for the case. He reassigned him to another investigation. Pérez left, furious.

Ramírez re-entered and stood by the window, playing with his ring finger, as if he was about to hit someone. He understood perfectly what had just happened. Falcón ordered him to take a forensic down to Eloisa Gómez's room and give it a thorough inspection. Ramírez left the office without a word. Falcón called Consuelo Jiménez who, as always, agreed to see him immediately.

They met in the office just off the Plaza Alfalfa. Sra Jiménez, sensing that this was a man with ammunition, played some diffusing tactics. She left him for five minutes while she supervised the making of his coffee.

'Not satisfied with Inspector Ramírez's report on our ... discussion?' she asked, sitting back from the desk with her coffee, crossing her legs, her foot nodding.

'Yes, as far as it went,' said Falcón. 'He's a good cop and a suspicious man. He knows when someone is lying, not telling the truth or withholding. You satisfied his curiosity on two counts.'

'We're all liars, Inspector Jefe. We are hard-wired to lie. I love my children and generally they are very good kids, but . . . they lie. They have an instinct for it. You think of the number of times your mother walked into the room to ask who broke this glass or that cup and how many times she heard the words: "It fell over." Human beings are built for deviousness.'

'Do you think that in my job I am dealing with people who *want* to tell the truth?' said Falcón. 'Murder brings out a stronger inclination to deny than any other crime, apart from perhaps rape. So if we find someone in an investigation with a powerful motive and a consistent propensity for dissembling, we naturally come back to them, again and again, to try to discover what they're hiding.'

'And so you waste your time with me,' she said.

'You are not being open with us.'

'I have one rule of conduct in life and that is that I never lie to myself.'

'And all other forms of mendacity are permissible?'

'Imagine going through a whole day just telling the truth,' she said. 'The damage you would do. Nothing would work. Political systems would collapse. The legal world would be a shambles. It would be utterly impossible to pull off a single piece of business. The reason for this is that they are all man-made systems for getting things done. Even in the worlds of Maths and Physics they still have to work with imperfect information in order to get to the ultimate truth. No, Inspector Jefe, you cannot have the truth without lying.'

'And where did you get the chance to develop such philosophical thoughts?'

'Not in Seville,' she said. 'Not even Basilio *El Tonto* could hold his own with me on that score, for all his stupid education.'

'My father would have agreed with you there,' he said. 'He thought university was an opportunity for other idiots to impress upon their students their ridiculous system of ideas.'

'I liked your father . . . enormously,' she said. 'I've even forgiven him his little deviousness in selling me his "original" copies.'

Falcón shifted in his seat. This woman knew how to knuckle down on the pressure points.

'One of the qualities you display in running your restaurants is,

I imagine, thrift,' he said. 'You've just extended it to the veracity department, that's all . . . I hope.'

'I'm neatly packaged, Inspector Jefe. I've learnt to present myself. You, and possibly half the Jefatura, now know things about me that only I knew. But I did know them. I've lived with them nearly every day. Naturally I'm distressed when they're brought out into the open, as they were recently, but I've suppressed any instinct I might have had for denial. Once you start on that road, you're on your way to oblivion. It is a road not easily back-tracked. My husband reached the only possible end of *Calle Negación*.'

'Except that he didn't kill himself, did he?' said Falcón.

'He became a victim. He began operating in a dangerous world. I've dipped my toe into that world and it was cold. My husband would have understood only one aspect of it, which is that its reptilian lifeblood is money. But what do you think the people who live in that world would see, when a man like Raúl Jiménez comes to visit? I can tell you: they don't see all the strengths that made him into a successful businessman. They see weaknesses. They see a blind man, stumbling about in an obscure world.'

'You're giving me a theory now.'

'I had to listen to Inspector Ramírez while he gave me *his* theory yesterday. I was a model of patience,' she said. 'I was also flattered that the powers that be in the Jefatura should credit a woman with the skills to execute such an elaborate plan, but then again, Raúl's death gives me control of his business empire, so perhaps the credit was not so misplaced.'

'An empire your husband was trying to sell.'

'Yes, Inspector Ramírez made much of that,' she said. 'But killing the prostitute, Inspector Jefe. Putting the body in the cemetery, in the Jiménez mausoleum. None of this strikes me as the work of a professional contract killer.'

'I'd be surprised if a woman such as yourself would have a choice of contract killers. I should have thought you'd have to go with anybody you could . . . *persuade* to do the work.'

'I would never expose myself to another person to that extent. They would have a hold on me for the rest of my life,' she said, lighting a cigarette. 'But believe me when I say this, Inspector Jefe, I know why you keep knocking on my door.'

'It's not because we've got no other doors to knock on,' he lied. 'It's because we never leave here satisfied. Something is always left hanging. The other day you said there are no files relating to your husband's presidency over the Building Committee for Expo '92. Yesterday you said to Inspector Ramírez that he can only look at the packing cases with the home movies in it and no other. You threaten him –'

'Well, now you reveal something else to me. The Jefatura is as fallible to the culture of deviousness as the outside world,' she said, delighted. 'You can look into any of those packing cases you like. They are ancient history to me. They don't relate to my life with Raúl at all. He's something of a bull, that Inspector Ramírez.'

'So that is all you're doing, is it?' said Falcón. 'Protecting your privacy.'

'Why should I let you intrude into areas which don't concern your investigation?'

'How do you know they don't?'

'Because I didn't kill my husband and I didn't have him killed.'

'Your reticence forces us to intrude.'

'Tell me what you've got, Inspector Jefe, I can't bear the suspense any longer.'

'I'd like to know what Marta Jiménez knows about the structure and design of high-traffic buildings in relation to security.'

She blinked, crushed her cigarette out.

'I'd like to know the nature of your husband's relationship with Eduardo Carvajal.'

She lit another cigarette.

'I'd be interested to know about any other business arrangements you might have with ... what was his name? One of Raúl's old Tangier friends ...'

'Don't play with me, Inspector Jefe.'

'Ramón Salgado.'

She swallowed, resumed smoking. The sound of sizzling nylon reached him as she sawed her legs together.

'I'm not discussing any of this without my lawyer present,' she said.

'That doesn't surprise me.'

'But I will tell you one thing: this line of inquiry will not solve your murder case.'

'How can you be so sure?' he said. 'You always speak as if you know things. You must have realized that it is this reticence which is breeding the ruthlessness down at the Jefatura.'

'I am protecting *my* interests, *not* a murderer.'

'Did you know Ramón Salgado before you came to Seville?' he asked.

Silence.

'From the Madrid art world?' he added.

More silence.

'Did Ramón Salgado introduce you to Raúl Jiménez?'

'You're like a bad surgeon, Inspector Jefe. You open people up and poke around looking for something diseased to cut out. What worries me is that you might cut out something perfectly good just to show that you've done some work.'

'Co-operate, Doña Consuelo, that's all I ask.'

'I have co-operated with you in the investigation into my husband's murder. You only encounter reticence when you stray into areas which should not concern a homicide detective.'

'Would you co-operate with someone sent down from Madrid? One of those investigators with special powers and an expertise in corruption and fraud?'

'Threats have a habit of putting people on the offensive.'

'We have become bellicose, haven't we?'

'I know who started it,' she said, stubbing out her cigarette.

They looked at each other through the drifting battle smoke.

'You're a perceptive woman,' he said. 'You know where my interests lie. I have a limited interest in embezzlement and fraud. I understand that businessmen have favours to repay. They have to show their appreciation to friends, pay an advance on the right words in the right ears or reward silence. That it can be done with public money is understandably expedient. Only the State has such depths to its coffers.'

'I'm glad you've rediscovered your urbanity,' she said.

'I can understand your husband's relationship with all these people . . . except one,' said Falcón. 'Eduardo Carvajal. And I am not in a position to ask him anything as he is no longer with us.'

'I think he died in a car crash.'

'A few years ago,' said Falcón. 'He was part of a paedophile ring, who were all subsequently convicted.'

'I pity you, Inspector Jefe,' she said. 'You have to spend your time in the darkest, coldest places on earth.'

'Your husband fell in love with his first wife when she was barely thirteen years old.'

'How do you know that?'

'Two sources. Your husband's eldest son and my father's journals.'

'Your father and Raúl knew each other?'

'They were in business together for some years in Tangier.'

'What business?'

'I think it's my turn to be coy with the facts now, Doña Consuelo,' said Falcón.

'Anyway . . . what you were saying . . . Raúl's attraction could have been quite innocent,' she said. 'It certainly wasn't illegal.'

'He was seeing the prostitute Eloisa Gómez who was not under-age but certainly looked it.'

'He was married to me and had three children by me, too.'

'Let's not go back to being bellicose, Doña Consuelo. I only want to know why he felt the need to reward Eduardo Carvajal,' said Falcón. 'This is off the record and anything you say will not be construed as an admission of guilt. I want a pointer, that is all.'

'I always tread carefully when everything that's presented to me appears to be to my advantage.'

'I'm sure, even here in Seville, you've maintained an ear well-tuned to the cracking of ice.'

'That's not much use to you if you're already a long way from the river bank.'

'Then tread carefully.'

She played with a new cigarette and the lighter.

'You have a new theory,' she said, pointing at him with the lighter.

'I'm running an investigation. My job is to think creatively around insoluble problems. I never give up on old theories, but in the absence of breaks I have to examine new possibilities.'

'I had no idea that police work could be so demanding.'

'It depends on how you approach it.'

'And *you* are the son of Francisco Falcón.'

'He never thought very highly of my decision to join the police force.'

'Even post-Franco I imagine it was full of undesirables,' she said. 'What made you join?'

'Romance.'

'You fell in love with a policewoman?'

'I fell in love with American movies. I was entranced by the idea of the individual struggle against the ranged forces of evil.'

'Is that how it turned out?'

'No. It's much messier. Evil rarely does us the favour of being pure. And we in the front line are not always as good as we should be.'

'You're rekindling my admiration, Don Javier.'

The thought that he might ignite anything in her gave him a strange satisfaction. Lights flickered in those byways of the spine. She lit her cigarette, blew smoke over his head.

'Eduardo Carvajal . . .' he said, to remind her.

'So you think my husband's killer might be an abused boy taking his revenge?' she said. 'I don't think so, Don Javier. He was never that way inclined . . .'

'A paedophile ring is rarely just abusing one child. They are numerous and with different tastes. Perhaps he is an abused boy taking revenge on behalf of others.'

'Do you think someone like that would kill the prostitute as well?' she said. 'Surely they would consider themselves fellow victims?'

'According to Eloisa Gómez's sister they had become intimate to the point that he had given her hope. If he then revealed that his relationship with her had been for the sake of expediency she could become a dangerous entity, someone who might at a later date find herself needing to cut a deal with the police, for instance. She would be too dangerous to leave out there.'

'You've thought this out.'

'I only pursue it because of the reward your husband gave to Carvajal.'

'You know what you're doing, Don Javier?'

'No.'

'You're putting me to work.'

'You don't know why?'

'I never met Sr Carvajal.'

'That might indicate that there was no business relationship between your husband and Sr Carvajal,' said Falcón. 'Had there been, you would have known him, no?'

'He wasn't involved in the restaurant trade.'

'He was a businessman is all I know,' said Falcón, getting up from his chair.

'You're leaving?' she asked.

'Our business is done.'

She leaned across the desk and looked up at him with her ice-blue eyes.

'You know, when this is all over, Don Javier, you and I should have dinner.'

'You might be disappointed,' he said.

'Why?'

'We'd never be able to recreate the tantalizing dynamic of you being a prime suspect in a murder case and me being the investigating officer.'

She laughed – throaty, unrestrained, sexy.

'There was one other thing,' he said as he reached the door. 'We'd like to have a look at your phone records both business and domestic over the last two years. Can you make those available to us?'

Their eyes met and locked. She shook her head, smiled and picked up the phone.

22

Thursday, 19th April 2001, Edificio de los Juzgados, Seville

Falcón paced the floor outside Calderón's office. He'd called him after his meeting with Consuelo Jiménez and they'd agreed to meet at six. It was already seven o'clock and the passing secretaries had given up on sympathetic glances. He was glad he wasn't being made to wait by a fiscal in their offices above the Palacio de Justicia in the building next door, where he would have been tormented by all those people who knew him through Inés. It would have brought back those winter evenings when he'd picked her up from work and found himself at the centre of her bustling world. Her beauty attracted the excitement of fame. He was her lover. The chosen one. People had looked at him with searching eyes and broad smiles, wanting to know his secret. What has Javier Falcón got? Had he imagined all that? The way women had sniffed the air as he went by, and men had glanced over the urinal walls.

Pacing the floor outside Calderón's office it suddenly hit him that it had all been about sex. He'd been caught up, not just in his own desire, but everybody else's, too. He'd mistaken it, as had Inés. They'd thought it was the real thing, but it wasn't. A fleeting physical attraction had been hijacked by everybody's need for romantic wish fulfilment. What should have been a few months of mad sex had been turned into a shotgun wedding – except it wasn't the father with the weapon. It was sentiment.

Dr Spinola, the Magistrado Juez Decano de Sevilla, came out of Calderón's office. He stopped to shake hands with Falcón and seemed on the brink of some intrusive questioning but gave up on the idea. Calderón called him into the office, apologized for keeping him waiting.

'Dr Spinola's not an easy man to throw out,' said Falcón.

Calderón wasn't listening. He searched the inside of his head, reached for a cigarette, lit it and inhaled deeply.

'That's the first time he's ever come to any of our offices to discuss a specific case,' he said, to the wall above Falcón's head. 'Normally I go to him and give him an overview.'

'What's he so concerned about?'

'Good question,' said Calderón. 'I'm confused.'

'If it's to do with our case, maybe I can help,' said Falcón.

In a fraction of a second Calderón weighed up the situation. Stripping his problem down to instinct he looked at Falcón, thinking: 'Can this man be trusted?' He decided no, but only just. If they'd had a few more moments like the one in the cemetery, Falcón thought that Calderón would have confided in him.

'What have you got for me, Inspector Jefe?' he asked. 'No Inspector Ramírez today?'

Falcón had arrived without Ramírez because he wanted to develop a personal relationship with Calderón and at the same time cut back Ramírez's access to information, force him out of the wider picture and into smaller parts of the puzzle. Now he'd changed his mind again. Seeing Dr Spinola had made him cautious. Perhaps it wasn't such a good idea to have the name Carvajal floating about the corridors of the Edificio de los Juzgados. There was no logic to this other than the tenuous link of Spinola being in Jiménez's celebrity photographs, along with León and Bellido, and Carvajal being on the MCA Consultores payroll. Leaking this in vague form to Consuelo Jiménez had been a calculated risk. First he'd wanted to see if she knew about it, which hadn't been conclusive and he was sure that she would only see it as a way of taking the heat off herself. If Falcón made this more official via Juez Calderón there could be unknown repercussions. The leak could find its way back to Comisario León. The only problem now was that he had nothing to talk to Calderón about, except the one thing he was anxious to avoid.

'You had an idea before we were sidetracked by Sergio's text message,' said Falcón.

'Sergio?'

'Our name for the killer. It was the one he used with Eloisa Gómez,' said Falcón. 'You remember, we were going to contact him, point up his mistakes and try to rile him into making more fatal ones.'

'He left her mobile on the body,' said Calderón.

'But he still has Raúl Jiménez's.'

'Do we know anything more about Sergio since he acquired a name?'

'Eloisa Gómez and her sister talked about him as a type. They described him as *un forastero*, an outsider.'

'A foreigner?'

'Forastero to them describes a mental state. He is someone who sees and understands things beyond the normal flow of everyday life. He knows how things really work. He has an automatic comprehension of what runs between the lines.'

'This sounds very enigmatic, Inspector Jefe.'

'Not on the margins of society, where people have detached themselves from normality. Where, for instance, every day they sell their bodies for sex, or shoot somebody because they haven't got the money. It's not so different at the other end of the scale. Those people with power, who know how to get more and how to maintain their position. None of these people see things as normal people do, who have jobs and children and houses to occupy their minds.'

'And you think an artist, such as you described our killer back in the cemetery, would have this same unusual perspective?' said Calderón.

'It fits the profile,' said Falcón. 'You mentioned "foreigner", too. Eloisa Gómez told her sister that although Sergio appeared to be Spanish there was something of the foreigner about him. He had foreign blood in him, or he'd been away from his Spanish roots.'

'How should this alter our approach?'

'I think pointing up a mistake is too obvious. He'd find it laughable. Forasteros know when they're being manipulated.'

'Maybe we should show him that we understand him.'

'But as an artist,' said Falcón. 'We mustn't be prosaic. We have to intrigue him as he does us. We're still no closer to understanding that last sight lesson. "Why do they have to die, those that love to love?"'

'Wasn't he just telling us that he'd killed her because she'd seen him – the gift of perfect sight?'

'But "those that love to love"? He's presenting her as an emblem and he's chosen a prostitute for his purpose. He's trying to alter the way we see things and we have to do the same. We have to try to make him see something as if for the first time.'

'So, all we need now is a resident genius,' said Calderón. 'Apparently this building is full of them, if you believe what you're told.'

'We borrow genius from the classics,' said Falcón. 'He's a poet and an artist . . . that's his language.'

'"*Los buenos pintores imitan la naturaleza, pero los malos la vomitan.*" Good painters imitate nature, bad ones spew it up. Cervantes.'

'That might do the trick of annoying him as well,' said Falcón.

'But what are we trying to do with this strategy?' asked Calderón. 'What do we want from him?'

'We're trying to draw him in, start a dialogue, open him up. We want him to start leaking information to us.'

Falcón, losing his nerve at the last moment, thumbed the Cervantes line into the mobile and sent it as a text message. The two men sat back in their seats feeling stupid. Their investigative world reduced to the absurdity of sending lines of Cervantes into the ether.

Now they had to fall back on their own resources, but with no point of contact apart from a recognition of each other's intelligence. Falcón wasn't going to talk about football and Calderón wasn't going to make him.

'I saw a movie last night on video,' said Calderón. '*Todo sobre mi Madre* – 'All about my Mother'. Did you see it? It's a Pedro Almodóvar film.'

'Not yet,' said Falcón, and an odd thing happened. His memory cracked open and for a second he was back in Tangier, splashing through the shallows and then up in the air, squealing.

'You know what struck me about that movie?' said Calderón. 'In the first minutes of the film the director creates this incredibly intimate relationship between the son and the mother. And then the boy is killed soon after. And . . . I've never had an experience like it; when he dies it's like being the mother. You don't think you'll ever recover from that terrible loss. That's genius, to my mind. To change a world in a few metres of celluloid.'

Falcón wanted to say something. He wanted to respond to this because, for once, there was something in this small talk. But it was too big. He couldn't get it out. Only tears welled in his eyes, which he pinched away. Calderón, unconscious of Falcón's struggle, shook his head in amazement.

'We've got something here,' said Calderón, picking up the mobile.

He read the small screen. A frown formed which transformed itself to pain.

'Do you speak French?' he asked, handing Falcón the mobile. 'I mean, it's simple, but . . . very strange.'

'*Aujourd'hui, maman est morte. Ou peut-être hier, je ne sais pas.*'

Falcón felt ill, nauseous enough to vomit.

'I understand it,' said Calderón. 'But what does it mean?'

'"*Today mother died. Or was it yesterday, I don't know,*"' said Falcón. 'And there's more: "Don't contact me again, *cabrón*, I will tell the story."'

'He's turned it back on us,' said Calderón. 'But what does it mean?'

'He couldn't resist it,' said Falcón. 'He had to show us that he could go one better.'

'But how?'

'I think he's probably had a French education,' said Falcón.

'*That's* a line of literature?'

'I don't know. I can't be sure. But if I had to guess I'd say that it comes from *L'Étranger* by Albert Camus.'

The Edificio de los Juzgados was almost empty at this time of night and Falcón's footfall echoed through his hollow body as he walked the long corridor to the stairs. He had to hold on to the bannister to get down the steps and stop at the landing to control the shaking of his legs. He was persuading himself that it was coincidence, that there was no bizarre telepathy between him and Sergio. Life was full of these odd moments. There was a word for it: synchronicity. It should be a good thing. Human beings liked things to synchronize. But not that. Not their discussion about outsiders, Calderón talking about the film with the unmentionable title and then Sergio slapping them down with that terrible line. A line that disconnected him from the normal world of human relations, from the profound filial–maternal bond. They were the words of the loneliest individual on the planet and they had torn into Falcón like a chain saw.

He made it to security, motor reflexes normalized. On the other side was Inés, putting her handbag and briefcase through the machine. This was the last person Falcón wanted to see and as he thought this, it all came rushing back – her beauty, the sex, his longings, their failure. She waited for her bags, looking directly at him, almost mocking.

'Hola, Inés,' he said.

'Hola, Javier.'

The hate was undisguised. He was condemned to be the unforgiven. He didn't understand this because he could find no trace of rancour in himself. They had made a mistake. It had been recognized. They had parted. But she couldn't stand him. The security guard handed over her bags and she dazzled him with a smile. Her lips returned to a hard red line for Falcón. He would have liked some inspiration at that moment. To somehow be able to make it instantly better, as people can in the movies. But nothing came. There was nothing to be said. This was a relationship beyond the possibility of even friendship. She despised him too much.

She walked away. The narrow shoulders, the slim waist, the swaying hips, the sure feet and the heels counting out the distance.

The security man gnawed his lip, looking at her, and it came to Falcón why she so loathed him. He had destroyed the perfection of her life. The vibrantly beautiful and brilliant law student who had become an exceptional young prosecutor, worshipped by men and women wherever she went, had fallen for him – Javier Falcón. And he had turned her down. He had failed to love her back. He had tarnished her perfection. This was why she thought he had no heart, because it was the only possible explanation for his failure.

Outside he took up a position by one of the pillars of justice of the adjoining building. It gave him a view of the main door to the Edificio de los Juzgados. A few minutes later Inés reappeared through that door followed by Esteban Calderón. She waited, kissed him on the lips, took him by the arm and headed off down the colonnade towards Calle Menéndez Pelayo.

Had they kissed? Was that a trick of the light?

His powers of dissuasion failed him. It had been too clear. And in the slanting shadows of the neoclassical columns he came across another anomaly of logic. The faultiness of human wiring that could shortcircuit even the clearest of thoughts. He did not love her. He felt no rancour. They were beyond repair. So why did he feel his blood, his organs, his sinew and tendon consumed by a monstrous jealousy?

Falcón ran to his car, drove back to the Jefatura clenching the steering wheel so tight that he had difficulty unbending his fingers to write his report. He tried to read other reports. It was impossible. His concentration flitted between the wreckage of his investigation and his inexplicable certainty of Calderón's indefatigable sexual athleticism.

A tranche of time disappeared. A journey was lost. One moment he was straining over those reports and the next he was sitting with Alicia Aguado, her fingers feathering over his wrist.

'You're upset,' she said.

'I've been busy.'

'At work?'

Laughter spurted from him like projectile vomit. He was hysterical in seconds, the laughter so intense that it wasn't coming from him – he was the laughter. She let go of him as he threw himself on the sofa, stomach straining. It passed. He wiped away the tears, apologized and sat back down.

'Busy ... that word is such an absurd understatement for the description of my day,' he said. 'I never knew a madman's life was packed so tight. I'm cramming an entire life into every tiny space I can find. Nobody can say anything to me without a whole world being dredged up. While a judge sits in his office, talking about his favourite movie moment, I'm running along a beach, splish-splashing through the waves, being launched high up in the air and squealing.'

'By your mother?'

Falcón faltered.

'Now that is odd,' he said.

Silence.

'It came back to me with the clarity of a dream,' he said. 'Except now I realize there was one feature missing, but I've got it now. I was being thrown up in the air by a man.'

'Your father?'

'No, no. He's a stranger.'

'You've never seen him before?'

'He's Moroccan. I think he must have been a friend of my mother's.'

'Was that unusual?'

'No, no. Moroccans are very friendly people. They love to talk. They're very curious and inquisitive. They have an amazing facility ...'

'I meant for your mother, a married woman, to be meeting a stranger on the beach. Allowing her son to be thrown up in the air by him.'

'I'm not sure he *was* a complete stranger. No. I'd seen him before. He probably owned a shop, which my mother used to buy from. It would be something like that.'

'What happened in the judge's office?'

He recounted the meeting: the attempted dialogue with Sergio, the Almodóvar film, the terrible reply from Sergio and what it had done to him.

'What shook me was the talk about outsiders beforehand and then the killer using a line from the book. I'm sure it's *L'Étranger*. The Outsider. It makes me feel as if I'm going mad.'

'Ignore it,' she said. 'Synchronicity. It happens all the time. Concentrate on the issues.'

'Which are?'

Silence from Alicia Aguado.

'My mother,' he said. 'That's an issue.'

'Why did the line from Camus have such a terrible effect on you?'

'I don't know.'

'How did your mother die? Was she ill?'

'No, no, she wasn't ill. She had a heart attack but . . .'

A long silence in which Falcón blinked once a minute.

'There was something . . . a crisis of some sort in the street. We were in the house, Paco, Manuela and I. And there was this big row in the street outside our house. I can't remember what it was about. It was afterwards though, that my father came to tell us that our mother was dead. But it won't come back to me . . . what happened.'

'What happened after she died?'

'There was a funeral. I only remember people's legs from that day and the general gloom. It was February and raining. My father spent a lot of time with us. He nursed us all through it.'

'Did you ever see the stranger on the beach again?'

'Never.'

'How long was it before your father married again?'

'We already knew Mercedes,' he said. 'She'd been a family friend for a long time. She helped my father a lot, marketing his work in America. They were having an affair before my mother died . . . did I tell you that? I only just found out.'

'Carry on.'

'Mercedes was still married when my mother died and then her husband subsequently died in America. Cancer, I think. She came back to Tangier in her husband's yacht. It must have been about a year after my mother died that they got married.'

'Did you like Mercedes?'

'I loved Mercedes from the moment I first saw her. I still have that vague memory of seeing her for the first time. I was tiny. She came to my father's studio and picked me up. I think I played with her earrings. I loved her from that moment, but then my father always said I was a very loving child.'

'What happened with Mercedes?'

'It was a very good time. My father was successful. The Falcón nudes were the talk of the art world. He was being hailed as the new Picasso, which was ridiculous given the size and quality of *his* oeuvre. Then tragedy. It was after a New Year's Eve dinner. Everybody went down to the yacht in the port afterwards to see the fireworks and then some of them went out on the boat at night and a storm got up. Mercedes fell overboard. They never found her body.

'But . . . but just before the party left the house I crept down from my bedroom and Mercedes spotted me,' he said, replaying it like film through the gate of his mind. 'She took me back up to bed. I was reminded of this the other day because . . . That was it. It's coming together. In my murder investigation the first victim, Raúl Jiménez, smoked these cigarettes, Celtas, and that was the smell in her hair. I only just found out that my father knew Raúl Jiménez from the forties and now I realize that he must have been at that party except . . . he'd already left Tangier by then.'

'I'm sure other people smoked that brand in those days.'

'Yes, of course,' said Falcón. 'So, Mercedes took me up to bed and kissed me and hugged me tight to her bosom. She was squeezing her love into me so hard I could barely breathe. She was wearing perfume, which I now know is Chanel No.5. Women don't use it so often these days. But years ago if I came across that smell in the street it would transport me back to that moment. Being in the grip of love.'

'And after Mercedes left you?'

Falcón grabbed his stomach with his free hand, stricken with pain.

'I hear . . .' he said, struggling. 'I hear her heels receding down the corridor and stairs. I hear the talk and the laughter of the other guests. I hear the door shutting. I hear the shoes pattering on the cobbles. And I remember that she never came back.'

271

Tears blurred his vision. Saliva filled his mouth. He couldn't swallow. The last words came out from under the shuddering wall of his stomach.

'There were no more mothers after that.'

Alicia made some tea. The cup burnt his fingers, the tea scalded his tongue. Physics brought him back into the room. He felt a strange newness, a cleansed satisfaction, as when he and Paco had scraped and rendered an old bullpen at the finca and whitewashed it to a solid white cube in the burnt-umber landscape. He'd photographed it. It had something of the simplicity of a great work of art.

'I've never remembered that all the way through,' he said. 'I always used to stop before I got to her receding heels.'

'And you know now, Javier, don't you, that it wasn't your fault that she didn't come back?'

'There's a question.'

'What question?'

He thought for a long time and shook his head.

'You know it wasn't your fault,' she said.

He nodded.

'Do you know what you've done this evening, Javier?'

'I suppose you'd say that I've relived a moment.'

'And seen it in its normal light,' she said. 'That's how the process works. If we deny things that are painful to us they don't go away. We only hide from them. You've just had the first success in the biggest investigation of your life.'

He drove back to Calle Bailén oddly refreshed, as if he'd been out running and sweated all the toxins from his body. He parked and walked through the silent, dark house until he reached the patio at its centre and its limpid pupil of black shining water. He turned the light on beneath the arched and pillared cloister. His hands shook as he entered the study. His eyes floated over the desk, the scattered photographs and the portrait of his mother and her children. He went to the old grey filing cabinet, unlocked it and took out a brown buff file from under the letter 'I'. He sat at his desk with the file, knowing that he would take the next step, beating back the guilt. He took out the fifteen black-and-white prints and laid them face down on the desk. He asked himself in the glass of the picture on the wall: 'How new are you?'

He turned over the first photograph. Inés lay face down, naked, on a silk sheet on the bed. She was looking back at him, resting her head on her fist. Her hair was all over. Falcón closed his eyes as the pain eased into him. He turned to the next photograph, opened his eyes. His neck shook with tension. Swallowing became impossible. Inés was propped up on the pillows, naked again apart from a piece of silk around her shoulders. She was looking at the camera with a deep sexual intent. Her thighs were spread wide, revealing her shaved sex. He was standing behind the camera in the same state. The wonderful excitement as they'd shaved each other, the giggling at their trembling hands. There'd been nothing perverse about it. The joy was in the innocence of it. The brilliance of that day came back to him. The torrid heat of that big fat afternoon, the cracks of intense light around the shutters brightening the dimness of the room so that they could see each other in the mirror. The privacy of the two of them alone in the big house, so that when they were too hot he'd picked her up and, still connected, walked downstairs, her thighs clenched around his waist, ankles locked, heels riding the tops of his buttocks. He'd stepped into the eye of the fountain and sank into the cool water.

It was so unbearable that he had to put away the file and lock the cabinet. He looked at the grey metal repository of his memory. Alicia was right. You could not lock things away. You could not obsessively order them, package them, file them under 'I' and hope to confine them to their place. No amount of order could stop the mind's inclination to leak. This was why desperate people blew their brains out. The only sure way to stop the leaking was to destroy the reservoir for ever.

That question came to him again. It still had no form. He didn't quite believe what Alicia had said he'd achieved tonight. He had *not* been certain that *he* was not the reason that Mercedes hadn't come back. He was responsible and the thought propelled him into his mac and out into the night air, which was now wet, the cobbles shining from some light rain. He went to the Plaza del Museo and found odd comfort pacing beneath the dark and dripping trees.

Just after 1 a.m. a taxi stopped at the junction of Calle San Vicente and Calle Alfonso XII. Inés got out and waited on the pavement. Calderón paid the driver from the back of the cab. Falcón came out from under the trees, his hair wet, and stood in the shadows of the kiosk on the plaza.

Calderón took Inés by the hand. She was staring up and down the street and across the plaza. They turned and walked up Calle San Vicente. Falcón loped across the square in a crouching run and found the shadows on the opposite side of the street to the lovers. He walked behind the cars parked on the pavement. They stopped. Calderón took out his keys. Inés turned and her eyes found him paralysed between a car and the wall of a building. He ducked and ran for the nearest doorway where he stood, back up against the wall, pressing himself flat into the darkness, heart and lungs fighting like a sack of wild animals. Inés told Calderón to go up. Her heels stabbed the street and stopped by the pavement close to him.

'I know you're there,' she said.

The blood thundered in his ears.

'This isn't the first time I've seen you, Javier.'

He squeezed his eyes shut, the child about to be found out, punished.

'Your face keeps coming out of the night,' she said. 'You're following me and I won't put up with it. You've destroyed my life once and I won't let you do it again. This is a warning. If I see you again, I will go straight to the courts and apply for a restraining order. Do you understand that? I will humiliate you as you did me.'

The spiky heels backed away and then returned, this time a little closer.

'I hate you,' she whispered. 'Do you know how much I hate you? Are you listening, Javier? I am going upstairs now and Esteban is going to take me to his bed. Did you hear that? He does things to me that you could never even dream of.'

Extracts from the Journals of Francisco Falcón

26th June 1946, Tangier
*I have terrible lower back pain and go to the Spanish doctor on Calle
Sevilla, not so far from R.'s house. He examines me, takes me into an
adjoining room and lays me face down on a cloth covered bench. Another
door opens and he introduces me to his daughter, Pilar, who works with
him as his nurse. She rubs an oil into my back which generates a
tremendous heat. She rubs the oil in down to my coccyx. By the end of
this treatment I am embarrassed by the state of my manhood. Her small
hands have magic in them. She tells me I have to come to her for a
session every day for a week. Were all afflictions like this.*

3rd July 1946, Tangier
*After endless negotiations I have persuaded Pilar to come and sit for me,
but a boy arrives at lunchtime to say she cannot come. In the late
afternoon Carlos Gallardo comes to visit. He is another of those 'fellow
artists', but he is not Antonio Fuentes. There is none of the ascetic about
him. He is louche. He drinks heavily and usually in the Bar La Mar
Chica, which was where we met. We have smoked hashish together and
looked at each other's work without comment.*

*He has brought a Moroccan lad with him who carries his groceries,
which he leaves at the door. We sit on low wooden chairs in one of the
dark cool rooms away from the heat of the patio. My houseboy puts a
hookah between us and fills it with a tobacco–hashish mix. We smoke.
The hashish does its work and I feel pleasant. Desultory thoughts float
into my mind like aquarium fish. C.'s boy is standing by his chair with
one of his brown feet resting on the other. He has had his hair shorn,
probably by C., against lice. He is smiling at me. He can't be more than
sixteen years old. I reset my vision and realize that C. has his hand up
the boy's robe and is caressing his buttocks. I didn't know this about C. It
does not disgust me. I make some comment. 'Yes,' he says,' of course I
like women, but there's something inhibiting about sex with a woman. I*

275

put it down to us Spanish and our mothers. But with these local youths it's so normal, something that has always happened and to which no stigma attaches. I feel free to indulge. I am a sensualist after all. You must have seen that from my work.' I muster some reply and he continues: 'Whereas you, my friend, are frozen solid. Bleak and chill. I hear the wind whistling through your canvasses. You should be thawing in this heat, but I can't see it. Perhaps you should take a boy for some guilt-free sensuality.' We smoke some more and my skin feels like velvet. C. says, 'Take Ahmed to your room now and lie down with him.' The idea sends a bolt of electricity through me. I find I am not appalled by the suggestion, quite the opposite. The boy comes over. I can barely speak but manage to turn down the offer.

5th July 1946, Tangier

P. comes with her mother. The heat is not so smothering and we sit in the patio under the fig tree. We talk. The women's eyes dart about like birds in a bush. I feel like a large cat planning dinner. P.'s mother is here to find out about me . . .

Because R.'s company, in which I am a partner, is one of the best known in Tangier's Spanish community, she is soon eating out of my hand as if it is chock-full of millet. I keep away from all the dull socializing and am not known. Were she to go down to the chabolas on the outskirts of town they would run away in fright at the mention of El Marroquí. But P.'s mother lives between her house and the Spanish cathedral so I am safe and I cannot see her ever straying into the Bar La Mar Chica.

She asks to see my work and I politely refuse, but relent under pressure. P. stands transfixed in front of the monochrome shapes and patterns while her mother rushes around trying to find something she understands. She settles on the drawing of a Touareg, which at least has some colour in it. I sign it and give it to her and ask to paint a portrait of her daughter. She says she will raise the matter with her husband.

They leave and moments later there is a fierce knocking on the door. It is the young lad who came round with C. the other day, Ahmed. He is eating a peach and the juice is dribbling down his chin and is smeared across his cheeks. He licks his lips. It is not subtle but it is effective. I haul him off the street and follow him, trembling, through the endless rooms and passages. He understands something of the urgency and runs kicking up his robe with his bare feet. By the time I arrive at the bedroom his caramel body lies beneath the mosquito netting. I fall on him like a demolished building. *Afterwards I give him a few pesetas and he goes away happy.*

3rd August 1946, Tangier
Trust has been established between myself and the doctor and P. is allowed to visit the house on her own to sit for her portrait. The sessions take place in the afternoon when the surgery is closed and can only last an hour. It is very hot. I have to work in one of the rooms close to the patio for the light. I am drawing. She sits on a wooden chair. I am close to her face. She does not flinch. We do not speak until I look at her hands. They rest in her lap, small, long-fingered, delicate instruments of pleasure.

Me: Who taught you to massage?

P.: Why do you think anybody taught me?

Me: The expertise in your fingers strikes me as coming from instruction rather than trial and error.

P.: Who taught you to paint?

Me: I had some help on how to look at things.

P.: I was taught by a gypsy woman in Granada.

Me: Is that where you're from?

P.: Originally, yes. My father was a doctor in Melilla for some years before we came here.

Me: And your father allowed you to mix with the gypsies?

P.: I am quite independent, despite what my parents might want you to think.

Me: You're allowed out?

P.: I do as I please. I am twenty-three years old.

The boy arrives with mint tea. We lapse into silence. I work on her hands and then we drink the tea.

P.: You draw figuratively but paint abstracts.

Me: I teach myself to see with the drawings and interpret it with the paint.

P.: What have you seen today?

Me: I have been looking at structure.

P.: How well am I built?

Me: With delicacy and strength.

P.: Do you know why I like you?

The question silences me.

P.: You have strength and individuality, but you are vulnerable, too.

Me: Vulnerable?

P.: You have suffered, but there is still the small boy in you.

This intimate exchange seals something between us. She has told me something she has kept from her parents. She has seen something in me which I have not denied. But she is wrong. I am those things . . . but I am not individual . . . not yet.

10th August 1946, Tangier
I am hobbling around again with my bad back. I have a lump on the right side of my spine. P. arrives for her sitting and immediately sees my problem. She leaves and returns with her little wooden case of bottles of oils. The bedroom is out of bounds. I lie on the floor. She tries to work on me from the side but it is hopeless. She tells me to shut my eyes. I hear her skirt slide down her legs. She lowers herself until she is astride the backs of my thighs. Only her bare legs touch mine on the outside. I can feel the heat of her above me. She kneads the lump in my back with the tips of her fingers while I take root in the ground.

She finishes with me. My whole body has been claimed by the floor. She puts her skirt on and tells me to get to my feet. We stand in front of each other. I have myself under control physically, but mentally I am in disarray. She tells me to walk around. I do this and there is no pain apart from a dull ache in my testicles. She tells me to keep walking. Activity is the secret of the healthy back. I must not sit to paint or draw. She leaves. I smoke some hashish until I feel liquid, like olive oil flowing greenly from room to room.

Ahmed turns up later with a friend. He is mischievous, this boy. I wonder whether C. is putting him up to it as an artistic experiment. Where P. and I are physically so demure, these boys are completely uninhibited. I smoke and they perform for me, their muscular adolescent bodies entwining like rope. They turn their attention to me. The release is explosive and they giggle like children playing around a fountain. Before they leave Ahmed presses a stoned date between my teeth. I lie there with the dreamy sweetness leaching into me, replete and satiated as a slumbering pasha.

11th August 1946, Tangier
It has been reported to me that two of my legionnaires have fought over a lover in a hotel room in town. The fight was long and bloody and the floor of the room was as slippery as a butcher's. One of my legionnaires is dead, the lover is badly wounded and the other legionnaire is in gaol. I ask the police chief if I can see the lover, thinking that this might be an

international incident if she dies; he tells me not to worry as the 'lover' is a Riffian boy. He shrugs, arches his eyebrows, opens his hands . . . es la vida.

I pay a bribe and the legionnaire is released on condition that he leaves the International Zone immediately. I take him to Tetuán and give him some money. On the trip over he tells me he was with the División Azul in Russia and stayed on with the Legión Española de Voluntarios and, after they were disbanded, he joined the SS. He was with the infamous Capt. Miguel Ezguera Sánchez when the Russians stormed Berlin. He shows me a handful of the leading currency at the end – cyanide pellets. He gives me two samples as an odd souvenir and as a novio de la muerte, *a bizarre way of thanking me.*

1st September 1946, Tangier
R. has taken out a loan and bought two more boats. I have been to Ceuta again and recruited more legionnaires. We train them to run the boats and pay them well for it. They like the work. They still have a weapon in their hands and there is adventure, although, because of our reputation for violence, nobody comes near us. The pirates pick on the small fry. My importance to the business is now paramount because trust is a rare commodity. The strong allegiances between legionnaires means we can rely on them and they will not steal. It releases R. and I from the grind of running the ships. R. is investing in property. We are building and I have to secure the construction sites. R. plays the gold and currency markets with the endless stream of cash that comes in from the smuggling operations. I do not understand these markets and have no inclination to involve myself.

Now that Barbara Hutton, the Woolworth heiress, has taken up residence in the Sidi Hosni Palace, R. tells me that Tangier will be the new Côte d'Azur. He plans to move more heavily into property 'to build hotels for all the people who will come here to warm their hands on our affluence'. He also tells me that La Rica *bought the palace for $100,000 – a quite unimaginable sum for all us Tangerinos to contemplate. The* Caudillo, *as General Franco is now called, had offered $50,000. He must be sitting in his El Pardo Palace fuming.*

3rd September 1946, Tangier
P. comes for another sitting. As soon as I open the door I see daring in her eyes, but also amusement and mockery. It is hot in the middle of the afternoon. We start to work in the usual silence until I lose concentration

and she walks around the room looking for anything she hasn't seen before. She finds a lump of hashish amongst the brushes and pots on the table and sniffs it. She knows what it is but has never tried it. She asks to smoke some. I've never seen her with a cigarette even, but I charge the hookah for her. Minutes later she's complaining that nothing has happened. I tell her to be patient and she releases a small moan as I imagine she would at the first sexual contact. Her eyes have distance in them as if she has retreated into her mind. She licks her lips slowly and sensually. I want to put my own mouth there. I drift and watch the light change in the room. P. says: 'I think you should draw me as I really am.' This I've been trying to do for weeks. In fast fluid movements she stands up, removes her blouse, lets her skirt fall, unharnesses her brassiere and steps out of her underwear. I am speechless. She stands in front of me, her long dark hair on her naked shoulders, her hands resting on the tops of her thighs, framing the triangle of her pubic hair. She slowly puts her fingertips to her shoulders and moves them down over her breasts to the brown pointed nipples, which harden to her touch. Her fingers trace the outline of her body. We are both so engaged in the sensuality of the moment that I think they are my fingers. 'This is who I am,' she says. I grab sticks of charcoal and sheets of paper. My hand flashes over them with bold, fluid movements. I must have drawn her six, seven, eight times in a matter of minutes. As I finish, each drawing slips to the floor. She continues to hold herself, utterly beautiful, and naked, with the supreme confidence of complete womanhood and it is that mysterious essence that I am 'seeing' and am able to draw. Then, as occasionally happens with hashish, we are in a different moment. She is pulling her clothes back on. She moves to leave and I stand with the drawings at my feet. She looks down at them and then up at me. 'Now you know,' she says. Her lips brush mine with the softness of sable and the coolness of water. The lightning touch of the tip of her tongue on mine stays with me for hours.

20th September 1946
I have returned from Tarragona to find that P. has gone back to Spain with her mother, whose sister has died. The doctor does not know when they will be coming back. I feel both bereft and oddly free. Ahmed and his friend come round at night and my mood is celebratory. A night of total hedonism comes to pass.

23rd September 1946
I show Carlos the charcoal drawings of P. He is astounded. For the first time he says something about my work and the word is 'Exceptional'. Later as we smoke a hookah together he says: 'I see the thaw has started. I hope Ahmed and Mohammed have been a help.' I look as if I don't know what he is talking about. He says he will send others to my door. 'I don't want you to get bored.' I say nothing.

30th October 1946
Still no word from P. and now her father has also left for Spain. The only possible address I have for them is Granada.
   R. has sold a plot of land to an American who wants to build a hotel. One of the conditions of sale is that we do the construction. It is our first major building contract. I want to be involved in the design, but R. insists that I keep my art and work separate. 'Everybody associated with me knows you as my security adviser . . . I can't have you designing the reception as well.'

23

Friday, 20th April 2001, Falcón's House, Calle Bailén, Seville

Clawing through oblivion was hard work. How could sleep be such toil? He surfaced, blathering like an old unvisited fool in a home for those close to the final terminus. His mobile was ringing, scintillating through the bones of his face. His mouth was as dry as bone meal. The phone ceased. He sank back into the felt grave of drugged sleep.

Was it hours later or just minutes? The mobile's trilling madness seemed to be tunnelling through his sinuses. He burst out of sleep, flailing. He found the light, the phone, the button. He sucked cool water in over the clod of tongue in his mouth.

'Inspector Jefe?'

'Did you call earlier?'

'No, sir.'

'What is it?'

'We've just had a report of another body.'

'Another body?' he said, his brain as thick as wadding.

'A murder. The same as Raúl Jiménez.'

'Where?'

'In El Porvenir.'

'Address?'

'Calle de Colombia, number 25.'

'I know that address,' he said.

'The house belongs to Ramón Salgado, Inspector Jefe.'

'Is he the victim?'

'We're not sure yet. We've just sent a patrol car out to investigate. The body was spotted by the gardener from outside the house.'

'What time is it?'

'Just gone seven.'

'Don't call anyone else from the group. I'll go on my own,' he said. 'But you'd better notify Juez Calderón.'

The name knifed through him as he hung up. He showered, head hung, arms weakened by the cruelty of Inés's words from last night. He nearly sobbed at the thought of facing Calderón. He shaved, turning his face interrogatively in the mirror. It would not be mentioned. Of course it wouldn't. How could something like that be laid out between two men? It was the end of his relationship with Calderón. 'Things . . . that you could never even dream of.'

He put his head under cold water, took an Orfidal, dressed and got into his car. He checked his messages at the first traffic light. There was one timed at 2.45 that morning. He played it back. The message began with some music, which he recognized as Albinoni's Adagio. Through it he could hear the muffled and desperate squeaking of someone trying to shout or plead through a gag. Furniture knocked against a wooden floor as the music soared, with the violins taking the exquisite pain of loss to new heights. Then a quiet voice: 'You know what to do.'

A terrible gurgling and rattling sound, that could only have been made by a constricted throat, came through the music. The struggle continued through the adagio's emotional peaks as the ricocheting furniture became frantic, until there was a crash and an abrupt silence before the violins returned on an even higher note and the message ended.

Horns blared behind him and he took off down by the river to the next red light. He called the Jefatura and asked to be connected to the patrol car. They still didn't have access to the house but there was confirmation of a body in the middle of the floor of a large room at the back of the house, which gave out on to the verandah and garden. The body was secured to a chair, which was on its side, and there was a lot of blood on the wooden floor. He told them to find the maid or check the neighbours for spare keys.

At the Parque de María Luisa he turned away from the river up Avenida de Eritaña, past a police station and the Guardia Civil, which were no more than a few hundred metres from Ramón Salgado's house.

There were still no keys by the time he arrived at the house, which gave time for an ambulance to turn up, followed by Calderón and finally Felipe and Jorge from the Policía Científica.

A neighbour found the spare set of keys at 7.20 a.m. and Falcón and Calderón entered the house, both wearing latex gloves. They went in to the large room at the back of the house with books lining the far wall. In the middle was a desk, which consisted of a sheet of three-centimetre-thick glass supported by two squares of black wood. There was an iMac, which was switched on with the 'desktop' showing. On the back wall behind the desk were four high-quality reproductions of the Falcón nudes. Between the desk and this wall Ramón Salgado was lying on his side attached to a high, ladder-backed, armless chair. One wrist was trapped underneath him, the other was secured so that the hand pointed down the back leg of the chair. One bare ankle was tied to the front leg of the chair and the other was high up in the air with a length of cord looped around the big toe. The cord ran up to a light fitting in the ceiling that consisted of four spotlights attached to a metal strip. Concealed in the metal strip was a small pulley. The cord ran through that and back down to Salgado's neck, which looked as if it might be broken. The cord was pulled tight so that Salgado's head, lolling on his neck, did not make contact with the ground. On closer inspection of the pulley they found it had been jammed by a knot in the cord.

'As soon as the chair went over,' said Falcón, 'he was a dead man.'

Calderón stepped around the blood on the floor.

'What the hell was happening in here before that?' he asked.

The Médico Forense, the same as for Raúl Jiménez, appeared at the door.

This was the first time Falcón had seen someone he knew murdered. He couldn't get it out of his head, the last occasion he'd seen Salgado, drinking manzanilla in the Bar Albariza. Now, to see him inanimate, his blood all over the floor, the gross indignity of the manner of his death, he winced with guilt at his dislike of the man. He moved further toward the book-lined wall to be able to look into Salgado's face. He could see that the cheeks were blood-streaked and stuffed full, gagged by his socks. The collar of his shirt was soaked, heavy with blood. The eyes stared up at Falcón and he flinched. In the coagulating blood on the floor he saw what he'd dreaded: a small flap with fine hairs.

Photographs were taken and Felipe and Jorge began taking samples of blood from every spatter mark on the floor until a path had been cleared for the Médico Forense to kneel by the body. He muttered his comments into his dictaphone – a physical description of Salgado, a catalogue of the injuries sustained and the probable cause of death.

'. . . loss of blood due to head injuries caused by the flailing of the

victim's head against the sharp edges and corners of the chair back
. . . eyelids removed . . . evidence of asphyxiation . . . possible broken
neck . . . time of death: within the last eight hours . . .'

Falcón handed Calderón his mobile and played him the message
that had been left at 2.45 a.m. Calderón listened and passed it on to
the Médico Forense.

'"You know what to do"?' Calderón repeated Sergio's instruction
to Salgado, mystified.

'This pulley isn't something installed by the killer,' said Falcón.
'It was already there. Somehow Sergio knew that Salgado had a
predilection for auto-strangulation. He was telling him how he could
end it all by taking his sexual proclivity beyond the limit.'

'Auto-strangulation?' asked Calderón.

'To be on the brink of asphyxiation during a sexual experience
intensifies the moment,' explained Falcón. 'Unfortunately the practice has its dangers.'

Things . . . that you could never even dream of, thought Falcón.

A patrolman came to the door. A policeman from the station down
the road wanted to speak to Falcón about a break-in he'd investigated
in Salgado's house two weeks ago. Falcón joined the policeman in
the hall and asked where the entry point had been.

'That was the strange thing, Inspector Jefe, there was no evidence
of a break-in and Sr Salgado said that nothing had been stolen. He
just knew that somebody had been in his house. He was convinced
that they'd spent the weekend here.'

'Why?'

'He couldn't tell me.'

'Does the maid come in at the weekends?'

'No, never. And the gardener only comes at weekends during the
summer to water the plants. Sr Salgado liked his privacy when he
was at home.'

'He's away a lot?'

'That's what he told me.'

'Did you check the house?'

'Of course. He followed me around.'

'Any weak points?'

'Not on the ground floor, but there's a room at the top of the
house with its own roof terrace and the lock on that door was almost
useless.'

'What about access?'

'Once you were up on the garage roof almost anybody could have made it up there,' said the policeman. 'I told him to change the lock, put a bolt on the door . . . They never do . . .'

Falcón went up to the top of the house. The policeman confirmed that the door and lock were the same. The key had come out of the lock and was lying on the floor. The door rattled in its frame.

In Salgado's study the medical examination was over and Felipe and Jorge were back on the floor taking blood samples. Falcón called Ramírez, filled him in, and told him to bring Fernández, Serrano and Baena down to El Porvenir. There was a lot of work to do just interviewing the neighbours before they left for work.

'There's an icon on the computer desktop,' said Calderón. 'It's called *Familia Salgado* and there's a card under the keyboard with "Sight Lesson No.3" written on it.'

It was after midday by the time Calderón signed off the levantami-ento del cadaver. It had taken Felipe and Jorge hours to take samples of each individual blood spatter in case one of them belonged to the killer. Salgado was removed, the crime scene cleaners disinfected the room. The chair was bubblewrapped and taken down to the police laboratory. It was 12.45 by the time Falcón, Ramírez and Calderón could sit in front of the iMac and watch *Familia Salgado*.

The film started with repeated takes of Salgado coming out of his house with his briefcase and getting into a taxi. These were followed by repeated takes of Salgado getting out of the taxi on the Plaza Nueva and walking down Calle Zaragoza to his gallery. There fol-lowed a succession of cuts – Salgado in a café, Salgado in a restaurant, Salgado outside the Bar La Company, Salgado window shopping, Salgado in the Corte Inglés.

'Yes, so . . . what's his point?' asked Ramírez.

'The man spends a lot of time on his own,' said Calderón.

The next scene showed Salgado arriving at the door to a house. It was a classic Sevillana door of varnished wood with ornate brass studs. He arrived again and again at this house, which had a very distinctive terracotta façade, with the doorframe and friezes picked out in a creamy yellow colour.

'Do we know where this house is?' asked Calderón.

'Yes, we do,' said Falcón. 'It's my house . . . my late father's house. Salgado was my father's agent.'

'If your father is dead,' said Calderón, stopping the film, 'why was Salgado . . . ?'

'He was always trying to get access to my father's old studio. He had his reasons, which he never told me.'

'Were you ever in when he called?' asked Ramírez.

'Sometimes. I never answered the door. I didn't like Ramón Salgado. He bored me and I avoided him whenever possible.'

Calderón restarted the movie. Salgado appeared at the intersection of a street. Above his head was a sign to the Hotel Paris and Falcón knew that he was standing on Calle Bailén looking in the direction of the house. Salgado set off. The camera followed him as he weaved through people bustling in the streets. Salgado was following somebody else. It was only as they came up to Marqués de Paradas that they could see that he was pursuing Falcón himself. They watched him go into the Café San Bernardo, which had an entrance on Calle Julio César. Salgado took the entrance on Marqués de Paradas and a 'chance' meeting ensued. The camera even came into the café, sat down and watched them talking at the bar. The barman set down a café solo for Falcón and a larger cup and saucer for Salgado. He returned with a steel jug of hot milk. Falcón recoiled as it was poured into Salgado's cup.

'What was all that about?' asked Ramírez. 'Did he say something to you?'

'He's always asking the same thing. "Can I just have a look in your father's . . ."'

'But why did you step back as if . . . ?'

'That's nothing, I just don't like milk. It's an allergy or something.'

'Now we're at the cemetery,' said Calderón.

'This is the Jiménez funeral,' said Ramírez. 'That's me by the cypress filming the mourners.'

The film showed Falcón and Salgado in conversation and then it stopped abruptly. Calderón sat back.

'Sergio seems to think that you are Salgado's only family, Inspector Jefe,' said Calderón.

'Salgado had a sister,' said Falcón. 'He'd just installed her in a home in Madrid.'

'Was there anything different about that last meeting after the funeral?' asked Calderón.

'He offered me information on Raúl Jiménez in exchange for access to the studio. He also said he didn't want anything from the studio but just to spend some time in there. I'd always thought he wanted to put on a final Francisco Falcón show, but he insisted that that was not the case. He made it sound as if it was something nostalgic.'

'What sort of information?'

'He knew Raúl Jiménez and his wife. He implied that he knew who the man's enemies were. He said that he picked up privileged information from the moneyed clients who frequented his gallery. He implied that he could point me in the right direction, towards people who had trusted Raúl Jiménez and been let down by him. We also covered such topics as the cleaning of black pesetas before the new euro currency comes in, how the restaurant business created black pesetas and how property and art were good havens for them. He was making everything sound full of promise, but I know Ramón Salgado . . .'

'And you have no idea what he wanted from your father's studio?' asked Calderón.

'Possibly there's a skeleton buried in all that paper,' said Falcón, 'but I doubt I will ever find it.'

'How well did Salgado know Consuelo Jiménez?'

'I know for certain that he introduced her to my father and that she bought paintings from him on three occasions. I am also convinced that Consuelo Jiménez knew Ramón Salgado from the Madrid art world and that it might even have been Salgado who introduced her to Raúl Jiménez at the Feria de Abril in 1989. She has not been clear about her relationship with Ramón Salgado from the beginning. This could be just her protecting her privacy – she really does not like our intrusions – or it could be that Salgado *did* know things about Raúl Jiménez and she wanted to keep us away from him. She referred to "a friend of her husband's from the Tangier days", who I am sure is Salgado. This would mean that the two men had known each other for over forty years.'

'There's a motive in there somewhere, isn't there?' said Calderón.

'She's had Salgado done as well,' said Ramírez. 'I'm sure of it.'

'Let's not jump to conclusions yet, Inspector,' said Calderón. 'It's something worth pursuing, that's all. We should look at this sight lesson now.'

Ramírez took the card out of the evidence bag. There were two names written on the reverse side. Francisco Falcón and H. Bosch.

'The card was tucked under the keyboard of the computer,' said Falcón. 'They could be access codes to files.'

Calderón double-clicked on the hard-disk icon and a box appeared demanding an access code. He typed in Francisco Falcón. The hard disk opened up to reveal twenty folders with nothing unusual about their names – Letters, Clients, Accounts, Expenses . . . They clicked them all open but only 'Drawings' demanded another access code. They typed in H. Bosch and it opened up another series of files. Calderón opened a file at random. It contained hundreds of photographs, each initialled and dated.

'I hope we don't have to go through Salgado's entire collection of drawings to find what Sergio wants us to find,' said Calderón.

Falcón scrolled down the list to the bottom.

'Those last five are movies,' said Calderón.

'Maybe the photographs aren't so innocent,' said Ramírez.

'They could be for insurance purposes,' said Falcón.

Ramírez grabbed the mouse and double-clicked on the movie icon. The opening image of the movie was framed by a small screen. It was of a young boy tied face down on an old-fashioned leather gym horse. His arms were bound so that he was hugging the horse and his ankles were attached to the metal legs. He was also strapped to the apparatus around the small of his back, and his buttocks had been grotesquely and obscenely thrust up in the air. He was helpless and his face, although slack and glazed over from drugs, still showed the worm of fear.

'We don't need to see this,' said Falcón.

'Check one of the photographs,' said Calderón. 'All these files could be disguised.'

Ramírez opened one up. Another pre-pubescent boy with blue eyeshadow and pink lipstick was graphically impaled on an adult penis. That was enough for them and they shut the computer down.

'We'd better let Vice take a look at this,' said Falcón.

'And where does this take us?' said Calderón. 'Why did Sergio draw our attention to that?'

'It was a sight lesson,' said Falcón. 'He was just showing us the true nature of the man. If before you thought that Ramón Salgado was an elderly, lonely, wealthy, well-connected, respectable director of a prestigious gallery in Seville, then now you think differently.'

'I think it's a blind alley,' said Ramírez. 'It's just another way to send us off on the wrong track. It's no coincidence that Sra Jiménez is intimately connected to both victims.'

'There was a third victim as well,' said Falcón.

'You know what I mean, Inspector Jefe,' said Ramírez. 'The puta was an unfortunate casualty and another way to confuse our investigation as well as use up our time. Consuelo Jiménez had all the information to set up her husband and, by the sound of it, Ramón Salgado, too. I still think we should take her down to the Jefatura and put her under some real pressure.'

'Before we even think about bringing her in for questioning I would suggest that we search this house from top to bottom and send a team round to the gallery on Calle Zaragoza,' said Falcón. 'To take *her* on you need ammunition.'

'And what are we looking for, Inspector Jefe?' asked Ramírez.

'We're looking for an ugly connection between Consuelo Jiménez and Ramón Salgado,' said Falcón. 'So, leave Fernández interviewing the neighbours here and take Serrano and Baena with you up to the top of the house and start working your way down behind Felipe and Jorge.'

Ramírez left the room. Falcón closed the door behind him, went back to Calderón sitting at the desk.

'I wanted to talk to you in private for a moment,' said Falcón.

'Look, er . . . Don Jav—, Inspector Jefe,' said Calderón, unprepared for this moment, the private and the official clashing in his mind. 'I don't know what happened last night. I don't know what Inés said to you. I know, of course, that you . . . but she told me that it was finished, that you were divorced. I think you have to . . . I don't know . . . I mean . . . What were you *doing* there last night?'

Falcón was rooted to the spot. The morning had been so full that he hadn't even thought about Inés. What he'd wanted to talk about in private was MCA Consultores S.A. and nothing to do with his private life. He stared into the floor, desperate for a time collapse that would bring him round a week later on another case with a different judge. It didn't come and he found himself in one of those titanic struggles of the sort he watched suspects go through on their way to confession. He wanted to say something. He wanted to somehow address the complexity of his recent experience, to show that he, like Calderón, was capable of overcoming this embarrassing situation, but all he came up against was an immense entanglement. Falcón sensed himself in retreat. He fingered the buttons on his jacket as if to make sure they were well fastened.

'It had not been my intention to talk about that at this juncture,' he said, appalled at the pomposity and restraint in his words. 'My only concerns are professional.'

He hated himself instantly and Calderón's dislike of him hit him like a bad stink. He'd been given a civilized opportunity to come to an understanding and he'd shown it the cold heel of one of his laced-up shoes and now it was irretrievable.

'What was it that you had on your mind, Inspector Jefe?' said Calderón, crossing his legs with glacial calm.

Everything had gone to ashes in that instant. Falcón had failed on the human level with Calderón and it had tarnished his professional credibility. He sensed that there would be resistance to his ideas and perhaps worse: the man's antipathy would turn against him. Calderón would never be an ally and any ideas that Falcón put to him might be furnishing an enemy with the means to destroy him. But he couldn't help himself and he realized that it wasn't his professionalism that made him tell Calderón about MCA Consultores S.A., it was his failure. It was because of the ridiculous and illogical thought that the young judge might now be able to agree with Inés and say: 'Yes, Javier Falcón has got no heart.'

24

Friday, 20th April 2001, Ramón Salgado's House, El Porvenir, Seville

Calderón took notes as Falcón spoke. At the end he lit a cigarette while Falcón looked out on to Salgado's abundant garden.

'Is this what you came to talk to me about yesterday?' asked Calderón.

'I think you'll agree there are some sensitive points to this theory,' said Falcón. 'And when I saw Dr Spinola coming out . . .'

'Dr Spinola was *not* on that list of directors,' said Calderón sharply.

'He was in Raúl Jiménez's celebrity photographs. There's a tenuous connection. It had to be thought about,' said Falcón, sensing Calderón's resistance, and his own pathetic need to side with him. 'You will also notice that the proof of Raúl Jiménez being involved in child abuse is circumstantial and weak. I only mentioned it because of the convicted paedophile ring in which Carvajal was involved and what we have discovered here today.'

'So, do you think we're looking for an abused boy and do you think Consuelo Jiménez is involved?' asked Calderón.

'Sergio is male. He was somehow able to make a connection with Eloisa Gómez, possibly through empathy . . . as another forastero. I have not read Carvajal's case notes so I don't know what his predilections were, but Salgado seemed to be interested in boys and Jiménez in girls.'

'In that case Sergio is either acting alone as an avenger of the abused or, quite possibly, he's having his targets pointed out to him,' said Calderón.

'Consuelo Jiménez loves her children. Admittedly, they are all boys but if she found any pornography in her husband's collection which was in any way related to child abuse, I am sure she would not tolerate it. She knew Ramón Salgado . . .'

'But how could she possibly know *this* about him?' said Calderón, tapping the computer.

'That, I don't know. I am only theorizing about her capability, not proving her involvement,' said Falcón. 'She has been evasive about all her husband's business affairs. When I demonstrated some knowledge to her about MCA Consultores she wouldn't speak without her lawyer present. She is a determined woman and although she says she abhors violence she did strike Basilio Lucena hard enough to draw blood. She is intelligent and calculating. In her defence it's possible she knew nothing about MCA and was just being cautious. She has also offered to find out about her husband's relationship with Carvajal.'

'It's flimsy, Inspector Jefe. As you said earlier, she could just be protecting her privacy, as well as her inheritance and that of her children. She struck Lucena, but that was under extreme provocation, given the dangers of his promiscuity. Intelligence and calculation are prerequisites for success in business.'

'You're right, of course,' said Falcón, loathing the obsequiousness that had crept into his own voice. 'Are we agreed that the murders are connected, Juez? I mean we're not looking at a series of random acts. This is multiple murder but not serial killing.'

Calderón pinched the cartilage of his ear and stared through the glass desktop.

'The punishment that Sergio has meted out to his two primary victims is consistent with what you'd expect of somebody who'd suffered sexual abuse,' said Calderón. 'The victims are clearly targeted and there is a link in that they knew each other. I agree with you that Sergio forces them to confront their deepest horrors. The removal of the eyelids and the subsequent mutilation both victims inflicted on themselves would indicate this. The question is: how does Sergio know these things? This is not available information. This is profoundly personal stuff. It is secret history. How does Sergio get inside people's heads?'

Falcón told him about the local policeman's burglary investigation.

'Well, if he did spend the weekend here that would suggest that he'd already targeted Salgado, perhaps he even knew this man's particular horror and he was just looking for the means to bring it back to him.'

'He's obsessed with film,' said Falcón. 'He sees it like memory.'

'You know how it is . . . films and dreams. People are always getting those words muddled up,' said Calderón. 'It's understandable. The enclosed darkness of the cinema, the images. It's not so different to what you'd see in your sleep.'

'We talked about his creativity before,' said Falcón. 'He is doing what every artist wants to do. He gets inside people's heads and makes them see things differently or, in fact, he makes them see what they already know but in a different light. And he has to be creative about it because people don't hold records of their horrors, do they?'

'They bury them,' said Calderón.

'Maybe this is the nature of evil,' said Falcón. 'The genius of evil.'

'What makes you say that?'

'Because it's beyond our imagination.'

Calderón turned in his seat to the four Falcón nudes.

'Fortunately there are other types of genius,' he said. 'To balance out the evil ones.'

'In my father's case, I think he wished he'd never had it.'

'Why?'

'Because he lost it,' said Falcón. 'If he'd never had it . . . he wouldn't have gone through the rest of his life with that sense of loss.'

Falcón drifted back to the window as the personal re-entered their dialogue. He wondered if he could do it now – salvage the situation. If he could talk about his father in this way, why not Inés? Why not bare his neck to this man? There was a knock at the door. Fernández put his head in.

'Inspector Ramírez has found a trunk up in the attic,' he said. 'The lock's been sawn through and the dust on the surface has been disturbed. Felipe is looking at it for prints.'

They got the trunk down to the landing after Felipe had declared it clean. It was heavy. They opened it up and parted the brown paper covering the contents – books and old catalogues, copies of a magazine called the *Tangier–Riviera*, manila envelopes packed thick with photographs. Slotted down the sides were four reels of magnetic tape of the sort used on the old reel-to-reel tape recorders. There was a single can of film but no camera or projection equipment. There was a diary whose first entry was on 2nd April 1966 and which ran out after twenty pages with a final entry on 3rd July 1968.

Calderón left for a meeting when he saw that the trunk offered no fast solutions. They fixed a meeting for midday on Monday. As Calderón left the house he was confronted by four journalists who were too well informed to be ignored. He held an impromptu press conference in which one of the journalists said that the media was dubbing the killer *El Ciego de Sevilla*. To which he automatically replied that there was no logic in calling the killer the blind man when, in fact, he was just the opposite.

'So you *can* confirm that the killer cuts the eyelids off his victims?' asked the journalist, and the press conference was prematurely terminated.

Falcón and Ramírez split the workload. Ramírez was happy to take Fernández down to the gallery on Calle Zaragoza when he heard that Salgado had a blonde, blue-eyed secretary called Greta. Baena and Serrano continued the search of the house with Felipe and Jorge while the trunk was taken down to the study and the contents laid out on the desk. A further search of the attic uncovered no camera or projection equipment, but there was an old reel-to-reel tape recorder which Felipe managed to get working.

The diary seemed the obvious place to start but was very badly kept up. The first entry showed why Salgado had started it. He was happy. He was getting married to a woman called Carmen Blázquez. Falcón, who'd never known that Salgado had had a wife, grunted as he read the words – Salgado already proud, pompous and unctuous at the age of thirty-three. '*Francisco Falcón has done me the great honour of agreeing to be my* testigo. *His genius will make the occasion one of the talked-about events of the Seville social calendar.*' It was no wonder he hadn't kept up the entries. The man had nothing to say. The only time he was moving was when he talked about his new wife. Then, all the artifice was stripped away and he wrote in unembellished prose. '*I love Carmen more with every day that passes.*' '*She is a good person, which makes her sound dull but it is her goodness which affects everyone who meets her. As Francisco says: "She makes me forget the uglinesses of my life. When I'm in her company I feel as if I have only ever been a good man."*'

Falcón tried to imagine his father saying those words and decided they were Salgado's invention. He opened up the manila envelope of photographs and found one of Carmen dated June 1965 in which she looked to be in her late twenties. There was nothing striking about her face except her eyebrows, which were short, dark and completely horizontal with no arch to them at all. They gave her an earnest, concerned look, as if she would look after her husband well.

Another entry dated 25th December 1967: '*Last night before dinner*

I was taken back to childhood. My parents always allowed us one present on Christmas Eve and Carmen has given me the best gift of my life. She is pregnant. We are deliriously happy and I get quite drunk on champagne.'

The diary charted Carmen's uneventful pregnancy, which was intercut with stupefying details of successful art shows and sale values. Salgado mentioned the purchase of the tape recorder, which he'd bought intending to record Carmen's singing, which he never managed to do due to her self-consciousness in front of the microphone. Salgado was also entranced by Carmen's pregnant belly, which was enormous. He even asked her if she'd let Francisco Falcón draw her. She was appalled at the suggestion. The final entry read: *'The doctor has agreed to allow me to record my child's first cry in the world. They are bemused by the request. It seems that men are never present at the birth. I ask Francisco where he was for the birth of his children and he says he can't remember. When I ask if it was at Pilar's bedside he is stunned by the notion. Am I the only man in Spain to be fascinated by such a momentous occasion? And Francisco, an artist of such genius, I would have thought he would find birth as compelling as inspiration.'*

A strange note to end on. Falcón counted back the months and reckoned that if Carmen had announced her pregnancy at the end of December then the baby should have been born in July. He went through the contents of the trunk to see if there was a record of the child's birth. In a stained blue folder was his answer – Carmen Blázquez's death certificate dated 5th July 1968. The medical report beneath it detailed a catastrophic birth marred by high blood pressure, fluid retention, septicaemia and finally death for both mother and child.

The thought of the padlocked trunk high up in the attic of Salgado's house took on a terrible poignancy for Falcón. The loneliness of the man – the solitary diner, the forlorn shopper, the desolate hanger-on – whose whole life had been dedicated to the genius of Francisco Falcón, walked the streets with his only possibility of happiness boxed away in a dry dusty place.

He turned to the next photograph from the manila envelope under the horizontal eyebrows of the undemanding Carmen Blázquez and there they were on their wedding day. Ramón and Carmen holding hands. Their whole happiness contained in that pocket. It was astonishing for Falcón to see Salgado so young. The subsequent thirty-five years had ruined his looks. The misery had been a weight he carried in his face.

The stack of tapes demanded Falcón's attention, but he continued to flip through the photographs until he came to a shot of his father sitting with Carmen in a garden, the two of them laughing. It was true of his father that he'd always been drawn to 'good' women. His mother, Mercedes . . . even the eccentric Encarnación was tolerated because she was 'a good woman'. He carried on through the stack of photographs and realized that this was Salgado's entire collection of shots of Carmen. They were all different sizes and taken with a variety of cameras. Salgado must have systematically removed her from the photographic record of his life.

The tapes. The thought of the tapes made his hands sweat. He didn't want to hear what was on those tapes. His hands trembled as he threaded the tape through the heads. He played it and was relieved to find that it was completely silent.

The second tape burst straight into a conversation between Salgado and Carmen. He was imploring her to sing. She was refusing. Her heels paced a wooden floor while Salgado pleaded with her, right down to begging her for something that he could remember her by if she happened to die before him. The conversation bled into classical music, followed by some flamenco and Falcón fast-forwarded to the end.

The third tape started with Albinoni's Adagio. There followed other stirring pieces by Mahler and Tchaikovsky. He barely managed to feed the fourth tape through the heads, his hands were so slippery. He pressed 'play' and heard only the ethereal hiss, but then came everything that he'd dreaded. There was screaming and exhortation and panic. There was the rushing of feet on hard floors, steel trays clanging on tiles, tables and screens toppling, material ripping. There was one last cry of someone being swept out to sea with no life line, with only the sight of their lover, helpless and diminishing on the shore: 'Ramón! Ramón! Ramón!' And then a harsh click and silence.

The glass desktop provided support. Carmen's final cries had hit him like three body blows and broken him in the middle. His organs felt ruptured.

He concentrated on his breathing – the calming effect of valuing a motor reflex. He turned the machine off, wiped sweat from his top lip. He was nearly overwhelmed by guilt at how brutal he'd been to this old friend of his father. All those times he'd seen him outside Calle Bailén and thought, no, not that pain in the arse. But then there were the appalling contents of the computer. What had happened to this man after he'd lost his wife? Had his misery goaded him? Had it prodded him down this worthless road to the ultimate, lonely depravity of auto-strangulation whilst calamitous images of ruined children passed before his eyes? Maybe it was in his nature and he'd seen that terrible capacity, but then Carmen had come into his life and given him a shot at goodness and he'd had her brutally torn from him. Yes, disappointment would seem a paltry word to describe Ramón Salgado's state as he left that hospital in the dreadful heat of a Sevillano July and taken his first feverish steps down towards hell.

Baena came in with a large plastic bag.

'We've finished in the house, Inspector Jefe.' he said and handed over the bag. 'Serrano's done the garden with Jorge. The only thing of interest was this. It's a whip. The sort religious nuts use to flagellate themselves. *Mea culpa. Mea culpa.*'

'Where was it?'

'In the back of the built-in wardrobe in the bedroom,' said Baena. 'No thorn tiaras or hair shirts though, sir.'

Falcón grunted a laugh and told Baena to make an inventory of the trunk and take it back to the Jefatura. He left Serrano to seal up the house and drove back to the centre of town. He parked in Reyes Católicos and had a quick *tapa* of *solomillo al whisky* and then walked up Calle Zaragoza to Salgado's gallery, where the showroom was in darkness.

Greta, Salgado's Swiss-born secretary, was sitting at her desk at the back of the showroom with her hands jammed between her knees, staring into space. Her eyes were puffy and wrecked from crying.

'You should go home,' said Falcón, but she didn't want to be on her own. She told him it was her tenth anniversary working for Ramón Salgado. They had a celebration planned for this year's Feria. She drifted off into old memories and stock phrases about 'what a good man Ramón was'. Falcón asked if there were any artists that she could think of who hadn't liked Ramón, who perhaps had been rejected by him?

'People come off the street all the time. Students, young people. I deal with them. They don't understand how the business works, that Ramón is not operating at that level. Some of them storm out, as if we don't deserve their genius. Others get talking and, if I like them, I let them show me their stuff. If it's good I tell them who they could show it to. Ramón never saw any of these people.'

'How many of them show you installations using film, video or computer graphics?'

'More than half. Not many of the kids paint these days.'

'That's not Ramón's style, is it?'

'It's not his clients' style. They're the conservative ones. They can't see its value. At this level it's mostly about money and investment . . . and a CD with some creative stuff digitalized on to it doesn't feel or look like a ten-million-peseta investment.'

'Were there any unhappy established artists that he was representing?'

'He worked very closely with his artists. He didn't make those sorts of mistakes.'

'What about in the last six months? Do you recall anything suspicious, an unpleasant or humiliating . . .'

'He's not been so concentrated on his work. He's been concerned about his sister and he's been abroad a lot. Mainly the Far East – Thailand, the Philippines.'

The thought of Salgado pursuing his needs with oriental boys congealed in Falcón's mind. He felt grimy in front of the blonde Greta – he with his new knowledge, she with her untarnished memories. He realized that he was diminished by the truth, and she, unsullied in her ignorance.

'Did Ramón ever talk about his wife?' he asked.

'I didn't know he'd been married,' she said. 'He was a very private man. I never thought of him as particularly Spanish even. There was a lot of Swiss reserve about him.'

We are such different things to different people, thought Falcón. Salgado was quiet, powerful, kind and private with a woman he had no need to impress, and yet to Falcón he was always oily, tedious, ingratiating and pompous. With a good memory we could be who we wanted to be, with whoever we liked – all of us actors and every day a new play.

He went upstairs to Salgado's office, now occupied by Ramírez and Fernández in their shirtsleeves on either side of the desk, leafing through papers.

'We're not getting very far here,' said Ramírez. 'The best we've got is what Greta gave us in the first half-hour, which was their client list, the list of artists he used to represent, those he still represents and those he's rejected. The rest is letters, bills, the usual stuff. No correspondence between him and Sra Jiménez. No little note from Sergio saying, "You're fucked." '

It was late. Falcón told them to pack it in. He went back to the Jefatura. The trunk from Salgado's attic was already there. He took the film and spooled it into Raúl Jiménez's projection equipment, which was still set up. The movie must have been a gift, perhaps even from Raúl Jiménez. It consisted of seven sequences of Ramón and Carmen. They were happy in every shot. Salgado clearly adored her. The look he gave her as she turned to the camera and his eyes remained fixed on her cheek, there was no mistaking it.

Falcón sat in the dark with the flickering images. He had no way of controlling himself. He had no one to control himself for. He wept without knowing why and despised himself for it, as he used to despise cinema audiences who wailed at the crass sentimentality on the silver screen.

Extracts from the Journals of Francisco Falcón

2nd November 1946, Tangier
An American came to see me yesterday. A sizeable piece of humanity. He
introduced himself as Charles Brown III and asked to see my work. My
English has improved with all the Americans suddenly appearing in the
Café Central. I don't want him leafing through my drawings and tell
him I have to show properly and to come back in the afternoon. This
gives me time to find out from R. that he is the representative of
Barbara Hutton, the new Queen of the Kasbah. I set up the work I
want to show and when he returns and we enter the room I say:
'Everything's for sale, except that one,' which is the drawing of P.

There's a rumour that inside the Palace of Sidi Hosni there is a world
of wealth beyond even R.'s imagination. Each of the thirty rooms has its
own gold mantel clock from Van Cleef & Arpels at a cost of $10,000 a
piece. Anybody who spends a third of a million dollars to tell the time can
only value things by price alone. 'She will not buy a drawing from you
for $20,' says R. 'She doesn't know how much that is. It's as little as a
centavo is to us.' I tell him I have never sold a piece in my life. 'Then
you should sell your first piece for no less than $500.' He gives me the
sales technique, which I have put into practice. I follow Charles Brown
around the room and talk him through the work, but all I can sense is
his desperation to get back to the drawing of P. At the end he asks: 'Just
outa interest, how much is the charcoal drawing of the nude?' I tell him
it's not for sale. It has no price. He keeps using the phrase, 'just outa
interest' and I say, 'I don't know.' He goes back to the piece. I play it by
R.'s book and don't go with him but smoke at the other end of the room
and look as if I'm amusing myself, rather than what I want to do which
is burst like a balloon of water so that all that is left of me is a puddle of
gratitude and a bladder.

'You know,' he says, 'this is all very interesting stuff. I like it. I mean
that. I like it. The interlocking shapes in the Moorish tradition. The
patterned chaos. The bleak landscapes. It all does something for me. But

we're not talking about me. I buy for clients. And this is what my clients want. They don't want the cool intellectual stuff . . . not the people who come to Tangier. They come for . . .what shall I call it? . . . eastern promise.'

'On the northwest tip of Africa?' I say.

'It's kind of a saying,' he says. 'It means they want something exotic, sensual, mysterious . . . Yeah, mystery is the thing. Why isn't this for sale?'

'Because it's important to me. It's a new and recent development.'

'I can see that. Your other drawings are perfect . . . meticulously observed. But this . . . this is different. This is so revealing . . . and yet, forbidden. Maybe that's it. The nature of mystery is that it shows something of itself, it entices but it forbids the ultimate knowledge.'

Has Charles Brown been smoking, I ask myself. But he is sincere. He pushes again for a price. I don't give in. He tells me his client has to see the work. I won't let it out of the house. He finishes our discussion with the words:

'Don't worry I'll bring the mountain to Mohammed.'

He leaves, shaking my damp hand. I tremble with excitement. I am in a sweat and tear off my clothes and lie on the floor naked. I smoke a hashish cigarette, one of the twenty I prepare for myself every morning. I look at the drawing of P. I am as priapic as Pan and, as if by telepathy, a boy arrives from C. and releases my steam.

4th November 1946, Tangier
I lie in my room in a state of controlled nonchalance for two days. My ear is trained and finely tuned to the faintest knock on the front door. I fall asleep and when the knock comes I burst to the surface like a man freed from a sinking ship. I wrestle with the bolster and try to dress at the same time. I do a comic turn while the houseboy waits at the side of the bed with an envelope. It is he who has prodded me awake. I tear open the envelope. Inside is a gold-embossed card from Mrs Barbara Woolworth Hutton, and in her own handwriting she asks if she may visit Francisco González in his home on 5th November 1946 at 2.45 p.m. I show the card to R., who is impressed, I can tell. 'We have a problem here,' he says. R. likes problems, which is why he is always creating them. The problem is my name.

'Name me a González who has done anything of note in the world of art,' says R.

'Julio González, the sculptor,' I say.

'Never heard of him,' says R.

'He worked with iron – abstract geometric shapes – he died four years ago.'

'You know what Francisco González says to me? It says button seller.'

'Why buttons?' I ask, and he ignores me.

'What's your mother's name?'

'I can't use my mother's name,' I say.

'Why not?'

'I just can't use it, that's all.'

'What is it?'

'Falcón,' I say.

'No, no, no, que no . . . esto es perfecto. *Francisco Falcón. From now on that is your name.*'

I try to tell him that it will not do, but I don't want to reveal more than I have to, so I accept my fate. I am Francisco Falcón and I have to admit it has something . . . Apart from being alliterative there is a rhythm to it, as there is to Vincent van Gogh, Pablo Picasso, Antonio Gaudí, even the simpler Joan Miró . . . they all have the rhythm of fame. They've known this for some time in Hollywood, which is why we have Greta Garbo and not Greta Gustafson and Judy Garland not Frances Gumm, never Frances Gumm.

5th November 1946, Tangier

She came as promised and I am completely delirious. I have not smoked this evening so that the diamond brightness of the moment is not lost in the hashish haze. She arrived, escorted by Charles Brown, who is monumental next to her and utterly deferential. I am struck by her extraordinary grace and elegance, the perfection of her dress, the softness of her gloves, which must have come from the underbelly of a five-week-old kid. What I like more is her natural disapproving look. Her wealth, which is an encasing aura, sealing her off from normal mortals, has made her demanding, but I think when she falls . . . she falls hard. Her heels click expensively on my terracotta floor. She says: 'Eugenia Errázuriz would love these tiles.' Whoever she may be.

I am mesmerized, but surprise myself by not being tongue-tied as we go to the exhibition room. I have refined R.'s technique and this time the drawing is not even on display. She walks around the room placing each foot carefully in front of the other. Charles Brown is murmuring words in her ear, which I imagine is lined with mother-of-pearl. She listens and nods. She is taken with the Moorish shapes. She moves swiftly past the bleak, Russian landscapes. She hovers over the Tangier drawings.

She turns on her heel. The kid gloves are off and hang limply from one of her small white hands. 'This is excellent work,' she says. 'Remarkable. Original. Quite strange. Very affecting. But Charles tells me you have something that is even beyond the excellence of these pieces, which you've had the good grace to allow me to view.'

'I know what you refer to and I told Mr Brown that it was not for sale. I thought it unfair to even show it to you.'

'I would only like to see it,' she says. 'I would never want to take something from you that was so important.'

'Then it is understood,' I say. 'Follow me.'

I have arranged the drawing so that it is perfectly lit at the end of a long dark corridor and displayed against an old terracotta brick wall beneath a white arch, which has been textured by decades of whitewash. This part of the house is quite dark and I know that she will suddenly come across it and will be drawn to it like a moth. I am not wrong. And, I don't think I am mistaken, when she first sees the drawing she lets out a little sexual moan. She walks towards it and I see that in her eyes she is lost. My work is done. I stand back and let her go on alone. She doesn't move for ten minutes. Then she bows her head and turns away. At the front door her eyes are glistening. 'Thank you so much,' she says. 'I hope you will do me the honour of being my guest at dinner one of these evenings.' She holds out her hand. I bow and kiss it.

6th November 1946, Tangier
The day starts with a dinner invitation from B.H. An hour later Charles Brown arrives. I arrange mint tea and smoke a cigarette. The conversation is long and meandering and includes enquiries relating to my past, which I lie about in monstrous fashion thinking, on the spur of the moment, that this is best, that in this way nobody will ever know me, including possibly myself, and so I will sustain the mysterious aura which will become the trademark of my work. I lose myself in this thought: that even after I'm gone and the laborious, scholarly effort is made to get to the bottom of Francisco Falcón (there, you see, the transformation is already complete, I wrote that without thinking – Francisco González has disappeared), the onion layers will be parted one after the other, leading to the kernel of truth. But, as everybody knows, the truth about an onion is nothing. When the last parchment of onion matter is teased open there is nothing. No little message. It is nothing. I am nothing. We are nothing. The realization of this gives me enormous strength. I feel a huge surge of immoral freedom. For me there are no

rules. I come back to C.B. with a start. He is asking me whether I will consider selling. I say no. He asks me whether I would bring it with me to dinner to show the other guests. This would be psychologically weakening, so again I say no. C.B. and I head for the door and he says: 'You realize that Mrs Hutton would be prepared to part with a significant amount of money for your piece.'

'There is no doubt in anybody's mind of the means of the owner of the Palace Sidi Hosni,' I say.

He leaves his parting shot until the last moment.

'Five hundred dollars,' he says, and walks off down the narrow street, turns left and heads back up to the Kasbah.

I use all my powers of restraint not to call him back.

11th November 1946, Tangier
I should have written this last night when the perfection of the whole evening was still fresh in my mind. I arrived back so drunk and in such a state of excitement that I had to smoke several pipes of hashish to bring me down into a fitful slumber. I have woken up thick-headed, with a flighty memory rather than one tethered to the facts.

I arrive at the gates of the Sidi Hosni Palace and am admitted, on showing my invitation, by a liveried Tanjawi in white pantaloons. I am instantly in a dream world, where I am handed from servant to servant and walked through rooms and patios, on which no expense has been spared by the previous owner, whose name escapes me. Blake? Or was it Maxwell? Or perhaps both.

The palace has been made up of a number of houses which have all been linked to a central structure where I am led. The effect is bewildering, magical and mysterious. It is a microcosm of the Moroccan mind. The servant leaves me in a room in which some of the guests are behaving as if they're at a cocktail party, and others as if they're in a museum. Both are right. I am in a suit but am swarthier from my outdoor life, which sets me apart from the predominantly white people in the room. One woman nearly asks me for a drink but realizes at the last moment that I am not wearing gloves or a fez. Instead she asks me what wood the floor is made of. C.B. rescues me and introduces me around the room. At each introduction a flutter bursts up to the chandeliers (which are to be replaced with Venetian glass) like a flock of doves. I realize this dinner has been set up for me, to present me to society, to flatter me. A drink is put in my hand. It is ferocious with alcohol. The colossal C.B. has his hand on my shoulder as if I'm his younger statue and with a bit more bronze poured into me I could command as large a square as he. No hostess yet. I am ill-equipped for the occasion, not through lack of language but lack of social niceties. The talk is of New York, London and Paris, about horses, fashion, yachts, property and money. I am told things about our hostess, about how she gave her London home to the American government as a gift, how the carpet on the wall is from Qom, the marquetry from Fez, the bronze head from Benin. They know everything about B.H.'s world but none of them had penetrated the carapace of her significant wealth. But I had. And that was why I was there. C.B. III had told everybody, in so many words, that I had got inside and done it with the simplest and yet most beguiling charcoal drawing that said more in its moment than the endlessly restructured, laboriously crafted, massively overstuffed palace of Sidi Hosni. As I moved around the room I picked up invitations to other social occasions as well as a number of sexual offers from women. The same depravity that trickles thickly and darkly down the alleys of the Soco Chico is here behind the gilded walls of the palatial home of the old Muslim Holy Man, Sidi Hosni.

B.H. comes straight to me, holds out her hand. I kiss it. We are the centre of attention. She says, 'I must show you something.' We leave the room. She heads for a door guarded by a tall, very black Nubian, who is in white pantaloons but stripped to the waist. She unlocks the door, which is heaved open by the Nubian, and we enter her private gallery. There is a Fragonard, a Braque, even an El Greco. A painting by that terrible fraud Salvador Dali, a Manet, a Kandinsky. I am stunned. There are drawings, too. I see a Picasso and others which I am told are by Hassan el Glaoui, the son of the Pasha of Marrakesh. Then comes the psychological point of the whole evening. B.H. leads me to a space on the wall. 'Here,' she says, 'I want to put something that sums up my feelings about Morocco. The piece will have to be elusive, apparent and yet untouchable, revealing and yet incomprehensible, available but forbidden. It must tantalize like the truth, just as you think you can put your finger on it, it slips away.' These were not entirely her words, some belonged to C.B. and I think others have been sewn in by me. She finishes with the words: 'I want your drawing to be part of this collection.' This was a planned assault. I knew I had to give in. To withhold any more risked boring my assailants. I nod. I acquiesce. She grips my arm at the bicep. We look enthralled at the space on the wall. 'Charles will talk to you about the details. I want you to know that you have made me very happy.'

The rest of the evening passed in a crystal blur, as seen at speed through a torrent of Venetian glassware. This had much to do with the savagery of the alcohol in the drinks. As I left for the night, B.H. had long since departed, C.B. took me to one side and told me that I had made Mrs Hutton very generous. 'She rewards genius. I have been instructed not to negotiate but to simply give you this.' It was a cheque for $1,000. He promised to drop by in the morning and pick up the piece. I am now worth one-tenth of a Van Cleef & Arpels gold mantel clock.

23rd December 1946, Tangier
Still no word from Pilar, I am desperate. I try to advance the work. I try to put into paint what I saw that afternoon, but it does not translate. Where it was so simple it has become complicated. I need P. to come back and remind me of what I saw that day. I have given up on society. I am bored by its gentility. I was much in demand after my triumph with B.H. but now the hungry beast has moved on. I am relieved but still swamped.

7th March 1947, Tangier
I have stopped work. I sit in front of the seven remaining drawings of P. with not an idea in my head. I have even worked under the influence of majoun. After one session I came back to reality feeling I had done something great only to find I had painted seven black canvasses. I hang them in a whitewashed room and stand amongst them in a state of total desolation.

25th June 1947, Tangier
I am repelled by my own rapacity. My inability to create has induced a need for endless change. I tour the brothels and hunt out new young men and tire of them instantly. I smoke powerful hashish and spend whole days fluttering like a flag in the enervating cherqi that knocks incessantly at the doors. My arms are weak, my penis flaccid. I spend whole nights in the Bar La Mar Chica surrounded by drunks, reprobates, idiots and whores. I have given up on majoun, under its influence I only revisit the old horrors – blood-covered walls, ramps of dead bodies, mud and blood, flesh and white bone churn in my head.

1st July 1947, Tangier
After ending up drunk on R.'s doorstep he has sent me back to work on
the boats.

1st January 1948, Tangier
A new year. It has to be better than the last. I still cannot face the blank
canvas. These are my first writings since July. I am in better shape
physically. I am no longer fat but I am unable to rid myself of this sense
of desolation. I have tried to find P. I even went to Granada only to find
that her home has been sold and that the family had moved to Madrid,
but nobody knew where.

I have nothing to report. The wind-whipped chabolas on the edge of
town contain nothing of the misery in my privileged body. I laid out the
seven drawings of P. in the hope of feeling a new surge of possibility. I
accomplished the reverse.

I have been allowed up, I have been granted the enormous privilege of
putting my eye to the crack and have seen the real nature of things and
I have brought it down and shown the same to ordinary mortals. But P.
was a part of it, she was my muse and I have lost her. I will not paint
or draw again. I am destined for the trough where everybody bends their
heads – eat, work, sleep.

25th March 1948, Tangier
I have seen her. In the market off the Petit Soco. I have seen her. Across
a thousand heads. I have seen her. Was it her?

1st April 1948, Tangier
Am I so desperate that I will pin my hopes on phantoms? I go to every
doctor in town to see if she is in their employ. Nothing. R. wants to send
me out on the boats again rather than have me crash to earth like a
sunstroked bird.

3rd April 1948, Tangier
I leave the house and there she is in the street, pacing this way and that.
At the sight of her I have to hold on to the door, my legs have gone. I
ask her in. She says nothing and crosses the threshold in front of me.
Her smell fills my chest and I know that I have been saved. The
houseboy makes us tea. She won't sit even when it arrives. She strokes
the houseboy's head. He slips out as if touched by an angel.

I don't know where to start. It is as if I'm in front of the canvas and my hand goes to this corner, that quarter, the middle and makes no mark. I have done this for hours and when finally I decide where I am going to touch the white, white canvas, I make no mark. There is no paint on the brush. This is how I am now. I force myself to speak.

Me: *I came looking for you in Granada ... when I didn't hear from you.*

Silence.

Me: *They told me that your aunt had died, that your mother was sick and that you had all gone to Madrid.*

P.: *That was true.*

Me: *They had no address for you. No way of contacting you.*

P.: *That was not true.*

Silence.

Me: *Why was that* not *true?*

P.: *They knew exactly where we were. My father had told them and he had also told them not to tell anyone answering to your description, coming from Tangier, asking questions about his daughter.*

Me: *I don't understand.*

P.: *He didn't want me to see you ever again.*

Me: *Was it something to do with me ... I mean, ... those drawings? Did he hear about them? That you had stood before me ... ?*

P.: *No. That was private between you and me.*

Me: *So what happened? I can't think how I could have crossed him. We only ever talked about my back.*

P.: *My father speaks Arabic.*

Me: *Of course he does, he was in Melilla. Where is your father ... I must talk to him.*

P.: *My father is dead.*

Me. *I am sorry.*

P.: *He died six months after my mother.*

Me: *You have been suffering.*

P.: *I have had eighteen months of sorrow. It has aged and hardened me.*

Me: *You still look as you did. You don't wear it in your face.*

P.: *I was telling you that my father spoke Arabic and because he spoke some of the Riffian dialects he was asked if he would spend a morning a week treating poor people in the chabolas on the outskirts of town. The American woman, 'La Rica', Sra Hutton had given money for medicines and food. He volunteered. He came across the usual things in malnourished people, but he also came across a surprising number of mutilations. Ears missing, fingers and thumbs cut off, nostrils split. Nobody would tell him how these injuries were incurred until he treated a woman who had been there the week before with her son, who had lost an ear. She was covered in shame at having to be handled by a man but was in such pain she had to succumb. He asked her about her son and why nobody would tell him what had happened. 'They won't talk because it is your people who are doing this,' she said. My father was stunned. She told him how these boys have to steal because they are starving and about the injuries they have to sustain to feed their families and the deaths that have resulted. My father was appalled and asked who was doing this. 'The men who are guarding the warehouses.'*

I am silent. The inside of my body is frozen. My chest is an ice cave through which the coldest wind is blowing. My muse has returned to tell me why she can never speak to me again.

P.: A boy with an infected wound was brought back to the surgery. This was unusual but he'd touched my father by his courage and his acceptance of pain without complaint. The boy recovered and my father employed him around the house. One lunchtime he disappeared. We searched the house. He was cowering in the back of the laundry. He couldn't speak except to ask, 'Has he gone? Has he gone?' His terror was pure. We asked him who he was afraid of and he would only say: 'El Marroquí.' It happened again the next day. My father looked in his consultation book and his only patients that day were Sr Cardoso, who was eighty-two, and . . . you.

The next day he took the boy to the Petit Soco. You took your usual seat at the Café Central. And the boy told my father that you were the one – El Marroquí.

I cannot move. The green eyes are on me. I know that this is the crux. I know it because life is tearing past as if both our lives are being compressed into this one moment. I decide I will ignore it. I will lie. Just as I have lied to all of them – C.B., the Queen of the Kasbah, the Contesse de Blah and the Duque de Flah. I will lie. I am Francisco Falcón. No. He is Francisco Falcón. I no longer exist.

P.: Were you responsible for what happened to those people?

The green eyes are willing me, beseeching me and I know that I am lost. I look into my hands, which contain life's water, and see it bubble and wink, mocking me, as it leaks through my fingers.

Me: Yes, I did those things. I am responsible.

She doesn't leave. She looks into me and I realize I have done the right thing.

P.: *My parents made discreet enquiries about the company you worked for. My father found out that you were a legionnaire and a contrabandista and that it was* your *capacity for violence which inspired fear in all your enemies and competitors. They decided to send me away. It was a coincidence that my aunt became sick.*

Me: *But why force you to leave? Why not just forbid you to see me?*

P.: *Because they knew I was in love with you.*

She finally sits down and asks for a cigarette. She can hardly hold it. I light it for her and put it in her fingers. She stares into the floor. I tell her everything. I tell her about 'the incident' (or nearly everything about it) that drove me out of my family home to join the Legion. I tell her what I did in the Civil War, in Russia, at Krasni Bor. I tell her why I left Seville, what happened in Tangier . . . everything. I tell her about my desolation. I tell her how she fits inside me, how she is my structure. She listens. The sky grows dark. The wind gets up. The boy brings more mint tea and a candle that wavers in the draught. There is only one thing I don't talk about. I tell her every hideous thing, but I don't tell her about the boys. That is not something for a woman's ears. The admissions have been of such staggering enormity that to introduce depravity would put me beyond redemption. I finish by talking about the work. How I have stopped the work. How I have been unable to progress beyond the drawings. How I need her to open my eyes again. I ask her if she remembers her last words to me on the day we made the drawings. She shakes her head. I tell her: 'Now you know.'

As I write this she lies on the bed, a vague form beneath the mosquito netting. A candle with a tall spear of flame burns by her bed. She sleeps. I reach for the charcoal and paper.

3rd June 1948, Tangier
P. tells me she is pregnant. I drop tools for the day and we lie in bed together with our throats so full we cannot speak about the wholeness of our future together and the children we will have.

18th June 1948, Tangier
After a civil ceremony at the Spanish Legation and a short Mass in the cathedral P. and I are married. R. arranges for a reception at the Hotel El Minzah. As they have begun to say now, in true Riviera style: le tout *Tangier was there. We are surrounded by strangers at our own wedding and leave as soon as it is polite. We disappear under the*

mosquito netting with a hashish cigarette. We float on each other's caresses and make love as man and wife for the first time.

She is tired and wants to sleep. I rest my head on her belly and hear the cells doubling within. I have too much energy and get up to work. I think it is an auspicious day so I take up paint and make my first mark on the canvas. It is a start. I become nervous and decide to take a walk through the Medina up towards the Kasbah to stand on the fortifications and look out over the night sea to contemplate my future. I am stopped in the Petit Soco by people who want to congratulate me and buy me a drink. They are insistent. C. is among them. I haven't seen him for months. I let him buy me a whisky. We talk and joke for a while and I take my leave. C. catches up with me on my way to the Kasbah. He takes my arm and asks why I have been ignoring him, why have I been sending his boys away? He tells me I have frozen up again, that marriage is for lawyers and doctors, that bourgeois living is the enemy of the artist. I remind him who P. is. We have been walking at a leisurely pace and he is now steering me towards a house. He tells me it is a bar and he would like to buy me one last drink. We take a seat in a courtyard and a drink is served. There is a walkway around this courtyard, like a cloister. Without my noticing, candles are lit in this walkway and suddenly young men are loitering there. C. is prattling about the subversion of sensuality, the anarchy of depravity. I don't listen but look at the muscular delineation of the boys' thighs as they walk beneath the uncertain light. I am stirred up. C. hands me a cigarette. There is hashish in it which slips into my blood like cream. My lips caress the cigarette. The night folds around me. More boys float past. C. leaves with one of them. They take me by the arms and lead me away. They undress me. They knead me. They massage my resistance away. I collapse to their touch.

I come round with my lips to a boy's back. I dress quickly. I find the courtyard. There is no sign of C. I walk back home. I strip in the bathroom and scrub at my genitals until they are raw. I stand naked at the end of the marital bed and look down on my sleeping wife. What sort of a man am I?

She stirs under my gaze and her head comes up off the pillow. 'My husband,' she says and smiles. She rubs the bed next to her. I lie down. What sort of a man am I?

25

What was the ingredient in sleeping pills that suppressed dreams? Was it the same one that dried the mouth and lined the brain with towelling? Falcón lay in the dark, pressing his fingers to his stiff face like a boxer inspecting last night's damage. And what about these black holes in the memory? The thought brought back Alicia's words to him last night.

'A neurosis is like a black hole in space. It is bizarre and inexplicable. How can something as catastrophic as the collapse of a star happen? How can something that has happened to a human being be so painful that we refuse to remember it, that we collapse that part of the brain?' she said. 'There's more to this analogy, because the collapsed star has such a powerful gravitational pull that it constantly sucks more matter into its negative world. So the neurosis draws all the positive things in your life towards it, consumes them and makes them anti-positive. You've described to me some important relationships in your life, with your first serious girlfriend, Isabel Alamo, and your ex-wife, Inés. They were both strong relationships, with passion on both sides, but they could not withstand the gravitational pull of the black hole within you.'

'With Inés it was just sex. I know that now,' he'd said.

'Do you?' said Alicia. 'You don't think that possibly it was you who wanted to maintain it at that level? Sex is manageable. Love is complex.'

'I know it was sex. That's why I'm suffering from this illogical jealousy.'

'Sex normally burns itself out.'

'And that's what happened,' he said. 'The sex burnt itself out and there was nothing left.'

'Except that you're still fascinated by her. You still want her.

There's a part of you that hasn't broken with her . . . which is one of the reasons why you can't talk to the judge about her.'

The cyclical thinking wore him down. He was too tired for it. He got out of bed. The hard thump of his father's journal hitting the floor brought back last night's reading. The pity and the disgust he felt for him. He was stunned by his father's weakness, this pathetic facet to his personality completely unknown to Javier. How strong his mother had been, how passionate to believe in his father and how feebly she'd been repaid by his ambivalence and restless sexuality. He was fragile, this genius, and another person with an instinct for worthlessness.

He dressed in his running clothes and went downstairs. The phone blinked at him. He played back the single message left for him, thinking: nobody calls me, I have a hundred messages at work and none at home. Paco's voice intruded, telling him that the torero Pedrito de Portugal had twisted his knee in training and that there was now a vacant slot for Monday afternoon on the same day that he was supplying the bulls. He was sure they'd give Pepe a chance.

Falcón ran down to the river and along its dark edge to the Torre del Oro. A runner nodded to him as he ran by and another gave him a half-salute. He'd become a regular since he'd finished with the mad, stationary cycling. These strange channels were opening up. He hadn't mentioned his ludicrous tears over the film of Ramón and Carmen to Alicia. Where had that sentimentality come from? There was no room for it in his work. The thought stopped him. He was completely out of breath. He'd been unconsciously sprinting to get away from his irritating thoughts. Had that been the reason he'd gone into police work? Did it suit his need for the dispassionate observation of life's terrible crises? Was that an insight? He ran back home, picked up an ABC and found Salgado's funeral notice.

By the time he'd stripped for his shower the progress he'd made on the run had evaporated. His back crawled with nerves and a pit had opened up in his stomach that had a terrifying similarity to Alicia's black hole. All his positive thoughts seemed to be drawn to it and that panicked him, the idea that everything, including his sanity, might collapse into it. He took an Orfidal.

Falcón called his brother before he went out into the pasture to round up the bulls to bring down to Seville for Monday's bullfight.

'How's your leg?' asked Falcón.

'The leg is good,' said Paco. 'Any news yet?'

'Not yet.'

'Look, another thing,' said Paco. 'There's going to be eight of us now on Sunday.'

Silence.

'You've forgotten, haven't you?'

'I've had my hands full,' said Falcón. 'You remember Ramón Salgado, Papá's dealer? He was murdered yesterday morning. I've got that and two other killings, so I haven't been . . .'

'Somebody *killed* Ramón Salgado?' said Paco.

'That's right. His funeral's this afternoon.'

'I can't think why anybody would go to the bother.'

'Well, somebody did.'

'Anyway . . . there's eight of us for Sunday.'

'Remind me.'

'We're coming to your house for Sunday lunch, we're all staying the night, we're going for lunch the following day down by the river and then the bullfight, followed by dinner out. We'll come back here to the finca on Tuesday morning.'

'I'd forgotten.'

'You'd better call Encarnación.'

He hung up and called Encarnación, who said she'd prepare the rooms but wouldn't be able to cook on Sunday, but she had a niece who would. She told him to leave some money out and she'd buy all the food later that morning. He went to the ATM on Calle Alfonso XII and took out 30,000 pesetas. The phone was ringing when he got back at nine. It was Pepe Leal saying he'd been given Pedrito de Portugal's slot. Falcón offered him a bed, but he preferred to stay with his team in the Hotel Colón.

'I'll come over on Sunday night,' he said. 'We can have a talk. You can prepare me for Monday, steady my nerves.'

Falcón told him about Paco's famous retinto bull and he sensed the boy's excitement that everything was finally coming together for him.

By 9.30 a.m. Falcón was calling Felipe, the forensic, to see if he'd come up with anything. No prints had been left in Salagado's house. They were working through the blood samples now, but so far it all belonged to Salgado. Falcón called the Médico Forense wondering what had happened to the autopsy report. The Médico Forense hadn't written his report because they were waiting for some blood-test results to come back from the lab.

'When I got the victim up on the slab I noticed that he had three contusions around his right eye,' he said. 'All the other contusions were at the back and side of his head, these were the only three on the front. They were also different. They had not been made by something hard and sharp but by something blunt and comparatively soft, like a fist. The killer had punched him three times in the face and I wondered why he would do that. The way the marks lay on the face I could see that he'd hit him with his left hand, but I know the killer is right-handed.'

'How?'

'If you're going to remove somebody's eyelids who's already secured to a chair you would stand behind them and tilt the head backwards. The initial incision with the scalpel on the victim's left eye was made from left to right and the same with the right eye.'

'So why do you think he hit him with his left hand?'

'Because his right hand was occupied.'

'In what way?'

'It was stuck in the victim's mouth. He was biting him.'

'Can you prove that?'

'After he chloroformed him to perform his operation he removed the socks from his mouth so that the victim wouldn't choke while he was unconscious. As the victim came round he stuffed the socks back in, but he either wasn't quick enough or there was a reflex action by the victim.'

'But how do you know all this?'

'I found blood that was not his own in his mouth and soaked into the socks. The victim is O+ and this blood is AB+. I've just given instructions for a DNA test to be done.'

He hung up and his mobile started ringing. It was Felipe with confirmation that one of the blood spatters was AB+ blood. The position of the spatter mark was 1.20 metres from the front chair leg in the direction of the doorway. As he spoke, the fixed line started to ring. This time it was Consuelo Jiménez.

'How did you get this number?'

'I called the Jefatura and they said you weren't in yet.'

'They don't give out this number and you already have my mobile.'

'I've had this number for years. Ramón gave it to me as a favour,' she said. 'Your father and I used to speak occasionally.'

'Have you got something for me on Sr Carvajal?'

'I read in the newspaper that Ramón Salgado has been murdered

316

by the same killer as my husband. You didn't tell me they cut off his eyelids.'

'The newspapers are being sensationalist,' he said and left it at that.

'We were good friends, Ramón and I,' she said.

'But not such good friends that you could remember his name at the beginning of my investigation.'

'I was very upset by the intrusiveness of the killer, I was just exercising some control over the intrusions of the investigator . . . that was all.'

'Did it occur to you that the delay in making the connection might have cost Ramón his life?' he said, pushing the limits of truth to the edge, to try to get some emotional purchase.

'He said he was going to meet you.'

'When?'

'We've spoken every day since Raúl was murdered,' she said. 'Didn't you check the phone records?'

'I haven't read that report yet.'

'Ramón was a very sensitive man and conscientious with it.'

'When did he tell you we were going to meet?'

'It was supposed to be yesterday for lunch.'

'Did he say what he was going to discuss with me?'

'No.'

'It doesn't sound as if it was going to implicate you, does it?'

'Why should it?'

'Did he tell you about our little deal?'

'No.'

'He would give me information that would point me in the direction of Raúl's enemies and in return I would allow him into my father's studio for a day,' said Falcón. 'Do you know why he would want to do that? I mean, spend a day in my father's studio. He said it was for no commercial reason.'

'He was devoted to your father,' she said. 'Ramón's whole life and success were due to your father's genius.'

'So what was it? Did he want to commune with my father's spirit?'

'Cynicism doesn't suit you, Don Javier.'

'How well did you know Ramón . . . how long?'

'Nearly twenty years.'

'Did you know that he'd been married?'

Silence.

'Did you know that his wife died in childbirth?'

Silence.

'Did you know that in his . . .' Falcón stopped himself; futility suddenly got the better of him. His suit was heavy on his shoulders.

'What?' she asked.

'Tell me what you know about Ramón Salgado,' said Falcón. 'He's been in and around my life for as long as I can remember. I was even featured in the killer's film *La Familia Salgado*. But now I realize that I didn't know the first thing about him, apart from the uninteresting surface of his existence.'

'I can't believe he didn't tell me he was married,' she said. 'We talked about everything.'

'Maybe not quite everything,' said Falcón.

'Well, for instance, he told me that he'd killed a man.'

'Ramón Salgado *murdered* somebody?' said Falcón.

'He said it was an accident . . . a terrible accident, but he had killed somebody and it weighed heavily on his mind.'

'Why would he tell you a thing like that?'

'Because I had just told him everything about myself. I was drunk and depressed after my second abortion and the end of my relationship with the son of the duke. I told him about the other abortion and how I'd earned the money and . . . you know, it became a very personal conversation.'

'These are big secrets to share.'

'We were two lonely and disappointed people and we opened up to each other in a café on the Gran Via, over brandy.'

'Did he say when he had killed this man?'

'In the early sixties in Tangier. He pushed somebody in a drunken argument. The guy fell over and hit his head in the wrong place and died. Everything was covered up. He paid some money and left the country.'

'You don't think he was lying?'

'Why should he admit to something as terrible as that?'

'Apart from making you feel better about yourself? Well, it gives Ramón a certain mystique . . . something that was totally lacking in his personality.'

'All I can say was that you didn't hear him say those words. You didn't see what it cost him.'

'All right,' said Falcón. 'It's true. That was forty years ago . . .'

'You went back that far when you were investigating Raúl's

murder,' she said. 'You said it was background. Here's some more background.'

'The problem now is that my superiors and I need some foreground,' said Falcón. 'I can't even show that your husband and Ramón were in Tangier together. Not even that tenuous link exists.'

'Raúl introduced Ramón to your father. He gave him a letter of introduction to take with him to Tangier.'

'What happened between Raúl and my father?' asked Falcón, momentarily fascinated by the digression. 'As far as I know once they arrived in Seville they never saw each other.'

'I don't know. He never spoke about it. I asked and he ignored me.'

'All right,' said Falcón, getting back on track. 'Tell me about the present-day relationship between Ramón and your husband.'

'What relationship was that?'

'Ramón introduced you to Raúl, didn't he?'

'Twelve years ago is present day to you,' she said. 'When does history start?'

'What about Expo '92? The names I gave you were linked by . . .'

'That's only nine years ago. You're becoming more modern, Inspector Jefe.'

'If you were abused as a child, how long do you think that would stay with you?'

A silence, so deep and prolonged that Falcón had to ask if she was still there.

'What names are linked and what do they have to do with abusing children?' she said, angry now.

'That is part of a police inquiry and will have to remain confidential,' he said. 'But you know one name . . . Eduardo Carvajal.'

'If you are saying that either my husband or Ramón had anything to do with a paedophile ring you will have me and my lawyers to answer to.'

'Keep reading the newspapers,' he said, and she slammed the phone down on him.

In seconds his mobile was ringing. He still hadn't moved from the phone since he'd come back from the ATM. The whole world was converging on him.

'Where are you?' asked Comisario Lobo.

'I haven't been able to get out of the house,' said Falcón. 'I've been taking one call after another.'

'Good,' said Lobo. 'I'll be in one of those cafés inside the Plaza de Armas at the end nearest the Avenida del Cristo de la Expiración. Fifteen minutes.'

Lobo had never met him outside the office before, and what a place to meet. This could only mean that whatever was up for discussion was too sensitive for the all-hearing concrete walls of the Jefatura.

Falcón reached the patio just as the fixed-line phone rang again. He went back, snatched the receiver to his ear. Silence.

'*Diga.*'

'What do you think of Ramón Salgado now, Tío Javier?'

'Hola, Sergio,' he said, the only thing that broke through the adrenalin burst.

'Don't call me that.'

'Then don't call me uncle,' said Javier.

'You didn't answer my question about your old friend's Hieronymous Bosch collection . . . the perfect place to keep them, wasn't it?'

'They were obscene, but, you know, we have laws in this country against child abuse and we have appropriate and severe punishment for offenders. You don't have to . . .'

'I see where you're going now, Inspector Jefe. Raúl's liking for young girls and Ramón's for tortured boys . . . very interesting.'

'And Eduardo Carvajal.'

Silence.

'Stop the killing, Sergio,' said Falcón. 'You don't have to do this any more.'

'I haven't killed any one,' he said. 'I haven't had to.'

'How's your thumb?' asked Falcón, and the phone went dead.

He clenched the receiver to his head. He'd lost him. All the questions and strategies arrived in his head seconds late. He slammed the phone down and went to meet Lobo.

As he walked up Calle Pedro del Toro he thought about the quality of that silence when he'd said the name Eduardo Carvajal. It was the silence of someone who'd never heard the name before and he knew that he was heading into another dead end.

The Plaza de Armas had been Seville's main station but had now been converted into housing for aimless people to wander about the shops, cafés and fast-food bars located there. Lobo was sitting on his own at a table close to the old entrance. He had two cups of coffee in front of him and he was wearing a coat that was too heavy for the weather.

'You look worn out, Inspector Jefe,' said Lobo.

'I've just been talking to our killer.'

'Is he still enjoying himself?'

'I wasn't ready for him after all the calls I've had this morning,' said Falcón. 'He confused me by calling me "uncle" and I didn't even have the presence of mind to ask him how he'd got my number.'

'Which number?'

'My father's old number . . . he never gave it out.'

'Perhaps he found it in Ramón Salgado's house.'

'Possibly.'

Falcón briefed him on the calls. Lobo played the edge of the table with his fingers.

'He sounded surprised at the connection you'd made,' said Lobo.

'I admit, it's unnerved me.'

'And no news from Sra Jiménez on the relationship between her husband and Carvajal, except to become furious at the implication,' said Lobo. 'What are you going to do now, Inspector Jefe?'

'I think I'll still send the computer down to Vice, there may be a link to Carvajal via the material.'

'The reason we're here may have something to do with this,' said Lobo. 'The name MCA Consultores has come back to me from a different source. There's been a leak. Have you spoken to anybody?'

'I mentioned some of the directors' names to Sra Jiménez, but not the company,' said Falcón. 'And when I saw the nature of the material on Salgado's computer I decided to tell Juez Calderón about my new theory, which involved mentioning MCA to him.'

'Then that is our leak,' said Lobo. 'That is how it got back to Comisario León, which is very interesting.'

'Would Juez Calderón have told Dr Spinola or Fiscal Jefe Bellido?'

'How do you think Juez Calderón became a judge before his thirty-sixth birthday?' asked Lobo.

'He seems very capable.'

'He is, but his father is also married to Dr Spinola's youngest sister. They are family.'

'So how did MCA come back to you?' asked Falcón.

'We are all at the mercy of our secretaries,' said Lobo.

'And how will this affect my investigation?'

'Whatever happens, we will be getting an indication of the level of guilt,' said Lobo.

26

Saturday, 21st April 2001, Salgado's gallery, Calle Zaragoza, Seville

The gallery was open but empty. Upstairs Ramírez and Greta were sitting next to each other going through the lists of artists that she'd given him the day before. She was looking down and speaking. He was admiring the top of her head. They jerked apart as Falcón reached the top of the stairs and he was sure he heard the snap of sexual elastic. He asked Greta if she would leave them to talk for a moment.

'We've drawn blood,' said Falcón, which got Ramírez's attention.

'In Salgado's house?'

'On the floor and in his mouth.'

'In his mouth?'

'Salgado bit Sergio when he was stuffing the socks back in his mouth.'

Ramírez sat back and smiled with his arms open wide.

'All we've got to do now is find him,' he said. 'Still, at least Juez Calderón will be happy to know that, when we do, he's got a case.'

'Work with Greta . . .'

'It's been a pleasure.'

'Develop a list of all artists who've used film or video in their works with addresses in either Seville or Madrid.'

'Madrid?'

'He posted us something from Madrid. He might still have an address there.'

'What age group are we looking at?'

'Take it up to forty-five just to be safe . . . as long as they're fit and healthy,' said Falcón. 'Do you know anybody in Vice who would look through that material on Salgado's computer and give us an opinion on where it's come from?'

Ramírez nodded, always a man who built up favours. They ran through Sergio's profile just to be sure. Falcón turned at the stairs as he was leaving.

'If Greta knows anybody on that shortlist who has had any kind of French education, or spent time in France or North Africa, highlight them.'

Falcón stepped over the police tape at Salgado's house and let himself in. The house was empty and, devoid of the activity of the crime scene, lifeless. There wasn't even any sadness. There was just the sterility of a man of borrowed tastes. The walls had been repainted downstairs. There was no bric-a-brac, no photographs, no clutter. The furniture was all clean lines. Only one painting hung in the living room, an almost colourless acrylic abstract. In the study, in the middle of the bookcase, was the only photograph on display – Francisco Falcón and Ramón Salgado, arms around each other, smiling.

He went upstairs to the room at the top, which gave out on to the small roof terrace, where they believed Sergio had got in. Felipe and Jorge had left the room exactly as they'd found it. Even the key to the door was still on the floor where it had originally been. He blinked at it and called Felipe on his mobile and asked him where he'd left the key.

'We put it back in the door rather than risk having it kicked about on the floor,' he said.

'In that case . . . he's been back,' said Falcón.

'Where was the key?'

'On the floor by the door where we first found it,' said Falcón. 'Why would anyone come back to the scene of the crime, Felipe?'

'Because they'd left something there?' said Felipe.

'That means he's lost something,' said Falcón, and a high palm in the neighbouring garden swayed in the breeze and rattled its leaves. The hairs came up on Falcón's neck and he listened hard. He wouldn't still be here? Not in daylight. He began a slow methodical search of the house. It was empty. He went back to the room where Salgado's body had been found. He stood in front of the desk and replayed the scene in his imagination.

Salgado came round as Sergio was stuffing the socks back into his mouth. He bit him. Sergio retaliated by hitting him three times in the face. Then he pulled back, holding his wounded thumb or forefinger. Where would he go? The kitchen was the nearest place. He went to the sink where he tore off the latex glove and washed the wound. He was probably in a panic and still bleeding with nothing to cover the cut, no plasters around here.

Kitchen roll. He'd have torn off a piece of kitchen roll, covered the wound and gone up to the bathroom. He'd be rattled by now, his nerve not quite as solid as it had been before. He might have been angry, too. He'd have wanted to finish the thing and get out as fast as possible. So he'd go back to Salgado, set up the terrible contraption, make his phone call and watch him die. Then he'd leave, fast.

Why did he call this morning? Was he worried? When did he end the call? When I asked him about his thumb. Did that give him the answer? It must have done. He knew that I didn't know it had been his finger.

Images shunted in Falcón's brain. Reels of memory unspooled their secrets. His mother coming in to the bathroom to wash him in his bath, rub his back with soap. She was all ready to go out to a party. She took off her rings and set them in a seashell on the edge of the bath.

Falcón went back to the sink in the kitchen. He understood it now. That was how Salgado hung on for three punches to the face. The ring was giving him purchase. He must have dragged the ring over the knuckle and when Sergio stripped off the torn glove it fell in the sink. Or did it? It was a stainless-steel sink. The noise of a metal ring hitting the sink, that would have drawn his attention – but if it went straight down the plug hole . . . He put his fingers to the hole. It had a rubber flap surrounding it. No noise. It would have gone straight down into the waste-disposal unit. He took out his pen torch. There was nothing visible in the hole. He called Felipe again and asked him about the sink, which the forensic admitted to giving only a visual inspection.

There was an unused box of tools in a cupboard under the stairs. In forty minutes Falcón had disconnected the waste-disposal unit and removed it whole. He drove it round to the Jefatura. Felipe and Jorge were still working. They cracked open the unit's housing and dismantled the grinders, which seemed to be jammed. They scraped out all the vegetable matter on to a sheet of glass and Jorge teased it all apart and there it was: one silver ring, mangled.

He must have tried to get it out,' said Felipe. 'Failed, decided to mangle it and that seized up the unit. Then he'd have had to face stripping it down, so he left it.'

'Can you straighten it out, see what it looks like?' said Falcón.

Felipe set to work and almost immediately asked Jorge to go back to the vegetable matter in the waste unit. He'd found evidence of a setting, which meant that a stone must be missing.

'The odd thing about this,' said Felipe, 'is that I'm sure that this was a woman's ring originally. Look –'

He had the ring under a microscope and when Falcón looked down it he pointed to the band of the ring.

'A different quality of silver has been used to enlarge it,' said Felipe. 'You can see where it's been cut and the new metal inserted. It's been well done. The only difference is in the colour of the silver.'

'What do you know about silver?'

Felipe shook his head. Jorge announced he'd found the stone. It was a small sapphire. They mounted the ring on some plasticine and laid the stone in its setting.

'That is a woman's ring, no doubt about it,' said Felipe.

'Why does a man wear a woman's ring?'

'A lover?' said Felipe.

'If a woman gave you a ring as a token, would you wear it? Would you go to the trouble of enlarging it and wearing it?' asked Falcón.

'Maybe not. You'd want to keep it whole and original,' said Jorge.

'I think this is more likely to have belonged to a woman who died,' said Falcón. 'This is an heirloom.'

'But you still haven't answered your question,' said Felipe. 'Why would a man wear a woman's ring? It must have some significance.'

'Ramírez wears a woman's ring,' said Jorge. 'Ask him.'

'How do you know?'

'Haven't you ever wondered why he wears that ring with the three little diamonds set in gold? I mean . . . especially Ramírez. So I asked him one night in a bar,' said Jorge. 'It was his grandmother's ring. He didn't have any sisters. He had it enlarged. He was very close to his grandmother.'

'What does that tell us about Sergio?'

'He didn't have any sisters,' said Jorge, and the forensics laughed.

'Do we know anybody who can tell us about silver?' asked Falcón.

'We've used an old jeweller in town before. He's retired now but he still has a workshop on the Plaza del Pan. I don't know if you'll find him there on a Saturday afternoon, though.'

The workshop was shut and nobody in the neighbouring shops had a home address or telephone number. Falcón tried other jewellers, but they were either busy or incompetent. He went back to Calle Zaragoza and knocked on the gallery door this time, in case Ramírez had advanced things with Greta. The door was locked. The other shops around were shutting for lunch.

He took out the evidence bag with the ring in it and something came back to him, fast moving, flashing like a jig in water to a fish's eye. He lost it in the gloom and remembered his father saying that they were the ideas that were worth something, the ones that came up from the depths and disappeared. He put the bag back in his pocket. The woman locking the shop next door told him that Greta had probably gone to El Cairo for something to eat.

Ramírez and Greta were there at the bar, eating tapas: squid and red peppers stuffed with hake. They sipped beer. Their knees were touching. Falcón showed Ramírez the ring. He took it and held it up to the light while Falcón briefed him on it.

'He didn't come back for it because it was valuable,' said Ramírez. 'Silver and a sapphire aren't so expensive.'

'It has to be significant,' said Falcón. 'That's why he called me this morning. He needed to know if I'd found it.'

'You think he was worried that we'd somehow understand the significance of it?'

'There's evident history to it. Just the fact that it's a woman's ring enlarged to fit a man's finger gives it a story.'

'But what is the story and how or why should we understand it?'

'Remember the call when he told me he had a story to tell and I wouldn't be able to stop him?' said Falcón. 'This is part of that story and I think we've got our hands on it too early. If we crack the story of the ring we will know too much about his work. It will point us to him in some way.'

'But we don't know it,' said Ramírez, baffled by the importance that Falcón was attaching to this small piece of evidence.

'But we *will* know it,' said Falcón, backing away to the door. 'We will *find* it out.'

He stumbled out into the street, their two faces imprinted on his mind. Greta appeared concerned, Ramírez clearly thought him deranged.

Back at the house on Calle Bailén he went straight up to the studio. He knew the rest of the house was empty of his father's effects. Encarnación had dealt with everything in the weeks after his death. He opened up the shutters in the room and paced around the cluttered tables in the middle. He was working on the memory he'd had of his mother bathing him with her rings removed. Where was all her jewellery? Of course, Manuela would have it. He called her on his mobile. She said she'd never seen any of it. She'd been too small for jewellery when Mamá had died and later, when she'd asked her father where it had all gone, he confessed to having lost it in the move from Tangier.

'Lost it?' said Falcón. 'You don't lose your wife's jewellery.'

'You know how it was between him and me,' said Manuela. 'He was convinced that I was only interested in money so if I asked for things he would always make me grovel. Well, over mother's jewellery, I didn't give him the satisfaction. None of it was that special as far as I remember.'

'What *do* you remember of it?'

'She liked rings and brooches but not bracelets or necklaces. She said they were the chains to enslave you. She never had her ears pierced either, so she only had clasp earrings. She didn't like expensive stuff and, because she was dark, she preferred silver. I think the only gold ring she had was her wedding band,' she said, as if she'd been expecting the question. 'Why, little brother, do you need to know this on a Saturday afternoon?'

'I need to remember something.'

'What?'

'If I knew that . . .'

'I'm joking, Javier,' she said. 'You need to calm down. You're taking your work too . . . personally. Get some distance from it, *hijo*. Paco told me you'd forgotten about lunch tomorrow.'

'Are you coming as well?'

'Yes, and I'm bringing Alejandro and his sister.'

He tried to remember the details of Alejandro's sister's diet and hung up. He went into the storeroom where he'd discovered the journals and sorted through all the boxes. He found nothing. The only thing he came across that he hadn't seen before was a roll of five canvasses which, as he opened them up, released a small diagram that fell among the boxes. He laid the canvasses out in the studio but didn't recognize them. They weren't his father's work. Layers and layers of acrylic paint giving a luminous effect, as of moonlight scarfed by clouds. He rolled them up again.

It was dark by now and he collapsed to the floor, realizing he'd forgotten to eat and forgotten to go to Salgado's funeral. He sat against the wall, his hands dangling between his knees. He was becoming an obsessive. The mess of his father's studio seemed to have got inside his head. His brain was as convoluted as a tangle of fishing line. He called Alicia and ran into her answering machine. He left no message.

He pulled a book out of the bookcase and realized that there was considerable space behind. His obsession resurfaced. He worked his way up and down the shelves until behind the art books he found a wooden box he recognized from his mother's dressing table. He even remembered his little fingers amongst the jewels, a treasure chest from an adventure book.

The box had a Moorish geometric design on the lid and sides. He couldn't open it and there was no apparent lock. He worked at it for over an hour until he twisted a small pyramidal piece of wood and the lid sprang open.

In front of his mother's jewels, she came back to him so vividly that he put his face to them to see if, after all these years, there would be a trace of her smell. There was nothing. The metals were cold to his touch. He laid out the pieces on the table. The clasp earrings, clusters of silver-black grapes, a silver scimitar brooch set with amethysts, a large agate cube set on a silver band. Just as Manuela had said, there was no gold. The wedding band must have been buried with her.

He looked down on all the pieces and waited for the sacred memory to come back, the one he'd nearly remembered outside Salgado's gallery. All that surfaced was the seashell full of rings in his bobbing vision as he sat in the bath while his mother's soapy hand rippled up and down his tiny ribs.

Extracts from the Journals of Francisco Falcón

2nd July 1948, Tangier
*I squirt the oil on to my palette. I stab it with the brush. I coax colours
into each other. P. lies on the divan. She is naked. Her arm rests over a
pink bolster. Her feet are crossed at the ankle. Her body is fuller in
pregnancy. She wears a necklace, which I have pulled tight around her
neck (she does not like this) and draped down her soft back. I press the
paint on to the canvas. It glides smoothly. The oil is pushing the brush. I
am close. I am very close. There is form.*

17th November 1948, Tangier
*P. is huge with pregnancy, her belly is tautly distended, the breasts with
their wide brown nipples have parted and lie in swags on her flanks. She
smells different. Milky. It makes me nauseous. I haven't touched milk
since I was a boy. Just the memory of its fat coating my mouth and
tongue and its cowy fumes filling the cavities of my head makes me gag.
P. takes a glass of warm milk before bed. It calms her and helps her to
sleep. I can't sleep with the empty glass in the bedroom. I have not
worked since August.*

12th January 1949, Tangier
*I have a son of 3,850 grams. I look at the mashed red face and blast of
black hair and am sure we have been given someone's Chinese baby by
mistake. The child's wails tear through me and I wince at the thought
of this massive presence in the house. P. wants to call him Francisco,
which I think will be confusing. She says he will be called Paco from the
start.*

17th March 1949, Tangier
*. . . I now run R.'s building projects. I work with the architect, a
brooding Galician from Santiago, whose dark ideas need enlivening. I
pour light into his sound structures and he flinches from it like a*

329

vampire. The American, for whom we're building the hotel, looks as if he might kiss me.

20th June 1949, Tangier
R. married his child bride today. Gumersinda (her grandmother's name, handed down) has the face and sweet nature of a cherub . . . He is a different man around her, quiet, respectful, attentive and, I suppose this is it, totally in love with the idea of her. I cannot get so much as a squeak out of her. I rack my brains for topics of conversation – dolls, ballet dancing, ribbons – and feel lupine in her presence.

1st January 1950, Tangier
The hotel was finished before Christmas and we celebrated New Year with an exhibition of my abstract landscapes to which le tout *Tangier came. I sold everything on the first day. C.B. bought two pieces and pulled me aside with the words: 'This is great, Francisco, really great. But, you know, we're still waiting.' I press him on this and he says: 'The real work. Back to the body, Francisco. The female form. Only you can do it.'*

This afternoon I take one of the charcoal drawings of P. out and tell her what C.B. said. She agrees to model for me. As she undresses I feel like a client with a prostitute and go to the drawing whose simplicity is still magnificent. P. says: 'Pronto.' *Just as a whore might say. I turn. Her shoulders and upper arms are heavy, her breasts look off to the side, her belly hangs above the bush of her pubic hair. Her thighs are thick, her knees have fallen. She has a bunion on her left foot. The green of her eyes comes swimming towards me like a tide of olive oil. She looks past me to the old drawing. 'It's not me any more,' she says. I tell her to dress. She leaves. I look at the drawing like a man who's found he can't perform with the whore. I put it away with the rest.*

20th March 1950, Tangier
R. calls me at the house to tell me that G. has given birth to a boy. The baby was big and the labour long and arduous. He is very shaken.

17th June 1950, Tangier
P. is pregnant. I move the studio out of the house to make more room. I have found a place on the bay with light from the north and which looks across to Spain. I set up a single bed and a mosquito net. I put a canvas up on the wall but no colour comes to mind.

20th July 1950, Tangier
C. arrives furious with some young Moroccan in tow. I haven't seen him
(it's no accident) since my shameful wedding night. He demands to know
why I haven't told him about the new studio. The boy makes tea. We sit
and smoke. C. drifts into a stupor and falls asleep. The boy and I
exchange glances and set to under the mosquito net. I wake later to find
C. in an even greater rage and the boy holding his face where C. has hit
him. It seems that C. had quite fallen for this boy and is enraged at
finding him behaving like a cheap whore. He won't be pacified and
leaves with the boy holding his nose with both hands and blood in flashes
down his white robe. The door shuts. I look to my blank canvas and
decide that red is the colour.

15th February 1951, Tangier
I have a pink and placid daughter who is a welcome relief after Paco,
whose first wails were just the start of a long campaign of relentless
demand. Manuela (P.'s mother's name) sleeps constantly and only wakes
to blow little bubbles at the purse of her lips and take a little milk.

8th June 1951, Tangier
I run into C. in the Bar La Mar Chica, which has become a late-night
haunt of aristocrats and other beauties. They press money on to
Carmella, who beguiles the air with the horrors of her armpits, and pay
no attention to her partner, Luis, who is a much better dancer. I have
not seen C. since the incident with the boy in my studio. Things have not
gone well for him. He is drunk and ugly. He looks drained and sucked
out. The anarchy of depravity has bitten back and taken great chunks
from him. He unleashes a tirade against me in English for the benefit of
the onlookers. 'Behold – Francisco Falcón, artist, architect, contrabandista
and legionnaire. The master of the female form. Did you know, he once
sold a picture to Barbara Hutton for one thousand dollars? No, not a
picture, a drawing. A little scratching of charcoal on paper and a
thousand notes fluttered down on his head.' I sit back. It is harmless, but
C. has his audience now and rises to it. He knows they're the sort who
don't want Luis but Carmella, and he rewards them. 'But let me tell
you about Francisco Falcón and his deep understanding of the female
form. He is an impostor. Francisco Falcón knows nothing of the female
form, but he is an expert on boys – oh yes, let me tell you of the bums
and cocks he has savoured. These are his real speciality and I should
know, because he used me as his pimp . . .' At this point Luis ventures

over and tells him to shut up. I am white with rage but cool to the touch. C. does not shut up but launches into a final bitter tirade which ends on the occasion of my wedding night. Luis grabs him and hauls him from the bar. They do not return. I leave, followed by the audience who assume that, having seen the dirt, they will now smell the blood. Luis has taken C. away and, despite feeling capable of tearing up palm trees, I walk calmly home.

12th June 1951, Tangier

C. has been found dead in his rooms in the Medina, his head bludgeoned to an unrecognizable pulp. The boy whose nose he had broken in my studio was found with the body and blood on his clothes. He's charged with the murder. This is the ultimate end of the sensualist – the kiss no longer satisfies, the touch is too delicate and so in time only a slap will do and then a punch and finally, down comes the cudgel.

18th June 1951, Tangier

I have decided to spend the summer months here in the studio. The house is in an uproar and stinks of caca and milk. The air is full of idiot talk. I'd rather lie here drowsy beneath my net, the world vague beyond, with only the muezzin calling the faithful to prayer to punctuate my day. His calls seem to come from the belly and resonate in his chest before issuing forth from his mouth – more plaintive than any of Luis's flamenco. The sound always comes from silence and its eerie spirituality needs no translation. Five calls a day and I'm moved every time.

2nd July 1951, Tangier

At one of the rare lunches I attend these days P. asks me what I am doing. I go into a long diatribe about painting the muezzin's call as an abstract skyscape and she interrupts. She has heard malicious gossip of depraved goings on. It seems that the proceedings in the law courts have penetrated her baby world. She probes and I am like a live oyster whose cold clammy world winces under the intrusions of her teasing blade. I ask her to visit my studio and see the work I am doing. I convince her of my ascetic life. She is satisfied that I am serious. I am such a monster . . . or at least so Paco thinks. He giggles and clasps my huge head as I feed on his tiny, tight belly. He knows no fear, this little fellow.

5th July 1951, Tangier
I wake up in a stupor with some Mohammed or other lying by my side
and P. knocking on the door down below. I send him up to the roof and
let her in. I make tea. She asks to see my work. I am evasive because I
have nothing to show. She touches me in a way that lets me know that
she has not come here with this in mind. I am spent after a whole
afternoon at play and I am dirty, too. She becomes irritable as I
procrastinate and spills scorching mint tea on my bare foot, so that I hop
about and the boy on the roof lets out a blurt of laughter, which I hope
she doesn't hear. She leaves soon after.

26th August 1951, Tangier
I glance back over the years, flicking through these journals, and am
aghast at the revelations. I now hope they will never be read. If I attain
any sort of fame from my work and these diaries come to light, what
will it do to the classification of my genius? They have become confessions,
not diaries. These aren't the noble notes one would expect of an exhausted
master but rather the tawdry jottings of a depraved rascal. I think I
must be smoking too much and not spending enough time in lively
company, although where I should find that I don't know. That
American Paul Bowles I mentioned earlier has had some success with a
book which I haven't troubled myself to read. I try to find him, but he's
always away. I go to Dean's Bar, but it is full of drunks and reprobates
with not one idea between them. The rest are tourists who have other
things to think about. I have failed to keep up with my contacts from
B.H.'s world. C.B. is not here. I give up on society.
   I hear from C.B. that he has sold two of my pieces to wealthy women
in Texas. The cheque is substantial, he tells me, but I had been hoping
for a space in MOMA. He tries to pacify me by saying that Picasso once
told him that 'Museums are just a lot of lies,' which is easy to say when
you hang in the best of them in every country of the Western world.

17th October 1951, Tangier
R. tells me that G. is pregnant again. He is both happy and terrified
after the last occasion. I am amazed how this monument to ruthlessness
can be reduced to the softness of dough. He quivers at the memory of her
suffering. When I tell P. about the pregnancy she looks at me with
longing and I realize why she came to my studio in July.

8th February 1952, Tangier
R. has sold all our boats to various competitors and they have paid the
top market price. He has also emptied the warehouses and rents them out
to the same people who bought the boats. I am astonished, but he assures
me that the smuggling business has peaked, that negotiations are
underway between the US and Spain. The Americans want to build
bases to counter the perceived Soviet threat. Franco will let them in
because he wants to stay in power. There will be a trade link.

20th April 1952, Tangier
G. went into labour and it was much worse than before. The
complications were such that the doctors even asked R. who they should
save, wife or child. He chose G. because he could not live without her.
Having decided this G. rallied and the baby was delivered, apparently
unscathed. This brush with near tragedy brings P. and I closer and we
go back to the old days and rediscover some of our passion. She comes to
the studio in the afternoons and I work and lie down with her. The
paintings are better than before, but they still haven't recaptured that
lost moment.

18th November 1952, Tangier
At a reception in the Hotel El Minzah I meet Mercedes, the Spanish
wife of an American banker. Her husband had bought my work at
C.B.'s gallery in NY and so she knows me like an old friend. After her
years in America, she comes across as very modern, not the typical
Spanish woman from across the straits. I ask her to my studio and she
arrives the next day in a chauffeur-driven Cadillac, which she sends
away. I make tea. She braces herself against the verandah rail and looks
out to sea. She has a boyish figure, narrow hips, small breasts and slim
muscular legs. I show her some abstract Tangier landscapes I have been
doing, which she notices have cubist elements from Braque floating in
blazing bands of colour, as she's seen in Rothko's work in NY. I am
taken with her intelligence. We are drawn to each other and it isn't long
before I find out what that taut little body, or rather, mind, is capable
of. There is a wickedness in the workings of it. As she reaches her
moment she goes into frenzy where nothing else matters (certainly not
me, on whom she is pounding her pelvis) and she howls like a she-wolf.
We come crashing to the floor, where she lies, eyes glazed, cheeks flushed,
lips white and a vein in her neck, thick as cord, thundering with dark
carnal blood. It's invigorating to find such sophistication shot through

with base animal desires. There's danger here, too. M. seems capable of taking me across boundaries to zones where there are no limits. It is an irony not lost on me that here we are in Tangier, captives of the International Zone of Morocco, in the cockpit of Africa, where a new kind of society is being created. A society in which there are no codes. The ruling committee of naturally suspicious European countries has created a permissible chaos in which a new grade of humanity is emerging. One that does not adhere to the usual laws of community but seeks only to satisfy the demands of self. The untaxed, unruled business affairs of the International Zone are played out in its society's shunning of any form of morality. We are a microcosm of the future of the modern world, a culture in a Petri dish in the laboratory of human growth. Nobody will say, 'Oh, Tangier, those were the days,' because we will all be in our own Tangier. That is what we have been fighting like dogs for, all over the world, for the last four decades.

15th March 1953, Tangier
R., having sold all our smuggling boats, has bought a yacht. A plaything for him to bob around on and look successful. I could probably afford one myself with the money from the partnership and the sales I am making through M.'s contacts in NY, but it would give me no satisfaction. I am nearly forty years old and ostensibly successful, but I am conscious of my problem. My mind drifts from it at the first opportunity. None of my fortune is as a result of my own doing. R. has structured my entire life in no less a way than the Legion did. P. was my muse, without her the charcoal drawings would never have been done. M. has built me a reputation amongst the Americans so that I sell well in NY. But I am a shell. Knock into me and my emptiness booms.

2nd April 1953, Tangier
The success of Paul Bowles has attracted a crowd of American writers and artists to our little Utopia. I met a man called William Burroughs who, it seems to me, has done nothing of any note except to carry a massive reputation before him. He shot his wife in Mexico in a William Tell stunt, in which he missed the glass she'd placed on her head and the bullet drilled a hole in her brain. The American who tells me this story does so in a state of appalled amusement, as if this is something from a film he's just seen. I look across the grubby floor of the Bar La Mar Chica to where W.B. sits and am prepared to be fascinated by the wife killer. Instead I see a bank clerk, just like the ones employed in town,

except this one has the skull of the figure in Edvard Munch's Scream. When we meet I tell him this and he says: 'How that bastard knew what was coming, we'll never know. Shit. And I tell you, that's how I see the sky sometimes . . . just like that. You know . . . like blood. Like fucking blood.' His magnetism lies in his instant access to savagery. He unleashes this on those around him he does not like, but I think he reserves the real ferocity for himself. He is like a howling animal and I think of that mad boy R. saw years ago in the village in the sierra, collared and chained up outside. It brings me closer to understanding why I put pen to paper.

28th June 1953, Tangier
I have three lives. With P. and the children I am decorous. The parameters are set for little minds. I am mild and approximately cheerful while my chest gapes with shuddering yawns. I look at P., the perfect mother, and wonder how she was ever my muse. I have my life in the studio. The work proceeds. The Tangier landscapes have developed into something different. Vast red skies bleed into a massive black continent and in between is smeared a momentary civilization. The work is broken up by a stream of boys who drop by to earn a few pesetas. My third life is with M., my society companion and deviant.

23rd October 1953, Tangier
C.B. invites me and P. to an evening with B.H. I am not happy about this one life bleeding into the other. We go to the Palace Sidi Hosni and as usual wait for our hostess amidst her fabulous wealth. P. is bored and C.B. takes her off and, being the man he is, manages to charm her even with his splintered Spanish. B.H. arrives as I am about to propose leaving. She works her way round to us and, on meeting P., is seized by an idea. She leads us off to the room guarded by the towering Nubian and it's only as we enter that I realize that I have never told P. of the sale of the drawing. B.H. takes her straight to the piece in its pride of place next to Picasso. P. blinks at it as if she's seen one of her children hurt. I know from the green look that finds its way to me that she considers this a betrayal of trust. B.H., who has had some drink, is unaware of this pain and it is C.B. who moves us on. On the way home P. is silent as she shimmers through the Kasbah, her heels clopping on the cobbles. I shamble behind, lying to her back like a beggar who's been refused some change.

19th February 1954, Tangier
R. has gone to Rabat and Fez to talk to the French and Moroccan administrators. He asked me to join him, but I am working on some huge abstracts which I hope will break me out of what M. tells me is the 'B List' of respected artists. She wants my name to join those across the Atlantic like Jackson Pollock, Mark Rothko, and Willem de Kooning. She thinks my landscape work is as strong as Rothko's. I look at Rothko and see him coming at his subject from a different angle. He aims high, seeking a spiritual element, I am pointed towards darkness and decadence.

3rd March 1954, Tangier
R. is back from his travels, much heartened by the bureaucrats. He alarms me by telling me that he has embarked on a piece of business with the Moroccans. I tell him that he does not understand the secretive nature of the Moroccan mind – they have ways of ensnaring even the sharpest operator. He dismisses the possibility and tells me not to worry. I will not be involved.

18th June 1954, Tangier
I drop by my home in the Medina one afternoon and am surprised to find P. is not there. The children are playing on the patio. Paco is being a torero, his little sister is the bull. He performs great flourishes with his shirt and she aimlessly toddles through and is enchanted to find herself on the other side. How this game developed I don't know, because Paco has never seen a bullfight. I am detached from their lives. But where is P.? Nobody knows. I play with the children, giving Paco a slightly more dangerous toro. I am surprised how deft he is with the shirt and understand some of Manuela's glee. I bore quickly though, and return to my studio.

20th December 1954, Tangier
We have been lucky to escape the worst of the débacle. Property prices have crashed. Everybody's hope that Tangier would become the Monaco of Africa has faded. It moves R. to take out all his capital and we fly to Switzerland, where he opens up an account in my name and deposits the fantastic sum of $85,000, which is the major part of my profit from our ten-year partnership. I have no way of disputing this and we have a celebratory dinner. This is the end of an era. R. is going his own way in business. At the end of the meal we embrace.

17th May 1955, Tangier
P. has been seeking me out in my studio for the first time in ages. She
has been here three days running and we have made love every
afternoon. M. is away in Paris with her husband and only the odd boy
comes knocking and has to be sent away with a bribe. I am puzzled by
her sudden ardour until I realize that I have been at home more in M.'s
absence and have rehabilitated myself with my family.

When she leaves I lie under the gathered knot of the mosquito net and
the dangling gauze makes me think of birth, waters breaking, and I
wonder whether I have been coaxed into fathering another child.

11th July 1955, Tangier
How things converge. Today I am forty years old. P. tells me I am going
to be a father again. R. has deposited another $25,000 in my account
and the partnership has been officially dissolved. M.'s husband has asked
for a divorce and is prepared to hand over a substantial sum to get it (a
twenty-two-year old Texan girl is the reason). I have moved away from
the abstract and back to the figurative. Perhaps I've been inspired by de
Kooning, who has moved away from the crowded and chaotic patterning
of his Execution *and steered himself more towards* Women. *Or not.*
Maybe I'm just chasing C.B.'s dream and my own. I have worked until
the light has faded. I am about to go for dinner with my family. I feel
nothing but total desperation.

1st November 1955, Tangier
Last month Sultan Mohammed V was recalled from his exile in
Madagascar where the French sent him three years ago. He is due back
some time this month. It is the beginning of the end, although you
wouldn't know it to see the expatriates here. They fiddle while Rome
burns, but what do they care? I am burning for M., who has been away
for months sorting out her divorce. We will all be consumed by fire.

12th January 1956, Tangier
Another son, whom I have decided to call Javier, which is a name I have
always liked and has nothing to do with family. For the first time I look
down on one of my children and feel, not so much a surge of paternal
love, but a wild feeling of hope. This child, with his fists clenched and
eyes screwed up, for some reason makes me think that great things are
possible. He is the one bright light in my forty-first year.

28th June 1956, Tangier
I lie on my back under the net with Javier on my chest. His legs are
braced like a little frog's, the toes are dug into my belly. My hand covers
his entire back. He sleeps and occasionally, unconsciously, kneads my chest
on the off chance that there will be some milk. How quickly
disappointment enters our lives.

    He lies on a blanket as I work. I talk him through the paintings, the
ideas, the influences. He slowly brings his hands and feet together as if
mocking me with silent, dawdling applause. I look down on him and
small cracks open up in me. His soft, tiny body, his large brown eyes, his
downy head, all come together and, as with a chisel slipped between my
ribs, I am levered open.

27

Sunday, 22nd April 2001, Falcón's house, Calle Bailén, Seville

Encarnación's niece, Juanita, was the first to arrive at 11 a.m. Falcón was still groggy from a heavily drugged sleep. The extra sleeping pill he'd taken at 4 a.m. had as good as interred him in concrete.

He showered, and put on a pair of grey trousers that were so loose at the waist he had to find a belt. The jacket, too, did not hold him at the shoulders. The weight was falling off him. His cheeks looked hollow in the mirror, his eyes sunken and dark. He was turning into his own idea of a madman.

In the kitchen, Juanita moved around on black stacked trainers, which squeaked on the floor. As she tossed her head, a river of black hair jumped off her back. Falcón checked the fridge was well stocked with fino and manzanilla and went down to the cellar to bring up the red wine to drink with the roast lamb.

The cellar was at the back of the house under the studio. He had used this enclosed space as his dark room but had not been in there since Inés had left the house. His developing paraphernalia was still there in the corner. A line of string hung across the room with clothes pegs still attached for drying prints. He missed the excitement of revelation, of the blank sheet slipping into the developer and, slowly emerging from the waters, a face coming to him. Was that what he had in his head? All these images that just needed some developer for the latent memories to find form, come through his consciousness and solve his crux.

The metal wine racks were divided into two. French and Spanish. He never touched the French, which was all expensive stuff bought by his father. But this time he felt celebratory. Those final paragraphs he'd read in his father's journals last night had sent him to sleep weeping and he felt like toasting the generosity of his dead parent. Their intimacy had been reaffirmed and he found traces of forgiveness for all his father's depravity and infidelity. He pulled out bottles of Château Duhart-Milon, Château Giscours, Montrachet, Pommard, Clos-des-Ursules. He took them up to the dining room and laid them on the dresser. On coming up from the cellar for the second time he saw an urn, which he'd never noticed before, in a niche above the door.

The urn was no more than fifteen centimetres high, too small to contain human remains. He put down the bottles and took it to the developing table, turned on the overhead light. The stopper was a simple clay cone that had been sealed with wax. There were no marks on the urn, which was of unglazed terracotta. He cracked open the wax and removed the stopper. He poured some of the contents on to the table. It was yellowish-white and grainy. Some of the larger pieces were quite sharp. He moved them around with his finger. There were some brown pieces in there too and the grounds suddenly struck him as macabre, something like crushed bone. He left it on the table, repelled by it.

Paco and his family arrived first. While the women went upstairs and the children careered about the gallery, Paco brought in a whole *jamón*, which he'd brought down from Jabugo in the Sierra de Aracena. They found a stand in the dresser and locked the jamón into position. Paco sharpened a long, thin carving knife and began slicing off paper-thin sheets of dark-red, sweet jamón while Javier filled glasses with fino.

Juanita set up a table on the patio and put out olives and other *pinchos*. Paco added a platter of sliced jamón. Manuela arrived with her party and they all stood on the patio, drinking fino and shouting at the children to stop running. The only adult who didn't tell Javier he was looking thin was Alejandro's sister, who was no fatter than a praying mantis herself.

Paco was happy and animated about his bulls, which had all been discharged in perfect condition that morning for tomorrow's bullfight. The horn wound was still visible in the retinto but he was very strong. He called him 'Biensolo' and the only warning he issued to Javier was that the horn tips were unusually upturned and the space between them quite narrow. Going in for the kill was always going to be difficult, even if the head was down low.

They sat down to eat the roast lamb at four o'clock. Manuela noticed the quality of the wine immediately and asked how many more bottles 'little brother' was hiding. Javier told her about the urn to divert her attention. She asked to see it and, when the meal was over and Paco was lighting up his first Montecristo, Javier brought it up from the cellar. She recognized it straight away.

'That's odd,' she said. 'I don't know how Papá lost Mamá's jewellery and yet *this* made it all the way here from Tangier.'

'Ach! Manuela, he never threw anything away,' said Paco.

'But this is Mamá's. I remember it. It was on her dressing table for two or three days . . . about a month before she died. I asked her what it was, because it was different to anything else she had on her dressing table. I thought it might be a potion from that Riffian woman, who was her maid. She said it contained the spirit of pure genius and must never be opened – strange, no?'

'She was just playing with you, Manuela,' said Paco.

'I see you've opened it,' she said. 'Any genie?'

'No,' said Javier. 'It looked like crushed bone or teeth.'

'That doesn't sound very spiritual,' said Paco.

'More macabre,' said Javier.

'I'd have thought after all the blood you've seen *you* could stomach some dry old bones, little brother' said Manuela.

'But crushed?' he said. 'That seemed violent to me.'

'How do you know it's human? It could be old cow bone or something.'

'But why the "spirit of pure genius"?' asked Javier.

'You know who gave her that, don't you?' said Paco. 'Papá . . . a long time ago. There were some strange things happening in the house at the time. Don't you remember? Mamá started a fire on the patio. We came back from school and there was a black patch by the fig tree.'

'He was too young,' said Manuela. 'But you're right, he gave her the urn the next day. And the other odd thing – that wonderful sculpture he gave Mamá for her birthday the year before . . . that disappeared. She had it next to her mirror. She really loved that thing. I asked her what had happened to it and she just said, "God gives and God takes away."'

'She started going to Mass almost every day around that time, too,' said Paco.

'Yes, she only ever went once a week before,' said Manuela. 'And she stopped wearing her rings, too. She only ever wore that cheap agate cube that Papá had given her for her birthday. You remember that, surely, little brother?'

'No, I don't.'

'Papá gave you her present to take to her at her birthday dinner. She undid the box and the lid sprang open and hit you on the nose as this paper flower burst out. Inside the flower was the ring. It was very romantic. Mamá was touched. I remember the look on her face.'

'She must have known something was going to happen to her,' said Paco. 'Going to Mass all the time, only wearing that one ring Papá had given to her. It was the same with me when I got gored in La Maestranza.'

'What was the same?' asked Javier, fascinated by these old memories, even touching his nose to try to remember the box hitting it.

'I knew something was going to happen.'

'How?' asked Paco's father-in-law, one of life's great sceptics.

'I just knew it,' said Paco. 'I knew I was coming to a big moment and being young and arrogant I assumed it was going to be greatness.'

'But what did you know?' asked his father-in-law.

'I don't know,' said Paco, hands all over the place, 'a sense of things coming together.'

'Convergence,' said Javier.

'Toreros have always been very superstitious,' said the father-in-law.

'Yes, well, when you risk your life like that . . . everything has meaning,' said Paco. 'Stars, planets . . . all that stuff.'

'Aligning themselves over *you*?' scoffed his father-in-law.

'I'm exaggerating,' said Paco. 'Maybe it was just a sixth sense. Perhaps it's only in retrospect that I attach greater significance to an event which, in a matter of seconds, ruined my youth.'

'Sorry, Paco,' said his father-in-law. 'I wasn't diminishing . . .'

'But *that* was why I wanted to be a torero,' said Paco. 'I loved the clarity of danger. It was like living life squared at that level of awareness. All that happened was that I misinterpreted the signs. Nobody could have predicted that disaster. Throughout my entire *faena* the bull hadn't hooked right and then . . . when I'm right over the horns, he hooks right. Anyway, I was lucky to survive. It's as Mamá said to Manuela: God gives and God takes away. There is no reason.'

The lunch broke up after that and Manuela left with her party.

Paco's family and in-laws went up to bed for a siesta. Javier and Paco sat with a bottle of brandy between them. Paco was on the edge of drunkenness.

'Maybe you were too intelligent to be a torero,' said Javier.

'I was always terrible at school.'

'Then perhaps you were *thinking* too much to be a good torero.'

'Never,' said Paco. 'The thinking came afterwards. Once the leg was wrecked I had to clear my head out. All those reports and footage of my glorious moments, which never happened and never would happen, had to go in the bin. It left me completely empty. I had nightmares and everybody thought I was reliving the terrible moment, but as far as I was concerned that was in the past. My nightmares were about the future.'

Paco poured himself some more brandy and slid the bottle to Javier, who shook his head. Paco rolled a cigar cylinder across and Javier rolled it back to him.

'Always the man in control,' he said.

'Is that what you think?' asked Javier, nearly blurting out laughter.

'Oh, yes, nothing ever gets through to you and disturbs your inner calm. Not like me. I was in a turmoil. My leg like a rag and no future. Papá saved me, you know. He installed me in the finca. He bought me my first livestock. He sorted me out . . . gave me direction.'

'Well, he was a soldier. He understood things about men,' he said, conscious of himself skewing things in his father's favour for Paco's benefit.

'Are you still reading those journals?'

'Most nights.'

'Does it make any difference to how you think about him?'

'Well, he's completely and terrifyingly honest in his writing. I admire him for that, but his revelations . . .' said Javier, shaking his head.

'From when he was in the Legion?' asked Paco. 'They were the hardest men of all, the legionnaires, you know that.'

'He was involved in some brutal actions in the Civil War and in Russia during the Second World War. Some of the brutality he experienced in those wars stayed with him when he went to Tangier.'

'We never saw any of it,' said Paco.

'He was pretty ruthless in some of his business operations,' said Javier. 'He used the same techniques he'd employed in the war . . .

terror. And that only stopped when he dedicated himself to painting full time.'

'Do you think the painting helped him?'

'I think he put a lot of violence into his painting,' said Javier. 'He's famous for the Falcón nudes, but a lot of his abstract work is infused with emptiness, violence, darkness, decadence and depravity.'

'Depravity?'

'Reading these journals is like working a criminal investigation,' said Javier. 'Everything gradually comes to the surface. The secret life. Society – and we, too – only saw what was acceptable, but I don't think he ever rid himself of the brutality. It came out in other ways. You know how he used to sell those paintings of his and then go straight upstairs and paint the same picture he'd just sold? I think that was a kind of brutality. He always had the last laugh.'

'You're making him sound as if he wasn't such a nice guy.'

'Nice? Who's *nice* these days? We're all complicated and difficult,' said Javier. 'It's just that Papá had some peculiar difficulties in a brutal time.'

'Does he ever say why he joined the Legion?'

'It's the only thing he doesn't talk about. He only refers to it as "the incident". And, given that he talks about everything else, it must have been terrible. Something that altered his life which he never came to terms with.'

'He was only a kid,' said Paco. 'What the hell can happen to you when you're sixteen?'

'Enough.'

The doorbell rang.

'That's Pepe,' said Javier.

Pepe Leal was reed-thin and tall. Standing in the street he held himself erect, feet together, head raised as if in constant expectation. He always looked serious and wore a jacket and tie on all occasions. He'd never been known to wear jeans, even. He looked like a boy returning from a private school and not somebody who would enter a ring with a 500-kilo bull and kill it with grace and poise.

The two men embraced. Javier escorted Pepe to the dining room with an arm around his shoulder. Paco embraced him, too. They sat down at one end of the table although, and Javier had always noticed this, the torero was always apart from ordinary people. It wasn't anything to do with the fact that he was in perfect physical condition, only drank water and sat some inches back from the table. His difference was that he was a man who regularly faced fear and overcame it. And it wasn't as if he'd attained a permanent state of fearlessness. He was that human. Every time he entered the *plaza* to risk his life he would still have to overcome more fear.

Javier had seen him trembling and ashen in the hours before a corrida, sitting in his hotel room, never praying because he wasn't one of the religious toreros, and never looking to anyone to calm his nerves. He was just a petrified human being who could not bring his terror under control. Then he would get dressed and that would start the process. As he was slowly bound into his *traje de luces*, the uniform of his profession, the fear was contained. It no longer drained off him, flooding the room with an invisible contagion. The 'suit of lights' did something to him, reminded him of the brilliant afternoon when he'd taken his *alternativa* and become a fully-fledged torero, or perhaps it just encapsulated the nobility of his profession and the wearer could only behave with the dignity it demanded. It did not, however, get rid of the fear, it just pushed it inside. Some toreros never even managed that level of containment and Javier had seen them in the *plaza* white and sweating, waiting for their moment and praying to be out on the other side of it.

'You look in good shape, Pepe,' said Paco. 'How do you feel?'

'The usual,' he said, cheerfully. 'And how are the bulls?'

'Javier has told you about my retinto – Biensolo?'

Pepe nodded.

'If you get him, I promise you, you'll never have to sit on your hands waiting for a contract again. Madrid, Seville and Barcelona will be yours.'

Pepe nodded again, his nerves too close to the surface to articulate. Paco gave him a rundown of the other bulls and, sensing that Pepe wanted to be alone with Javier, made his excuses and went for a siesta. Pepe relaxed about two millimetres into his chair.

'You look as if you're working too hard, Javier,' said Pepe.

'Yes, I'm losing weight.'

'Will you be able to come to the hotel before the corrida?'

'I'll try, of course. I am sure my investigation can do without me for a few hours.'

'You always help me,' he said.

'You don't need me any more,' said Javier.

'I do. It's important to me.'

'And how *is* the fear?'

'Still the same. I am consistent in that. My level is fixed . . . but higher than most,' he said.

'It would interest me,' said Javier, suddenly seeing the opportunity, 'to know how you control your fear.'

'No different to the way you do when you confront an armed man.'

'I was thinking of a different fear to that.'

'It's all fear, whether you're about to die or someone says: Boo!'

'You're an expert,' said Javier, laughing, and grabbing Pepe by the neck, unable to restrain his affection for the boy. Maybe this was the wrong thing to talk about, he thought, I'll just infect his mind with my idiocies.

'Tell me what's bothering you, Javier,' he said. 'As you say, fear is my speciality. I'd like to help.'

'You're right . . . we're afraid of these outside things . . . You fear the bull, I fear the armed man. They're both unpredictable. But they are only *moments* of fear. We feel terrible apprehension, confront them and they are gone.'

'There you are. You know as much as I do. Controlling fear is in your training, in your willingness to confront, in the inevitability of it.'

'The inevitability?'

'You are bound by the state to deal with dangerous criminals on behalf of the citizens of Seville. I am bound by a contract to fight a bull. These are inevitable responsibilities that we must not shy away from or we will never work again. Inevitability helps.'

'Your fear of failure is greater than your fear of the bull.'

'If you think of all those soldiers who fought in all those wars with some of the most destructive weaponry known to man . . . how many of them were cowards? How many ran away? Very few.'

'Perhaps that means we have an enormous capacity for accepting fate?'

'Why try to control the uncontrollable? I could give up being a torero tomorrow because I fear injury and death too much and yet I'll still cross crowded streets, drive on the roads, and fly in aeroplanes, where I could easily meet an inglorious end.'

'So, it's inevitable. What about the willingness to confront?' said Javier. 'That sounds like bravery to me.'

'It is. We are brave. We have to be. This is not fearlessness. It is recognition. It is the admission of weakness and the willingness to overcome it.'

'You talk about this a lot?'

'With some of the brighter toreros. It's not a profession known for its great thinkers. But we all have to deal with it, even the greatest of us. What did Paquirri say when an interviewer asked him what was the most difficult thing to do when confronting a bull? "To spit," he said. *Nada mas.*'

'The first time I had to face an armed man a senior officer said to me before I went in: "Remember, Falcón, courage is always retrospective. You only have enough of it once you've been through it."'

'*That* is true,' said Pepe, 'which is why we can talk, Javier.'

'But now I'm in the grip of a different fear,' said Falcón, 'one that I've never come across before. I'm living in a permanent state of fear and the worst of it is that there is no armed man and no bull. It doesn't matter how brave I am, because I have nothing to confront . . . except myself.'

Pepe frowned. He wanted to help. Falcón brushed the problem away.

'It doesn't matter,' he said. 'I should never have mentioned it. I was just wondering if there were any tricks of the trade, a way in which toreros, who live with fear, dupe themselves into thinking . . . ?'

'Never,' said Pepe. 'We never cheat ourselves on that score. It's one of the great ironies. You *need* the fear. You welcome it, even though you hate it, because it's the fear that helps you to see. It's the *fear* that will save you.'

Extracts from the Journals of Francisco Falcón

7th July 1956, Tangier
I should be more concerned with what is going on. I still have coffee with
R. in the Café de Paris and all the talk is of an independent Morocco
and what will happen to us, the lotus eaters, in Tangier. (Perhaps it is
only I who am the lotus eater and everybody else is firmly in a tax
haven.) But I don't care. I am floating. I rarely need to smoke because
my natural state seems to be so light and feathery. My studio, with
Javier mewling (never wailing), is ambrosial. I frighten myself because
my mind suddenly turns on me late at night, as my pen hovers over this
journal, and pokes me – it says: 'You are happy.' I think this and
immediately the contentment is ravaged by uneasy thoughts. No word
from M. still. There's tension in the Medina, as if the narrow alleys are
filled with gasoline vapour – a spark, and the whole lot will go up. The
people sense independence. They are on the brink of it and are convinced
it will mean that they will be as free and wealthy as the expatriates are.
The slowness of political progress brings their anger and frustration to
the surface.

18th August 1956, Tangier
Riots in the Medina, which spill out into the Grand Soco. No European
or American ventures out on to the streets. Windows are smashed and
shops looted. At night the women ululate, a noise that Europeans find
terrifying. It is animal, potentially savage, like laughing hyenas or
vixens on heat. In the morning the streets are filled with men and boys
singing the Istiqlal *(independence) song and giving the three-fingered*
salute (Allah, the Sultan, Morocco). Portraits of Mohammed V bob
along on a tide of humanity and then it all goes bad again. I stay at
home. P. is nervous, especially at night, and the effects of the warm milk
are not so calming. The Riffian woman now passes the warm milk
through crushed almonds, which settles the stomach and eases the mind.
It works. These people know things that we have forgotten.

26th October 1956, Tangier
It is done. The Statute of Tangier has been abrogated. The international
regime is finished, but the existing financial, monetary, economic and
commercial conditions of our business Utopia will remain in force until
the Sultan can come up with his own ideas. R.'s contacts assure him these
will not differ dramatically from the ancien régime. *How money talks*
so much louder (even over the din of national pride and Islamic fervour),
although they have banned the sale of alcohol within 50 metres of a
Mosque, which has put an end to all my drinking holes in the Medina.
R. has no plans to leave. I still see him in the Café de Paris, but he is
now surrounded by men in robes, wearing fezes and thick-framed glasses.

26th October 1956, Tangier
I now know why M. has been so silent. An American writer (every other
one is a writer these days) who claims to be a friend of de Kooning met
M. at a dinner in NY. M. was with her new husband, a
sixty-nine-year-old philanthropist and collector called Milton Gardener.
The news leaves me stunned and blinking foolishly. My instinct is to feel
betrayed, but then later I ask myself, what had I been expecting? I have
no intention of leaving P.

15th June 1957, Tangier
M. arrived three days ago with her new husband whose full name is
Milton Rorschach Gardener IV. We meet at a function in the El
Minzah Hotel. I am delighted and at the first opportunity try to run M.
upstairs into one of the spare rooms, but she quickly puts me in my place.
She introduces me to M.G., who is not a doddery old fool but a very tall,
imposing and impressive man. He has a cane and a knee which, when it
bends, snaps with a metallic click. They ask to come to the studio.

They arrive the next day just as I'm explaining my new interlocking
figurative landscapes to Javier, who has now had to be caged in a wooden
pen. A worrying development is that in creating these patterned human
landscapes I seem to be implying some wonderful network of human
connection, which I don't think I believe in. M. takes one look at Javier,
picks him up and takes him away on to the verandah. It's love at first
sight from both sides. As M.G. and I talk we can't help but glance over
at the two of them, feeling like jilted lovers at a dance.

M.G. is taken with my new work but he has seen the drawing of P.
in B.H.'s collection. He asks me if I've developed that idea into paint and
says: 'There's your future, if you ask me.'

M. tells me later that M.G.'s 'old money' came from steel but his 'new money' came from playing the futures markets. Apparently in these markets you can bet on the future price of a product like wheat, sugar or even pork bellies (this doesn't sound like work to me) and I realize how small my world has become. Because of my talent I think art important but now see that I rely on a small group of wealthy people to buy my work, who in turn can make a fortune by putting chips on bacon. It's an epiphany of sorts, perhaps a reverse one, as I now see myself as one of M.G.'s futures markets. He's looking at my pork bellies and wondering if they're worth putting money on. I tell M. that he should buy Chaim Soutine's Carcass of Beef, *which she doesn't find funny but I think the old Lithuanian Jew himself would have laughed. Come to think of it, even Chaim Soutine's landscapes were like offal. I put this to M.G. who says: 'Yeah, truly offal,' which joke is spoilt because he has to explain it to me.*

3rd September 1957, Tangier
R. is happy about Mohammed V's Royal Charter, which came into effect a few days ago. The money market is still free and exports and imports unrestricted. The business community is euphoric. I am in a black depression. M. and M.G. have left. They bought one of my 'peoplescapes' so all was not lost. I gave M. a present of a (very) small painting of a line of carcasses hanging in a butcher's cold store. Amongst the carcasses is a little self-portrait. I am hanging upside down, thorax and belly split, meat-hook through my Achilles heel. M. chides me for being a cynic but keeps it, 'Because I know you will be famous one day.' I call the piece Futures in Art. *I am now reeling from my stupid joke because I have touched on the wretched truth. I am not operating in a sacred world. I am in a market. Here we all are aiming at some high truth, when in fact we are mired in the mud of commerce.*

I leave the studio and on an impulse take out the drawings of P. (which I keep at home or I'd spend my day gawping at them). I pace up and down as if inspecting the troops until I find P. is in the room with me. I tell her that I'm trying to find a way to take this work forward. She says in a prophetic voice: 'You won't be able to take these forward until you can see beyond them.' I ask her what she means. 'You only see what is there,' she says and leaves me no better off than I was.

28

Monday, 23rd April 2001, Plaza del Pan, Seville

At 8.30 a.m. Falcón was waiting outside the jeweller's workshop. The old man turned up ten minutes later. Falcón followed him in to a room that had clocks all over the walls and, hanging from hooks on various shelves, hundreds of watches. On the work bench were the entrails of various timepieces.

'Aren't you a jeweller?' asked Falcón.

'I was,' said the old man. 'I retired. I think this is suitable work for a man of my age. It's always good to keep an eye on the time when there's so little of it left. What have you got for me?'

'I want you to identify the quality of some silver in a ring,' asked Falcón, producing his police ID.

The old man sat down, took out an eyeglass and emptied the plastic evidence sachet on to a piece of velvet on the work bench. He screwed the eyeglass into the socket of his eye and held up the ring.

'It's been enlarged,' he said, instantly. 'They've used a different grade of silver. The original is sterling silver, which is 92.5 per cent pure, minimum. This other silver is much less pure. You can tell from the greyer quality of the material. It's maybe 20 per cent alloy instead of 7.5.'

'Where would you find silver like that?'

'It's not of European origin. Nobody would accept it. If you told me you'd found it in Seville or Andalucía I'd say it had probably come from Morocco. They use this grade of silver there and a lot of it comes over here in the form of cheap jewellery. When you take off a ring like this it leaves a greenish, greyish mark on your finger. That's the high copper-alloy content in the silver.'

'What about the original ring?' he asked. 'Where did that come from?'

'I wouldn't be able to offer any proof on this in court because it's not hallmarked, but in my opinion this is Spanish, from the thirties. There was a fashion then for parents giving their daughters silver rings on reaching womanhood. It didn't last. You don't see them any more.'

At the Jefatura he went straight to Felipe and Jorge in the laboratory and gave them a twist of newspaper that contained a small quantity of the ground substance from the urn he'd found at home. He asked them to identify the material.

Ramírez and the rest of the group were waiting in the office. Ramírez was handing round the list he'd extracted from the artists' names he'd found in Salgado's office. There were over forty names on the list, divided into three levels of probability.

'There's a lot of names here,' said Falcón.

'They're not just Salgado's clients or his rejects,' said Ramírez. 'Greta put this together, it's a list of anybody in the Seville area who's been involved in the art world using film, video or high technology. She's started on a list for Madrid, too.'

Ramírez handed over six sheets of paper, which Falcón put on the desk. He saw a letter there addressed to him; he ignored it.

'I think you should work in pairs on this,' said Falcón. 'He could be dangerous and he might be expecting a visit from us ... if he's on this list. We're looking for a male, about 1.80 metres tall and about 70 kilos in weight with a dark complexion. He could have foreign blood in him, possibly North African. He has knowledge of French and might have had a French education at some stage, although he is Spanish and speaks it perfectly. The most important identifying mark at this stage is a bite wound to the forefinger of the right hand and possibly grazed or bruised knuckles on his left hand.'

Falcón held up the evidence sachet with the ring in it.

'This was found in the waste-disposal unit of the sink in Salgado's house. It's a woman's ring, which has been enlarged to fit a small man's finger. The silver used to enlarge the ring is low grade, possibly of North African origin. This does not mean we are looking exclusively for a North African male. He is quite possibly naturalized Spanish and from some generations ago. Keep an open mind on this.

I don't want any racial harassment complaints. Inspector Ramírez will divide up the list and give you your assignments.'

Ramírez took the men into the outer office. Falcón opened the letter on his desk, which was an appointment to see Dr David Rato in the Jefatura at 9.30 a.m. He called Ramírez back in and asked who this doctor was.

'He's the police psychologist,' said Ramírez.

'He wants to see me.'

'Probably just a routine assessment.'

'I've never had one before.'

'Officers in high-stress situations get given them,' said Ramírez. 'I had one after shooting a suspect dead three years ago.'

'I haven't shot anybody.'

Ramírez shrugged. Falcón reminded him about the meeting with Juez Calderón at midday. Ramírez left, taking the rest of the group with him. Falcón called Lobo, whose secretary said he was out for the day. Sweat trickled from the high point of his forehead. He clamped a handkerchief to his head as if it was a wound. Damn this leaking, he thought. His palms moistened. He went to the bathroom, washed his hands and face, and took an Orfidal.

The psychologist's office was in some unvisited part of the Jefatura on the second floor with a different view of the car park. He was called in immediately. They shook hands and sat down. The psychologist was in his early fifties and wore a charcoal-grey suit with a waistcoat. There was a single sheet of paper on the desk in front of him.

'I don't think I've been to a police psychologist before,' said Falcón.

'What about the two times in Barcelona?' asked the doctor.

Panic swept through him. He'd walked straight into a memory blank. Twice in Barcelona?

'You investigated a car bombing in which the twelve-year-old daughter of a politician was killed and there was a shooting in a lawyer's office which left a mother of three dead.'

'Sorry, of course, I meant since I'd been in Seville.'

The doctor gave him a physical examination, which included weighing him and taking his blood pressure. He resumed his seat behind the desk.

'Why am I here?' asked Falcón.

'You're handling a very difficult case with some gruesome details to the murders.'

'I've seen worse,' he lied.

'Everybody in the Jefatura thinks it's one of the worst cases ever.'

'In Seville,' said Falcón. 'I was in Madrid before I came here.'

'You're five kilos under your normal weight.'

'Cases like this use up a lot of nervous energy.'

'In those two cases you looked after in Barcelona you weighed in at 79 kilos. Now you're 74 kilos.'

'I haven't been eating regularly.'

'You mean, since you separated from your wife?'

A small abyss opened up as Falcón realized how many factors might be taken into consideration.

'My housekeeper cooks meals for me. I just haven't found time to consume them, that's all.'

'Your blood pressure is high. At your age I would expect it to be above your normal 12/7 but you're 14/8.5, which is borderline, and you look hollow-eyed. Are you sleeping well?'

'I'm sleeping very well.'

'Are you taking any medication?'

'No,' he said fluently.

'Have you noticed anything different in your bodily functions?' asked Rato. 'Sweating. Diarrhoea. Loss of appetite.'

'No.'

'What about mental functions?'

'No.'

'Any cyclical thinking, memory loss, obsessive tendencies . . . like washing your hands again and again?'

'No.'

'Any joint pains? Shoulders, knees?'

'No.'

'Can you think why anybody inside or outside the Jefatura might have become concerned about your behaviour recently?'

More panic surged through him. The diarrhoea he'd just denied suddenly became a possibility.

'No, I can't,' he said.

'Stress acts on people in different ways, Inspector Jefe, but the fundamentals are the same. Mild forms of stress – overwork with a problem at home – can induce physical reactions to make you stop. A pain in the knee is not unusual. Extreme forms of stress release the same atavistic mechanism known as "fight or flight" – that burst of adrenalin which will give you the strength to strike out or run away. We are no longer in the wild, but our urban jungle can induce the same reaction. The combined pressure of a heavy workload with distressing details, the death of a parent and the divorce of a wife, can trigger a permanent adrenalin rush. Blood pressure goes up. Weight goes down as appetite is suppressed. The brain speeds up. Sleep becomes elusive. The body reacts as if the mind has encountered something to be feared. There's sweating, anxiety, rising to panic, followed by memory loss, and obsessive circular thinking. Inspector Jefe, you have all the symptoms of a man under great stress. Tell me, when was the last time you took an afternoon off work?'

'I'm taking one off this afternoon.'

'When was the last time?'

'I don't remember.'

'Since you arrived in Seville nearly three years ago you haven't taken any time off apart from a single two-week holiday,' said Dr Rato. 'What was your work load before you took on this latest investigation?'

Blank. Panic splashed like ether against his chest.

'I'll tell you, Inspector Jefe,' said Rato. 'You investigated fifteen murders last year as against thirty-four in your last year in Madrid.'

'What's your point, Doctor?'

'Do you think you're hiding in your work?'

'Hiding?'

'There are attractive things even about the ugly work you have to do. There's routine. There's structure. You have colleagues. And it is endless, if you want it to be. You could fill your year with paperwork alone, I imagine.'

'True.'

'Real life is messy. Relationships don't work out. Friends come and go. And, at our age, people start dying. We have to face loss, change and disappointment, but within all this there's the possibility of joy. However it is only achieved by making a connection. When was the last time you had sex?'

Another jolting question, that nearly had Falcón out of his seat and pacing the room.

'That wasn't supposed to be offensive,' said the doctor.

'No, of course, I just haven't been asked that question since I was at university.'

'No male friends have asked you that question?'

Male friends, thought Falcón. Female friends, even. It nearly squeezed a tear up to his eye, the thought that he had no friends. It seemed impossible that his life had slipped away from him like this without him noticing. When was the last time he'd had a friend? He hit the blank wall of his memory until he thought that Calderón could have been a friend.

'When was the last time you had sex?' asked the doctor again.

'With my wife.'

'When did you separate?'

Blank.

'Last year,' said Falcón, struggling.

'Month?'

'May.'

'It was in July, which was probably why you didn't take a holiday,' said Dr Rato. 'When was the last time you had sex before you separated?'

Falcón had to calculate using the ugliest of algebra. If we separated in July and she hadn't let me touch her for two months then that must equal May.

'*That* was May.'

'A year without sex, Inspector Jefe,' said the doctor. 'How is your libido?'

Libido sounds good, he thought. Like a private beach. Let's go down to the libido.

'Inspector Jefe?'

'It probably hasn't been so good, as you might have guessed.'

That image of Consuelo Jiménez came to him, the one with her kneeling in the chair with her skirt rucked up. Was that libidinous? He crossed his legs.

The doctor terminated the meeting.

'Is that it?' said Falcón. 'Don't you have to tell me something?'

'I write a report. It's not up to me to tell you anything. That is in the hands of your superiors. I am not your employer.'

'But what are you going to tell them?'

'That is not a subject for discussion.'

'Give me the general idea,' said Falcón. '"Stick him in the madhouse" or "Tell him to take a holiday"?'

'This is not multiple choice.'

'Are you going to recommend me for a full psychological assessment?'

'This was an initial inquiry following some outside concerns.'

It's Calderón, thought Falcón. That business outside his apartment with Inés.

'Tell me what you're going to say in your report.'

'The meeting is over, Inspector Jefe.'

It was more by luck than judgement that Falcón came out of the bullpens of the Maestranza with Biensolo in his *lote* for Pepe to fight that afternoon. He'd nearly hit a moped on his way from the Jefatura, and just missed shunting into the back of a horse-drawn carriage full of tourists. Seven bollards were now missing from the roadworks on Paseo de Cristóbal Colón. The bull selection process had shot past him. There had been some vague talk about the horn wound in No.484, which had reached him, and the other confidants had taken advantage of his distraction to give him the lote that none of them wanted. He called Pepe at the Hotel Colón and gave him the news.

He went home. He was ready for nothing. His concentration fluttered like a blasted flag. His memory sieved disparate thoughts and images into his brain. He dragged himself up to his room and flung himself face up on the bed. His body shuddered with each sob that lifted his shoulders. The pressure was just too great. Tears ran down his face into the pillow. He gagged against the massive thing that wanted to come up through his throat. Then he slept. No sleeping pill. Pure exhaustion.

His mobile woke him. His eyes felt like hot stones, his lids thick as leather. Paco told him they were down at the restaurant and he was about to eat all his *chuletillas* for him. He showered like a gaping inmate. He dressed and it returned some of his equilibrium. He even felt mildly positive, as if his breakdown had repaired some small but vital mechanism.

During the Feria de Abril the area outside the Hotel Colón was always busy. The bellboys never stopped as cars and minibuses glided in and managers and promoters and team members got out. Fans always hovered around the cafés opposite. There were fewer today because there were no big names on the bill – Pepín Liria was the best known, followed by Vicente Bejarano and then the unknown Pepe Leal.

Falcón went up to Pepe's room. One of his *banderilleros* was standing in the corridor outside, hands behind his back. He opened the door, as if on a mourning wife. He murmured something to Pepe and let Falcón in.

Pepe was sitting on a chair in the middle of the room. His shirt was undone and outside his trousers. He wore no jacket, tie, shoes or socks. His hair was a mess from where he'd been gripping his head. There was a slick of sweat on his forehead and in the middle of his chest. He was white. His fear was naked.

'You shouldn't see me like this,' he said.

He took a sip from a glass of water on the floor and embraced Javier, then he ran for the bathroom and retched into the lavatory.

'You've caught me on the way down,' he said. 'I'm nearly at the bottom of my fear. In a moment I'll be blabbing and in half an hour I'll be a different man.'

They embraced again. Falcón caught the sharp smell of his vomit.

'Don't worry about me, Javier,' he said. 'It's good. Things are coming together. I can feel it. Today will be my day. *La Puerta del Principe* will be mine.'

He was gabbling. They embraced again and Falcón left.

Both the bar and restaurant were heaving with people. The noise was cacophonous. He squeezed into the *comedor* and kissed and embraced his way around the table. He sat down, wolfed the tuna and onions, dipped his bread in the juice of the roasted peppers, gnawed on the slim bones of the chuletillas and drank glasses of dark-red Marqués de Arienzo. He felt whole again, full and solid. His nerves were intact. There'd been some release in being found out. He didn't care any more. Seeing Pepe so profoundly scared had marshalled him. He would embrace everything, including his fate.

At five o'clock they made their way through the warm streets to La Maestranza. The smell of cheap and expensive cigars mingled with cologne, hair oil and perfume. The sun was still high and there was the lightest of breezes. The conditions were near perfect. Now it was up to the bulls.

Their group was split up. Paco and Javier took their privileged debenture seats in the *Sombra* while the family took their complimentary seats in the *Sol y sombra*. Paco and Javier sat two rows up from the ring in the *barreras*. Paco handed his brother a cushion with the finca's crest embroidered on it. They breathed in the atmosphere of *la España profunda*. The murmuring crowd, the Ducados and *puros*, the men with their hair combed back in brilliantined rails helping their silken wives up the steps to their seats. A line of young women in traditional mantillas of white lace sat beneath the president's box. Boys with buckets of ice full of beer and coke patrolled the terraces. Cans were expertly hurled and caught by customers, who handed down change through the obliging crowd.

The toreros led their teams out, all in their trajes de luces, following three perfectly groomed, high-stepping, dappled-grey stallions who necked at their bridles. Pepe Leal had rebuilt himself and was resplendent in his royal blue and gold suit. He wore the serious expression of a man who'd come to do his work.

The stallions retreated, followed by the mules, who would drag the dead bull out of the plaza, nodding under their red pompoms. The three toreros practised slow, beautiful passes with their pink capes. The crowd's anticipation tightened. The toreros moved behind the barriers leaving Pepe Leal, who was to face the first bull, out alone in the plaza with his cape.

The door into the dark swung open. Silence. A single voice shouted encouragement and the half-ton bull burst into the sunlit plaza and the roar of the crowd. The bull looked about, charged, gave up and eased to a trot. Pepe called the bull, which thundered past him with no interest in the cape and savaged one of the barriers with his horns. Pepe brought him back and executed two *media verónicas* with the cape and the crowd broke their silence for him.

A trumpet announced the picadors, who trundled out with their lances on their blindfolded, mattressed horses. Pepe drew the bull into one of the picador's horses. As the bull hit, the picador leaned down on his lance and drove the point into the hump of muscle. The horse's front legs came off the ground. The crowd cheered the bull's willingness to charge and its strength.

The picadors left the ring. Pepe's team lined up with their banderillas, which they placed efficiently into the bull's neck. Pepe came out for his faena and Javier and Paco leaned forward to study the final act.

The nervousness and disinterest in the cape the bull had shown at the beginning became more apparent in the faena. It took Pepe nearly half his faena to persuade the bull to take to the muleta. When the bull finally responded the band played a slow *pasa doble*. Pepe went on to kill the bull well. Javier and Paco thought it had been a creditable performance with a distracted bull. The crowd applauded, but no white handkerchiefs dabbed the air asking for an ear.

Pepín Liria's first bull did not take to the ring. It burst out into the bright roar, took ten strides and turned tail. It trotted around, butting the barriers. Its only moment came when, running through the cape, a horn caught in the ground and the bull performed a perfect half-ton somersault.

Vicente Bejarano's bull was strong and fast and interested in the muleta. The crowd took to the animal, but it was not Bejarano's day. He could not forge any connection with the beast and, although he produced some fine sculpted moments, never controlled the bull.

At 18.40 the sun was still shining on the expectant crowd sitting in *Sol* when the door opened into the plaza and Biensolo trotted out and took stock. There was no rushing madness, there was no charging at barriers or senseless butting. He looked around the plaza and decided it was his.

The crowd murmured, unsure of this bull, worried that it might know more than it should. Pepe walked out towards him and laid his cape at his feet. The bull took exception to the intrusion and charged him, fast, direct, head down. From that moment the crowd knew that this was the bull of the day and that if Pepe could control him then they would see something unique.

'This should have been Pepín's bull,' said the man sitting next to Paco.

'You watch,' said Javier. 'You'll be crying with the rest of us by the end of this.'

Pepe performed two full *verónicas* and a *chicuelina* with the cape. The crowd went wild with anticipation. Words were spoken between the torero and the picador and when Biensolo drove into the mattressed side of the horse with such stupendous violence that both man and horse were carried aloft right to the barrier, the crowd erupted. They loved this bull.

Paco grabbed Javier around the neck and kissed his brother on the forehead.

'*Eso es un toro, no?*'

One of Pepe's banderilleros excelled in placing the banderillas.

The horn tips were practically in the man's armpits as he leaned over on his slanting sprint and there was a breathless, frozen moment when man and beast became one, before miraculously separating.

Pepe came out for his faena and the crowd stilled to the purest silence in Spain. The silence of respect for the bull.

The bull, mouth closed, shoulders heaving, a red sash of blood running down his right flank to the top of the foreleg, looked at Pepe. Pepe screwed the baton, which brought the muleta out to its full extension, into his palm. He walked towards the bull, pointing the toe of each shoe at him, holding the muleta behind him. The bull was patient. At four metres Pepe turned a shoulder to the beast and opened out his chest and slowly produced the muleta, as if to say: 'May I offer you this?' The bull took to it, ran hard and fast and dropped his horns. Pepe seemed to hold him there, forcing him to slow down, so that only when the nose met the muleta did Pepe allow him to go forward, drawing him on, telling him that this was the royal pace. And it was a beautiful thing to see, the gradual tensile twisting of Pepe's body, smooth and strong as red-hot wrought iron.

He brought Biensolo back and forth, and with each pass the dance improved, the relationship grew stronger, the mutual respect deepened. It was done so slowly that the audience didn't notice that the connection had been made, the pact understood, that man and beast would play this out to its only possible conclusion.

At no point in the faena did Pepe try to dominate too much and it was this that he'd understood about the bull from the moment Biensolo had entered the ring. This was the bull's space and he'd allowed Pepe into it.

He performed his *naturales*. Biensolo thundered past him as if he was moving the whole of Spain forward on his horns. Then Pepe stood before the bull and just showed him one corner of the muleta, no bigger than a terracotta floor-tile, from behind his back. Some women in the audience couldn't stand it and gasps and squeaks of fear broke out. The bull crashed past the lonely figure, the reed in the wind bending slightly in the draught. Without turning, Pepe showed him another corner of the muleta and again Biensolo tore past him. Even the men broke at that. Paco had his fists buried in his eyes. The man next to him was crying. They knew that they were seeing it. The impossible genius of man and beast in their dance of death.

The silence was so absolute when Pepe went to exchange the

straight sword for the curved killing sword that Javier believed he could hear the sound of Pepe's light-black pumps on the sand of the plaza. The bull watched him, front legs slightly splayed, foreleg and shoulder still slick with blood, chest heaving in silent bellows, the banderillas clacking a death rattle on his back. His dance partner returned, the muleta under his arm, the new lethal sword at his side. Pepe's long shadow met the bull's head and walked into him.

The horns came up. Their minds re-engaged. The crowd, who knew that if Pepe killed Biensolo well he would get everything – ears, tail, *La Puerta del Principe* – tightened their already constricted silence. Pepe released the muleta. It dropped like a bucket of blood. The bull nodded, assenting to his kind collaboration. Pepe looked at the position of the bull's feet and, with several short passes, manoeuvred him to the barrier and then teased him with flicks of the muleta until he stood just right with his horns pointing into the Sombra crowd. Pepe, with his back to Javier now, moved lightly as if he might disturb a sleeping child. The sword came up. Pepe aimed at the coin-sized target between the bull's shoulders. His feet braced themselves against the plaza floor. His body was no longer human but had assumed the shape of a brilliant wading bird.

The moment. The speed was breathtaking as the two forces shunted together.

But it was wrong. Pepe's head came up. The sword struck bone and span away. The right horn sliced into his inner thigh and with a derisive flick Biensolo tossed him in the air. It was so fast nobody moved as Pepe tumbled in the triumphant updraught from the bull's horns. The reed body came down, as broken as a torturer's victim, and the horn disappeared into his belly. The bull drove forward, head down, a recollected atavism at work now that their pact had been broken. He rammed into the planks of the barrier with a splintering thud that seemed to wind the entire audience.

Pepe's team erupted over the wall. The stillness went out of the crowd and a keening cry went up from the women. Javier ran down, stumbling over the heads of the horrified spectators. He sprinted to the barrier where Pepe was pinned. The bull savagely rammed his quarry with brand new, brilliant strength. Pepe grasped the horn in his stomach with both hands like a general who'd seen disaster and dispatched himself. His face bore only the sadness of regret.

The team worked to distract the bull. Hands reached over the barrier to hold Pepe. His rag legs, with a ghastly slash of red where the femoral artery thumped out thick, dark, vital blood, flapped and slapped against the wooden planks.

The bull pulled away, turned viciously on the waving capes around him and eyed each one individually like a victorious but unpopular emperor who has to endure the frivolity of peacetime politics.

They lifted Pepe over the barrier, arms now open, the red burgeoning from his stomach, and for a moment he was as pitiful as a *pietá* as they rushed him from the ring towards the infirmary.

Javier ran after the six men holding Pepe, who reached out a hand to him. The news travelled fast and they didn't bother with the infirmary but took him directly to the ambulance. The paramedics put him on a stretcher and threw him into the back.

Pepe called for Javier, his words hardly more than breath.

Falcón leapt over the back of the paramedic who was already slapping a compress on to Pepe's stomach wound. The ambulance lurched away from the plaza. The other paramedic cut away the trouser and plunged his hands into the gaping wound in Pepe's thigh. Pepe arched his back, cried out in agony. The paramedic called for a clamp. A packet was thrown at Javier, who tore it open and held the clamp out to the paramedic whose hands were in the wound, trying to find the artery. Javier took hold of Pepe's hand, cradled his head in his lap. There was no blood in Pepe's face and the pallor of death was creeping over him. Javier gripped his shoulders, whispered in his ear everything that he could think of that would help him hold on.

The ambulance careered down Cristóbal Colón, sirens blaring, and headed down the underpass by the Plaza de Armas. Pepe ran his tongue over his lips. His mouth was as dry as cardboard from the catastrophic fluid loss, his hand as cold as dead meat. The paramedic cut up the sleeve of Pepe's *traje de luces* and tore a sack of blood from the fridge. The other paramedic shouted for the clamp. Javier leaned forward and they clamped the femoral artery. He turned to help plug in the litre of blood to Pepe's arm. Javier roared at Pepe to hold on. He saw him trying to speak. He put his ear to his lips. Even the boy's breath was chill.

'I'm sorry for that,' said Pepe.

29

It had rained during the night. The new day arrived rinsed and
refreshed. The sun played over the beads of moisture on the dripping
trees and the first jacarandas came into high purple flower. Falcón
stopped when he saw them, pulled over and dropped his window.
He had rarely done this in the city – found in nature an expression
of the complexities of the human condition. But the high, fragile,
fern-like green leaf of the jacarandas feathering against the clean
blue sky with the clusters of pale purple flowers hanging in the
windless morning spoke the same language, could talk to anyone
about pain.

He turned on the car radio. The local news was all about Pepe
Leal. The media were trying to make a story about the fact that just
as Pepe was going in for the kill his head had come up. A bullfight
journalist talked inconclusively about the incomprehensible distraction. Someone on the panel mentioned camera flashes, the number
of people trying to capture the moment. Another person said he
remembered a bigger flash. The bullfight journalist scoffed. The
myth had begun. Falcón turned off the radio.

By the time he arrived at the Jefatura the men had already dispersed. Only Ramírez remained. They shook hands. Ramírez
embraced him and offered his condolences. He handed him a message, which told him that Comisario León wanted to see him as soon
as he arrived. He took the lift up to the top floor, looking at his
vague reflection in the stainless-steel panels. He was held together
by threads. There would be no resistance from him.

Ten minutes later he was going back down. The weight of command had been lifted from his shoulders. He had been given two
weeks compassionate leave and would have to undergo full psychological assessment on his return. He had said nothing. He was

defenceless. He went to his office and cleared out his desk to find there were no personal items, only some letters, which he put in his pocket, and his police-issue revolver, which he should have returned to the armoury but didn't.

At 6 p.m. he attended the funeral of Pepe Leal. The whole bull-fighting community was in attendance. Paco was there, inconsolable and uncontrollable. He bawled into his hands, his shoulders shaking, the whole tragedy weighing down on them. Everybody cried. The mourners, the cemetery workers, the flower sellers, the onlookers, the grave visitors. And the grief was genuine, except that it wasn't for Pepe Leal. He was almost unknown to these people. He was not a great name. As Javier stood in dry-eyed suffering amongst the weeping and the snivelling, he understood what this grief was for. They were mourning their own losses – youth, prospects, health, talent. The death of Pepe Leal had, temporarily at least, brought an end to possibility. It was for this reason that Javier found it kitsch and he wouldn't cry with them, and he wouldn't join them afterwards but went home to his bruised and silent house and the compassion of his enforced leave.

He sat in his study, still in his mac, doodling on a paper with a pencil. He wanted to get out of the city. Biensolo's horn had punched a hole in the Feria and Falcón would leave the city to bleed over Pepe's death. He took out a map of Spain, placed the pencil over Seville and span it three times. Each time it pointed directly south, and south of Seville there was nothing apart from a small fishing village called Barbate. But beyond Barbate, across the straits, was Tangier.

The phone rang, startling him. He didn't answer it. No more condolences required.

The following morning he packed a bag, including the unread journal, found his passport and took a cab to the bus station at the back of the Palacio de Justicia. Five and a half hours later he boarded a ferry in Algeciras to Tangier.

The ferry journey lasted an hour and a half. He spent most of it watching a Moroccan version of himself taking down the details of a group of six boys – illegal immigrants, who were being returned. They were cheerful. Tourists gave them the thumbs up and cigarettes. The policeman was firm but not unkind.

Tangier appeared out of the mist without dredging up a single memory. The long rainy winter had left the surrounding country a deep, lush green, which was not a colour he associated with Morocco. There was something familiar about the cascade of grubby white-washed houses within the walls of the old town, which fell from the Kasbah at the top of the cliff to the Grand Mosque at the lower end. Beyond the walls the *ville nouvelle* had pushed further around the bay. He tried to find the old house where his father's studio had been but it was either hidden amongst the apartment blocks or had been destroyed to make way for them.

The taxi driver took him from the port to the Hotel Rembrandt and tried to charge him 150 dirham, which involved an ugly argument and a dishonourable discharge with half that amount changing hands. The reception, still in its fifties marble splendour, gave him the key to room 422 and he took his own bag up there.

The hotel had suffered in the intervening half-century. There was a glass panel missing from one of the doors in his room. Paint peeled off the metal windows. The furniture looked as if it had taken refuge from a violent husband. But there was a perfect view of the bay of Tangier and Falcón sat on the bed and gaped at it, while thoughts of deracination spread through his mind.

He went out to get some food, knowing they ate early in Morocco, but found the time two hours behind Spain and at 6 p.m. nowhere was open. He walked to the Place de France and then down past the Hotel El Minzah to the Grand Soco and entered the Medina through the market, which brought him out in a street not far from the Spanish cathedral. From there he tried to remember the route to his old family home. He must have walked it a thousand times with his mother. It didn't come back to him and he was soon lost in the maze of narrow alleys until quite by accident he found himself in front of a house he recognized.

The door was opened by a maid who spoke only Arabic. She disappeared. A man in his fifties wearing a white burnous and white leather babouches came to the door. Falcón explained himself and the man was stunned. It had been his own father who had bought the property from Francisco Falcón. Javier was welcomed in. The man, Mohammed Rachid, showed him around the house, which was structurally exactly the same, with the fig tree still in its place and the strange high room with the window at the top.

Rachid invited Falcón to dinner. Over a vast shared bowl of couscous Javier revealed that his mother had died in the house and asked if any of the neighbours would have been alive at the time. One of the boys was sent out with instructions. He was back in minutes with an invitation to take a coffee next door.

The neighbouring family included an old man of seventy-five, who would have been thirty-four at the time of his mother's death. He remembered the incident very well because most of what happened took place outside his front door.

'The unusual thing was that *two* doctors turned up,' said the old man, 'and there was a disagreement as to who was to see the patient. As it happened, the woman, your mother, was already dead and so your father had called his own doctor to deal with the matter.

'Your father had arrived back from his studio for breakfast to find his wife dead in her bed. In his distress he called the only doctor he knew, which was his own. A German. Your mother's doctor, a Spaniard, seemed quite satisfied with this and was about to leave when the Riffian woman, your mother's maid, burst out of the house and announced that her mistress had been poisoned. She held a glass of something in her hand, that she said had come from her mistress's bedside. Nobody believed her and she took the drastic step of drinking some of the liquid. Your father tore the glass from her grip and with great drama she fell to the ground. There was consternation. The Spanish doctor leapt forward. But it was a sham. She wasn't dead. There was no poison. And the maid was dismissed as a hysteric.'

Falcón couldn't control the trembling in his hands, not even by clasping them together. Sweat trickled down his cheek and nausea swooned in his head at this light-hearted recounting of the drama. He staggered to his feet from the cushions on the floor, knocking over the undrunk cup of coffee. Mohammed Rachid stood to help him.

They walked to the taxi rank on the Grand Soco, and a battered Mercedes took him back to the Hotel Rembrandt. Once out of the house and the Medina he calmed down, brought the panic under control. It was just that the old man's benign recounting of the story had brought it all back to him. The horror of that morning. His mother dead in her bed and this unseemly commotion in the street outside. He remembered it and yet there were still gaps and he hadn't wanted the old man to continue because . . . He didn't know why. He just wanted to get out of there as soon as possible.

Back at the hotel he sank on to the bed in the darkness of the room and looked out to sea over the lights of the town and harbour. He was desolate. His body shuddered under a spasm of loneliness and all his deferred grief at Pepe's death came to the surface. He fell back, drew his knees up into a foetal position and tried to hold himself together, afraid that if he didn't do this he would fragment beyond repair. Some hours later he released himself and stripped off his clothes. He took a sleeping pill, scratched the bedclothes over himself and passed out.

The morning was nearly over by the time he woke up. There was no hot water. He showered under cold, which brought his mind back sharply to the inexplicable fact that he was quietly weeping a stream of tears that he was powerless to stop. His hands hung limp at his sides and he shook his head in misery. His body, now, was out of his control.

He walked up to the Place de France and took a coffee at the Café de Paris. From there he went to the Spanish consulate and, showing his police ID, asked if there was anybody Spanish still living in Tangier who had been there in the late fifties and sixties. They told him to go to a restaurant called Romero's and ask for Mercedes of the same name.

The restaurant was in a garden wedged between two roads leading to a roundabout. The door was opened by an elderly man in a white jacket and a fez, whose breathing difficulties were manifest. As they made their way to the table a Pekingese dog attacked them. Javier winced at its penetrating yap.

He ordered steak and asked after Mercedes Romero and the old man pointed to an elderly, well-coiffed, blonde woman who was playing patience at a single table on the other side of the empty restaurant. He asked the old man to give her a note of introduction, which he wrote out on a page of his notebook. The old man staggered away, placed the note before Mercedes, told her the order and was given some money to buy the steak.

Mercedes came slowly across the room. She grabbed the Pekingese by the scruff, rubbed its tummy and threw it under an empty table. She sat opposite him and asked him if he was the son of Francisco Falcón, which Javier confirmed.

'I never knew him,' she said. 'Nor Pilar, but I was a good friend of your stepmother, Mercedes, who was about my age. She used to eat in the restaurant my family owned then in the Grand Hôtel Villa de France. We were very close and I was devastated by her death.'

'I never called her my stepmother,' said Falcón. 'I always referred to her as my second mother. We were very close, too.'

'Yes, she told me that she thought of you as her own son and how desperate she was for you to follow in your father's footsteps. She hoped that you might be an even greater artist than he.'

'I was barely eight years old at the time.'

'You don't remember that then,' she said, nodding behind him.

In a simple black frame on the wall above his head was a line drawing of a woman. Underneath was written *Mercedes*.

'No, I don't.'

'You drew that in the summer of 1963. Mercedes gave it to me as a Christmas present. It's of her, of course, not me. I asked her why she was giving it to me and she said something very strange: "Because with you I know it will be safe."'

Tears brimmed in Falcón's eyes. He'd given up any attempt at control of his emotions.

'She drowned,' he said. 'I still remember the night she left and didn't come back. They never recovered the body and I think not seeing her again made it harder. I saw my mother in her casket . . .'

'Where is your father now?' asked Mercedes.

'He died two years ago.'

'Maybe you remember someone else from that time – your father's agent, Ramón Salgado?'

Falcón nodded madly and told her how Salgado had just been murdered and that he was the investigating officer. It all came out why he was in Tangier, which was when the old man in the fez came staggering back with the steak and salad, which he breathed over heavily as he served.

'Perhaps if you'd been a detective back then you might have dealt with the matter of Mercedes' death with a more penetrating eye than the local police.'

'Why do you say that?'

'I don't believe in gossip – I hear too much of it running a restaurant – but there was a lot of it about at that time. Enough gossip to have made anyone seriously investigating that tragedy ask harder questions than they did.'

'What are you implying, Sra Romero?' said Falcón quietly.

'I shouldn't speak ill of the dead, but Mercedes was my friend and I was very sorry to lose her, especially in a boating accident. She had spent a lot of time on boats. Her husband, Milton, owned one. She had sailed across the Atlantic several times. She was a very experienced and sure-footed sailor. She did not make mistakes. They said it was rough that night, that a storm had got up in the straits, but I can tell you it was nothing compared to some of the storms she'd been through coming over the Atlantic. They said she fell overboard and I'm afraid that I for one did not believe it. I did not believe the gossip that ran along the lines of how careless it was of your father to have lost two wives. That disgusted me. But both your father and Ramón Salgado should have been forced to account for their actions in an official inquiry, at least.'

Falcón got up from the table, his steak untouched, and walked out of the restaurant. He wasn't prepared to listen to that sort of stuff. That was what happened when you became famous. People loved to speculate at your expense. Fine. But he was not going to be a party to that. He walked flat out back to the Hotel Rembrandt, sprinted up to room 422 and threw himself on the bed, wrapped a pillow over his ears and clamped his eyes shut.

It was night-time when he woke up and a great storm was playing itself out across the straits over Spain. The sheet lightning ran for hundreds of kilometres, illuminating the vast, stacked clouds boiling in the night sky. Outside it was spitting. He found a restaurant and ate a lamb tagine and drank a bottle of Cabernet Président. He staggered back to the hotel, collapsed on the bed and woke up sweating and fully clothed. He stripped and crawled back into bed. The rain slashed and raked at the windows.

The Friday morning was drear and sodden. He had one more enquiry to make, which was probably going to be more fruitless than the rest. He checked out of the hotel and took a *grand taxi* to Tetuán, which broke down on the way so that he arrived in the late afternoon. He made a quick tour of the town's Spanish community, trying to find somebody who might have known the González family who ran a hotel business back in the thirties.

By seven o'clock he'd lost his guide in the Medina and was wandering aimlessly through the alleyways, following carts piled high with fresh mint, when he came across a sight in a narrow street that totally paralysed him with panic.

A man with a cart of steel churns was pouring milk into local women's calabashes, in which they would make their yoghurt. The gush of white liquid induced nausea. The flat white calm of the full calabashes turned him and sent him on a wild run through the streets and out of the Medina.

He gave up on trying to find someone to explain 'the incident' from his father's journals. He found a cheap hotel with a bar. He drank beer and ate *albondigas* in a crowd of Moroccan men, under a pall of cigarette smoke. He engaged in their small talk so as not to slip back into more despairing thoughts.

That night he was woken by a dream, a terrible dream, which he had to walk out of himself in his small room. The dream had been of nothing, of a terrible whiteness – an amorphous, consuming blankness that contained no memories, no past, no present and no future. It was the end of time and it seemed to want him.

Extracts from the Journals of Francisco Falcón

12th January 1958, Tangier
I come back home early to take Javier out for a little treat on his second birthday but P. and he are not at home. The other children are at school. There is only the one maid at home, a Riffian woman, who speaks some impenetrable Berber dialect that only P. understands. I am fuming and go back to the studio and paint a canvas with terrible slashing strokes of red, as if I'm carving my way through the ranks of the enemy. The result is a work of terrifying energy, of appalling violence such as I've only ever committed on the battlefield. I burn it and watching the sickle slashes of paint being consumed by fire gives me near-sexual pleasure.

15th July 1958, Tangier
R. has turned up at the studio (he's never been before). G. is pregnant again and he's in a terrible state. He waits for my admonishment. I say nothing and he calls me a true friend. The doctor had been savage with him. He tells me over and over that it was an accident so that I stop believing him. 'This time I will lose her,' he says, and I see his passion for her, a passion I used to have for P. and now have for Javier. I'm moved and try to calm him. She will have to stay still for the entire pregnancy, he says, and for the first time I think there's something else at play here. He seems scared by the fact that she can't be moved and when I press him on this he suddenly says: 'We should all leave and go back to Spain.' I think he has a problem in his business, but he won't be drawn on the matter.

25th September 1958, Tangier
I have been naïve. I should have known that, while R. can conduct himself in business with ruthlessness and tact, when it comes to affairs of the heart he is a small boy, incapable of objectivity and subject to the whim of his, still youthful, passions. I now know why he couldn't speak to

me before. He was ashamed. It seems amazing living in Tangier, where the orgies of Ancient Rome appear as staid as English tea parties, that a grown man is capable of shame. R. is an island of virtue in a sea of shamelessness. He has never indulged in the local young men and is appalled by the idea, calling it 'unnatural'. Since he met G., as far as I know, he has not transgressed, not even with a prostitute before they were married. Just the thought of the frenzy on their wedding night leaves me weak.

R.'s revelations are quite a shock and are drawn from him at visible cost. We are on the verandah of the studio and, when he is not holding his head in his hands giving me his confession (who has begun to feel like a fat, corrupt prelate), he is pacing from side to side and casting about in case there is someone in the vicinity who can hear. R, at the age of thirty-five, has now transgressed in a spectacularly irresponsible fashion. I realize that I have been making light of this, but what R. has done is serious. I'm not sure that it has been done without the guile of the Moroccans with whom he has been doing business. We Europeans and Americans in particular are impressed by strengths, we like to see them displayed before us, especially in business. The Moroccan, however, and perhaps the African in general, is not so interested in strengths, which are always overt, but in the weaknesses which are hidden. It is sad that virtue should be seen as a weakness . . . or is it virtue? I was always disturbed by R.'s passion for G. when she was still a girl. He has succumbed again. He caught sight of one of the young daughters of a business associate of his in Fez. The girl was not veiled so might even have been as young as twelve years of age. R.'s interest was noted, the girl was made available, R. transgressed and now perhaps the most serious thing in Moroccan society is at stake – honour. R. is expected to take the girl for his wife. This is impossible. And here we have the cultural clash and the reason for R.'s torment. There is a solution: he must leave the country. He will lose his entire investment in the Moroccan project, which amounts to $25,000. But G. cannot be moved and he cannot uproot the family without making some unpleasant revelations. He fears that now the International Zone no longer exists, his family could be at risk. Of what? He leaves his final revelation to the last moment. The Arab girl is pregnant. He thinks that if he leaves Tangier there could be some revenge attack on his family.

7th October 1958, Tangier
As a security measure R. has rented a house nearly opposite his own and
we have put four legionnaires in there. Pressure is mounting on him and
he is buying time by continuing to invest money in the Moroccan project.
It costs him thousands of dollars, but he is prepared to pay any amount.
P. has been to see G. and she is in no fit state to be moved, let alone
undergo a sea journey across the straits in winter.

14th December 1958, Tangier
The pressure on R. has been too great. His health has suffered and he
has been laid up with a lung infection. I tell him that as soon as he is
well he should leave, which is what he did yesterday, taking Marta, the
six-year-old, (who, after her difficult birth, is a little simple) with him.
R. has done everything possible. He has bribed the whole of Tangier. I
don't know how deep his resources are, but they must be considerable for
him to have raised his investment with the Moroccans to close to
$40,000. He has given them some excuse or other that he has to go to
Spain and that they have nothing to fear from a man of honour. I wish
I knew more about these people, but R. will not let me near that end of
things. I have no idea whether they are rogues who've seen a way of
milking a vulnerable European, or genuine traditionalists who adhere to
some ancient code of behaviour and mores. R. says they do not
understand why he can't simply divorce G. In their culture they only
have to say the words three times and it is done.

22nd January 1959, Tangier
G.'s waters have broken and she goes into a prolonged labour of what P.
describes as almost constant contraction. P. is convinced that the baby will
not be able to survive the trauma. I call R. in Spain. He receives the
news in silence. Twelve hours later he appears in the house, which is
tomb dark on a grim winter morning. The fifty-year-old Spanish doctor
and midwife are doing everything to get the baby out, but it is the
wrong way round and also stuck. The atmosphere in the house is one of
hopelessness. There is something of the torture chamber about it, with
G.'s screams, the attentiveness of the medical staff and the black, lightless
desolation of us all. After fifty-two hours the boy is delivered. He weighs
three kilos. G. is so exhausted that should she sleep too deeply she might
slip away. The doctor delivers a savage monologue to R., who asks when
G. can be moved. 'She might never leave this house alive, but you should
know within the week,' he says.

7th February 1959, Tangier
I go down to the port with my pockets full of dollars. It is better for G.
to be moved on a quiet sea than driven to Ceuta on rough roads. The
night is calm. The officials are malleable. We bring G. down to the port
in a lumbering Studebaker and load her on to the yacht R. has
chartered. As they're about to cast off a police car arrives on the quay
and a row develops in which the travel documents are confiscated,
permission to leave the port is revoked and we all have to go back to the
terminal for questioning. We ask on what charge and are stunned when
they say it is fraud and mention the company that R. has been investing
in. R., believing that the game is up, parts with $200. The sum is so
vast that a deep silence ensues in which the situation could go one way or
the other. The money is pocketed. Documents are returned. Permission is
granted and a salute goes up.

12th February 1959, Tangier
As the legionnaires I had positioned opposite R.'s house were leaving, a
group of Moroccans turned up with some police and a warrant. They
broke the door down to R.'s house and removed all contents. Later a
letter arrived at my home written in Arabic script, which I cannot read.
I take it to the Spanish Legation where even the translator blanches at
its contents.

> I am Abdullah Diouri. I was a business associate of your
> friend whose name I cannot bring myself to write. You may
> know that he has deeply offended the honour of my family.
> He has treated one of my young daughters as nothing more
> than a common prostitute. Her life has been ruined. There is
> no amount of money that can repair the damage done to
> her or my family name. You should know that I have
> withdrawn from the business in which my associates and I
> had invested.
>
> You should tell your friend that the family of Abdullah
> Diouri will be avenged and the price that we shall exact will
> be the same as exacted from us. I have lost a daughter, my
> family has been dishonoured. I will seek out your friend to
> the ends of the earth and I will reclaim my family honour
> from him.

There was a crudeness and a lack of affectation to this letter that gave
it the ring of authenticity. The dots above and below the lines of script

376

had been added in red ink. The effect was one of spattered blood. I send the original and translation to R., who has not yet been able to move G. from hospital in Algeciras, where she arrived unconscious after the crossing.

17th March 1959, Tangier

I have been too occupied by R.'s problems these last six months to contemplate the end of an era. It has stolen up on me and left me in its roiling wake. R.'s departure has hit me harder than I thought. I sit alone at his table in the Café de Paris and the talk is like an ongoing lament. Offices have closed down. No alcohol or tobacco can be loaded in the port. The hotels are empty. We have to use the dirham. The smart shops on the Boulevard Pasteur have closed down and been taken over by Moroccans selling tourist rubbish. Were it not for B.H. in Palace Sidi Hosni we would slip completely off the world stage. My work has foundered. All I seem to be doing is copying de Kooning, even though M. writes to tell me how admired my 'peoplescape' has been by those allowed into M.G.'s apartment. Even these words cannot stem my sense of decline. I feel like an old Roman, post-bacchanal, jaded and listless, prone to ennui and anxiety at the demise of empire.

R. sends word that he is living in the Sierra de Ronda. The clear dry air agrees with G.

18th June 1959, Tangier

The first heat of the summer is brutal. My brain is a seethe of nothingness. I lie about on carpets in my studio drinking tea and smoking. I sleep all afternoon and wake up at eight in the evening to find the temperature nearly bearable. I suddenly remember it is P.'s birthday and that I've failed to buy her a gift. I rummage about in the drawers and find an agate cube on a cheap silver ring. It must be a cast-off of M.'s. I fashion some coloured paper around it so that it looks like the pistil of a flower. I press it into a box and crush a lid on top so that when opened it will spring out. I tie it up with strips of red cloth and go home.

By midnight we have eaten. The children are about to go to bed when I remember my present. I send Javier round the table to her with my little box. P. opens it with great ceremony. The flower springs out and the box lid hits Javier on the nose. Everyone is delighted, including P., but then a look of complete puzzlement crosses her face. I panic that it was one of her old rings that I have given back to her. But I'm sure it's *not. I would have noticed it. The moment passes. She puts on the ring. I kiss her and notice that it is the only ring on her finger apart from her wedding band. This surprises me, because there was always one ring that she never took off – a silver band set with a small sapphire, which was given to her by her parents when she became a woman. I nearly ask her if she's lost it, but that look on her face when she saw the agate cube has left me uneasy.*

30

Saturday, 28th April 2001, Tetuán, Morocco

Falcón was up early to catch a *grand taxi* to Ceuta before dawn. From there he took the hydrofoil to Algeciras. The last entry of the diary was burnt on his mind. The silver ring with the single sapphire was his mother's ring. The killer had been wearing his mother's ring. That was why he'd had to come back to find it, because now Falcón knew the journal was the key. The killer had somehow had access to his father's house, read the journal, stolen the vital section and set out on his avenging spree. But how had he come into possession of a ring his mother never took off? Uneasy truths slipped into his mind, along with the memory of being lifted high in the air at the edge of the sea on the bay of Tangier, legs kicking, above a face that would not come back to him.

By two o'clock he was in Seville. There was a message from Comisario Lobo on the answering machine. He was furious and used up a lot of tape telling him that it was no coincidence that Comisario León's lackey, Ramírez, had officially removed Consuelo Jiménez from the suspects list as soon as he'd assumed control of Falcón's investigation. He didn't care. He went straight back up to his father's studio. The jewellery box was still open on the table where he'd left it. He clenched the agate cube in his fist as if the impression of its geometry would take him through the lock of his memory. He paced the floor, kicked at a pile of magazines under the table which fell at his feet.

The cover of one of the magazines was totally black and its English title was *Bound*. He opened it with his foot and reared back. The two photographs he saw were visions of hell – two blindfolded women being tortured by heavily tattooed men. He kicked the magazine away.

Was that what his father had been driven to? Had the loss of his genius polarized him to the extent that, having painted the sublime and lost his grasp of it, he was drawn to the ugliest of pictures . . . to do what? To disturb his mind back to greatness? To bury himself in the philosophical hope that beauty can only exist if there is ugliness? Falcón couldn't wait to get the appalling images out of the house and in kicking it away he saw that the whole pile consisted of pornography – hard core, bestial, depraved beyond imagination.

On the table above the pile of magazines was the roll of five canvasses, none of which he'd recognized. He unrolled them again and pinned them up on the work wall. He noticed that the canvas was old but the paint was acrylic, which his father hadn't started using until the late seventies. He was also sure that this was not his father's work and he wished Salgado were alive to tell him about these paintings.

Then he remembered the copyist. The half-gypsy guy who lived in the Alameda somewhere, the one he hadn't liked, who'd stood in his black underpants and scratched his genitals while his father spoke to him. What was his name? There was something odd about it. It wasn't a real name. Something came back to him about the day he'd gone to the copyist's workshop with his father. All the paintings were upside down on their easels. He copied upside down. El Zurdo – that was it. The left-hander. To imitate a right-hander's brushstrokes he used to paint upside down. Falcón found an address for the copyist but no telephone number in his father's old address book under 'Z'.

He picked up a taxi outside the Hotel Colón and went to Calle Parras, not far from the Alameda. There was no answer from El Zurdo's apartment, but the neighbour told him that he'd gone to lunch in his usual place, a bar on Calle Escuderos called La Cubista.

There were six lone men sitting at individual tables, eating and watching the television. He recognized none of them.

'I wondered how long it was going to take,' said a voice, as Falcón walked to the bar.

The cutlery activity stopped, the soap on TV continued. The dark-faced man with horse teeth who'd spoken stood up. He had grey hair just visible under a black hat, which had a number of badges and brooches pinned to the band. He was dressed head to toe in black.

'You must be Javier Falcón,' he said.

'Why do you think that?'

'Because you've just walked in here with a roll of canvasses under your arm, looking like someone's lost child.'

'El Zurdo?'

The man pointed him to a chair opposite his own.

'Have you eaten?'

'You were wondering how long it was going to take . . .'

'For Javier Falcón to come and find me,' he said, looking over his shoulder to the blackboard menu. 'Now, *cordero en salsa, escalopinas de cerdo* or *atún en salsa*?'

'*Cordero*,' said Falcón.

El Zurdo shouted the order across. Falcón leaned the canvasses against the adjoining table. Red wine was poured for him.

'We only met once,' said Falcón.

'I have an eye for faces,' said El Zurdo. 'You didn't like me, I remember that.'

'We didn't even speak.'

'You wouldn't shake my hand.'

'You'd just used it to scratch yourself.'

El Zurdo laughed. A woman put a plate of lamb stew in front of Falcón.

'What have you got?' asked El Zurdo, nodding at the canvasses.

'Five paintings. I don't recognize them. They're not my father's work. I wanted to know if you copied them.'

El Zurdo pushed his empty plate back and took a toothpick from a jar on the table. Falcón started eating.

'Why do you want to know about these paintings?' asked El Zurdo. 'You're a cop, aren't you? Your father told me.'

'I'm not working, if that's what you mean,' said Falcón. 'I'm on leave.'

'Do you want to sell them?'

'I want to know what they are before I burn them.'

El Zurdo lit a cigarette, stood and pushed two tables together. He undid the roll of canvasses and leafed through all five dismissively.

'They're all mine,' he said. 'They're copies I did for your father, but they're not his work. He asked me to do him a favour and make copies of these paintings for a Swiss painter who'd just sold them at Salgado's gallery and wanted to avoid paying tax. Of course, the Swiss guy should have taken the copies with him to show Customs that they hadn't been sold. So I don't know what they're still doing in your father's studio.'

'Did my father give you the canvasses?'

'Yes. They were all old and there was something already on them which he'd painted a wash over.'

'Something he'd done?'

'I didn't ask.'

El Zurdo smoked some more. Falcón ate his food.

'Do you want to know what's under there?' asked El Zurdo.

'I think so.'

'You don't sound so sure.'

'You think you want to know until you find out what it is.'

They caught a cab, which took them through to Calle Laraña and the Bellas Artes Institute. They went across the internal patio and up to the first floor. For 15,000 pesetas a friend of El Zurdo's put the canvasses through an imaging machine and gave them five print-outs of the original work underneath. What came out looked like nothing: a mass of cross-hatching, swathes of black on white with the occasional discernible detail such as an eye, a leg, a hoof, an animal's tail.

El Zurdo could make nothing of them. They parted at the building's steps. El Zurdo told him if he needed to talk again he was always in La Cubista for lunch. Javier walked home. He dumped the canvasses and print-outs, called Alicia and arranged to see her that evening.

'I've been relieved of my command,' he said, as Alicia took hold of his wrist. 'I go back in ten days' time for psychological assessment.'

'That doesn't surprise me,' she said. 'Your behaviour was probably becoming quite strange.'

'That business with Inés and the Juez de Instrucción decided it. She thought I was stalking her, but I was only coming across her in the street as I would in my own mind.'

'You've told me all this before.'

'Have I?' he said. 'Yes, to a madman a few days becomes eons. I keep reliving my life until I hit a memory blank, which I hammer at until I'm weak and then I go back and relive the same stretch again, until I hit the same closed door. It's exhausting, and it makes the time between the real experiences of everyday life seem like ancient history. Did I tell you that I went to Tangier?'

'Not yet,' she said. 'Why did you decide to go there?'

'I was given compassionate leave.'

He told her about the death of Pepe Leal.

'What did you hope to find in Tangier . . . forty years later?'

'Answers. Life doesn't move at the same pace in the Third World. I thought I'd be able to find people who could remember things I'd forgotten and that would jog my memory.'

'But why Tangier? You lost your job because of Inés. Why not resolve that? What was the impetus?'

'I was drawn there. I made no conscious decisions. I went where fate led me. I put myself in others' hands . . . and I ended up in front of my old house in the Medina.'

'No conscious decisions?'

'None.'

'Remind me how this madness of yours manifested itself in the first place?'

'I felt the change when I saw the first victim's face.'

'And what was the first thing that happened, outside of your investigation, that made you think that the change was not, for instance, shock at a gruesome sight?'

A long silence.

'I went into the centre to pick up the victim's address book and I got caught up in a Semana Santa procession. For some reason, seeing the Virgin . . . I nearly fainted. It was a very affecting experience.'

'Are you religious?'

'Not at all.'

'And after that?'

'I saw the shot of my father in one of the victim's photographs and I learned he was having an affair before my mother died.'

'But in *your* life?'

'Finding the journals with his letter . . . that started up something. I mean, it stirred up . . . some sort of darkness. I behaved very strangely that night. I thought there might be something evil in me. I'd never seen that side of my nature. I've always been relentlessly good. Determined to be good.'

'Because you're afraid?'

'Yes.'

'Of what?'

'There was something else that night,' said Falcón. 'I was trying to find the prostitute who'd been with the victim on the night he died. She'd gone missing. The killer made contact with me for the first time. He asked me: "Are we close?" and then he said: "Closer than you think," as if he knew something about me, which I now know he does.'

'What did you think he knew about you?'

'I thought he meant that he was physically close to me, that he was following me. But later I thought that perhaps he meant that we weren't dissimilar people,' said Falcón, stumbling over the words. 'And I knew he'd killed the girl and I felt guilty about that.'

'Guilty?'

'We suspected a link between the killer and the girl and we didn't follow it up. We should have tried harder. We failed . . .'

'You didn't *fail*,' said Alicia. 'She wouldn't tell you. She was protecting him for her own reasons.'

'I still felt guilty.'

'But guilty about what?'

Long silence.

'I ran into another procession that night. One of the silent orders. One of the accusatory orders. And you know . . . she was so beautiful . . . the Virgin. Ridiculous that a mannequin in robes could be so . . . moving,' he said. 'I couldn't bear it. I couldn't bear everything she stood for and I had to get past her. I had to get away from her.'

'And this was bound up with your sense of guilt about the girl?'

'Yes. My failure.'

'You know who the Virgin is?'

'Yes.'

'You know what she stands for?'

He nodded.

'Say it,' said Alicia.

'She is the ultimate mother.'

'The Ultimate Mother,' she repeated it for him. 'Tell me why you went to Tangier.'

'I wanted to know how . . . I wanted to know what happened when she died.'

'Did you find out?'

'It was inconclusive. I found out what had happened in the street, which was a memory that had bothered me. But it was just my mother's Riffian maid going through some histrionics. It's not uncommon in Arab women. You've probably –'

'You don't believe what you're saying, do you, Javier? You've attached some importance to this.'

'I don't think so,' he said.

Alicia breathed out slowly. The brick wall hit again.

'What else did you find out in Tangier?'

'Some nonsense gossip about how my second mother had died.'

'Your second mother?'

'I'm not going to give it the credibility of repetition.'

'What else?' asked Alicia, snapping at his resistance to talk.

'I have an inexplicable fear of milk,' he said, and told her about the incident in the Tetuán Medina and the dream that followed it.

'What does milk mean to you?'

'Nothing.'

'And that was what you dreamt about?'

'I meant that it has no meaning other than that I have always hated dairy products . . . just as my father did.'

'And what do mothers produce to feed their babies?'

'I have to be going,' he said abruptly. 'The hour is up. You should have been stricter with me.'

They walked to the door. He stepped into the stairwell without looking at her. He didn't turn on the light. He pattered down the stairs.

'You will come back to me, won't you, Javier?' she called out after him.

He did not reply.

At home he sat in the study, leafing over the black-and-white print-outs from the imaging machine while guilt and failure tumbled in his mind. He stuck the print-outs up on the wall and stood back from them. They were meaningless. He switched them around, thinking that it might have something to do with the order, but soon realized there were thousands of permutations.

The wind buffeted around the patio, rattling the door. He went out and sat on the lip of the fountain and tapped his feet on the worn marble flagstones whose rectangular shapes reminded him of the diagram that had fallen out of the roll of canvasses.

He tore the print-outs off the wall and sprinted up to the studio. He found the diagram on the floor of the storeroom amongst all the boxes. Five interlocking rectangles, each one numbered. He ran back down the stairs, possessed by the idea that this would be the key that would unlock the whole mystery. But of what? He slowed to a stop on the patio.

The certainties, the idea of their collapse, came to him in a series of Biblical film clips, statues keeled over, keystones plummeted, arches folded in on themselves, columns toppled into colossal fluted fragments. His view of his father had already changed – the violent legionnaire, the shell-shocked veteran of Leningrad, the murderous smuggler and finally the tortured artist. And yet somehow this was all explicable. This wasn't nature, it was the nurture of history's most savage century. The brutal and bloody Civil War, the catastrophic Second World War, the left-over brutality that eventually slid into hedonism in post-war Tangier. He could always point to the outside influences that had worked to brutal effect on his father's fragile state. But perhaps this was different. It could be that this would reveal something deeply personal, some terrible weakness that would expose the hidden monster. Did he want that?

What had Consuelo called him and Inés at their first meeting? A union of truth hunters. The whole reason he'd started this terrible journey was because of the irresistible urge to discover. Was he going to shy away from that now, and end up at the only end of *Calle Negación*? Then what? He would live his life as if none of this had happened, and Javier Falcón would sink without trace.

He took the rolls of canvas up to the studio and matched each one to the relevant print-out, but could find no numbering system. There was nothing written on the backs of the canvas except the letters 'I' and 'D', and he suddenly felt tired and desperate for bed. Then he saw, at the edge of the print-outs, some ink marks. He realized his father had numbered the canvasses on their fronts, beyond where the canvas would stretch over the frame. He worked out the numbers and got the order right through a process of elimination. Then he understood that the 'I' and 'D' were *izquierda* and *derecha*. He marked off the print-outs accordingly and then trimmed the A3 sheets down to the edges. He turned them over and stuck them together as shown in the diagram. He took the finished piece up to his father's work wall and stuck it there with tape. He walked away from it. He reached the bookshelves on the far wall and was about to turn when he felt the sweat break – the familiar trickle down his cheek.

It was his last chance to walk away.

He turned with his eyes tight shut.

He opened them and saw what his father had done.

31

Sunday, 29th April 2001, El Zurdo's workshop, Calle Parras, Seville

Falcón pinned the print-outs up on the wall while El Zurdo busied himself rolling and lighting a joint. Javier tapped him on the shoulder just as he took the first toke. El Zurdo turned.

'*Joder!*' he said. 'Who is that?'

'That?' said Falcón, spitting it out. 'She. *She* is my mother.'

'*Joder,*' said El Zurdo, moving closer, fascinated. 'This is quite a piece of work.'

'It's not a piece of work,' said Falcón. 'It's a piece of shit.'

'Hey, I'm not involved in the same way you are,' said El Zurdo. 'I'm just looking at this . . .'

'As art?' said Javier, incredulous.

'Technically. I mean, it's extraordinary to create five interlocking pieces which are meaningless and apparently disconnected . . . I didn't even see the joins in the jigsaw and yet when they're put together . . .'

'They become the most vile expression of a man's hatred for his wife and the mother of his children, that only the mind of a monster could possibly produce,' said Javier.

The two men stood in silence with the horror work filling the room. The picture had revealed a woman entwined and under the ministrations of two ravening satyrs, one thrusting from behind while the other graphically filled her mouth. But it was not a rape. There was compliance in the single visible eye of the woman. It was nauseating. Javier strode past El Zurdo, tore the piece off the wall, screwed it up and hurled it into an empty corner of the workshop.

'What could possibly have made him want to produce . . . ?'

'Take a toke of this,' said El Zurdo.

'I don't want a toke of that.'

'It'll calm you down.'

'I don't want to be calm.'

'Look . . . maybe he found out she was having an affair.'

'Oh,' said Javier, 'while he was a total innocent? While he wasn't off sodomizing young men at every opportunity . . .'

'It was different for women in those days,' said El Zurdo.

'While he didn't go sodomizing on his *wedding* night. While he didn't start having an affair with a mistress, who was to become his second wife, before his first wife had died.'

'He hated women,' said El Zurdo, matter-of-fact.

'What did you say?' said Javier. 'I didn't hear that . . . what . . . ?'

'I said that he hated women.'

'What are you talking about, El Zurdo?'

'Just what I said . . . and I'm not talking about the completely normal level of misogyny that existed in those days. It was beyond that . . . well beyond.'

'He was married twice, he's painted the four most sublime nudes of women the world has ever seen and *you* think he *hated* women?' said Javier.

'I don't *think* anything,' said El Zurdo. 'That was what he told me.'

'*He* told you that? Since when were you so intimate with my father that he would reveal something like that to you?'

'Since we were lovers.'

A long silence developed in which Javier slumped into a battered armchair. All his strength sapped out of him. He was conscious of himself gaping, his face flabby with shock, his arms weak.

'When?' he asked, quietly.

'From about 1972 for eleven or twelve years, until he got scared by *SIDA*.'

'So . . . that time I came here with him . . . ?'

El Zurdo nodded. More painful time eased past.

'And you don't think that this is the bitterest irony of all time?' asked Javier.

'That he should have painted those nudes?' said El Zurdo. 'That was just his work . . . it didn't have to be his life as well.'

'Where did it come from . . . the hate?' asked Javier. 'I don't understand where that could come from.'

'From his mother.'

Javier's brain ticked like a metronome counting out the seconds before insanity struck.

'In his journals he refers to "the incident",' said Falcón. 'Something that happened when he was a boy, which made him leave home and join the Legion. I think he might have told people about it, my mother being one of them, but he never wrote it down. Did he tell you?'

'He told me,' said El Zurdo. 'I'll tell you if you want. I mean . . . these things, the further they slip into history, the less important they seem to be. They just happen to decide the direction of a life at the time.'

'Tell me.'

'What do you know about his parents?'

'Next to nothing.'

'Well, they ran a hotel business in Tetuán in the twenties and thirties. They were very conservative. His mother was a devout Catholic and his father was a drunk. He was a nasty drunk, who took out his weaknesses on his children and his employees. That's all you need to know to understand what happened.

'One morning his father caught Francisco in bed with one of the houseboys and he went completely berserk. While Francisco cowered on the bed in the corner of the room, his father bludgeoned the houseboy to death in front of him. Only when he came out of his terrible rage did the father realize what he'd done. The two of them disposed of the body somehow and Francisco was kept in his bloodstained room until he'd cleaned every drop of blood and whitewashed the walls.'

El Zurdo sat back with his hands open.

'How did his mother come into it?' asked Falcón. 'You said . . .'

'She never spoke another word to him. She withdrew all maternal affection and acted as if he didn't exist. She didn't even have a place laid for him at the dinner table. As far as she was concerned, in her small Catholic mind, he'd transgressed beyond any possible forgiveness.'

'When did he tell you that?'

'A long time ago. More than twenty years.'

'When you were lovers?'

'Yes. It took a while for him to come back to men after something like that. It wasn't until Tangier after the Second World War that he . . . although he did have a passion for another legionnaire who was killed in Russia – Pablito . . . But nothing ever came of it and, of course, Pablito was betrayed by a woman . . .'

'He talks about him in the journals. My father was on the firing squad that shot the woman,' said Falcón. 'He purposely aimed for her mouth.'

'Do you know how he and I stayed lovers for so long?' said El Zurdo. 'Because I never made any attempt to understand him. I never probed. Some people don't like intimacy and your father was one of them. Women do like it. They want to know their man. And when they find out who you are and they don't like it, they do one of two things: they set about changing you or they abandon you. These are your father's words, not mine. I've never been with women. My tastes are more singular.'

They went down to La Cubista for lunch. Javier ordered the tuna, El Zurdo the pork. He drank wine through Javier's tormented silence and encouraged him to do the same. The food arrived.

'You know the other reason your father liked me?' said El Zurdo. 'This is strange. He liked me because I was a copyist. Odd, no? He admired it. He liked the fact that I painted upside down. He interpreted it as a lack of respect for the original, even though I told him that I only did it because I didn't want to be distracted by the structure and wholeness of the piece when all I was doing was trying to copy it precisely. You know, sometimes he thought my copies were actually better than his originals. So there are two American collectors with my copies signed by him on their walls. That, he said to me, is art. Nothing is original.'

Falcón sipped his wine, picked up his knife and fork and started eating.

'When did you last see him?' asked Falcón.

'About five years ago. We had lunch here. He was happy. He'd solved his problem of loneliness.'

'He was lonely?'

'All day, every day. The famous man in his big dark house.'

'He had friends, didn't he?'

'He told me he didn't. The only friend he had he lost back in 1975.'

'Who was that?'

'Raúl Jiménez . . . I heard he was murdered recently,' said El Zurdo. 'Your father wouldn't have been sad about that.'

'So why did they stop being friends?'

'That's interesting. I didn't understand why it incensed him so much. He told me that he bumped into Raúl in the street one day in Seville. They'd both been living in the city, on either side of the river, apparently without knowing it. They went for lunch. Your father asked after Raúl's family and he said they were all fine. They talked about your father's fame and Raúl's business success – all the shit you'd expect two old friends to talk about – except your father didn't ask him why he hadn't been in touch with him. I mean, given your father's fame, Raúl must have known he'd been living in Seville for ten years or more. But this is explained by what happened. At the end of lunch Raúl told him something out of the blue . . . nothing to do with what they'd been talking about. You may have read in the journals that your father left the Legion and came here to paint. He had money saved up from the army. Combat pay from Russia.'

'And someone stole the money,' said Falcón, 'which was why my father ended up in Tangier.'

'Right,' said El Zurdo. 'And that's what Raúl told him at the end of the lunch, that *he* had stolen the money. And they never spoke to each other again.'

'Why?'

'Your father didn't think that Raúl Jiménez had the right to alter the course of another man's life. I said, if it was for the better, so what? He'd made his fortune out there, he'd become famous . . . But he wouldn't listen. He stormed around the house shouting: "He ruined me, that *cabrón* ruined me." And for the life of me, Javier, I couldn't see the ruination in all he'd achieved.

'He was also maddened just by the fact that Raúl Jiménez had *told* him what he'd done. He couldn't understand it, until he found out what had really happened to the man's family. The wife had committed suicide. The little boy died. The daughter was in a mental institution and the son didn't speak to him any more. It was a disaster and that's when he realized that the last thing Raúl Jiménez wanted at this stage of his life was an intimate friend. What he wanted was a new life . . . one without Francisco Falcón.'

'You said earlier that my father had solved his loneliness problem.'

'He told me he didn't want any friends, that what he really wanted was companionship.'

'What about Manuela?' asked Javier. 'Didn't Manuela ever go and see him?'

'She did, but he never liked Manuela. She came for a few hours a week, but that wasn't what he was looking for. He just wanted somebody to fill the empty spaces in the house. He liked the idea of young people, uncomplicated and forward-looking people, who would be relentlessly cheerful. And he came to an agreement with the university here and in Madrid that they could send him the occasional student for a month at a time. It worked for him. I'd have hated it.'

'He didn't tell me about that.'

'Maybe he didn't want to admit that to you,' said El Zurdo. 'Maybe he didn't want to alter the course of *your* life.'

It was nearly dark by the time Javier had taken a long circuitous route home. As he entered the house he kicked two packages across the floor. Both had been pushed through the letter box and neither was addressed. Only the numbers 1 and 2 were written on the outside.

He took them to his study, where he had a pair of latex gloves. He opened the first package and took out an envelope that had Sight Lesson No.4 written on it. Inside, the card read: *La muerte trágica del genio*. The tragic death of true genius.

There was something else in the package with more weight to it. He laid paper on the desk and emptied out what he thought was a piece of glass, until he saw that it was the back of a shard of mirror. He turned it over with the nib of a biro. The initials P.L. were written in what looked like dried blood.

Falcón sat back in his chair. He knew what Sergio was doing. He was hijacking the media's myth by telling him that he'd used the shard of mirror to distract Pepe Leal when he went in for the kill. Javier didn't believe it. It just wasn't possible. But it interested him because he realized that he'd finally forced Sergio's hand. There was some desperation in this arrogant and unsubtle ploy.

He tapped the card with the sight lesson written on it. The same words his mother had used when telling Manuela about the contents of the clay urn. Hints pressed against the membrane of his consciousness, but nothing came through. He flipped the card across the desk. He opened the second package, which contained a set of photocopies. He could tell from the handwriting that these were his father's journals.

7th July 1962, Tangier

*I have quite lost track of Salgado since our return from NY when, just
as that thought had drifted across the flat calm of my horizon, a boy
arrives with a note from him written on Hotel Rembrandt notepaper
and telling me to come immediately to room 321 alone. I'm not so
surprised by the note. There is no phone here. It's only as I make my
way to the Boulevard Pasteur that I become unnerved. What could have
happened that he should think to interrupt me in my work time? I am
intrigued and disturbed. The lift in the Hotel Rembrandt, which is only
a few years old, is one of those halting affairs that make me feel as if the
cable is about to snap at any moment. I arrive at the door to 321 in a
state of impending doom. There's a short corridor between the main door
and the door to the room, one of those perplexing design features that
seem to be made for just this kind of occasion. It means that Salgado can
pull me inside and explain the direness of his circumstances without the
full horror of the incident overwhelming us.*

The short version – there's a dead boy in the room.

Salgado tells me he's accidentally been killed.

'Accidentally?' I ask.

*'He fell over and hit his head,' he says. 'He must have hit himself in
the wrong place, but he's definitely dead.'*

'How did he fall over?'

*'Tripped on his way to the bathroom . . . but I've put him back on the
bed.'*

'Then why don't we call the police and explain the incident like that?'

Silence from Salgado.

*'Shall I just take a look at him?' I ask, and don't wait for an answer
but push into the room and find the naked boy growing out of a twist of
sheet. An arm is flung out. His tongue protrudes from his mouth and his
eyes are bulging. There are bruise marks round his windpipe.*

'I don't think he knocked his head, did he, Ramón?'

'It was an accident.'

'I don't know how you accidentally strangle someone, Ramón.'

'I was trying to make it better.'

*We blink at each other and Ramón suddenly turns to the wall and
starts hitting his head against it and intoning something which sounds
like Basque. I sit him in a chair and ask him what happened. He presses
his fists into his head and repeats over and over that it was an accident.
I tell him I'll call the Chief of Police and he can tell him just that, with
the boy lying on the bed sodomized and strangled. He gets up and starts*

striding about the room, throwing his hands about and making great declamations in the same strange tongue. I slap his face. He turns into a pathetic creature and sinks to the floor. He cries and his bird-like shoulders convulse. I slap him again, which turns him to me.

'Tell me what happened,' I say. 'I am not your judge.'

'I murdered him,' he says.

'Were you in love with him?'

'No, no, no que no!' he says emphatically. Too emphatically.

I stare into him and see his corruption, so terrible that he cannot admit it to himself. I know Ramón Salgado has killed this boy for no other reason than for what he was making him into. Salgado is vain. He is a great flatterer of women. M. and he adore each other. He has affairs which never last. He is now wealthy, famous in his small world and reputable, but . . . he likes to sodomize boys and that interferes with his gilded self-image. That's my reading of it, anyway. He's killed the boy because he was forcing him to see what he hates.

He says the fateful words:

'I couldn't face a scandal.'

I don't despise him, even for that. Who am I to despise anyone? I sit at the boy's feet. I light a cigarette for him.

'Will you help me?' he asks.

I tell him a story, which I first heard from a friend of B.H. back in the forties, about a wealthy homosexual who'd picked up a bunch of servicemen from a well-known bar for queers in Manhattan and taken them back to a party at his mother's apartment on 5th Avenue. They were all drunk and one of the soldiers passed out. They removed his pants and for a joke started to shave off his pubic hair. And, accidentally – I emphasize that – they chopped off his prick. So what did they do? Salgado looks at me like Javier does when I'm telling him a bedtime story, all hunched and wide-eyed. They wrapped him in a blanket and dumped him on a bridge somewhere. He was lucky, because a policeman found him and got him to a hospital before he bled to death.

'What do you make of that, Ramón?' I ask.

He blinks, desperate not to say the wrong thing and be sent out of class.

'If you help me, Francisco,' he says. 'I will never do anything like this again.'

'What? Kill somebody?'

'No, no, I mean . . . I will never go with boys again. I will lead an exemplary life.'

'I will help you,' I say, 'but I want to know what you think of my story.'

More silence. He's too panicked to think.

'They paid the soldier off,' I add. 'So that he wouldn't press charges. How much do you think?'

He shook his head.

'Two hundred thousand dollars, and that was in 1946,' I say. 'You made a lot more money from losing your prick in those days than you did from painting pictures.'

Salgado rushes past me and vomits in the toilet. He comes back wiping his mouth.

'I don't know how you can be so cool about this, Francisco.'

'I've killed thousands of people. All of them as guilty or as innocent as you and I.'

'That was war,' he says.

'I'm just pointing out that once you've seen slaughter on the scale I have, a dead boy in a hotel room is not so terrible. Now, give me your comment on my story.'

'It was a terrible thing to have done,' he says, drawing on his cigarette.

'Worse than murdering a boy?'

'He could have died for all they cared.'

'Right. And what does that reveal about the people you're so desperate to impress?' I ask. 'The perpetrator is still free, by the way, and he's still a friend of Barbara Hutton.'

Ramón is too muddled to work it out for himself.

'We are their lapdogs,' I say. 'We are their little marvels – yes, even me, Ramón. They stroke us, feed us morsels, tease us and then grow tired of us and throw us out. We are nothing to the very rich. Absolutely nothing. Less than toys. So remember, when you sip their champagne, that it is for these worthless people's high opinion of you that you have murdered this boy.'

The words shunted into his chest like high-calibre bullets. He thumped back into his chair.

'For them?' he said, puzzled.

'You killed the boy because you did not like the idea of those people knowing this about you. You killed him because it is the one thing you find hateful in yourself, and you think others will, too. And you have been very wrong.'

He sobs. I pat him on the back.

'Francisco,' he says, 'where would I be without you?'
'In a far happier place,' I reply.
It wasn't so difficult to dispose of the body. We took it out into the garden of the hotel at three in the morning and heaved it over the wall. We put it in the car, we took it to the cliffs out of town and threw it into the sea. On the way back to town Ramón stared into the window utterly wordless, a man coming to terms with a changed world, in which, because of a moment of blindness, nothing will ever be the same. If you have to kill. If there's nothing to be done. Then always kill with your eyes wide open.

Falcón let the photocopied sheets fall from his lap. They scattered on the floor. He was mesmerized by his thoughts, the confirmation that the killer had access to his father's diaries and now, with the additional information from El Zurdo, he realized that it must have been one of the art students his father had taken on to relieve his loneliness.

The Bellas Artes would be closed. El Zurdo was uncontactable. He went through his father's address book and found the name of somebody at the university with a home telephone number. He called but there was no answer.

His thoughts turned to Raúl Jiménez and the revelation that had broken his friendship with his father. He thought it unlikely that his father would let that pass without comment in the journals, but it had taken place on a date after the final entry in which his father had announced his total ennui.

Javier shunted back his chair, ran up the stairs. He slowed to a walk around the gallery and stopped outside the studio. He stared into the black pupil of the fountain on the patio. An apparently disparate thought had come to him. One of the insoluble elements of the case was what Sergio had shown Raúl Jiménez. Where had he got his images? Salgado's horrors had been easy enough to solve. They'd found the trunk in the attic and the necessary images and soundtrack, but with Raúl Jiménez they'd never succeeded. Despite endless inquiries at Mudanzas Triana there'd been no evidence that any of Jiménez's long-term storage had been touched.

He pushed himself away from the wall of the gallery and went into his father's studio. He found the last journal in the storeroom. And there it was, some ten pages after what he'd thought was the final entry.

13th May 1975, Seville
I am in such a rage that I have had to return to the confessional in the
hope that it will calm me.

The entry told the story he'd heard from El Zurdo and finished with
the line:

I cannot think what possessed him to tell me this now, and I roar that at
him as I storm out of the restaurant into the street. He says to my back:
'If it hadn't been for me, you'd be painting window frames in Triana by
now.' It was an enormous and calculated insult for which he will receive
appropriate punishment.

17th May 1975, Seville
A postscript to my last vent of outrage. I have discovered that
punishment has already been served on my old friend R. It seems that his
youngest son died in Almería, his wife committed suicide by throwing
herself into the Guadalquivir here in Seville, his daughter, Marta, has
ended up in a mental institution in Ciempozuelos and his eldest son lives
in Madrid and no longer speaks to him. Whatever I had in mind seems
like fly-swatting after this series of calamities. I think now that he only
told me what he'd done to get rid of me. I was just another relic from
that troubled era.

Falcón leafed through the empty pages to the end. He went back
to the last entry and read it again. Ciempozuelos stuck in his mind.
Sergio would have known everything from this entry – the whole
family tragedy – and there was an opening for him: Marta in Ciempozuelos. But Marta could barely speak. Falcón replayed his last visit
there. Marta's wound being tended to by a doctor. Ahmed taking
her back to the ward. She vomiting after the shock of her fall. Ahmed
going off to get the cleaning equipment. And that's when he saw it
again, as clear as a creative idea: the trunk underneath Marta's bed.

32

Sunday, 29th April 2001, Falcón's house, Calle Bailén, Seville

Ahmed had never told him what was in the trunk. Falcón checked his watch, it was ten o'clock at night. He went down to his study, found his notebook, tore through the pages to Marta's doctor's name – Dra Azucena Cuevas. He called the hospital in Ciempozuelos. Dra Cuevas was now back from her holiday and would be on duty in the morning. Falcón spoke to the night nurse on Marta's ward, explained his problem and what he wanted to see. The nurse said that the only time Marta allowed the chain to be removed from her neck was for her daily shower and she would talk to Dra Cuevas about his request in the morning.

Falcón had taken one sleeping pill too many and overslept. He just managed to board the midday AVE to Madrid, which, on a Monday, was full. He was back in his suit, carrying his mac and wearing his fully loaded revolver. He called Dra Cuevas from the train. She agreed to delay Marta's daily shower until the afternoon.

From the Estación de Atocha he took a taxi straight out to Ciempozuelos and by 3.30 p.m. he was sitting in Dra Cuevas's office waiting for the cleaning lady to bring up Marta's trunk.

'What do you know about her nurse – Ahmed?' asked Falcón.

'Nothing about his private life. As far as his work is concerned he is excellent, a man of infinite patience. He never even raises his voice to these unfortunate people.'

The trunk arrived and some minutes later a female nurse brought the key and locket on Marta's chain. They opened the trunk. Inside it was a small shrine to Arturo. The lid was stuck with salvaged photos. There was a handmade birthday card with a stick woman with her eyes off her head, stiff hair and 'Marta' scrawled out underneath. In the body of the trunk were small metal cars, a grey child's sock, an old school exercise book, crayons with teethmarks chewed into the ends. At the bottom were two rolls of 8mm film, just like the stock they'd found in the Mudanzas Triana warehouse. He held one up to the light. There was Arturo in the arms of his sister. He put it all away, closed the trunk and re-locked it. He flipped open the locket. It contained a single curl of brown hair. He handed the chain back to the nurse. The cleaning lady took the trunk back to the ward.

'Where's Ahmed now?'

'He's walking two of the patients in the gardens.'

'I don't want him to know anything about my visit.'

'That might be difficult,' said Dra Cuevas. 'People talk. There's nothing else to do here.'

'Has there ever been an art student who's worked on Marta's ward?'

'Some time ago we did a three-month experiment with some art therapy,' said Dra Cuevas.

'How did that work?' asked Falcón. 'Who were the art therapists?'

'It was something we did on the weekends. The work was unpaid. It was just to see if the patients responded to a creative activity that might remind them of childhood.'

'Where did the artists come from?'

'One of the board members of the hospital is a film director. He recruited people from his company with an artistic background. They were all young.'

'Is there a record of who they were?'

'Of course, there had to be. We paid their travel expenses.'

'How were they paid?'

'Once a month by cheque, as far as I know,' she said. 'You'd have to go to the accounts department for details on that.'

'Do you remember any of the names of the males who helped with the course?'

'Only their first names – Pedro, António and Julio.'

'Was there a Sergio?'

'No.'

'I'll go and see the people in the accounts department.'

Dra Cuevas was right. There'd been a Pedro and an António, all of whose names were completely Spanish. It was the third name that the secretary in the accounts department gave her that attracted Falcón's interest, because in full it was Julio Menéndez Chefchaouni.

It was 9 p.m. by the time he got back to Calle Bailén and as he opened the door he kicked another package across the floor. No address again. The number 3 written on the front.

He was exhausted. He put the package in his study. The answering machine was blinking. There was one message from Comisario Lobo, giving a home telephone number. He didn't have the strength for it and took a shower instead.

The kitchen supplied him with bread and chorizo, which he washed down with red wine. He took some ice with him to his study and found a bottle of whisky in the drinks cabinet. He poured a couple of fingers over the ice. He stretched before he sat down and thought that for the first time he'd managed to get a move ahead of Sergio. He wasn't chasing any more, but circling. He opened the package. There were more photocopied sheets of his father's journals.

1st July 1959, Tangier
I have a new toy, which is a pair of binoculars. I sit on the verandah and look at people on the beach and sketch their bodies, the unaware still lives. Rather than the lithe bodies of the young, I find I am more drawn to the collapsing geography of the old and out of condition. I draw them as landscape – escarpments, interlocking spurs, ridges, plains, and the inevitable mud slide. As I train my new far-seeing eyes across the beach I come across P. and the children. My family at play. Paco and Manuela are constructing some Gaudiesque castle, while Javier annoys P., who takes him down to the water. P. walks while Javier high-steps through the shallows, holding his mother's hand. I am entranced by this everyday sight, which seems more wonderful for their being unconscious, until P. stops and Javier sets off at a sprint and is caught up in the arms of a stranger, who hurls him up in the air and puts him down again. Javier stamps his feet in demand and the stranger complies and throws him up again. He is a Moroccan in his mid thirties. P. approaches and I see that she knows this man. They talk for some minutes while Javier forms mounds of sand over the stranger's feet and then P. walks off, towing

*Javier, who is turning and waving at the man. I refocus on the
Moroccan, who is still standing with his head held high to the sun. He
looks at P. and the boy for as long as it takes them to merge with the
crowds on the beach. I see admiration in his face.*

1st November 1959, Tangier
*The first rains and there is nobody on the beaches. There are few people
in town. The port is empty. Last month Mohammed V's decree, giving
Tangier special status, was abrogated. The Café de Paris is empty apart
from the grumbling few, who blame the recent move on Casablanca's
business community, who have always been envious of Tangier's
competitive advantage. I go to the Medina and sit under the dripping
balconies of the Café Central where they now only serve poor coffee or
mint tea. I am aware of being watched, which is unusual as I am
normally the watcher. My eyes move over the turbanned heads, the
burnouses done up to the chin, the babouches clapping against hardened
heels until I come across the face of the man on the beach who was
talking to P. He has a pencil in his hand. Our eyes meet and I see that
he knows who I am. He leaves soon after. I ask the waiter if he knows
him, but he's never been seen here before.*

*R. tells me he is moving again. Abdullah Diouri's letter has got under
his skin.*

3rd December 1959, Tangier
*M. writes, v. depressed. M.G.'s stomach pains have been diagnosed as
liver cancer and no surgeon is prepared to operate. It seems he will die in
months, if not weeks. She has fallen hard for M.G. and I know this
news will be a savage blow. She asks after Javier, another male who has
dived into her heart. Her letter makes me nostalgic for how P. and I
used to be. This thought jolts me out of my seat and I pace the room.
There is an intruder in my head. I root around for the lie and find the
face of the man on the beach. I know I will not find peace of mind until
I know who he is.*

7th April 1960, Tangier
*I do not work any more. I cannot. My mind has no sticking point. I
cannot bear to be in the studio. I wander the town and Medina looking
at faces, watching and waiting to find the stranger. He is my new
obsession. I am living in my head, which has the bizarre logic of the
Medina, but all I come up against is dead ends.*

402

10th May 1960, Tangier
I had almost given up hope when, walking down the Boulevard Pasteur,
I am oddly drawn to a piece in the window of one of the tourist shops,
which is of carved bone. As I lift my eyes from the sculpture I see the
stranger from the beach serving in the shop. At first I think it is his shop
until I see an old man running the money. I go in and, ignoring the
stranger, who is serving some tourists, I ask the old man about the piece
in the window. He tells me it is made by his son. I am impressed and
ask for his name, which he tells me is Tariq Chefchaouni. The old man
says his son has a workshop on the outskirts of town, on the road to
Asilah. As we talk I see next to his cash box a small basket of cheap
rings. Four of them are agate cubes mounted on simple silver bands.
Now I understand P.'s puzzlement, or was it fear?

When he'd read that name for the first time Falcón got to his feet
and did a tour of his study with a clenched fist. By tomorrow morning
he'd have the killer's ID number and an address. He drank more
whisky, poured himself another glass.

2nd June 1960, Tangier
A letter from M. telling me that M.G. IV has died, having survived
two months longer than expected. She is desolate. I write her a letter of
commiseration telling her to come to Morocco, leave the city, leave the
scene of her grief. This is selfish. I am in need of a companion. P. and I
move around each other like strangers, or rather, with a stranger in our
midst. I should ask her about Tariq Chefchaouni. I should, as her
husband, demand to know who she was consorting with on the beach. But
I don't. Why not? I rummage through my mind, looking for reasons and
find none, other than that I seem to be frightened at the prospect. Does
this seem possible of me, the veteran of Krasni Bor? But this is not
physical fear. I am scared to reveal my vulnerability. I am stunned to
discover that this all started last summer and I have been tormented for
a full year.

3rd June 1960, Tangier
I go back to the Boulevard Pasteur and stand outside the shop, waiting
for the younger man to leave. I go in and ask his father how much he
wants for the bone sculpture in the window. He says it is not for sale (a
technique I recognize) and we haggle. I play the game badly because I'm
too concerned about T.C. returning. I pay $30, which seems like a

fantastic sum, until I get the sculpture back to my studio and see that it is indeed quite a piece. There is a stunning beauty to the lines and shapes, which is offset by the macabre quality of the material used. It says something ambiguous about the quality of being human. I begin to think that the old man, rather than being crafty, has in fact done something unforgivable.

18th June 1960, Tangier
This is how I am. It is P.'s birthday. Rather than give her the usual piece of jewellery I wrap the bone sculpture. I ask her to the studio in the early evening and serve champagne on the verandah. It is still light and very warm with a gentle breeze blowing off the sea. We are hovering around a perfect moment when I give her the present. She is animated, because I normally give her a small box, rather than something which stands 40 cm high. She tears the paper off like a small girl. I watch like a wolf and see it the moment she has stripped it down to the bone. Her face, for a fraction of a second, breaks in two. Her eyes enlarge and stand off her face. She recovers. We go back to the champagne. The sky darkens. I am aware of her looking at me as if I am a strange beast that has assumed human form but been careless about leaving a hairy hoof showing. I have what I want. She has what she desires. The piece sits on her dressing table.

A letter from M. saying she has been delayed by a legal battle. It seems that the children from M.G.'s previous marriages don't think that she deserves half his fortune.

3rd August 1960, Tangier
I find T.C.'s workshop and am told he is never there in summer. The house, I'm sure, consists of no more than two rooms with a garden behind. It is unattached to any other building so is not part of the family home. I come back at night and wait and watch. It is silent. I return the next night and slip over the wall into the lush garden, which smells of damp earth. There is a large brick tank in the middle, brimful of water. The lock at the back is very loose after the summer and the door opens easily. Inside is a straw mattress on a wooden pallet and a calabash in the corner, nothing else. I hesitate as I reach the door to the next room, as if I have some premonition that my life will be changed by crossing the threshold. The room is his studio. It is full of the same paraphernalia as my own. My torch ripples over ironwork, stone sculpture, horn carving and jewellery until it catches the edge of a painting.

I fix my beam on it and am drawn to it as if falling on my own sword. At the end of the room are three abstract nudes. Looking at them down the mote-filled flute of light is not the best way to see such works, but even in that wretched dimness their quality stands out. Two nudes reclining and one standing. I know immediately, even though they are abstracts, that the subject is P. I am eviscerated by the sight of them. They are the perfect and beautiful developments of the charcoal drawings of P. that I'd accomplished fifteen years before. Hot tears roll down my face as the thought enters my head that this should have been the rightful end of my work.

On the table there's a sketch book which I cannot resist leafing through. The drawings are of the highest quality. They are figuratives of details. A hand, an ankle, a throat, large heavy breasts, buttocks, a waist and a belly. They are entrancing. Then I arrive at my own face, brilliantly dashed off. I see developments from that. Caricatures. Uglier and uglier until, in the bottom right-hand corner, I am a brute, a cartoon horror. My hand trembles with rage. His vision gives me righteousness. I am capable of anything now.

30th October 1960, Tangier
Summer is over. The tourists have abandoned us. I leave the house and wait for P. in the market. She goes through the Petit Soco to the taxi rank on the Grand Soco and gets into an old Peugeot. I follow in the next taxi, pressing more dirhams on the driver as I tell him which way to go. The Peugeot stops at T.C.'s workshop. She gets out and is welcomed in. I tell the taxi driver to wait for me. I climb over the garden wall. The bedroom door is open. I hear T.C.'s talk and P.'s laughter from the studio. The door is ajar. I see her naked as she steps out of her underwear and walks to a rumpled sheet spread out on the floor. She kneels with her back to T.C., whose robe is already showing the ludicrous signs of arousal. He works with pencil first. He has a way of putting his whole body into creating each line. The lines become balletic flourishes, as if he is dancing the work out of himself and on to the paper. He goes through three sheets and then asks P. to change her position. He moves behind her and gathers her hair up and pins it with a brush. He moves in front of her and pushes her shoulders back so that a ridge forms down her spine. P. sees his arousal and, with instinctive intimacy, pushes up his robe and strokes him until he is shuddering. She drops her head to him and he gasps. She brings up a hand to his buttocks and pulls him to her. She slowly bows her head as if in prayer. His

405

hands tremble on her shoulders and he lets out the cry of a child woken suddenly in the night. She drinks him in. I leave.

I go back to my studio in the taxi and take up my brush for the first time in months. There are five blank canvasses which I tack up on the wall. I prepare black paint. I take up a pencil. My mind is like steel. The thoughts rifle down the channels like bullets and within moments I have sketched out a drawing of utter obscenity, with P. amongst satyrs of appalling priapism. I paint with vigour and viciousness, but with clarity and precision so that when I take the paintings down they are nothing to the viewer but five black-and-white canvasses. My revenge only takes shape with a precise configuration.

3rd December 1960, Tangier
I am not working. I only watch. My eye rests solely on the entanglement of two people. I have cooled to ice. My mind works with the clarity of a shout across a still, snow-covered field. I have established T.C.'s winter routine. He wakes up late, always after midday. He walks to a small café and eats breakfast and drinks tea. He smokes three or four cigarettes. In the afternoon he rarely goes back to the workshop. Sometimes he goes to his family home. He has a wife and three children, two boys and a girl, aged between five and eight. Other days he goes to the beach. He likes the bad weather. I watch him from my studio, standing in the wind and rain with his arms spread out, as if he's welcoming the cleansing powers of the elements. At night he works. I have watched him. He is so absorbed he notices nothing. Sometimes he works naked, even in the freezing cold. Occasionally he drops, literally, to the studio floor, exhausted. He has completed a fourth nude. P. kneeling. It is phenomenal. A marvel of the mysterious simplicity of form, but with the same quality that distinguishes the previous three – the joys and dangers of the forbidden fruit.

28th December 1960, Tangier
It is a freezing night, perhaps the coldest night I've known in Tangier. The wind blows from the northwest bringing the chill of the Atlantic. I walk through the silent city. Not even the dogs are out. It is a long walk to T.C.'s studio and it takes me more than an hour. I do not think but climb over the wall in my usual place (I have found a spot where I land on a path rather than leave a print in the earth). I go into his bedroom and hear his feet moving over the floor and I know that he is working. I step into the light of his studio. It is warm from a wood-burning

salamander in the corner. He continues to work. I move towards his back. The muscles are tense beneath his robe. I stop very close to him and still he does not notice. He lays on paint as thick as flesh. I breathe on his neck and he sets solid as stone. He does not turn. He cannot bring himself to turn.

'It is me,' I say.

He turns. His eyes search mine for reason and, when that is fruitless, pity. I have no need of, or desire for verbal redress and so my hand flashes out and I chop him across the throat with such brutal force that his throat cracks loudly. The brush and palette fall from his hands. He drops to his knees. I hear him desperately trying to breathe over his shattered larynx. I step behind him and hold my hand over his mouth and grip his nose. All the strength has been taken out of him by the savagery of my first blow. Only as death crowds his mind does the survival reflex shoot strength into his arms, but it is far too late. I hold him tight and snuff out the last flickering flame. I lay him face down on the floor. I take the four nudes and remove them from their stretchers and roll them up. I put them by the door. I take a five-litre can of white spirit and pour it over the floor and T.C.'s inert body. There is turpentine and alcohol, too. I drop a lighted match and leave. I walk back to my studio. I hide the canvasses above my bed in the roof. I lie down. My work is done and sleep comes easily to me.

Javier drank the last of the whisky in his glass. As the enormity of what he was reading had burgeoned off the page to fill the whole room with its tumorous ghastliness, he had steadily filled and refilled his glass until he was drunk. His earlier sense of triumph had disappeared. His face felt like slapped rubber. His feet were covered in the photocopied pages that had fallen from his weakening grasp. His head nodded against his shoulder. His neck cracked back as his reflexes shunned sleep and what lay in wait for him there, but he lost all resistance; exhaustion won, his mind and body were completely played out.

His dream was of himself asleep, but not as an adult, as a child. His back was warm and he was safe under the mosquito net. He was in that half-sleep where he knew that the heat on his back was the sun and that through his half-closed eyes he could see the shallow crater he had picked from the whitewashed wall by his face. He felt the wriggling happiness of childhood come up from his stomach as he heard his mother calling his name:

'Javier! Javier! Despiértate ahora, Javier!'

He came awake instantly, because he knew she was going to be there in his room and he would be happy and loved.

But she wasn't. Whatever was there rolled in his vision for a moment until it snapped into focus. He was back in his study. He was in his chair, except that it wasn't his normal chair. It was one of the high-backed chairs from the dining room and he couldn't move forward out of it because something was cutting into his neck, his wrists and ankles. His feet were bare and cold on the tiled floor.

33

Monday, 30th April 2001, Falcón's house, Calle Bailén, Seville

There was nothing on the desk in front of him. The pictures had been removed from the wall.

'Are you awake, Javier?' said a voice from behind him.

'I'm awake.'

'If you try to shout I will have to gag you with your socks, so please be sensible.'

'I am beyond screaming now,' he said.

'Are you?' said the voice. 'I see you've been reading. Did you finish?'

'I finished.'

'And what do you think of the great Francisco Falcón and his dependable agent, Ramón Salgado?'

'What you'd expect me to think.'

'Tell me. I'd like to hear it.'

'I'd just begun to think that he was a monster . . . I'd found those five terrible paintings in his studio . . . and now . . . I know it. What I didn't know was that he was a fraud as well. That adds . . . or rather that takes away the final dimension. Now he's just monster. There's nothing else left.'

'People are very forgiving of genius,' said the voice. 'Your father knew that. These days you can rape and murder, but as long as you're a genius you will be tolerated. Why do you think we tolerate evil in someone with a God-given talent? Why will we put up with arrogance and boorishness in a footballer, just because he can score great goals? Why will we accept drunkenness and adultery in a writer, as long as he gives us the poems? Why will we rape, maim and murder for someone who is able to give us the illusion of belief in ourselves? Why do we let genius get away with it?'

'Because we are easily bored,' said Javier.

'Your father was right,' said the voice. 'You do see things differently.'

'When did he tell you that?'

'It's in those diaries somewhere.'

'He always told me I was blessed with normality.'

'That was because he suspected something.'

'Like what?'

'This is not the order of things,' said Sergio.

'Then tell me the order.'

'How terrible a monster do you think your father was?' asked the voice. 'So far we know he was a murderer, a pirate, a depraved hedonist, a fraud and a thief. The world is full of those sorts of people. They are quite ordinary monsters, I would say. What would make somebody extraordinary?'

'My father was charismatic. He was charming and witty, intelligent . . .'

'You can't go out there with blood dripping from your lips,' said Sergio. 'You have to be two-faced or society deals with you straight away.'

'He understood the ambiguity of being human, that good and evil resides in us all . . .'

'That's an excuse, Javier,' said the voice. 'It's not what made him extraordinary.'

His brain slopped from side to side as he strained against the flexes.

'He's a desecrator of innocence,' said Javier.

'Normal.'

'He's an abuser of trust.'

'Normal, but warmer,' said the man. 'Try thinking of the most extraordinary, incomprehensible . . .'

'I can't. My mind doesn't work like that. Maybe yours does. You find out about people and show them their most secret horror. Now *that* is extraordinary.'

'You think it monstrous what I have done?'

'You've killed three people in the most brutal . . .'

'I haven't.'

'Then you are insane and I can't talk to you.'

'Ramón Salgado hanged himself rather than face his music.'

'So facilitating his suicide makes you innocent?'

'Raúl Jiménez writhed himself to death.'

'And what about the innocent Eloisa?'

'Oh, I'm probably just in denial . . . like you,' he said.

'Only society is guilty,' said Javier, dismissive.

'Don't be trite. I haven't come here for received opinion. I want creative ideas.'

'You'll have to help me.'

'Who do you know that loves or loved you?'

'My mother loved me.'

'That's true.'

'My second mother loved me.'

'How touching that you don't call her your *madrastra.*'

'And, whether you like it or not, my father loved me. We loved each other. We were intimate.'

'Were you?'

'He told me. He even wrote it to me in the letter that came with the journals.'

Silence, while the horizons changed in his head.

'Tell me about the letter,' said the voice. 'I haven't seen it.'

Javier recited the letter verbatim.

'How interesting,' he said. 'And what do you understand from this document, Javier?'

'He trusted me. He trusted me over and above my elder brother and sister.'

'It's interesting that he made you the guardian and destroyer of his works,' said the voice. 'What do you think was in his mind when he imagined you reading that letter in the storeroom, surrounded by those trashy attempts at copying my grandfather's work?'

'Your grandfather?' said Javier, to himself, the sweat breaking out from his hairline and trickling down his face.

'You didn't mention the date on the letter,' said the voice. 'When did he write that?'

'It was the day before he died.'

'Extraordinary timing.'

'He'd already had one heart attack.'

'What about his last will? When was that dated?' asked the voice.

'Three days before his death.'

'I suppose coincidence isn't *that* extraordinary.'

'What are you implying?'

'Where was your father found after the second heart attack?'

'At the bottom of the stairs.'

'He would have known by then that the journal was missing, that he was on the brink of exposure and the end of his world,' said the man. 'So easy to throw himself on the unyielding marble and leave it all in his *favourite* son's hands.'

This silenced Javier. He sat with the pressure building in his mind, the floor of his memory creaking under the old weight.

'This is how consciousness works. It's slow. Scaling the high-security walls of denial is painstaking,' said the voice. 'But we do not have the luxury of time. Tell me why you think your father wanted you to read these journals?'

'He didn't. The letter made that clear.'

'What did it make clear?' said the voice sharply. 'Do you seriously imagine he expected you, a detective, to put the letter away and carry on with the rest of your life?'

'Why not?'

'Look, Javier, I'll say it for you. That letter is *telling* you to read the journals. And why did he want that?'

'So that ... so that I could share the pain of his tormented life?'

'Is that a line from a movie? Something nice and sentimental from Hollywood, perhaps?' said the voice. 'I won't tolerate that stuff in here, Javier. Now tell me why – I'm sounding like your father with Salgado now – tell me *why* he wanted you to read the journals?'

'So that I could learn to hate him?'

'You are so pathetically needy, Javier,' he said. 'Why did he praise your police skills so highly and tell you they would be useful in finding the missing journal?'

Javier fought hard against the idea that had just entered his head. Even now he clung on. It was all he had left. It was one of the few things that sustained him. His father's love of forty-three years. Even the love of a monster was hard to give up.

'Some help for you Javier,' he said. 'I won't read it all ... just the pertinent bits. Are you ready?'

7th April 1963, NY
On the way to NY Salgado proposes that prior to the showing of the final Falcón nude I should publish my journals. I choke with appalled hilarity at the prospect. What a fantastic undoing that would be. I laugh in great hiccuping gulps. It is Mercedes who's put him up to this. I've seen them hatching their plans and M. has unnerved me on a number of occasions by wafting past as I jot my dysenteric jottings. (She has a pair

of very supple and silent gold sandals – I shall have to scatter nutshells to catch her out.) I give Salgado an emphatic no, which tweaks his fascination.

31st December 1963, Tangier
I have been careless and it has changed everything. M. and I were in the studio yesterday. The children were playing in the street below, so excited about their game that they didn't wait to get on to the soft sand of the beach. Javier, desperate to keep up, fell and hit his head. His face was covered in blood. I ran from the studio and threw him into the car and took him straight to the hospital where they put a few stitches in his head. By the time I returned to the studio I could see that everything had changed.

So what is actually different? We are still man and wife, we still live in the same house, we are still having the New Year's Eve party tonight.

When I returned from the hospital M. did not immediately ask after Javier, who was at home with the maid. She was on the verandah looking at me as if I was a lone wolf across an ice field. I walked towards her, telling her about Javier, as if auditioning. She manoeuvred around me back into the room. I said he was at home and wanted to see her. She practically ran for the door. We drove back in a frosty silence, with Paco and Manuela fighting in the back. She went upstairs and I to my study.

I am still here now, twenty-four hours later, watching her shadow on the ceiling of Javier's room. It is already dark. It is only a matter of hours before the guests arrive for dinner. Later we will go to the boat and watch the British fireworks display in the port. I am nearly paralysed with sadness. I watch her shadow, which has enlarged because she is holding Javier. They come to the window and look into the dark patio and the inkier blackness of the fig tree. I have tears in my eyes because I know that she is saying goodbye to Javier, that she will be my wife at this party and then no more. She is going and in going she will betray me. I shall go to my room now and put on my white dinner jacket.

5th January 1964, Tangier
I am ruined with fatigue but I have to bring myself to the page, my pristine confessional. This is what my journal has become. I vomit and the ghastly nausea of my existence subsides. On the evening of the party I was dressing. She went straight to the bathroom as if to hide. She waited

for me to leave before putting on her evening dress. I went to check the children. She didn't come down until the guests arrived. My eyes followed her as she mingled, occasionally our glances clashed and we'd switch away. Dinner was loud and boisterous, but I experienced it as a child under the table. After the meal we gathered in the hall while the women put on their coats and Javier suddenly appeared at the foot of the stairs. M. carried him back up to bed with his face buried in her neck. We left the house in a crowd, M. on Salgado's arm. Champagne corks popped as we arrived at the yacht. The fireworks happened. The guests began to leave.

I said to Ramón that I wanted to take the boat out and asked him to put it to M. 'She'd do anything for you,' I said. 'But she can easily talk me out of it.' The three of us put out an hour later. It was flat and cold and a half-moon added to the chill. We drank champagne at the wheel with M. wrapped in a coat of Arctic fox. The stillness out there was terrible. Then the wind got up from nowhere and Ramón, who was drunk, went down below. I turned the boat back towards Tangier.

Finally M. said: 'I'm leaving you . . . you know that now, don't you?' I asked her how she'd found the diaries. She'd persuaded Javier to tell her where I kept them. Her face was very close to mine as she spoke and she added: 'Your secret is between us.' If I thought about it, even for a moment, I would not be able to go through with it, so I rapped her with my knuckles on her solar plexus and she doubled up over my arm. I shoved her hard, firing her backwards to the rail, which hit her below the buttock. She vaulted over and, like a comic turn, her feet flipped into the darkness. The splash was inaudible. I didn't look back. The sea grew before me and there was quite a storm blowing as we came into Tangier. As we entered the port I called to M. and Salgado to come up on deck. Salgado appeared bleary-eyed. I told him to wake M. and he went back down. In seconds he was back saying she wasn't in her cabin. We went mad searching the boat before facing the awful truth and calling the coast guard. We never found her. The following day I told Javier what had happened. He was heartbroken.

The voice continued, but at a distance because now Javier was back in that moment, heading for the room that used to be his father's studio. He's been called there to be told the terrible news, which has already reached him through the thick whitewashed walls earlier that morning. A damp gloom has filled the house and all he can hear is his own heart as he slips through the door into his father's presence.

414

His father calls him and he thinks that he will draw him into his chest and kiss his head. but instead he takes him by the arm, squeezing and twisting the bicep so that Javier comes up on his toes. His father's huge face and head come down level to Javier's own. He points his finger at Javier's eye, as if it's loaded.

'You know why Mercedes isn't coming back, don't you, Javier?'

Javier was mute through this double pain of his pinched flesh and what I could see was the plummeting emptiness of what he feared most.

'This is important,' I said, pulling him to me so that his wincing face was right next to mine. 'You must never tell anyone where I keep my journals. That is my secret. I want you to remember that . . . From now on, Javier, there are no journals.'

Back in the corridor outside his father's study, he's looking down at his arm. Tears well in his eyes and trickle cleanly and quickly down his smooth face. His mouth is thick with saliva and he knows that Mercedes is never coming back. Her smell is never coming to him again as his lies under the tight sheets. His small fingers will never trace those ears again. And it is his doing. He should never have told her. He breaks into a run, down the corridor, up the stairs, into his room, on to his bed, but still the black emptiness of his realization stays with him and the twisted pain of his burning arm.

'Does that clarify things?' said the voice, and Javier had the sense of rush as on a crowded street, until he popped back into reality still looking at his bicep, as if examining the bruising he'd sustained all those years ago.

'He still loved me,' said Javier, blurting it out through the saliva in his mouth. 'He was just warning me, but he still loved me. We didn't live all those years together . . .'

'You still don't want to believe it. I can understand that, Javier. It's a difficult thing to give up . . . like life itself is difficult to give up . . . until it becomes completely intolerable. Until one's actions become . . .'

'Who *are* you?' asked Javier. 'Who the fuck are you?'

'I am your eyes,' said the voice. 'Through me you will learn to see. How brave are you, Javier?'

He shook his head, not brave at all, still crushed by the weight of Mercedes' death on his conscience and terrified at the new possibilities, the fresh horrors, the ones he knew but still didn't.

'You're afraid, aren't you, Javier? You're afraid of what you will see.'

His face trembled under restraining flex.

'What did you show the others . . . Raúl and Ramón?' asked Javier, desperate to put off the moment. 'What did you find to show them that was so terrible?'

'You must know that by now,' said the voice. 'I didn't show them anything terrible. No abandoned children or dead babies. No raped girls or strangled sodomized boys. You can see that sort of thing on the news, in the cinema, in magazines, on the Internet, on TV. We are inured to the brutality of the human condition. Nothing can horrify us now. Did you see those pictures Ramón Salgado had on his computer? Did you see what Raúl Jiménez watched while he screwed his puta? These were men well versed in horror. There was nothing more I could show them in that vein.'

'Then what *did* you show them?'

'I showed them the happiness that they had forsaken.'

'The *happiness*?'

'Arturo playing on the beach with Marta. She was tickling him, you know. She was tickling him until he couldn't bear it. I added a soundtrack. Did Manuela ever do that to you? Tickle you nearly to death? Tickle you until it wasn't tickling but torturing. Oh, the mind plays such tricks, Javier . . . after decades of denial.'

'And Ramón? What did you show Ramón? His happy wife . . .'

'I think Raúl must have given them that footage as a wedding present. The happy married couple, Ramón and Carmen. Did you listen to the tapes?'

Javier nodded.

'There was another tape, which I took with me. Carmen sang in the end. Her voice wasn't that good, but she sang for Ramón . . . an aria of love. Ramón clapped at the end and I could hear the emotion in his voice. I changed it a little. There was no clapping . . . just those last three desperate shouts – "Ramón! Ramón! Ramón!"'

Javier shuddered at the terrible exquisiteness of that torture. The men facing the double horror of the irrevocable surgery and the last

416

moments of true happiness cruelly disfigured by the added soundtrack.

'And me? What will you show me?' asked Javier, his fear making him angry while he tried to remember when he'd last been happy. 'What happiness have I forsaken?'

'I am going to blindfold you for a moment,' said the voice. 'When I take away the sleeping mask, you will see.'

Elastic snapped at the back of his head and the soft darkness of a padded mask descended. It was beautiful in the velvet, quilted dark. He thought he should never come out from under it. Something was placed on the desk. His chair was manoeuvred forward. Adrenalin pounded in his system. The purity of his seething panic thinned and cooled his blood to ether. He was cold and shaking. Fingers eased off the mask and Falcón kept his eyes tight shut.

'Open your eyes, Javier,' said the voice. 'You, better than anyone, know what happens if you don't open your eyes. It really is nothing terrible.'

'I will open them. Just give me some time.'

'You see it every day of your life.'

'Even you know that it's not what's on the table,' said Javier. 'It's what's in my head.'

'Open your eyes.'

'I will.'

'Time is short.'

'I will do it.'

'I will make you. You know I will make you. You know how I do it.'

Javier felt his head gripped in the crook of an elbow and tilted back so that his neck was stretched tight, so tight he couldn't scream. He felt its touch. It was like ice. The cold burn of the unfeeling blade. Warmth trickled down his cheek, thicker than sweat or tears. His eyes sprung open as his head tilted forward.

On the table was a single glass of white milk. He reared back from it but it was too late, the image stuck in his brain like a splinter of glass. He had no idea why he was so scared. There was no accompanying logic to the fear flashing in pulses from synapse to synapse, nerve to nerve, until his whole body convulsed in chair-rocking spasms.

The blindfold came down, shut out the ridiculous reality of a glass of milk. A hand sheaved his hair, a body reached forward past him.

'Breathe in.'

He breathed in a smell of cloying, nauseating richness. Sulphur sprang into his saliva and a cold sweat broke out over his body. He vomited.

The smell was taken away, the glass replaced on the desk. The man settled down behind him.

'I knew you would be brave,' said the voice.

'I don't feel brave,' said Javier, still gasping and coughing from the vomit.

'What did you smell?'

'Almonds and milk,' he said. 'How do you know I hate almonds and milk?'

'Who used to drink almond milk before she went to sleep every night?'

'I think it was my mother.'

'You *know* it was your mother,' said the voice. 'Who brought her the almond milk for her to drink every night?'

'The maid took it . . .'

'No, she *made* it for her. Who *took* it to her?'

'I didn't,' he said quickly, childlike. The instinctive lie. 'I didn't do it. It was Manuela.'

'Do you know why your father hated you?'

Javier hung his head in misery. He shook it from side to side, denying it, denying everything that came to mind.

'Why did your father make you love him?'

'I don't understand you any more.'

'Quiet now, Javier. I'm going to read you a story, just like your father used to at bedtime. What will it be tonight? Yes, tonight it will be: "a small history of pain which will become yours."'

3rd January 1961, Tangier
For six days I have sat in front of P. and watched her face turn to ash. Only the children bring any animation to her being. I ask her what is the matter and she says the same thing every time: 'Nada, nada.' I pass T.C.'s workshop. The walls are intact, the door has been burnt out and there is no roof. I hear from the café that T.C. used to frequent that there will be no police inquiry. It was a tragic accident. P. has started going to Mass regularly. I look out to sea with my binoculars. It is flat and grey as steel. The beach is empty. I watch the seagulls plummet.

12th January 1961, Tangier

*It is Javier's fifth birthday and we have a small party for him. P. is in
high spirits throughout. I am amazed at her capacity. I am the star of
the afternoon as the monster from the deep. Shoals of children flee from
me, screaming. The odd one I capture and eat with relish – the giggling,
thrashing mass of elastic child – until one little girl wets herself. End of
the monster. The children go to bed early and P. and I have dinner
alone in the customary silence. Even the servants walk as on broken
glass. The meal is finished. The servants leave for the night. We are
alone. I sip brandy and smoke. I make my usual observations about her
demeanour of late and this time she hits the table with both fists. It's like
a rifle shot. Her eyes narrow and she leans across the table at me.*

P.: I know it was you.

Me: What?

P.: I know that you are responsible.

Me: For what?

P.: For his death.

Me: Whose?

*P.: You are as cold as those landscapes you used to paint. Those frozen
wastes. You have no heart, Francisco Falcón. You are empty, you are cold
and you are a killer.*

Me: I have already admitted my past to you.

*P.: Oh, may God forgive me, I should have listened harder. I should
have listened to my father. I should never have let your icy hands near
me. You are a brute. You are the perfect monster. It chilled me to my
bones to see you with the children today, because that is you, that is
what . . .*

Me: What are you talking about, Pilar?

P.: I will say it to your face if you wish.

Me: I do wish it.

P.: You murdered Tariq Chefchaouni.

Me: Who?

Her contempt is almost too massive for the room.

*P.: You know I'm not a fool. When you gave me that ring, when you
gave me his bone sculpture . . . didn't you think that I would know
precisely what you were doing? It didn't stop me though, Francisco. It would
never have stopped me from enjoying the true passion of a man with more
genius in a single hair than you have in your entire, vacated soul.*

*The words come down on me like cudgels, each one reaching some vital
organ or crucial joint.*

P.: So tell me, Francisco, why did you kill him? I can't believe that it was because he was . . . fucking me. Or was it? Was it because he was pleasuring your wife while you played games with that rich whore, or sodomized young men with your cronies from the Bar La Mar Chica? Was that it? When did we last make love? Did we ever?

Me: You're taking this too far, Pilar.

P.: I'm taking this too far for you, am I? This is the mother of your children speaking. She is telling you what you are. You are unfaithful. You are a sodomite. Deny it!

Me: You don't speak to me like this.

P.: I do. I am telling you, Francisco. It's all going to come out. Everything . . . right down to the fact that you were even off sodomizing young men on our wedding night with that revolting character . . . I can't bear to say his name.'

Me: Who told you that?

P.: I hear everything. It all comes back to me. I know it all, Francisco. I even know why you married me, you cold-hearted brute.

Me: Why did I marry you?

P.: Because you thought that I could tap your genius, that with me it would flow. But genius, Francisco, is God-given. You were offered it. You caught a glimpse of it. You took it. And what did you do with it? You sold it. And that's why God never came back to you. He recognized you for the puta that you are.

Me: Shut up! Shut up! Shut up!

P.: No, no, no que no! This is the end, Francisco Falcón. You will hear it all. You were given sight. You were given a special sight. You were allowed to see into the nature of things and you treated it like coin. When I came back to you, oh, you were so pathetic. You were so grateful. Your muse had returned. And you asked to look again but, because of the man that you are, you couldn't see inside. You saw only the surface. And anybody can paint surface. They whitewash the Medina every day.

Me: I won't stand for this.

P.: Stay seated then. But admit it to yourself, even if you can't to me, that the reason you murdered Tariq Chefchaouni and destroyed his work . . .

Me: Shut up, Pilar!

P.: . . . was that he, some poor Arab boy from the Rif, was succeeding where you had failed. He went quite mad with rage when he discovered that his father had sold his bone sculpture. He only relented when he knew that I had it. His work was not for sale. It was between him and his Creator. That was his principle. That was his morality. You do not sell your sight to the highest bidder.

I get to my feet on shaky legs. All my strength is pouring into some central rage. I am like a volcano preparing to erupt. I have to support myself on the table with both hands to contain myself. She leans across to me so that our faces are close and I can see the sharp, hard whiteness of her teeth. Her eyes are roaring at me, burning green flames.

Me: So what was his sculpture doing in a shop window?

P.: None of us are without vanity, only a few are totally consumed by it.

I hit her. I lash her with the back of my hand across her face. It is a terrible blow, which sends her flying across the room so that she collides with the wall and drops like a befuddled beetle. She crawls directionless to the corner and sits there, retrieving her senses. The bones in my hand crackle. I feel completely murderous and savage, but something holds me back. P. pushes herself up off the floor, bracing herself against the whitewash wall, which crumbles in flakes. She is blinking, shaking her head. She is determined.

P.: I have one thing more for that ravening beast in your head to feed on. You should know that you have murdered the father of my last child and you will never be forgiven.

She leaves the room. My enraged brain has trouble deciphering the complex words, whose every letter seems as sharp as an 'X', a string of them, that wrap themselves around my chest like barbed wire pulled tight. I have to sit. I am in a paroxysm of agony. My heart seems to have contracted, gone into cramp. Through the stupefying howl in my head I hear her heels retreating down the terracotta-tiled corridors. A door shuts. A lock clicks. I want to call her back to save me. But I am alone with something terrible going on inside me, which I am not sure my ribcage can contain. I screw my eyes into a prolonged wince of agony. I sob and on the back of it comes a stentorian belch which fills the room with the stink of rancid chorizo. The relief is immediate. Death wanders off. I leave the house and go to my studio to sleep. I wake in the morning with a clear head and write this as if it were an unsettling dream. I do not believe what she has said to me about Javier. Her spite was her only defence against my spontaneous violence.

13th January 1961, Tangier
I go back to the house in the afternoon. As soon as I open the front door I smell burning, or rather old smoke, a cold fire. There is a black patch

on the patio and the wind has stirred up the black flakes of burnt paper, which swirl and drift like a plague of insects with no escape. I move amongst this world of moths, black flecks attach to my cool but sweaty face. I cannot think why a fire should have been started here until I see a scrap of paper, its edges scorched to a black frill. I turn it over and see the vestiges of a charcoal line. I go to the room which had been my studio. I stand in front of the chest whose bottom drawer is open. The seven remaining drawings of P. have gone.

I go wild and tear through the house to her bedroom, which is locked. I throw my shoulder into the door and it blasts open. It is empty. I take the bone sculpture and go straight back to my studio on the bay. I take up hammers and go to the roof. I smash it to pieces with a hammer in each hand. I collect up the shards and with mad, obsessive strength I grind them up in the pestle and mortar. I bag the bone dust and go to a cheap tourist shop and buy a simple clay urn. I pour the bone dust into it. I take it home and place it on the dressing table.

18th January 1961, Tangier
Nothing has been said. The black patch on the patio has gone. I don't know where the urn is. It remained on her dressing table for a few days and then disappeared. We move around each other as if we're at the heart of a collapsing empire, as if we are emperor and empress with designs on each other's power in the midst of this final demise. We know what it will take. Suspicion lurks in the corridors. We are drawn to each other's company, which is mutually abhorrent but we have to look on what the other is doing. She will only take drink and food prepared for her by her Riffian maid. I profess disinterest and take my meals in the restaurant at the Grand Hôtel Villa de France. I watch her routine and wait. There was a story from Ancient Rome of a man and wife in exactly our situation. The wife noticed the husband eating figs from the tree. She painted them with poison and watched him die. We are not in the season for figs.

25th January 1961, Tangier
I sit in the studio. It has taken me all day to find this screw of paper that I have in front of me. I smoke and smooth out the paper. I finger the two glass capsules of cyanide given to me by the legionnaire I'd saved from gaol. I sniff them. Nothing. From the recess of my brain I remember that cyanide smells like almonds.

2nd February 1961, Tangier
P. has been going to bed earlier and the Riffian woman now calls one of the children to take her warm almond milk to her. Paco and Manuela always send Javier, who is delighted to perform the task. I watch from the patio. P. puts the milk on her bedside table and kisses Javier and hugs him before sending him off to bed. She drinks the milk and turns out the light.

I ask myself whether this is what I want. To be an uxoricide. Have I no morality? The question doesn't seem relevant. The pressure is from a different quarter. The nights are longer and longer and my thoughts spend more time in the solitary dark. I lie at the centre of my studio, the mosquito net tied above my head, and an image comes to me of those first days in Russia. I see Pablito's betrayer in my sights. Her panting breast is in the pinhole of the sights. I shift my aim, and on the command, shoot her in the mouth. Her jaw shatters. I have my answer.

5th February 1961, Tangier
I sit beneath the fig tree on the patio. I have both capsules with me. I roll them in my palm. I am not consumed by hate but moved by inevitability. We are at the crux. There is no way to change the outcome.

I hear the Riffian woman call out. Moments later Javier's bare feet thud over the terracotta tiles. I hide in one of the rooms off the corridor to P.'s room. I hear the approach of Javier's rustling pyjamas.

Again Sergio's voice receded as the words tumbled down inexorably. Javier finds himself looking down at his bare feet on the terracotta tiles, the glass of almond milk chin-high. He chews on his lip with concentration, trying not to spill a drop and is startled by his father suddenly appearing at shoulder height. His big face emerging from the dark with such suddenness that Javier nearly drops the glass which, thank God, his father takes from him.

'It's only me,' he says, and opens his eyes wide and squeezes his fingers over the glass with the word, '*Abracadabra*.'

He gives him the glass back.

'It's all right now,' he says and kisses his head. 'Go on. Take it. Don't drop it.'

Javier clasps the glass and his father pats him on the shoulder and his feet are on the move again across the terracotta tiles, the contour of each crater and join is imprinted on his bare soles. He reaches the door, puts the glass on the floor; it takes two hands to work the handle. He picks up the glass and goes in. His mother looks up from her book. He closes the door by backing into it until he hears the latch click. He places the glass on the bedside table and clambers up on to the bed and his mother squeezes him to her bosom and he is momentarily lost in the squashiness of her nightdress. He feels her hand, the ringless hand, holding his taut tummy and her breath and the touch of her lips on his head, the way it tickles him. She is warm and the cotton smells of her and she crushes his ribs into hers and gives him a final hard kiss on the forehead, which marks him with her love forever.

Javier froze in his chair as he came back into the dark reality of the sleeping mask. The flexes still cut into him, his eyelid still burnt at the edge, the velvet of the mask was soaked from his tears and the voice behind him rolled out the final words from his father's journal:

Moments later Javier runs past on his way back up to his bedroom. I go to the window and look through the cracks of the shutters. P. holds the glass of milk. She blows on it and drinks the first centimetre. She puts it back on the table. By the time she turns back the cyanide has reached her system. I am shocked by its speed. It's as fast as the blood itself. She convulses, reaches for her neck and falls back. The Riffian woman goes to the children's bedroom and their light goes off. She goes to her own room soon after. I go to P. and remove the glass. I wash it thoroughly in the kitchen and fill it to the halfway point with a bottle of almond milk I prepared earlier in the studio. I replace the glass by P.'s bed and turn out the light. I go back to the studio to write this down. I must sleep now because tomorrow I have to be up early.

Sergio finished and there was silence in the house. Javier's tears, which had soaked into the sleeping mask, mixing with the blood from his cut eyelid, now broke down his face. He was drained. There was some movement behind him. A rag closed over his nose and mouth and a hard chemical smell as ugly as ammonia batted his brain into another soundless galaxy.

34

It was a respite. His chloroformed brain toppled through space silently. The return to reality was fragmentary – bits of audio and then shards of visual. His head came up, the room tilted. Slices of light penetrated his eye and suddenly he was jerked awake by his own fear that something terrible might have been done to him.

He could see and his eyelids still opened and closed. Relief spread through him. He coughed. The flex was no longer around his face and his feet were free from the legs of the chair, but his wrists were still attached. He orientated himself in the room. He was facing away from the desk now. He leaned forward, trying to swallow back the turmoil rising in his chest and up his throat. He sobbed, straining against the memories, the shattered certainties. Was there any possible recovery from this?

A noise. Castors on tiles. The rush of something passing too closely. A thump of air. A man – Sergio, or was it Julio now? – shot past him and sailed to the far wall on his castored desk chair.

'Awake?' he asked, and nudged himself away from the wall so that he drifted nauseatingly to a point in front of Javier.

Julio Menéndez Chefchaouni sat back in the chair, relaxed. Javier's first impression was one of beauty. His looks were almost girlish, like a star from a boy band, with long dark hair, soft brown eyes, long lashes, high cheekbones and a clear, smooth complexion. It was the sort of face a camera would love, but only for a moment.

'Here it is, Inspector Jefe,' he said, framing his jaw with his hands. 'The face of pure evil.'

'Still not finished?' said Falcón. 'What more can there be, Julio?'

'I think the project needs ... not an ending exactly, because I don't believe in endings – or beginnings or middles for that matter – but it needs to make its purpose known.'

'The project?'

'As I think your father noted: "Nobody paints any more," ' said Julio. 'Daubing canvasses is not so far from what cavemen used to do. You know, *Ceci n'est pas une pipe* and all that. Art is all about progress, isn't it? We can't stand still. We constantly have to show people new things, or show them that old things can be seen anew. Carl André's *Equivalent VIII*, Damien Hirst's pickled sharks and cows. Those plastinated real dead bodies from Gunther von Hagens' show *Body Worlds*. And now Julio Menéndez.'

'And what's your project called?'

'Even that is new. The title is constantly evolving. It is three words in English which can be placed in any order, using any preposition in between. The words are: Art. Real. Killing. So it could be the Real Art of Killing or perhaps Killing Real Art.'

'Or the Art of Real Killing,' said Falcón.

'I knew you'd understand it straight away.'

'Where is this project going to be shown?'

'Oh, that is not really in my hands,' said Julio. 'It will be all over the media, of course, but, well, you've heard of people who've devoted their lives to things such as literature. This is an extension of that. I think it will probably insist on being posthumous.'

'Start at the beginning,' said Falcón. 'I'm conventional like that.'

'As you now know, Tariq Chefchaouni was my grandfather, my mother was his only daughter, who married a Spaniard from Ceuta. His art gene missed a generation but it got me. After my first year here, at the Bellas Artes, my mother and I went to visit the family in Tangier. I asked to see some of my grandfather's work and was told that everything had been destroyed in the fire which killed him, apart from a few effects and some books. It was a couple of years later that the family called to tell me that, in doing some building work, they'd found a small pewter box under the floor in his room.

'I was here in Seville, studying art, and I knew a great deal about the Falcón nudes because I'd done a project on them in my second and third years. In fact, I was obsessed by them even before I came to Seville and, when I found out that your father was still living here, I even met him on a couple of occasions to iron out some technical things I didn't understand. Of course, he only knew me as Julio Menéndez. He was very . . . gracious. We liked each other. He said I could call him if there was anything else I needed to know. So when I went back to Tangier and opened this pewter box I was completely fascinated to find that my grandfather seemed to have had the same obsession, except . . . how could he? He was already dead by the time the Falcón nudes came into existence.'

Julio opened the box and took out four postcard-sized pieces of canvas. He held each one up to Falcón. They were perfect reproductions of the Falcón nudes.

'You can't really see them without a magnifying glass and good light, but I can assure you they are perfect . . . each brushstroke is a perfect miniature of its original.'

'Now look on the back.'

He held up the reverse side of the miniatures and each piece was inscribed to Pilar, followed by the dates May 1955, June 1956, January 1958 and August 1959.

'There was one other thing in the box, which is no longer in my possession.'

'The silver ring with the sapphire,' said Falcón. 'My mother's ring.'

'My first reaction when I saw the miniatures was that I would show them to your father, that he must have lost them and they had strangely come into my grandfather's possession. But then I remembered that the Falcón nudes were all painted in the space of a year, which didn't fit with the dates inscribed on the backs. I was confused.'

'When was this?'

'The end of 1998, beginning of 1999.'

'And when did you think that there was something more sinister to this?'

'While I was in Tangier your father had a heart attack and there was a piece in the paper accompanied by an old photograph of him in the sixties. One of the older family members said that this was the man who'd come round to the house after my grandfather died and bought up his few remaining drawings.

'I went back to Seville and I heard at the Bellas Artes that he was still taking on students for a few weeks at a time. I called him. He remembered me and I volunteered to be his companion. He was frail after the heart attack and I had the run of his studio. The storeroom he kept locked, but I soon opened it. And there I found all the confirmation I needed, through the stunning mediocrity of his attempts to reproduce my grandfather's work, and then again in the journals. I read them all and when I finished I stole the crucial diary and walked out. I never went back. I never spoke to him again. I was mad with rage. I was going to publish the journal, to show the world the real Francisco Falcón . . . but then he died.'

'Why didn't you publish it anyway?'

'I could see the whole thing being taken away from me,' said Julio. 'I wanted to have control.'

'But then something must have happened.'

'Why?'

'For it to have become your project.'

'Nothing happened,' said Julio. 'That's the nature of the creative process. One day I decided it would be interesting to know everything about Raúl Jiménez and Ramón Salgado. The men as they are today. So, I started filming *La Familia Jiménez* and it grew from there.'

'And what about Marta?'

'It's amazing how once you start working on something these things find you, rather than you finding them. I knew, from the journals, that she was in Ciempozuelos. I was very interested to see her, to find out about her, but I had no way of doing that without drawing attention to myself. At the time I was doing some freelance computer effects work for a film company up in Madrid and one of the directors asked if any of us would be interested in helping some mental patients in Ciempozuelos with some art therapy. I volunteered, but Marta was not one of the patients involved in the course. I still had to find her.'

'And that's why you became Ahmed's friend?'

'Once I saw that metal trunk under her bed I knew I had to get inside it and Ahmed was my only chance. I have a talent for friendship, especially with people like Ahmed – you know, forasteros . . . like me.'

'Like Eloisa.'

'Yes,' said Julio smoothly. 'Ahmed showed me Marta's file and once I read the letter from José Manuel Jiménez's psychoanalyst, I knew I had a project.'

'And where did you get the idea of killing people?'

'From you, when I found out that you were the Inspector Jefe del Grupo de Homicidios de Sevilla,' said Julio. 'To have the son of the great Francisco Falcón investigating the crimes of his father seemed too perfect an opportunity to miss. It made sense of the whole idea.'

'That was not a rational decision.'

'Artists don't have rational minds. How am I supposed to disturb the minds of others if my own is a flat calm?'

'Killing is not art.'

'You missed out the word "real",' said Julio, on his feet, the pupils in his eyes suddenly massive and shiny black, but not seeing out, only sucking in. 'You should have said Real Killing is not Art or . . . or . . . Killing is not Real Art.'

'Sit down, Julio. Just sit down for a moment . . . we haven't finished,' said Javier.

'You know, the problem is,' said Julio, 'is . . . is . . . that I see things too clearly now. I can't seem to lower my visual scale. Once you kill somebody everything becomes intensely real, and it's unbearable. Did you know that, my uncle, did you know that?'

'That's right, I *am* your uncle,' said Javier, trying to keep Julio under control. 'And I do know that.'

'That's why I didn't kill you. I only tried to do you good. To save you from your blindness.'

'Yes, I can see now and I'm grateful,' said Javier. 'There's just one more thing I need to know from you.'

'It's all been said and done and written and filmed . . . there's only one thing left now,' he said.

He went behind Falcón and pivoted the chair around so that it was facing the opposite wall. On the desk was the glass of almond milk, the leather-bound journal and his police revolver. Julio took a knife and cut through the flex securing Falcón's right hand.

'I have to go now,' he said, throwing the knife on to the desk. 'You know what you have to do. You shouldn't have to face any more of this than you've had to.'

Their eyes met and turned to the revolver sitting on top of the journal, next to the glass of milk – the reminder of all that he had done and all that he had lost.

'There's your solution,' said Julio. 'The only way to close everything down and leave it behind for ever.'

Sweat came up on Falcón's hands, trickled from the hairline. How could he still have so much juice in him? He picked up the revolver, flicked open the barrel and saw all the chambers were full. He thumbed the safety off. He looked down at the gun in his trembling hand and brought it slowly up to his face. Suicide had its attractions for him at that moment. It was the simplest solution in the face of this sudden nothingness. His past gone and the future frail and uncertain. His father's love . . . never there. Only hate, which he, Javier, had fuelled . . . just by living. And, yes, who was he now? Was he still even Javier Falcón? The threads that held him together were guilt and grief; tug at them and he would fall apart. And now it could all be over. With one small pull of the trigger he could blow away the reservoir of all his pain.

A wall in his memory suddenly gave way and, rather than more suffering flooding through to his tangled mind, he remembered that kiss, the one from his mother, that had marked him with her love forever. And, under the remembered pressure of her lips, he found out who he was, recalled the boy he had been for her. It undid something, unravelled part of the vast knot, and he was suddenly able to see clear lines of thought that were not uncomplicated but at least thinkable.

He was relieved of one pressure. He did not belong to the man he'd known as his father and yet . . . there had always been something. They were inextricably joined, but . . . by what? Had it been as simplistic as Julio had said? That Javier walked the earth as a constant reminder to his father of all his failings? Was he the emblem of hate? Or was his father's final act as ambiguous as we all are. Our constant needs make us weak. Adversity leads us down some treacherous paths to worthlessness and despicable acts, but there is always that draw to the power of the original connection. Raúl to Arturo. Ramón to Carmen. Francisco Falcón to Javier.

His father, in forcing the journals on him, could as easily have been saying: 'Now you know the kind of man I was, feel free to hate me and absolve yourself.'

Javier turned. Julio was still standing in the doorway, waiting. Shaking, Javier stretched his arm out and pointed the gun at Julio's face whose facile beauty had disappeared, leaving his features dislocated by his insanity.

'Come to me,' said Javier, not unkindly and Julio complied.

He walked right up to him until the gun barrel touched him between the eyes.

'I'm not going to shoot you,' said Falcón, whose other wrist was still tied to the chair.

It happened quickly. Before Falcón could even think of words that might penetrate the deranged mind before him, the boy's hands flew up into his face. One gripped Falcón's wrist and the other pressed his trigger finger and the colossal noise of the gun shot filled the room and the patio and echoed through the empty house.

Julio cannoned backwards and crashed through the glass doors on to the patio. His blood spread across the marble flagstones towards the stone circle of the fountain.

By 11.00 p.m. the levantamiento del cadaver had been completed and the Juez de Guardia, who was not Esteban Calderón, had left. Ramírez finished taking Falcón's preliminary statement with Comisario Lobo in attendance while all the relevant evidence was removed.

By 11.30 p.m. Lobo was driving him to the hospital to have a stitch put in his eyelid. Lobo recounted how he'd secured Comisario León's resignation. Javier didn't respond.

'You know,' said Lobo, as they drew into the hospital, 'there's going to be heavy media interest in this case, especially . . . due to your father's unusual involvement.'

'That was Julio's intention,' said Javier. 'He wanted the maximum and most shocking exposure possible . . . as any artist would. It's out of my hands now. I'll just . . .'

'Well, I hope . . . I think I can help you control that.'

Javier raised an eyebrow.

'We should confine the story to a single journalist,' said Lobo. 'That way you can put your version of events forward, rather than having it torn from your hands and transformed into some lurid fantasy.'

'I have no fear of that, Comisario, only because I don't think any editor could think of anything more lurid than my father being a brute, a pirate, a thief, an impostor, a double uxoricide and a fraud.'

'At least, this way, the first airing of the story will be as close to the truth as possible. I think it's always best that the first impression is the . . .'

'Perhaps you've already reached an agreement with a journalist, Comisario,' said Javier.

Silence. Lobo offered to go in to the emergency room with him. Javier turned him down.

He went into the hospital and sat under the bright neon of his new life while they put two silk stitches in his eyelid. His mind recoiled from the harsh operative light and he shut his eyes while his thoughts writhed. How would Manuela and Paco react to the media onslaught? What would he say to them? Your father . . . but not mine, was a monster? Manuela would throw it off or it would just bounce off her. She wouldn't let it in. But Paco ... His father had 'saved' him after his goring, given him the finca, set him up in a new life. There would be no easy rejection from Paco. And Javier was relieved to find that the connection was still there, that this would not change anything for him.

'Am I hurting you?' asked the doctor.

'No,' said Javier.

'Nurse,' said the doctor, 'swab these tears.'

He was out by midnight, still in his bloody shirt. He took a taxi home. He stood in the middle of the patio looking at the bronze statue leaping out of the fountain. Always on the move, that boy. He went upstairs to the studio; the black pupil of the fountain followed him round the gallery. He went into the storeroom and removed all his father's attempts at copying Chefchaouni's work and the five canvasses that made up the obscene painting of his mother. He threw them down into the patio. He followed them with the box of money and the pornography. He took a five-litre flagon of alcohol down and drew everything into a pile next to the fountain. He poured the alcohol on top and threw a match on it. The flames thumped into life and jaundiced light flickered in the silent patio.

He went into the study where the pewter box was still on the desk. He lifted out the priceless miniatures and laid them out one by one. His father's work. His real father's work. And for a moment he was up in the air again, looking down into the face he'd never remembered and seeing him for the first time.

He showered and put on a new shirt. He had no desire for bed or to stay in the house. He had a sudden need to be with people, even strangers ... especially strangers. He walked out into the night and was drawn to the lights along the black leathery river and then across it into the Plaza de Cuba, where the crowds drew him on up Calle Asunción towards the Feria ground.

He ended up in front of the Edificio del Presidente where it had all begun, a lifetime ago, and Consuelo Jiménez came to mind with her daring eyes. He admired her strength. She had never wavered despite the continuous onslaught. Calderón was right, she'd held them all together. He remembered her dinner proposal and the click of her kitten heels on the marble flagstones. He shook his head. Too early for that.

He turned and entered the Feria de Abril through the massive, garishly lit portals of the main gate and walked into a surreal world, where everybody was beautiful and happy. Where the girls flounced in their figure-hugging *trajes de flamenca* with flowers and tortoiseshell combs in their hair while their men struck poses in grey bolero jackets and flat-brimmed hats. He walked, looking about him with childlike fascination under the lanterns and the bunting, past the endless marquees where everybody was eating, drinking fino and dancing. The air was full of the incense of enjoyment – music, food and tobacco. Under the silken tented ceilings women plaited the air above their heads with sinuous arms, the men upright, chins raised, shoulders braced torero-style.

He walked amongst the people, all of them smiling and laughing, as if drugged. How could there be so many and so happy? In this small galaxy he seemed to be the only human present with a direct line to misery, the only one with memories and guilt, hopelessness and fear. He wondered if he would ever be able to plug himself back into a whole life from the half-life in which he'd been living.

A burst of handclapping snapped him back into the fantasy world of the Feria. The rhythm of the Sevillanas being sung and danced all around him insinuated, and as he passed one of the smaller casetas he heard his name shouted.

'Javier! Heh! Javier!'

A small, dumpy woman in a white traje de flamenca with big red polka dots appeared to know him. She danced a few steps, her feet suddenly dainty and her hands turning and twisting, beckoning the air, as if encouraging him.

'You don't recognize me. I'm Encarnación. Welcome, stranger,' she said. 'Will a stranger dance a Sevillana with me on the first night of the Feria de Abril?'

His housekeeper, the perfect stranger, one who represented all that was uncomplicated in the world, had finally taken bodily form. He followed her into the caseta. She insisted that they start with a dance and a glass of fino. She took two sips of her pale Tio Pepe while Javier knocked his back in one. He slammed his glass down, raised his head, clicked his heels together and they started their first Sevillana.

Encarnación was instantly transformed. The sixty-five-year-old woman became elegant and smouldering, coquettish and daring. They danced four or five Sevillanas, one after the other. He ordered more fino. They ate a plate of paella and some calamares and he remembered how good food tasted. They danced again. His anguish subsided, his misery drifted off. He forgot everything and concentrated on one thing – the mood of his Sevillana – and he threw himself into the dance, each sequence drawing him closer to the perfect expression. And he realized that he'd found it again – the Sevillano solution to misery – *la fiesta* – and he danced his problems out of his head, down his body to his feet and stamped them into the ground.

AUTHOR'S NOTE

About half way through writing *The Blind Man of Seville* I realized that the journals I wanted to integrate into the story did not exist. So in the summer of 2001 I took three months to write the diaries of the periods in Fransisco Falcón's life that I wanted to use. I didn't know how I was going to fit them into the narrative but it helped me to develop the fully rounded character. By the time I had finished the book I was left with material from the latter part of Fransisco Falcón's life in Tangier which, although interesting from the characterization point of view, were not integral to the story. You can read them on www.HarcourtBooks.com.